We are all
teachers and students —
Always —

[illegible]

The Impersonators

Cover designed and created by Tom Greene and Jens Trumpa. Special thanks to Jens Trumpa and Paul Nussbaum for their invaluable suggestions, encouragement, and guidance. This novel would never have been completed without their input.

Introducing...

The Impersonators

Mark McLane

I dedicate this book to all my students I have met in my life of teaching. Thank you for giving me the inspiration to thrive as a teacher and love life as an author.

Chapter 1

It is a strange little quirk of human nature that fills the apartments of the Villa Verdugo. Folks never do ever seem to feel quite settled about things. They always feel deep down that they are missing something out there and that they have to go poking around for it. Most of the time, they don't know what it is. Or, if they do, then something always gets in the way, slowing them down, or wanting to control them.

Felix felt that way, like he was living a cartoon, that some unknown hand was drawing his lines and shapes for him, making him talk cartoon talk, giving him cartoon friends, making him run off cliffs, shooting him out of a cannon. It was always something. He could count on it.

The Villa Verdugo was a quiet gray building that didn't intrude quite too much into a neighborhood of green squares with quaint cottages drawn behind white picket fences. Felix especially liked the balcony, suspended over a courtyard of blooming bougainvillea and birds of paradise. Everything in southern California blooms with lust and certainty, ignorant of frost or thirst, oblivious to the walls and zip codes that divide the ranks, that set the boundaries, that keep one in one's place. Felix had just arrived and so those lines had not yet been drawn.

He decided that the Villa Verdugo would do and so he signed the lease. It was within easy presence of the graceful

Verdugo Mountains that loomed above Burbank. There was no nearby heavy traffic or noisy neighborhood bars to distract him from his sleep or his thoughts. Within a mile or so were the lifelines of LA, the twelve lane chains of concrete that dissect the San Fernando Valley, connecting and separating neighborhoods at will and admitting columns of cars to the major studios to the east and the Pacific Ocean to the west. Down the street far enough, beyond the neat rows of lanky palms on Hesby Street was the village of North Hollywood, a place of littered alleys and sidewalks as broken as the spirits of the street campers who lived there, those who came looking for something and failed to find it, condemned to panhandle for coins and cigarettes by day, then retreat to store doorways or the recesses of the nearby 170 overpass by night.

Felix had left the southern Indiana hill country, driving the old Ford pick-up across America's midriff to a collision of cultures and customs and colors all splattered together in some exotic urban variation by the hand of Pollock. Sometimes he had to squint, tilt his head, and stand with his back against the wall to make any kind of sense out of it. His only kin here were the other Midwesterners, those who had run away to Los Angeles to flee their families, to reinvent themselves, or to escape their past. Some came seeking attention in a world that generally ignored them, believing strongly in their fantasies that Hollywood Boulevard was the only avenue to the attention and adulation they so desperately sought. But few had a sensible road map. There was no yellow brick road to follow and so they wandered around until the money ran out, and then reluctantly traded their delusions for reality, or they joined their kin in obscurity in the darkened doorways down the street. A fortunate few found a little luck, had a season in the limelight. It was nothing more than that, but they could claim their place and they would have a story to tell.

In LA, everyone has a story to tell. Felix's story was a joke, told in comedy routines polished by years of gigs in Midwest bowling alley bars and old folks' home, amid the cadence of jukeboxes and respirators. He had fought hard and thought he was ready for more. But he soon discovered that he did escape his past, that anything that had been written in the past doesn't matter anymore, a page already written and read. It was just a line or two on a resume and nothing more. So there was another new page to draw, of someone bouncing anvils off his head.

The Mainstream Talent Agency lay only a few miles north of the Villa Verdugo, in the quiet Latino barrios of Sun Valley. Barbara McGill ran her business from her home there, an unimposing two-bedroom bungalow crammed with head shots and demo reels and fax machines and phones. She always worked, rising every day at early dawn from her bed in the only room off-limits to the interns and her associates who helped her run her business. She would click on the computers while she waited for the coffee to brew, then sit in her pajamas viewing the morning breakdowns, the bloodline of her business, those daily faxes and emails from casting directors seeking talent. It was always quiet and she could relax. Within a few hours, the machinery would light up, but for now there was peace in Sun Valley.

It was a modest operation, but through hard work and determination she had established herself as a viable player, earning the trust and respect of the casting directors and studio reps. Many shoestring operations come and go, but Barbara watched the cash flow carefully, used interns to do most of the drudge work, traded favors with her contacts on her fat Rolodex, and with no crushing overhead to endure, she would survive the periodic strikes and economic slowdowns with more dignity than most. Life in Los Angeles is a struggle. The weak and the foolish are separated quickly from the herd and devoured.

Felix had never been in California before, and he knew no one. He brought nothing with him, so he slept on a blanket in the middle of the living room. In fact, he felt that he should.

It was part of the sacrifice, keeping things pure. People want you to work hard for your success. They like you more when they know you had to sleep on the floor for a while. They had to a time or two themselves. They don't care much for people just being handed stuff.

LA is the City of Transience so it wasn't too long before he found what he needed at curbside, the cast-offs from others who came before him, those who had moved on up. Or on out. He seldom thought of what he had left behind, which really wasn't much of anything or anybody anyway, except Maggie. She couldn't come with him. There were no rabbits to chase across the meadows, no tractors to follow across the fields, no woods to walk in nighttime. It was another part of the sacrifice, a painful one. Nothing had ever been easy in his life. He was here now, and there was no looking back. No need to.

This was a new life. He had Barbara's phone number in his wallet. Someone he knew had drawn that line for him before he had left and he was grateful. It wasn't easy for him to make the phone call. It was something he didn't like to do. Ask for help. He wrote out on a piece of paper what he would say. He was so nervous that his hands trembled. He had read the trade books before he left and he knew that finding a good agent is difficult so he had to make sure that he did things right. There would be no margin for error here. Many actors arriving in LA never find agents. Some that do, discover that they have been hip-pocketed, forgotten by an agent that represents too many clients, or an agency that goes belly-up, too deeply into arrears ever to recover.

But Barbara liked him and offered him an internship and so he relaxed a little bit. Felix knew there would be no pay involved, but he also knew that she would send his headshot out to the hosts of casting directors in Hollywood. It was a tit for tat, a quid pro quo kind of thing. He would arrive every morning at 8:00 to take his seat at the glass-topped kitchen table that doubled as the submissions desk and work until noon matching the description on the breakdown with the forty or so actors in

Barbara's talent bank, arranged alphabetically behind him in blue plastic milk boxes. He snipped labels from big sheets, filled out the name of the project and the role, clipped them to headshots and addressed the big manila envelopes, preparing them for the couriers who arrive twice a day to deliver them to the casting directors. Barbara told him that the whole way of doing things was changing, though, gearing up to use the new technology. "Point and click would replace the snip and clip," she said. He ran for supplies or lunch and worked the phones.

It was there that he learned first hand of the realities of the fantasy, the realities that the trade books forgot to mention. He learned it straight from the horse's mouth, so to speak, those actors out there in the field. He learned about the heartbreak and the debilitating toll that years of rejection has on the human psyche. "Sorry, you're not right for this" that they hear again and again and again, the months that go by between auditions when an actor was in a slump. Felix could hear the self-doubt creeping into their voices. "Anything for me today? Anything at all? I'll do anything, even a music video." He could hear hope turn to bitter disappointment in the voice when an audition led to a callback that led to a producer's session that led to an availability check that led to nowhere after that.

"Any word yet?" the actor would ask.

"No, sorry," Felix would answer.

"They said for sure they were going to use me. Told me to stay by the phone."

"I haven't heard anything yet," Felix would say softly.

"Can you call them again for me? Please?"

"I did. Three times. Left messages but they haven't called back."

He heard from penniless actors who wondered when they would receive the check for the gig they did months ago. He heard the humiliation, the shame in the voices of the actors who called to report that their talent did not surface to the expectations of the producer or who were harassed all day by a temperamental director. "It happens to everyone sometime,"

Felix would offer, "even the biggies. Just let it go." He would hear, too, of success, a national commercial with thousands of dollars in residuals, or a series regular with a regular paycheck in a soap or sitcom somewhere, or an above-the-line role in a big budget picture. There would be celebrations and high fives and everyone would be heartened by the news. "If he can do it, then so can I!" Barbara's fifteen percent cut would buy another couple of months.

Soon, it was his turn. He was new in town and the casting directors were curious about him and so the phones would ring for him. With his thick Thomas Guide in his lap, Felix made the rounds, plying the streets of Hollywood and beyond to take his place in line, headshot in hand, sweat on his brow. On days when he had multiple auditions, Felix became a quick-change artist in his truck as he drove, transforming from businessman to cowboy at red lights, often driving bare-chested to the next red light, which was sometimes several blocks down the street, before he could pull on his shirt. On side streets near casting suites, he would stand behind the open door of the truck in his skivvies and morph into a sleazy punk; an ignorant, backwoods huckster; or a neurotic Woody Allen type, confused and confusing. And he played along. Whatever was drawn out for him on the story board. He bought some nerdy eyeglasses, found an old cowboy hat at a yard sale, and brushed up on his bad grammar. He wouldn't shave so that he could look the part, unless he had to shave to look the part. He learned to carry rolls of quarters in the truck and study all the attachments, restrictions, and conditions tacked onto parking signs. He warily watched the clock and when auditions ran longer than expected, scurried out to reload the hungry meters with quarters to avoid the $58 parking ticket or the $200 towing fine. Actors with no rolls of quarters to spare carry spray cans of gray paint to cover over red curbs, or cut the bottoms from plastic garbage containers to place over fire hydrants, or become adept at whittling down pennies on concrete sidewalks to make dimes for the meters.

Hollywood could find whatever she needs, and in spades. If the need is for a fat banker type or a pencil-necked geek or a tight-lipped bitch, long lines of the best of them would wait in crowded holding pits, each sizing up the competition with leery eyes. Talent agencies fill casting suites with the pierced and tattooed, pretty faces, actors in lab coats or polo shirts, sumo wrestlers and love children. Clones in gray business suits line up to audition for the multitudes of casting directors who conduct their trade in far-flung corners of Los Angeles, in offices in Hollywood and Century City, in spare rooms of their homes and rented suites in West Los Angeles, in the city parks of Santa Monica and Venice, and in the shadows of the mega-studios in Studio City, Burbank, or Culver City.

Most of the actors in Barbara's talent bank had night jobs. Felix knew that he would join them, sooner rather than later. He had brought enough money to trade a tall stack of twenty-dollar bills for the key to Apartment 211. Everything up front had to be done in cash or cashier's check, the damage deposit, first month's rent. No checks or credit cards or IOU's accepted. It didn't leave him with too much left. He passed the credit check, and when the manager asked him if he were an actor, he said he was a teacher. He knew about the Catch-22. Apartment managers loathe renting to actors because they know that during the lean months, rent will be slow in coming, if at all. Employers loathe hiring actors because they know that they will miss work with little notice for an audition or a booking. Talent agencies loathe representing actors who have day jobs because they know about unsympathetic bosses. If the actor does not show up at an audition, he soon finds himself with no agent. Casting directors won't call agents if their clients don't show up when called. If an actor misses work because he does show up for an audition, he soon finds himself with no job. If an actor misses his rent deadline because he has no job, he soon finds himself with no place to live.

So the actors and the models, the singers and the dancers, the production assistants, the set dressers, the wardrobe folks, location scouts, and everyone else who live on the edge do what they can. Some team up with three or four others to split the cost of a one-bedroom flat in the cheap rent district north of Ventura Boulevard in Van Nuys or Panorama City. Some pay a few hundred dollars a month to sleep on a futon mattress in someone's living room or in a makeshift apartment in someone's garage. Most take night jobs at bars and restaurants to be free during the days. It's part of the sacrifice, part of the pain, sleeping on the floor.

Rusty Ford Country Squire station wagons and sagging Chevrolet Impalas line the streets in the Fairfax District. There are no new or expensive or exotic cars to be seen anywhere, a wasteful extravagance in the eyes of those who live here. Traffic moves slowly here. Everything and everyone moves slowly here. It is an old-world place where old Jewish men gossip as they resole shoes, repair clocks, or order bagels and latkes from café signs written in Hebrew. They craftily barter prices until the deal is set, complete the transaction, and then sweep the sidewalk until the next deal is offered. On Saturday mornings, families walk in small groups to nearby temples, the men in solemn black suits, the women modestly covered from head to ankle, their children restrained in uncomfortable deportment. Nearby, on a quiet side street is the yeshiva, a boarding school for young Hasidic Jews who will become the family rabbi. They wear names like Yanki and Yossi and Yitzi as comfortably as they wear their black fedoras and prayer shirts and black cloaks. They are protected against the underbelly of Hollywood by high walls, immunized from the influences of television, movies, newspapers, magazines, books, radios, computers, and females, safely cloistered against those sins and the sins of the nearby Melrose District.

Felix answered a small classified ad in the LA Times. The yeshiva needed someone to teach the boys how to write. The rabbi who taught that class had left for London and the yeshiva was in a pinch so the Rosh Yeshiva ran that ad. It was all so new. He had never known a Jew. There weren't any in the rolling hills of southern Indiana so they were a curiosity to him. When he arrived for his first day of teaching, he found the boys as wary of him as he was of them. His hands shook, and he fought the urge to head out the back door to his truck parked below in the courtyard. But he needed the job and the late afternoon hours were right for him. So each afternoon at 3:00 he would enter through the heavy iron gates, where his students would wait to follow him up to his classroom on the third floor, all the while crowding him with questions about the current state of affairs in Israel or wishing to negotiate the grade they received on the last assignment.

Chapter 2

Beth Ann had fled a colorless life in the rust belt of northern Ohio, taken up residence at the Villa Verdugo, and became an independent producer. Chased back to a steady income during one too many lean months, she now worked in the corporate legal offices of Videmantics, a large, rich cable channel that charted the Golden Years of Hollywood. She lived with piles of books on metaphysics and two fat, old, long haired cats named Archie and Veronica. Whenever she arrived home, she would always call out to them, "Mama's home! Mama's home!" Even if she stepped out for just a minute or two to check the mail, when she returned, she would still holler out, "Mama's home! Mama's home!" She was a good soul; and eager to be of service to those on the planet with her, she trained to become a practitioner, as they were called, at a large metaphysical church in Santa Monica. She fed on the holy classes, religiously visited the jails and sick beds, and monitored the church help hot line as part of her holy diet, until she took her holy vows, when those responsibilities were passed on to the novitiates in line behind her.

She required that every meal, or any other event for that matter, should begin with a blessing. She would form a ring in the middle of the living room and insist that everyone hold hands, then ramble on for so long about the beauty and glory of life that by the time the final amen was said, the vegetarian meatloaf was cold and Archie and Veronica had had their fill of the gravy. If the hamster or canary of an acquaintance left the planet, she would arrive immediately for hours of prayers, holding the hands and sobbing quietly for the bereavement of the bewildered and beleaguered next of kin.

Good health was an anathema to her. There wasn't much to talk about with others if she felt just fine so she preferred illness. There was the added benefit that it afforded her the opportunity to exercise her metaphysical sensitivities, commiserating with others who felt poorly, walking in their shoes. They would share and compare their stories, nodding sadly and murmuring little reassurances to each other. Her ailments served Beth Ann well and she relied on them for comfort and support.

She propped her bed up to a steep angle to enhance the blood flow and regularly visited the bottles and jars of herbal supplements that lined her kitchen counter tops. She knew all the terminology, symptoms, and treatments of every disease, and every caveat of her company's generous employee health plan. She arrived well informed at the physician, and routinely visited her physical therapist, metaphysician, metaphysical-therapist, acupuncturist, sonic-therapist, chromo-therapist, chrono-therapist, tono-therapist, aroma-therapist, music-therapist, thermo-therapist, hydro-therapist, thermo-hydro-therapist, hippo-therapist, hypno-therapist, aural-therapist, primal-therapist, and thera-therapist.

Recently she had acquired a most unusual and peculiar tickle in her throat which grew more serious as the tickle became a tackle and the tackle became a tuckle, ballooning into a full-blown gale of epic proportions, a gurgling, gasping, strangling, choking, spasmodic HAHAKAKAROOM! HAHAKAKAROOM! HAHAKAKA ROOM! ROOM! ROOM! AHEM AHEM, which would utterly baffle the physical and metaphysical sciences alike, and alarm the movie audiences or restaurant patrons in her frequent nights out. There was no henna, no witch hazel, no rhubarb in the apothecary's jar that had any influence over her ailments. Her bladder, which held no more than a teaspoon of pee, was continually replenished from the water bottle always at her side.

She claimed legions of friends. Any unwary stranger who expressed concern about that strangling cough or that cane was promptly and deeply clutched within the ample folds of her bosom. Once you were there, you were immediately indentured and there was no escape. There was no chore too big or too small for others to handle, no time of the day or night too early or too late. "Would you be a dear?" she would say.

Woodrow had been scientifically engineered to assist and then tested for his strength and endurance before he was assigned to duty. Yes, he could hold up under extreme pressure. Yes, he was ready to lend a foot. "Exist to Assist" was his handle, his mantra, tattooed for inspection on his sturdy leg. He remembered when he was first commissioned how honored he felt, ready at a drop of the foot, eager to serve. He had waited only a short while before he was called on to report to duty. He remembered when she came in and chose him from the line-up in the Wood rack, how proud he was when she examined him closely, looking for weakness and flaws and discovering none. Beth Ann held him up, felt him, weighed him in her hand, leaned on him, testing him, and then pronounced him suitable. At first, he felt that he was truly needed, but it wasn't too long before he realized that it wasn't going to be quite as he had imagined, not being the mainstay, the leg up he had envisioned. It wasn't it at all. Not at all. In fact, he felt quite uncomfortable almost right from the start, uneasy when there were long lines at the movie theater or post office. Then she would lean heavily on him, whisper, "Would you be a dear?" to the person next in line at the customer service counter, and then deftly cut to the front.

If she were lonely and needed someone to talk to, once again he was front and center, flourished with fanfare. Ta da! Strangers would ask about him as if he were an oddity, a curiosity from an old shop, a monkey's paw or something. She would tell the stranger her story. He had heard it so often that he knew it by heart. It was all about this peculiar numbness in her leg that left her unable to walk unassisted, how it would come and go without explanation, about how no doctor seemed able to identify the problem and she had seen the best of them, and so on and so forth. A tear would escape and then the two of them would stare at the Woody and nod their heads in sympathy. Then the tickle would trickle, creeping in slowly at first with a quiet cough and gaining steam until it tackled and then tuckled into HAHAKAKAROOM! HAHAKAKAROOM! HAHAKAKA ROOM ROOM ROOM AHEM AHEM thing, a guttural thing that frightened him, sounding something like an angry rooster with bad diction. Then she would tell that story, too.

Woodrow wasn't just real sure about how he felt about all of this or what he should do about it. Humans weren't the easiest of all the species to understand. He had a gilded friend who had been assigned to a man who used him to enhance his position as a distinguished gentleman, but that was harmless enough. Another friend of his was wielded as a weapon, on hand to rise against attack. Specially constructed to serve as a part time cane, part time cudgel. But this was something else entirely. There was no mention of it during his training sessions, nothing in any manuals anywhere about this kind of assignment. There was no support group to turn to for solace and comfort. He realized now, after much due consideration, that it was just his bum luck that the woman was sporting a Woody.

Beth Ann pulled into the parking lot a full half hour before her appointment. She had spent most of last Saturday on line seeking a new doctor. The last one had been a little abrupt with her. She didn't think he had examined her thoroughly enough, that he had not spent enough time with her, like he had more important business to attend to. She had been suspicious of this doctor before, like when she told him about the tickle in her throat, the little cough. He told her it was acid reflux. She had heard that old song and dance before. They say that when they have no other explanation for something, like a parrot trained to say "Acid Reflux! Acid Reflux! Acid Reflux! Awk!! Awk!!" She was sick of hearing it. It was something worse than that, something very much more serious. She knew it. She could feel it. Nevertheless, she would accept the prescription and use it as directed, carefully laying out the pills in a neat row next to her napkin at restaurants and downing them in five minute intervals, drowning them with tall glasses of water with no ice. The pills never helped. They only made her have to pee all the time.

So she pretty much decided on a new doctor. Most post their pictures now on line, and she appreciated that. She had scrolled down slowly, scanning each face carefully. She could get a good sense of someone's inner soul and sensitivity by the look on that person's face, a talent for reading physiognomy that made her immediately able to recognize whether kindness, compassion, and caring held sway or was dominated by primal depravity, degeneration, or debauchery. The Dimmesdale and Chillingworth Dilemma. As the universe is comprised of all matter and manner, she accepted the co-existence of the good and the bad, of salvation and damnation, the dual human nature. The Jekyll and Hyde Syndrome.

Then she spotted a very nice looking doctor.He was really quite handsome, and young. She had studied the picture for some time. She felt the good vibes. She liked younger men. Their faces were easier to read, less encumbered by distracting wrinkles and warts and eye glasses. She relied on her skills of discernment. Photoshop might do wonders doctoring up the smudges on one's visage, but it is quite useless against thick stains on sick souls.

And then also, there was something else she needed to consider, and she thought of it often. Though she was proven and true in matters of the heart, the mind, and the soul, she was untried, untested in the matters of the flesh. Pure as the driven snow. At fifty-three, she could not rule out any possibilities. Time was slipping by. She always dressed up when she went to the doctor, but this morning, she had taken an extra little time, digging out the lacy panties that she wore for special occasions, like her birthday or payday. She had been looking for a good excuse to wear her new bra, the one she paid full price for, not the cheap sale bin bras in her top drawer. This would be the day for the new one. She wanted to look especially nice. "You don't get a second chance to make a first impression," her mother always told her. Perhaps this doctor would be a little bit more sympathetic about her need for a handicapped placard to hang from her rear view mirror for all to see that she needed a parking place up close to the front door of places.

She looked around and then hurried across the parking lot. It was such a long walk and there were the new patient forms to be filled out. The numbness left her leg. The strain on Woody lessened considerably. When that happened, he knew the worst was imminent; he was about to be lifted up and shoved into the warm, wet depths of her armpit.

Beatrice appeared one afternoon at the Villa Verdugo, like a stray cat at the back porch, quietly, with no fan fare. She carried up a few boxes from her car and that was that. Just about everyone else living at the Villa Verdugo arrived just like that so no eyebrows were lifted. It was just part of that starting-all-over thing, leaving the past behind. There would be no need to ask any strangers for help, no need to make any compacts with others until there had been enough time to sniff things out.

She was tall and blonde and prone to bursts of garrulity. Prim and proper in her movements and English upbringing, she walked in long, confident strides, easily out pacing her companion and then waiting at a door for it to be opened for her. She moved that way everywhere and always, her long legs jumping over hedges, onto curbs, and into the street to pass amblers, moving in the fast lane and passing people who slowed her down. And that was the way she lived her life and got things done. By the time she reached thirty, she had amassed a small fortune from an import-export business she founded in England.

She sold it, and looking for new opportunities, turned to America.

She always had a clear vision, able to set and determine priorities, able to cut though thick fog and see the truth. She didn't know until she was a grown-up that most people simply wander through life and if something interesting or important happens to them, it is because of circumstance and not by design. So she became a life coach, helping others to make sensible plans, clear away distractions, prioritize, discriminate, making something interesting or important happen. Word spread around Richmond, Virginia and she soon had a steady flow of customers who became successful people who wanted to become more successful people, now that they were rich enough to afford her steep consultation fees. Paul was one of those, a smart, likable gentleman, a lawyer on an upward path who wished to become a partner in his law firm. She was seduced by his good looks and his charm, and she cleared away the distractions, prioritized his game plan, and fulfilled all his objectives. But everything had gone badly. For the first time in her life, she became a victim of circumstance and not design.

She had a flair for the finer things in life, a trained and appreciative eye for classic English autos and haute couture. She liked a smart-talking, well-mannered, clean-shaven gentleman walking on her right side and she liked mingling with people. So she found her kin in Beverly Hills, wedged between gay West Hollywood and intellectual Westwood. She would motor her black Jaguar along the broad boulevards, past the headquarters of the Screen Actors' Guild and the La Brea Tar Pits, under the shadows of the monoliths that house LA's well hung art galleries and through the neighborhoods of the dead rich and famous, now the mansions of the plastic surgeons and the entertainment attorneys.

The movie stars have opted out, heading for Malibu, Pacific Palisades or the Hollywood Hills, well outside of the range of all but the most diligent of tour buses that haul bus loads of wide-eyed tourists past the homes of Jack Benny and Lucille

Ball and Gene Kelly. Guides on mikes point in solemn gestures to the home where the gangster Bugsy Segal was shot one sunny June Sunday morning while he sat on the sofa in front of the picture window reading the Sunday LA Times.

"The bullet," the guide confides, "entered the back of his skull and exited through his eye socket, sending the Bugster's eyeball shooting across the living room and bouncing off the opposite wall."

"Up ahead here, folks, is Dead Man's Curve. If you look closely, you can still see the deep scar on that big oak tree... riiiiiiiiiiight THERE!...that ended the singing career of Jan and Dean."

"On your left here, on the sidewalk... riiiiiiight HERE!... is where River Phoenix dropped dead of a drug overdose on Halloween Night while waiting in a long line to get into the Viper Room riiiiiiight THERE!"

But mostly the tour guides point to the invisible. Behind those ivied walls and royal palms is the mansion where they shot "Falcon Crest." Behind that steep hedge at the top of that knoll is the Playboy Mansion. "The Beverly Hillbillies" mansion is on the other side of that big, black gate and up the long drive. What high walls, iron gates, and long driveways can't shield, hired security can. Rent-a-cops cruise the neighborhoods in official-looking squad cars, highly visible. The signs and the sentries are posted. The handsome Beverly Hills police officers wear white gloves and drive big white Chevy Suburbans and are trained in matters of diplomacy, etiquette, good manners, and discretion.

Tiffani lived in the Villa Verdugo for nearly six years and so felt that she pretty much had seniority over just about anything that goes on there, demanding the best of all available amenities of the Villa Verdugo. She was a large, dark chocolate woman from East Saint Louis with a perpetual appetite for pot and dark chocolate cake with butter cream icing. She was always well supplied with both. She spent her waking hours sunk into an easy chair wedged between her computer monitor and her television screen and sucked on a snake head of her hookah.

Ever since she was a young girl, she didn't believe much of what anyone told her. In fact, she didn't trust much of anything she heard or read. Just because someone said something or something was on the television or reported in the local paper didn't automatically make it so. In fact, Verify, Verify, Verify was what she spent most of her time doing, instantly clicking her long fingernails onto her computer keyboard to double-check anything and everything uttered even in casual conversation. She could spot deception a mile away. She had had long experience learning from the best of them. The world is filled with hustlers and hucksters and if you're a patsy and you fall for it all, you deserve what you get. It's your own fault. Don't come crying to her about it.

She rented the floor of her apartment to Harold, a struggling black musician who had agreed to pay half of the rent and half of the utilities for the privilege of sleeping there. But she fibbed about the rent, inflated the electric and gas bills, able to snooker him into paying more than his fair share of the costs of Apartment 213 and leaving him with little left of his paycheck. When his behavior was subservient enough, she would reward him with occasional use of the computer or a visit with the hookah. If he objected to anything, she would remind him angrily about his stinky bowel movements she had to endure, or the fact that he was using her computer to look at pictures of naked, young white boys in full bloom.

She would sleep until 3:00 most afternoons, rising just as soon as she heard the door click behind Harold, the Dim-witted, leaving for his job as a security guard. She would make her coffee. She knew that soon the cell phone would begin ringing, starting her business day. Her clients knew that she was a late riser, and fearful of waking her and her wrath, would wait until after late afternoon to place their order. On any given day, she would buzz up seven or eight to the second floor there. She had her regulars, but she didn't call them customers. She called them friends. To protect herself from the law, she told them that she was giving the pot to them, but that they could leave a donation on her kitchen counter for her if they so wished. Most of them left a twenty dollar bill for a little bud in a little thumbnail-sized baggy. Occasionally, someone would leave a stack of twenties for a fist-sized bag. Those who did not leave the appropriate donation ever found their phone calls returned. Once the donation was made, she would fire up the hookah and offer the snake head as a courtesy, following the business model she noticed at See's Chocolates, which offers a free piece of fancy candy with every purchase, or Krispi Kreme, which presents customers waiting in long lines a free donut fresh from the oven, and staying open into the late nights seven days a week to accommodate her needs.

She believed in her product, that it was the best in LA, and no one would disagree with her. It was either that her friends agreed with her or thought it wasn't worth opening up that can of worms. If there were a complaint, that name would be scratched from her little black book after a severe tongue-lashing and the unfortunate soul left to lament his lack of good judgment.

She feared the federal, state, and local government, the subway, everything white except for butter cream icing, bathrooms with no windows, and most of all, the LAPD. Her anger surfaced at the slightest provocation, an anger rich with the coarse language and aggression gleaned from her eight years in the Army. She bought dozens of cartons of eggs as ammo against anyone in the neighboring Otsego Arms complex that had barking dogs or noisy motorcycles. But nowhere was her ire more evident than when she got behind the wheel of her old Ford Taurus.

Traffic is as predictable as the weather, a constant that can be counted on. There is no ignoring it. It never changes. Traffic in early morning and late evening is barely more bearable than the rush hours. The surface streets are no more comfortable than the freeways, whose waysides are cluttered with broken glass, shards of sharp metal, and fender parts. Flat tires are commonplace. Drivers swerve to avoid stepladders, old mattresses, kitchen appliances, bales of cardboard, palm fronds and everything else that falls from the overloaded pick-ups of overworked day laborers. Cars overheat on the 405 over the Sepulveda Pass and catch on fire. Semi-trucks and smoky diesel-powered school buses spew their noxious emissions into the fresh-air intake ducts of the cars trapped behind or between them.

Angelenos deal with the stress of the traffic in their own ways. Some develop road rage and resort to shooting at some offender who cut them off. Others buy motorcycles and become quite deft at lane splitting, a legal thing that allows hog riders to drive between the lanes of traffic, often startling an unwary car driver and readjusting his side mirror. Others throw their manners by the roadside and drive to the front of the long lines waiting to exit, and then cut in, avoiding eye contact to avoid culpability.

Tiffani had her own foolproof system, lane hopping. She would begin in Lane One. If she believed that the lane next to her was moving a little faster, she would push in to Lane Two. It didn't matter how anyone else felt about it. If it was there, it was hers. If another driver had an issue about it and honked, he or she would immediately back off after seeing the look on her face. Then Lane Three would beckon her. A quarter of a mile down the road, it was back to Lane Two. A bit farther down the road, it was back over to Lane Three, then Lane Four, then Three again, back to Four, Five, Six, back to Five, Four, Three, back to Two, back to Three, back to Two and finally back to One, firmly believing in her heart that everyone else on the freeway were there simply to spend a good part of their day getting in her way. No passenger riding with her would dare point out that in spite of all of her maneuvering, that same black BMW that was in back of them three miles ago was now in front on them. That same delivery van that was on their right was now on their left.

If she were annoyed by a slowpoke in front of her, she would tailgate within an inch of the offender's rear bumper and blink her headlights on and off in rapid succession, and wave her hands in a friendly "move-aside" gesture. If that didn't work, she would dispense with the politeness and blow a long insistent honk to get the driver's attention, then shrug her shoulders, lift her palms up, and shoot over an exaggerated look of "what the…?" It didn't take very long for a first-time passenger in her car to slump down into the seat to hide, too embarrassed to surface until her car pulled safely into the darkness of the underground parking garage of the Villa Verdugo, and swearing under solemn oath never to step foot into a car with her again.

Chapter 3

The High Holy Days would be approaching soon, Rosh Hashanah, then Yom Kippur, back to back. It would be one of those rare occasions when the boys were released from the confining walls to prepare for the trip back to their families in Miami or Chicago or Brooklyn or Houston. Zealous rabbis in Old Testament beards would hurry the boys past the temptations of Melrose, where loud pulsating hip-hop emanates from trendy fashion stores featuring black leather bustier and $200 T-shirts, where tattoo parlors and piercing joints prick their way between the dank nightclubs, their outside walls plastered with spooky glossies of the grungy, where Japanese girls loaded down with heavy bags teeter in steep platform shoes down crowded sidewalks.

They boys would arrive at Fairfax, purchase their tickets and the tins of tuna and cartons of crackers needed for the flight, and return to their sanctuary to pack for the trip back home. Before they left for the airport, they begged Felix for his forgiveness for any transgressions that may have happened in the classroom anytime during the semester and then celebrate their release from guilt with pious davenings of thanksgiving, bobbing toward the east in unison like the big boats in the Marina Del Rey harbor at evening tide. They are as fervent in their remorse as they are in their celebrations and when it's all over, they return to their life of study and discipline until the festival of Hanukkah in December releases them once again from the sacred duties of their holy vows.

Mainstream Talent was closed for the day. Most of the industry was shut down. It was the Day of Atonement and things would be quiet. The fax machine would hum alive only occasionally, mostly apologies from Jewish casting directors seeking forgiveness. Barbara would not need to slip out of her pajamas. Today she had time to think, to catch up on some stuff. She had wanted to purge a few from her talent bank. It wasn't her favorite part of being an agent, having to clean up her ranks, cutting back a little bit.

It was time to unload that prima donna who had a little luck, and then became a bigger pain in the ass than it was worth. It would be the same sentence for Which Way Walter, who called in every five minutes, lost in Century City somewhere, "Which way am I supposed to turn?" then five minutes later, "Okay, now which way?" Then, "Okay, what was that address again?" She was too busy for that. Casting directors would call and tell her that he was doing the same thing at audition sessions, slowing them down with all of his stupid little questions. "Now what is my motivation again?" They were too busy for that, too.

Then there were always a few that never get called in. No reasonable explanation for it, other than they just never get called in. Can't do anything about it but send them on their way. Make room for some new blood. She would call them personally. She didn't like doing it, but she felt she owed them that much at least. They were always shocked. Some would say they were sorry and swore to do better. Some just swore. But it didn't matter. She would be firm. "Sorry," she would say. She might as well do it today, the Day of Atonement.

But the talent showcases were another thing. They had become an everyday thing. There were lots of them going on in LA all the time, groups coming in from all over the country and abroad. Someone was always calling, asking her to come over to a showcase for a while, look around. Sometimes it was a friend calling, someone to whom she owed a favor. "We got someone you really must see, a young Tom Cruise. He'll knock your socks off!" If she couldn't, could she send someone from her office, an associate, maybe? So she sent Felix.

It is a strange, Felix concluded, after working his first showcase, how many people believe they are born actors, that no training or experience is necessary, that they can just feel how to do it, sense it. Some actually are born actors. Trial lawyers in packed and hushed courtrooms rival the talents of the great Sirs Lawrence Olivier or Ian McKellen. Televangelists hypnotize congregations of millions in unctuous tongues with fervent promises of a better life in the one hereafter. Politicians learn how to win votes with patriotic staging, flattering camera angles, and intimacy with teleprompters. Two different actors became the governor of the most powerful and richest state in America, and one of them became president of the most powerful and richest nation in the world. But for the most part, most people are not born actors and Hollywood is quick to recognize the untrained or untalented.

Felix took his seat at the judge's table in a small and stuffy conference room at the LAX Harrison Hotel and Convention Center. Across the hall a few paces was the cavernous convention hall for the big events. Today's group was from Louisiana and Mississippi, mostly. He knew that when they arrived, they believed they would be performing on the main stage in front of thousands. But they meekly submitted to the conference room, seated on uncomfortable folding chairs, impatiently and nervously waiting their turn to strut and fret their five minutes upon the small, makeshift stage. It didn't take him long to learn that this group had fallen prey to well-oiled hucksters that had charged them exorbitant fees for poor head shots and demos, inflated the costs of transportation and their hotel rooms at the Harrison, and made worthless promises of inside connections.

Felix dreaded the obligatory one-on-one interviews that

followed the showcase where he dispensed the advice and the bad news. He tried to be polite and helpful, but avoided creating any false hopes or high expectations. He figured they needed to know the truth, and that frankly, they were not going to make it, telling the wannabe high fashion models to get braces on their teeth, to lose weight, and to stay in school.

He told hopeful young actors to get experience in their home town first, take acting classes, and get involved in local theater, anything but coming out unprepared. Felix would talk in calm terms and ask the frank questions. To the mother and father of some 13-year-old freckle-faced rural boy, Felix would ask if they both would quit their jobs, pull the kids out of school, sell their house, move all the way across the country to Los Angeles, find a new place to live, find jobs, and enroll the kids in the Los Angeles Unified School District, all to try their hand at the biggest crapshoot in town.

Felix knew, too, that many of those lined up to see him were more interested in the bucks in the deal than they were in the actual craft itself, blinded by unreasonable expectations about the amounts of money they would earn and the fan clubs and paparazzi they were expecting. Then there were those who believed that all they needed to do was park their car on the street in front of a studio and pose for a while and then everything would fall right into place. To those, Felix didn't feel quite so bad about delivering the bad news. "Go buy a lottery ticket," he wanted to tell them. "Your chances are much better." But he didn't. It just sounded rude. And you really never knew for sure. That is the thing about Hollywood. Anything can happen.

Last Saturday in San Diego, there were more than a thousand young children. He sat there at a folding table at the far end of a long room for a long, long time. There wasn't even a makeshift stage, either, just a long, long line lined up all the way out to the street. Each lovely young child wanted to sing or pose or do a monologue, standing there right in front of him. He would give them sixty seconds, take their headshot, say a kind word, and move on to the next in line. At the end of the long, long day, when no one was looking, he tossed all the head shots, demo reels and comp cards into a nearby dumpster. He felt badly. They were such nice kids, hopeful, innocent, sincere. But there wasn't anything that anybody could really do for them, for one reason or another.

But this afternoon was easy. There were only forty or so. Once they were sitting nervously at the table across from Felix, after the interminable wait in line, they did not wish to be rushed. This was what it was all about. This is what they had paid for, contact with an industry insider. They spread out their portfolios filled with their head shots of every conceivable pose, expecting Felix to examine every one carefully and closely. Then they would ask how they did on the stage. Some would flirt. Then they would ask for contact numbers or business cards. When he sat through his first showcase, he did provide that information. He didn't know any better. He didn't know that for the next month or two, the offices of Mainstream Talent would be inundated, utterly overwhelmed with phone calls and faxes and emails and drop-bys and Barbara was angry. She didn't get anything done for a long time so she was angry for a long time. He didn't provide that information anymore. Felix knew they would all go home and wait by the telephone, not leave the house. But the phone would never ring. He knew that like last week, there wasn't really much he could do for any of them. Like last week, he would take no head shots back to Barbara. It was just something he had to do, just part of the process.

None of the agencies want to be bothered. The scores of small boutique agencies scattered around LA, as well as with the big players, the impenetrable suites of Creative Artists Agency, International Creative Management, William Morris Endeavor on Wilshire Boulevard, where the really big deals are made and reported by Variety magazine and the Hollywood Reporter. Entry is strictly restricted. Unsolicited mail is dutifully stamped Return to Sender! or dispatched unopened to the dumpsters in the back alley. No showcases. No newbie's. No manuscripts. No screenplays. No novels. No head shots. No demo reels. No phone numbers. No fax numbers. No email addresses. No visitors. No entry. No parking. No standing. No talking. No breathing. No, thank you, but **NO!**

Occasionally, there are those who steadfastly refuse to take no for an answer. They had been to several showcases but have never heard a word from any of them so they don't believe anything they hear anymore. They become more aggressive, pushy even, refusing to leave until they have contact information. Some agencies have post office box numbers to give to these types, which they empty only when the post office complains. Others give dead-end email addresses that funnel everything into the trash can. Felix would give them his landline number, which he monitored only when the message machine was full, hitting the play button for a quick sample, then the fast-forward button. Zip! Then the erase button Zap! in a quick succession of jerks. Zip-Zap! Zip-Zap! Zip-Zap!

But Heath Charles Harley was there that afternoon. Felix had not been particularly impressed with the young man's monologue. It seemed that he had forgotten his lines or something, but Felix was impressed by his teeth, which rested well over his lower lip. There was no escaping them. They would have filled an entire dam of over-achieving eager beavers with a gnawing admiration. Jerry Lewis would have been one-upped. He had a peculiar manner, nerdy somewhat, perhaps Billy Bob Thortonesque, an interesting aura, good head shots, a gentile Louisiana drawl, impeccable manners, and a rich father. He was in his last semester of college, majoring in theater. Felix wondered, though, as he talked to him, whether his aspirations had staying power, legs. It takes time and money to develop new talent. Some never develop or never get a break. Some actors get bored with the process or tire of being broke all the time. And if an actor does make it, will he or she stay loyal or jump ship when the going gets good, headed for one of those bigger agencies on Wilshire. And the biz is rife with stories of agents who passed, who said no to nerds like Jim Carrey or Will Ferrell.

So Felix bit. For Heath Charles Harley, the phone call would come.

There are millions of people in LA and they all have names. Jesus, Treniqua, Ho, Stanislaus or Irving. River, Sequoia, First Born, Waterfalls, Blueberry. Donner and Blitzen. Little Bit and his little brother Tiny Bit. You name it. It's out there. After all, this is California. And it's usually no problem until an actor finally becomes eligible for membership in the Screen Actors Guild and then discovers that someone else is already registered with the same name. Sometimes things are just out of your control. There is always someone out there, somewhere, with your name. Albert Brooks was born Albert Einstein. Too bad. Zip Zap. Someone else had that name and so a name changes. Sometimes ethnicity is a problem. An unpronounceable eastern European name, a name changes. Sometimes politics is the problem. Before World War II, there were about a dozen Hitler's in the Greater Los Angeles phone book. After the war. Zip. Zap. A name stained forever. No longer usable. Pretty much took Adolf off the shelf as well. One of Barbara's clients was named Jihad. He couldn't get any auditions in the largely Jewish dominated entertainment industry until he became Jay. Young hopefuls, eager to shed their Midwest heritage and christened Sheila or Theresa, become Brook or Ashley.

But Heath Charles Harley had been called Heath Charles Harley from the day he was born, and he answered to nothing else. It was all one word, Heathcharlesharley. "Heathcharles-harleyhoney, pleasecometodinnerdeah." He was fourteen before he even learned how to spell it. He had special status in his family. His mother had conceived him in a steamy Motel Six during a drunken one-night stand with a smooth, clean-shaven likeable Southern gentleman who walked on her right side and who disappeared before the sun rose the next day over the steamy Louisiana bayou. To atone for his mother's careless ways and to discourage any conjecture from their gentile neighbors, his grandfather adopted him, becoming his father. And with that simple stroke, Heathcharlesharley's grandmother became his mother, his uncle became his brother and his mother became his sister.

The days were getting shorter and Beatrice added another layer of clothing. It was one of only a few concessions that she would have to make. She had no complaints about the southern California weather. It was always pretty much predictable, like the traffic. If the temperature fluctuates more than a few degrees or the wind picks up, Angelenos call it weather. "Weather is moving in," the would say as they reach for the sweater. For the eight months of summer, there was never a need for rain dates for picnics and ballgames, no umbrellas or sweaters needed for the walks through Runyon Canyon. But now the days were becoming shorter, the evenings chilly. Weather was approaching. Fall. Then the LA Winter. But she knew she would not be forced out into dark, frigid January mornings. She would not have to shovel a heavy wet British snow or scrape a little hole in the frozen windshield big enough to be able to see well enough to drive home. But there would be rain. It would become the main event. Beverly Hills radio and television stations would interrupt their regular programming with bulletins advising residents not to wear their silk shirts and suede jackets. Long lines form at Mercedes and BMW dealerships, where roof technicians raise convertible tops. Rodeo Drive boutiques fill with patrons shopping for the newest look in hooded raincoats and matching galoshes for the family's matching Italian bulldogs.

On the freeways, the rainwater mixes with the eight-month accumulation of engine oil and brake fluid across twelve lanes, making them slicker than any good Virginia road on the iciest day of the winter. Squealing with delight, young Angelenos in their glass-packed BMW's plow through puddles at top speed, sending torrents of water onto on-coming cars or into the hapless pedestrians brave enough to venture out. If Angelenos have any complaints at all about the weather, it would be about the marine layer in the spring, affectionately nicknamed May Gray and June Gloom, brought in by Coastal Eddie and keeping skies overcast until three in the afternoon before burning off into an azure sky.

It was almost three years ago when Beatrice first settled into her new home in Richmond. She had been so puzzled when she first arrived. Virginia was certainly different from the Isle of Jersey in the English Channel. She remembered her first evening there. She had just finished unpacking for the day and had settled in for a spot of tea. Then the doorbell rang. There, standing on her stoop, were two young children, one dressed like a little fairy of sorts, and the other rather like a pirate. Clutched in their little hands were little tote bags brimming with chocolate bars and cakes. “Trick or treat!” they shouted in unison.

“How quaint,” she thought, “they must be here to welcome me to the neighborhood with a trick or a treat.”

“Well,” she said, “I think I would so enjoy a nice little trick.” Perhaps it would be a card trick or a rabbit appearing in one’s hat.

“We don’t know any tricks, lady.”

“You don’t know any tricks? Then why did you offer me a trick or a treat, when you don’t know any tricks? Why didn’t you just offer me a treat?”

“It’s trick or treat, lady,” repeated the pirate. The little fairy held her bag open towards Beatrice. Completely puzzled, she decided that since the children were so young, that perhaps it would be better for her to opt for the other prize.

“Well, then since you don’t know any tricks, I guess I will take a treat.” Beatrice then leaned long into the bag of each child, fished around for a few moments and selected a large chocolate bar from the pirate’s bag and a popcorn ball from the young fairy.

“Well, thank you ever so much!”

“Weird,” muttered the young pirate and the two clumped back down the steps.

Beatrice set her treats on the little table next to her rocker, unwrapped the candy bar, and returned to her tea. She knew she was going to like it here. "Nothing like this ever happened on Jersey. These Americans are a friendly lot," she thought as she rose once again to answer the door. "Who could this be now?"

There on her front stoop were three more children, a small tot of a ghost, an alien from Mars, and a cowboy in a ten-gallon hat and plastic leather vest. "Trick or Treat!"

"Well," thought Beatrice, "here are more. These Americans are so quaint." She smiled down on the three. These children look a little older. Perhaps they would know a trick."

"Well, I would like a nice trick, if you please. The last children here didn't know one and I was so disappointed. But they were so young."

"Whacha talkin' about, pardner?" drawled the cowboy.

"I would so like a trick, love."

"A trick? I ain't never heared of anyone wantin' a trick. And don't call me love. My name's Tex."

"Don't you have a little trick, Tex? Can't you pull a rabbit out of that big hat you have?"

"Well, I can rub my nose and my belly at the same time," said the ghost in his spookiest voice.

"That will do, I guess, if that's all you have."

Dutifully, the young ghost put down the little plastic orange pumpkin he was carrying and performed the trick. "How's that, lady?"

"It's okay, but I sort of expected a little more. What with going around offering tricks or treats and not knowing any good tricks."

Nodding to the cowboy and the alien, "Okay, you two, since you don't have any tricks, I guess I will have to settle for a treat." Leaning over, she selected a most wonderful looking red apple from the cowboy and a bag of salted nuts from the alien. "Okay, now off with you before my tea gets cold."

"That's not fair, pardner," grumped Tex as he yanked his six-shooter from the holster, took dead aim, and pulled the trigger with a click, then turned and disappeared into the darkness.

"Oh dear," thought Beatrice, as she shut the door. "This new country is a little strange. Little children dressed up in costumes walk about the neighborhood offering tricks and treats to people, but not knowing any tricks and then complaining that it's not fair." And then it dawned on her. "How silly of me. I am supposed to provide a trick for them and then I get my treat. That's why the children seemed upset. Silly, silly, silly me."

Why, she knew plenty of tricks. She used to torment her father and her little sister for long hours with an endless parade of tricks. That was one of her real loves. That and practical jokes. That was the mischievous side of her. Her friends all knew to be on the lookout while good old Beatrice was around. She giggled. This was even better yet. She so much loved to perform. What could be better? She regretted that she had left her large box of tricks and gags safely stored in the dry basement of her father's house, never for a moment thinking she would actually need them over here. But she could make do with a simple coin or two for now. Should she ever move again, she would be sure to ask her father to send her the box so that she would be better prepared. "Would there be more coming," she wondered, and the heavy pounding on her door sent her hurrying to her handbag. So she was ready for the next round.

"Trick or treat!" they all shouted in unison, a skinny skeleton, a funny little clown with a white face and a big red nose, and a young Elvis Presley. Behind them were four more, all squeezed onto the stoop. Another ghost, Harry Potter, a young boy dressed like a tart, and a little fairy queen. "Trick or treat!"

"Okay, I have a nice trick. Move back a little bit so that I have some room." She palmed the quarter, reached up to the ear of the clown and proudly produced the coin she pretended to have taken from it. "Ta da!" she proclaimed. The tart laughed. Encouraged, Beatrice flipped the coin into the air, deftly caught it, closed it into a fist, and then opened the palm to reveal that the coin had disappeared.

"So, said Beatrice proudly, "there is my trick." She

reached into each bag and selected an especially yummy looking cupcake, a peanut bar, and a peppermint stick, some chewing gum, an apple covered with caramel, and two rolls of Life-Savers. There were no more complaints. By the end of the evening, she had enjoyed a dazzling array of costumes and get-ups, exhausted her complete routine of coin tricks, juggled apples and oranges and popcorn balls selected from the offered bags, and in the process, amassed another small fortune and there wasn't a single complaint. She knew that she had come to the right place.

But that was back then, when everything was fun and carefree. But things had happened and now things were different, lots different, actually. That smart-talking, clean-shaven gentleman lawyer had come along and taken her peace, piece by piece, leaving little left for her to enjoy about life.

Felix could do it quickly, two index fingers all that was needed, one finger to zip, one finger to zap.

Beep."Hi, there! Did you know that your vehicle warranty is about to expire? If you act now..." Zip-Zap.

Beep. "This is Officer Knotts and we want to offer you the opportunity to help our local Police Activity Program..." Zip-Zap.

Beep. "Uh, hi, um... this is Jimmy DeMarco and ummm you told me to call you about ummm... finding ummm... someone to ummm help m..." Zip-Zap.

Beep. "Hi, there! Did you know that your vehicle..." Zip-Zap.

Beep. "Hello! This is Roger Hopkins and I am calling because I need your vote..." Zip-Zap.

Beep. "Hi, there! Did you know that yo..." Zi- Zap.

Beep. "Good morning, Sir. I met you at the show case and you t..." Zip-Zap. Next!

Beep. "Hi, Felix. This is your mother calling. Someone told me you were somewhere in California now and he tracked down this number for me. I hope you're doing well, honey. It's such a beautiful fall day and I was thinking of you. Do you remember how we used to rake the backyard together and then when we were all done you would jump into the big pile of leaves? I miss you so much. We haven't heard from you in so long. You sound pretty much the same, a little older, maybe. Can you give me a call, Felix? It's still the same old number. I love you so much. Goodbye, honey."

Beep. "Is this Mr. Felix? This is Charlie Wilson and you told me to call you about the..." Sorry, Charlie. Zip-Zap.

Beep. "Hi, there! Did you..." Zip-Zap

Beep. "H... Zip-Zap

Beep. "H...Zip-Zap

Beep. "Hello, Felix! This is Lenore Anderson. Guess what? Frankie is coming to Los Angeles. His college showcase. Maybe you could help him. Can you call me back?"

Colleges and universities across the nation bring their theater and film majors to showcase their talent. An effort is made to bring in real insiders and to serve fancy noshes with elegance and grace. They have nifty programs with state-of-the-art graphics and finely tuned multi-media presentations of live student performances and film screenings on large stages and screens in darkened theaters on La Cienega Boulevard for a relatively decent audience of industry insiders. One or two of the students may actually receive a phone call, but the rest return to Yale or Ball State and ponder what else they can do with their degree in acting.

After the showcase, Frankie would stay in LA. Mom was uncomfortable about the whole thing. She was as much disturbed by his decision to remain in Los Angeles as she was by his decision to become an actor. She had preferred that he would become a teacher or insurance agent. But an actor? That was just a little too unsettling. But he was always a little different from the other ones. And Frankie, with his dyslexia, had good teachers who taught him how to invent a path of his own to get around obstacles.

Los Angeles. It was so far away. Nobody in the family had ever been out there. She had acquiesced. She had no choice. She knew he would go out regardless of how she felt about it. She wanted him to take along one of the family handguns. She heard all about all the problems out there. Worried about something happening to her baby. She counseled against the move, but he refused to heed her advice and now he was on his way. So that's when she called Felix. Felix knew Frankie's family. They had nursed on the same milk from the same Indiana breast. Felix knew the boy and his brothers and sisters and mother and father and cousins and nieces and nephews and friends. That's the way small towns are. Lots of the dots are connected.

"Will you keep an eye on him?"

"Sure," said Felix.

"Maybe you could help him find a place to live?"

"There's a place downstairs here, a two-bedroom."

Chapter 4

"Do you smoke," asked Frankie?

"No," said Heathcharlesharley. "Do you?"

"No," said Frankie.

"Do you have a cat?" queried Frankie. He so much hated cats.

"No," assured Heathcharlesharley.

"Are you a queer?" queried Heathcharlesharley. He so much hated queers.

"No," assured Frankie.

So Heathcharlesharley joined Frankie among the birds and the birds of paradise of the Villa Verdugo. Neither of them was much acquainted with housekeeping in general and vacuum sweepers or kitchens in particular. Frankie preferred his daily diet of ramen noodles and peanut butter sandwiches. His art minor in college surfaced as he carefully loaded the smooth peanut butter evenly onto the knife and then in short and precise strokes painted it onto a slice of bread, covering the total surface of the bread and wiping any excess off the crust with the deft swipe of a paper towel, like Leonardo Da Vinci, slowly and painstakingly daubing pigment onto the canvas of the "Mona Lisa," then dipping the brush clean.

The father of Heathcharlesharley had been forced to eat things against his will when he was a child, so the old man swore that any son of his own would not be forced to eat food that didn't look or sound good. So Heathcharlesharley never had a visit from zucchini or a pear. He had never sampled a milkshake or salad or strawberry short cake, an egg, a piece of chocolate, or a supermarket. Every afternoon a plain cheeseburger with a side of fries, and a liter of Coke would be delivered to the apartment. In the evenings it would be a large pepperoni pizza. A bite or two, a slice, or a sip was always enough and the leftovers were left as they lay. And that was how he dined during the 22 years of his life.

Frankie was very, very tall and blond and physically very well fit from years of working in the family canoe business. He could heave a hefty aluminum station-wagon of a canoe over his head with ease and load it unaided onto the top rack of the trailer attached to the old school bus the family used to haul Buckeyes back up the Whitewater River after their long and drunken excursions down to Cedar Grove. It was in that family owned business where Frankie learned the values of hard work and good old Midwestern frugality. He knew he was on his own. If this was what he wanted to do, he would have to provide his own resources. So he bought a bunk bed. He would rent the top bunk to someone for half of his half of the rent. Then he found a job, working as a server at the Coral Reef, a popular tropical restaurant just a few miles down Ventura Boulevard in Sherman Oaks. He had gone through the training, memorized the four page menu, and passed the test. It was the first real job he had ever had outside of the family business.

Heathcharlesharley never had a real job of any kind anywhere and wasn't entirely sure what one even was, but he figured from what everyone said about it, a job was something definitely not for him. So that, he figured, left him only two choices, becoming either a priest or actor, and he was still sorting through the details, testing himself, keeping one foot in each neighborhood.

When he moved from Lafayette, he carted along scores of expensive leather-bound volumes of plays from the early classics of Sophocles and Euripides and Shakespeare to the American treasures of Edward Albee and David Mamet, none of which he ever read completely, but he knew the titles and the signature lines from these plays that he insisted to his father that he must have. They were tools of the trade, he argued.

As an actor in his high school and college plays, he could never remember his lines and often times found himself ad-libbing long monologues that would become the talk of the next day around the school hallways and in the teacher's lounge. It wasn't his fault that he had trouble concentrating on much. He had attention-deficit disorder, a rather profound case of it, to boot. That is just the way it was. But now he had an internship in Hollywood, sitting right next to Frankie at the glass dining room table, filling out submission slips and licking envelopes. He had an inside connection now.

"Come on out," he urged his only friend. "I'll make you a star."

Ronald Beauchamp happened to become Heathcharlesharley's best friend one afternoon by mistake, rescuing him from the high school bully in the bathroom. After graduation, they never saw each other again, with Heathcharlesharley heading for college and Champ for the oil rigs in the Gulf of Mexico.

A self-described coonass, a Cajun, a guy from No Man's Land, Terrebonne Parish, he came from Creole parents who believed in the virtues of hard work and fierce independence. You worked hard for it or you didn't have it. A quiet man, never saying much to anyone, Champ was a bull of a guy, short, stocky, and strong as an ox. In his early twenties, he was already an old man. His round fat head, punctuated with studs and a jet black Ho Chi Minh, was shaven bald. He washed down each day of his hard life with heavy swigs of Jack Daniels chased with XXX beer.

His story was told in his music, in exquisite tones and remarkable range, in beauty belied by his physicalness, a beauty enhanced by virtuoso skill on Ruby, his red guitar. There was always a song bumping around in his mind, like there was some kind of radio receiver up there with no on-off switch. "Radio Head," he called it. It was his solace, his tutor, his constant companion, his escape from whatever the harsh realities of his current station in life happened to be. And right now the realities happened to be quite harsh, after being given the heave-ho from the rigs for failing one too many drug tests. So Champ arrived carrying everything he owned in a big brown Piggly-Wiggly bag and took up residence on Frankie's top bunk

West Hollywood, known locally as WeHo, is the vibrant and bustling center that celebrates the gay and lesbian community in Los Angeles. Santa Monica Boulevard winds through the heart of it among the neatly trimmed cottages and throbbing nightclubs and eclectic cafes with their exotic dishes and specialty drinks and the art shops and home decorating boutiques, event planners, and top-end hair salons. Billboards portray ads with scantily clad handsome men touting products and services enjoyed by a gay community with plenty of disposable income.

Its biggest event and one of the largest celebrations in all of the Southland is their annual Halloween Parade, when more than half a million spectators and participants gather. It is a political affair as much as it is a social one. Politicians running for election are out in full force, pumping flesh and passing out campaign buttons, waving, blowing kisses, and bowing to the celebrities and judges in the viewing stands. The gay vote can often carry a politician into office in tight elections. The Rainbow Coalition cotillion carries pro-rights and pro-marriage banners and chant slogans decrying homophobia, sexism, and racism. Teens from the LA Youth Center for Gays and Lesbians pass out explicit fliers about safe sex and AIDS awareness and distribute rainbow condoms to spectators, who tuck them safely into their hip pockets for use later than night. Something about a rainbow condom to get the juices flowing.

But primarily it is a Halloween party. Like any good

party, days of preparation take place, the menu planned, the wine cabinets checked and restocked, guest lists reviewed, the day of the event cleared of duty and responsibility.

Santa Monica Boulevard disrobes, soaks in her perfumed bath, shaves her legs, paints her nails, powders her nose, and dresses in her finest tinsels and garlands, ready for her close-up. Young introverted boys don their g-strings and stiletto heels and make their first public gay debut, doing in the full West Hollywood spotlight what they can only do in the shadows back home. Truck drivers haul out their sexy strapless black gowns and push up their pectoral muscles to form boobies. Corporate lawyers dig out their studs and black leather and crack whips and leer at the spectators through long eyelashes. School teachers in Dionysian frenzy waddle down the middle of The Boulevard wearing exaggerated phalluses strapped onto their chest or heads and revel in pretended foreplay. Alice in Wonderland and Dorothy and Toto and Pan and Mab, with all of her attendant faeries bejeweled, glittered and dazzling. There is plenty of hand-holding and lip-locking and confetti and floats and banners and bands in bandannas and dancing brigades and everyone stays until the third crow of the cock.

The new Metro subway station opened on Chandler and Lankershim in the center of North Hollywood and another name change was in the works, the NoHo Arts District, a haven for the artists and the theaters, the cafes and coffee shops, and those who had been left out retreated farther back from the darkened recess of the storefronts and the cheap tenement flats to the darker recesses under the overpass. Felix spent his Friday and Saturday nights in NoHo, now the home to dozens of non-equity theaters, small theaters with seats for an audience of thirty or so, all swaddled in the shade of the Academy of Television Arts and Science and the Sanford Meisner Center. They sprout up like mushrooms in the first warm rain in April and perish in the first hot, dry day of May, the venues retired storefronts with tiny lobbies and back alleys as green rooms. Props are minimal, an elderly sofa, a wobbly table, a wooden chair or two, borrowed from the apartments of the cast and crew. Non-equity is nonunion, which means to the cast and crew that the thrill and the pleasure of plying their craft is their greatest, and only, reward.

Felix enjoyed the creativity, the edginess of the place, the cast, crew, and audience standing outside together on the sidewalks during intermission, smoking. It is here that the fledglings test their wings, earning credits, field-testing one's newest creative endeavor, networking with others. It is here where new actors learn how to learn lines, lighters learn how to light, sounders learn how to sound, and directors learn how to direct. Novice, angst-ridden writers under the heavy influence of Eugene O'Neill and Tennessee Williams fill the stages with dramas of incest, suicide, forbidden love, rape, mental illness, and alcoholism, as black as the paint that covers every square inch of the theater interiors. On a good night, a troupe may play to an audience of a dozen or so. On particularly slow nights or when a reviewer is scheduled, the cast and crew, usually one and the same, cruise the sidewalks and local coffee shops, enticing an audience with the promise of a free ticket and a good show.

Tucked in among these fledgling theaters are the equity theaters, Deaf West, El Portal and the NoHo Arts Center, which present full production musicals or classical or avant garde theater to full houses at $50 a pop and union wages to the actors and crews. They have thick glossy playbills and assigned seating. None of the cast and crew in these venues have to slip out a few minutes before the opening curtain to solicit an audience.

El Pueblo de Nuestra Senora la Reina de Los Angeles de Porciuncula is her full god-given name, but those who live there call her LA. She is the City of Angels. She is the City of Immigrant Angels. They are Latino, Asian, European, and African. They cram extended families of ten or fifteen into the two bedroom apartments in the low-rent districts in the San

Fernando Valley and South Central LA. They find comfort and support in the barrios and places called Little Italy and Little Armenia and Little Bangladesh, and China Town, Thai Town, Korea Town, and Filipinotown. They arrive from Jordan and Syria and Iran and Iraq and Germany and Great Britain. They are Israeli, Chinese, Japanese, and Korean and Vietnamese. They come from India and Pakistan and Malaysia and Indonesia and Australia and a hundred other nations and speak two hundred different languages, drawn by the promise of freedom from autocratic regimes and intolerant religious fanatics and crushing poverty. And they work as strawberry pickers and maids and gardeners and restaurant servers and cooks and car washers and they slowly save enough to take a place of their own. They send their children to the Los Angeles Unified School District and monitor their progress carefully. They are decent and honest and proud, and they blend in and become Angelenos and Americans.

The Chabad Lebovitcher Jews are followers of the Rebbi Menachem Mendel Schneerson, who died in 1994 in Brooklyn. They believe that the spirit of a great wise man and prophet such as the rebbe remains after death, and some Lebovitchers believe that the rebbe was not only a sage, but also the messiah. Unlike other Jewish sects, the Lebavitchers proselytize, becoming shluchim, or missionaries, spreading Lebavitcher practices in the hopes of hastening the arrival of the messiah and redemption. So every Friday afternoon for a few hours, the older boys of the yeshiva load into private vans for the short excursion to the Farmer's Market in the shadows of CBS Television City in the Fairfax District, on the lookout for fallen-away Jews, hoping to convince them to return to traditional Jewish practices.

Felix wasn't exactly sure how his students were able to pick out fallen away Jews from the crowds that flood the market place. He knew it couldn't be by the size of their nose because nearly all of his students had normal sized noses and many even had very small ones. He knew it couldn't be by the color of their hair as several of his students had red or blond or brown hair, as well as thick, curly black locks. And there were fat Jews and skinny Jews and tall Jews and short Jews and Jews with green eyes and blue eyes and brown eyes and such.

Maybe it was the way they walked. Or the expression on their face. Maybe the students had their own physiogonometer, or radar systems, like bats. Probably, though, they just hang around the garlic stand. Chances were very good that they would hit pay dirt there. Some habits are just hard to break. But he couldn't be sure. It just became another mystery, one that was meant to go unsolved since Felix was reluctant to probe too deeply into the mysteries of the universe with Rabbi Horowitz.

Lebavitcher Jews are generally forbidden to touch a razor to their body so a bearded Jew is generally considered a devout Jew. Felix figured that was the reason why the Lebavitcher women wore their skirts down to their ankles. To hide their hairy legs. But that theory went up in smoke when someone mentioned in passing that orthodox Jews were allowed to wax, but there was little evidence that men exercised that option on their face.

The Lebavitchers isolate themselves as much as possible from the frenetic and modern megalopolis around them, living in their own self-sustaining communities, free as much as possible from the influences and the provocations of the secular world. But the Christian world surrounding them is more difficult to escape. After all, the early fathers of California were proselytizing Christian shluchim who honored their deities by naming their missions after them. And these early missions became the major cities of today, San Francisco, San Diego, Santa Monica, Santa Cruz, San Jose, Sacramento. So the yeshiva rabbis did what they could to purify the language. "San" and "Santa," omnipresent Latino-Christian words in California, become "Simcha," as in Simcha Diego, Simcha Francisco, Simcha Monica, Simchamento, and Simcha Claus, if one must refer to him at all.

There were no text books or novels to seduce the boys from their spiritual quests, but the Rosh Yeshiva had okayed, after much careful consideration, deliberation, solitary anguish, and prayers for guidance, the sports section of the LA Times, but only on the conditions, terms, and stipulations spelled out in articulated detail, that it be closely scrutinized by the authorities, mainly himself, before public dissemination to his young charges. Advertisements featuring women or other inappropriate subjects were snipped out or inked over. Stories about wrestling, boxing, poker, horse racing, beach volleyball, swimming, and other salacious sporting activities would always fail to meet the standards for approval.

So Felix spent his time teaching writing and whenever possible, delicately narrating a timeless tale.

"Thousands of years ago, when the father god Zeus ruled the universe, there…"

"Uh, Sir?" That was a cool thing at the yeshiva. The students called him "Sir."

Yes?

"You can't say that here."

"Say what here?"

"The pagan god. If the Rosh Yeshiva would hear about this…" The Rosh was a frightfully hoary rabbi who knew the Dead Sea before it was even sick. Felix was diligent in staying away from his path, lest he remind the Rosh Yeshiva of his materialism and spiritual depravity that would evoke his choler.

"Oh…Okay, Let me start again. Once upon a time about twelve hundred and fifty years before the birth of Christ…"

"Uh, Sir?"

"Yes?"

"You're not allowed to say that."

"Say What?"

"That 'C' word."

"The 'C' Word?"

"The 'C' word."

"Oh. Well, what do you do when you **have** to say the words "Jesus Christ," like when you hit your thumb with a hammer?"

"We say cheese and crackers, Sir."

"Cheese and crackers?"

"Yes sir, cheese and crackers."

"Okay, about twelve hundred and fifty years before the birth of Cheese and Crackers, there lived a beautiful woman named Helen…"

"Uh. Sir?"

"What!"

"You're not allowed to say that?"

"Now what!!?"

"A beautiful woman…The Rosh would…"

"Okay! Okay! Okay. About twelve hundred and fifty years before the birth of Cheese and Crackers there was a famously fat and ugly mensch, but who would in Jewish circles be known as respectfully good enough looking to qualify as possible fodder for mudderhood…"

Chapter 5

Ruby had languished for years in a black coffin in a very black closet under the basement stairs of an old house of a very old man on old Rue Entombe, wasting away, forgotten about until she was rediscovered during a particularly thorough spring housecleaning by the old man's particularly thorough in-laws, then condemned to hang in the window of a storefront, like a side of beef at a butcher. She had been there for some time at the Fair Deal Pawn and Resale Shop, watching the sun every morning rise over the steaming savanna across the way. She figured that was just the way things were going to be. Until Monsieur Ronald Beauchamp showed up one afternoon. She liked the way he handled her, like he had been around a real lady before. He had caressed her long stiff neck, massaged her smooth flanks, looked her right in the eye, and then pulled her strings. Boy, did he pull her strings. This boy could have his way with her, she was sure of that. They even looked alike. Full waisted. Broad in the shoulders. Strong. Well strung. Both persons of color, he with his dark Creole patina and she with her exotic red. It was right then and there that she knew they would make beautiful music together. He must have felt the same way because he slapped down a handful of bills on the counter, picked her up carefully, double strung her perch on the back of his Harley and roared away.

He called her Ruby. She loved that name. Near as she could remember, nobody ever bothered to give her a name. They would be together all the time, inseparable. At the pier down on the bayou. The back porch on rainy days. Later, in the balmy gulf breezes of the oil rigs. Now the sunny southland of the San Fernando Valley. She never really knew what to expect. That was one of the things she liked the most.

With Monsieur Beauchamp, anything could happen. One night he would be governed by his loneliness and melancholy, the next night, by his loveliness and softness. Sometimes he was gentle and unhurried, a peaceful energy, like when you wait for the light to change before crossing the street, even when there is no traffic, even when no one is watching, even in the middle of an empty night. Or smiling at a child in a stranger's arms for no good reason. You are just there at that point, like it's the heart of something. Other times, deep into the darkest hours, his energy and emotion could become raw and angry and powerful. Sometimes it was a destructive energy, the type that would make you go out and do something ugly, like key a particularly fine automobile because it wasn't yours, or scratch profanity into a park bench frequented by children. For no good reason other than you just feel like doing that at the moment.

But whatever the energy, whatever the emotion, Ruby was always there for him. Whenever she was needed. Rising and falling on request, acquiescing to his demands, showing her metal, sharing equally his power and anger, his vulnerability and needs. And he for her.

Tiffani sat at her control panel, an astronaut at the helm of the spaceship. Green lights and red lights and blue lights blinked in the darkness like an alien monster. The glow of the hookah brightened as she drew on the snakehead, deep in thought. Above her, the ceiling fan fluttered. Her log was opened to a clean page carefully lined with fresh headings and columns and rows. She settled deeply into the cockpit, took a deep breath, focused, and then resolutely reset the clock to zero hundred hours, pausing for a moment to relish the first step in a gargantuan task. She was on a new mission, one that would require Herculean concentration, research, and long hours of arduous labor, consuming all of her energy and thought for months and months. But in the end, all of her efforts would be worth the price. She was eager to start the long trek, an important journey with both scientific and ethical ramifications. It would be quite a challenge. She had done her homework, had previewed the data, and tonight was Day One. She slipped the disc into the drive, leaned closely into the screens, one hand holding the snake head, the other holding the remote, and summoned forth "Titanic."

This was going to be an official inquisition. The task was daunting. It was an extraordinarily long movie and every inch of it demanded an excruciating, frame-by-frame scrutiny. She did not want to miss even one little water spot on a single lens, one ringlet out of place in the female lead, one can label turned slightly out of place in a series of inserts, one shirt collar that had been adjusted.

She knew already when she previewed the film that she would need to check to see when things were first introduced, looking for anachronisms. She was kept really busy with "Forrest Gump." Mello-Yellow hadn't been developed yet and there was Mr. Gump sucking on one. USA Today hadn't been published yet and there he is reading one. She had to check to see what year the Chevrolet Impala had fender skirts and static straps, what month Charley Company of the First Air Cavalry Division charged up the hills at An Loc, then checking those statistics against the year the movie was set in. She would carefully record each indiscretion into her log, correlating the notation to the minute and second posted on the digital counter. By the time she finished "Forrest Gump," she had seventy-two pages of entries in her log.

She sent her audit results in an anonymous manila envelope to that fancy agency on Wilshire that represented that Robert Zemeckis guy who directed that nightmare. She didn't include her return address because she didn't want anyone coming over late at night to settle any scores. After all, it's people like her who keep people like him honest and they don't like that. They figure that if no one is really watching, they can be as sloppy as they want. Now it was time for the Titanic to sink.

It was open mike at Ho Ho's. Felix had called ahead of time to ask for a place on the roster. There was still one position left out of twenty so his name was jotted down at the bottom of the line-up. The only audience members were the other comics and a few of their friends. Those on the line-up weren't watching, but sitting silently scribbling down last minute ideas onto yellow legal pads or pacing outside, chain-smoking cigarettes until their name was called. He had done open mike nights years ago to empty rooms and thought he had passed that stage. But this was LA and not the Midwest.

He knew no one here and that suited him quite well. Back in the Midwest, it was the same way. He would never tell anyone if he was doing a show somewhere. It was the best way to handle things, a matter of preserving his dignity, saving face if things went badly. There would be no one to remind you about it or to spread the word around. No one to say, "Oh yes, ten years ago you did a Christmas show for the Kiwanis. We spent our entire $20 entertainment budget on you and you sucked!" You just never knew what kind of a night you would have. Joan Rivers once remarked that she died on stage more often than Hamlet. Phyllis Diller had been fired after her opening set at a big famous nightclub in Miami, her first big gig. That's the way it goes.

There were other pitfalls to avoid, too. Back home he had to stop going to social gatherings like retirement parties or wedding receptions. The family of the retiree or the father of the bride would invariably come up to him halfway through the reception just as he was getting comfortably stewed and people were eying the door to leave.

"Come on, be a good sport and tell some jokes. Do me a personal favor. I told them I would ask you. Come on, now... This is their special day. Come'n now. Do it for me. Please!"

What could he do? Some people think that singers or musicians or dancers or actors or joke tellers can just walk right up there and do something right at the spur of the moment. There was something else, too, and he never could get over it. He could never recall a show when he didn't have it. Pure, unadulterated stage fright. It was very real, palpable and he had to fight it every time. It was always the same way. He would wait the long wait for his introduction, a cigarette between sweaty fingers. He couldn't eat or drink a thing. He would stare at the black back exit door and know that all he had to do was push it open and walk out into the comfort of the night. Then he wouldn't have to be afraid anymore. Someone told him that Johnny Carson was like that, and Barbra Streisand, too.

It wasn't like he was elevating himself to their status. It was just that if the biggies could feel that way, then it was alright for him to feel that way. He wondered why, if it is such a tough thing, that people do this sort of thing, exposing themselves in front of an audience, leaving themselves open to criticism. What was it out there that made them do this kind of thing?

Felix thought he would get used to it, like when he first started to teach. He was nervous then and he had to micromanage everything, spending endless hours in the town library looking through endless books and magazines for stuff to say. He had to write everything down, working every night for five or six hours filling in every single second of a six fifty-minute class periods. Then he would present it the next day. His lips would be so dry, his tongue paralyzed, the arm pits of his neatly pressed shirt showing large round darknesses. But he eventually got used to it. But it was easier with kids than it was with adults. With the children he was in charge. He had his teaching notes on the lectern in front of him to keep him on course. If they didn't like his performance, he could always give them extra homework. But on a stage in front of adults, in front of strangers, with no lectern to hold his routine, well, that was a different ride entirely. Would he ever find the comfort zone? Was there one?

Felix studied his joke list. He worried about "going up," as they call it, forgetting, freezing, drawing a blank. He had seen it happen to many comics on stage. It had happened to him, too. It was an easy thing to happen, especially when he had to do forty minutes. There would be an awkward silence. There wasn't much he could do, but say something stupid like, "Thanks, everyone... you've been a great audience," not leaving them laughing, just leaving them, then slipping out the side door. When he had two shows in one night, he always worried about using the same routine twice to the same audience. "Uh...did I already say that?"

He had seen an interview one time with Frank Sinatra, who said he always worried about forgetting the lyrics of a song he was singing to a sold-out audience. Later in his life, Sinatra would have an electronic prompter in front of him on the stage floor that spelled out all the lyrics, word for word. One time Felix went to the Tonight Show and saw that everything that Jay Leno said was written in heavy dark lettering on cue cards, even the ad libs. And there was a teleprompter, as well. Nothing left to chance.

But the regular Stand-up Joe doesn't have those luxuries. He has to be a little more subtle. One of Felix's comic friends would always take a guitar on stage with him with his routine written on a piece of tablet paper taped on the back, strum a bar or two and get a quick peek. The trouble with that, though, was that when people saw the guitar, they expected the comic to sing a long funny song, like Adam Sandler's "Happy Marijuanukah" song. Another comic he knew had his line-up pinned on the inside of his jacket. Adjust the jacket and see what was next. Felix had even seen some just hold their notes in their hand, not giving a whit what anyone thought about it. Felix once had written out key words on a small index card that he placed on a stool that held a glass of water. Trouble with that was that he had to have a reason to walk over there to look at it, but he couldn't pick up the glass of water because his hands would shake so violently that the water would go sloshing around. He couldn't take the mike out of the stand for the same reason. He just had to leave it in the stand and his hands in his pockets. He would wear baggy pants for that, and to hide his knocking knees.

Felix stared through the smoke. Nearly everyone was gone by now. That's the way open mikes are. You do your thing and leave. No need to watch the others. Now you have a little story to tell now. You were on a stage somewhere. Maybe someone will listen. You feel important, for a while, anyway.

"Okay, ladies and gentlemen, next up is a very funny guy. Give it up for old Whatshisname!"

Champ settled in comfortably in the top bunk. He was a man of few needs. He had inherited the full impact and responsibility of his father's fierce independence so it hadn't been easy for him to accept the largess of Heathcharlesharley's father, the daily visits to Friendly's Liquors for the XXX beer and the Jack Daniels, which he needed to fall asleep at night, the Marlboro menthols. That was all fine. But Heathcharlesharley had drawn the line on weed, though. It was a moral thing, he said, conflicting with one of the amendments in the bible.

Champ had inquired down the street at the construction sites for the trendy new loft apartments being built, but with no union card for such work, he resorted to the noon shift at Epic Heroes, sandwiched between Java Juice and Dairy Doodle. He could eat there for free, and use his paycheck for the rent and what he needed. He knew the hooker with the red Taurus who lived above the pool had weed. He saw the late night guests tramp up to her apartment, smelled it through the open bathroom window. As soon as he got his first paycheck, he would pay her a visit. What the hell. First things first, then everything else after that. Heathcharlesharley's charity, Epic Heroes, the upper bunk, all of this was just temporary. Just a soon as he and Ruby could get things rolling, everything would be different. He wasn't real sure what it was he had to do to make all that happen.

Heathcharlesharley had urged him to come out, to bring his guitar. So he did just that. Dropped everything and came out with Ruby. Of course, there really wasn't much that he had to drop, but here he was now anyway. Okay, so now what?

Felix had a heart that wasn't as hard as the folding steel chairs occupied by those sitting in front of him and sometimes it would ache. He tried to be tough. He knew it was a “don't call us, we call you” kind of world. He knew well why agencies had to shield themselves from the flotillas hoping to dock at their piers. But occasionally there was a prince or princess in the tides and what was he to do?

Sometimes it was a lovely young child who pierced his armor. He was always a sucker for children. A few agencies specialize in representing children, some agencies represent one or two perhaps, but most prefer to take a pass. It's a tough gig. Very young children aren't called in too often for auditions, maybe with a little luck a few times a year, if that, and usually they are just go-see cattle calls for print work for a diaper company or something like that. Casting for older children is usually done in the late afternoon when they are finished with the school day, but Mom and Pop aren't finished with the work day. Somebody has to leave work early to drive through late afternoon LA rush hour traffic to an audition where there is a high probability that nothing will come of it. And if something did, it was usually for only a couple of hundred bucks.

Then there are all sorts of legal restrictions and conditions that must be followed to protect children from danger and exploitation. And if all of that isn't enough to make an agent hesitant about representing children, then there is the notorious omnipresence of the most pernicious and despicable curse in the entire entertainment industry, a scourge with the power of the pestilence of a plague of the Middle Ages, the avatar of the Great Baal Zevuv:

THE STAGE MOTHER

It is easier just to submit to a beating for twenty minutes. So Barbara would say no.

Sometimes it was an adult who was sitting on the hard steel chair in front of him, someone in his or her thirties or forties maybe, with the talent and the charisma, the ways and means of surviving a long quest, a solid resume of plenty of fine work back in Omaha or Pittsburgh, and Felix would really like him or her, but he knew he couldn't help. Sometimes he would even try to pitch the actor, but Barbara would say no to that as well. "I already have what I need in that category."

In the early morning quiet, while Heathcharlesharley and Champ were still in bed, Frankie would slip onto the balcony where the light was particularly true, to his easel set up at the opposite far end of the balcony, far enough away as not to trespass into Champ's space. He would carefully remove the veil which protected it in repose, soften up the brushes between his thumb and index finger, squeeze pigment onto the palette, and compose. He didn't have to think while he painted. He never cared too much for thinking. Someone one time tried to teach him how to play chess, but he gave it up real soon. He didn't see much point sitting there all evening thinking about the next move, and then his opponent doing something that stops him dead in his tracks and makes him have to start thinking all over again about what to do next. Same with life. Wasting all that time thinking about things today when there's always something that happens tomorrow that he didn't count on that changes everything. It's too much trouble. Nothing much you could do about things anyway so it's so much easier just to let things go wherever they go. Why fly against the wind? Take yourself where that day will go without resistance.

He wasn't at all like Felix, the list maker, neatly writing down everything he wanted to do that day, and then checking off each item as he finished it. He had daily and weekly and monthly and yearly lists. He kept track of everything on lists. Mileage, meters, movies, whether or not there was room in the day to take a nap and when and then checking it off when he woke. He had a list for all his lists. Felix told him he did it because it allowed him to get things done in his life. Frankie didn't like having to get things done. It uses up too much energy, takes up too much time. Lists were like rules to follow.

Okay, it wasn't that he spent all of his time unthinking. He did have to think when he was sitting at the glass-covered table at Mainstream or carrying a big tray of cheeseburgers and fries at the Coral Reef, but he didn't have to think at full speed. Maybe just five miles per hour, but even then, there was still some thinking to do. But it was all just a temporary thing. It wouldn't be around forever. He would arrive at a point where he didn't have to think about anything ever at all, just idle all afternoon wandering and wondering.

He was more interested in wondering, especially about wonderful things. Things were out there for you to wonder about. Not think about. Not analyze until it is no longer full of wonder. Things like wondering what color that was in last night's sunset. Wondering what dogs wonder about when they lay in the shade. Wondering if birds dream, if trees sneeze, if whales snore.

The days were long and the nights longer for Champ. He never slept well. He slipped onto the balcony amid the rubble of cans and bottles and butts with Ruby and slid the door quietly behind him. The balcony was his space. He took a peek behind the curtain that Frankie had hanging over his canvas. It wasn't finished yet, but it appeared to be a naked pussy laying in bed, craning his neck to look out at a full moon shining through the window above his head, his butt rearing up invitingly and gleaming in the moonlight.

"Two full moons," he thought, then dropped the cloth back over it and took his seat on the upturned five gallon paint bucket that served as his roost, and lost himself, isolated, alone. Every night was the same, except some nights when the search for Shangri-la was a little more elusive. But not tonight. He was almost there. He hit the last of the doobie, held it full, slowly released it, then rocked back against the rough stucco wall. Ruby would call out for him soon and when she did, he would pick her up and tease her, cuddle her, caress her in foreplay. She was his Jesus. His sun. His South. But she wasn't much fun to take out for dinner and a movie on a Saturday night.

He had always liked girls a lot. Especially if she had long, flowing curls that bounced on her shoulders when she walked. That was a real turn-on. Just one time he would love to run his fingers through those locks. Smell them. Taste them. But he was always afraid to. Ever since Natalie in tenth grade. He spent a whole week getting up the courage to ask her out and then she says she'll go out with him when pigs fly. That's what she said. When pigs fly. What the hell. She couldn't have found a little nicer way to say it. Like, "Aw...gee whizz...sorry, Champ. I'm a lesbian," or "Go Fuck Yourself." But no. It's "When Pigs Fly." He thought about that a lot. "When Pigs Fly." Whatcha you gonna say to something like that? "Oh... okay, catcha later, alligator." What the hell.

Chapter 6

Frankie rose on the special day. It was finally here. He would start with his mom. He always told her everything. Well, almost everything. Then he would call his dad, his three brothers, his little sister, one by one.

"Mom, it's National Gay and Lesbian Coming Out Day.

"Uh?"

So, guess what?"

"What, honey?"

"I'm coming out."

"You're doing what?" she said. "You're coming home!? Oh, thank god!"

"No, Mama, I'm coming out."

"Coming out? Coming out of what?

"Hmmm... Well... I guess the closet."

"Coming out of the closet? What are doing in there? I thought you outgrew that. Aren't you a little old for that now, Frankie?"

"I'm gay, Mama."

"Gay?"

"Yes, Mama."

"Aw… Honey. That's okay. You're just like your father. You know, he's gay, too."

"No… Mama."

"That's why I married him. It sure is!"

"Uh… No Mama."

"What is it, honey?"

"I'm a queer, Mama."

There was the hesitation.

"Mama, You still there?"

Then she found her voice. "We was afraid something would happen to you in California."

"Mama."

Another pause. He knew she wouldn't know what to say. She didn't expect this. She had told him often that he would have his own children some day, that she had expected beautiful grandchildren from such a handsome boy as he.

"Maybe if you come home, you'll be okay again."

"No, Mama."

You wasn't like that before you left, Honey" she said.

"Yes, I was, Mama.

"What about Becky? What about all that? You shoulda stayed in Indiana. This wouldn'ta happened."

He would tell her later about Ricky. About he and Ricky.

"Love ya, Mama. Bye-bye."

Back in high school, he had heard the guys in the locker room talk about guys being gay. At first, he thought it meant being happy and fun so he didn't see anything wrong with that. Later he learned that being gay was where guys would be attracted to other guys instead of girls. He didn't see anything wrong about that either, as that was the way he felt. But then he heard the other guys make stupid jokes about it so he decided that it was best just to keep things to himself. Then in college he found out that most people didn't see much wrong with it again so he was happy and gay again. There was no more pretending to do, no more Becky, but Ricky, and he liked how it all felt, and that's why he called Mom. Next he would tell Heathcharlesharley and Champ.

Felix stood in the stall of the third floor bathroom at the

yeshiva. The old building never had been outfitted for separate faculty bathrooms. He quickly dragged on his cigarette, and then exhaled. He hated that he smoked. It was pretty much ingrained into every part of his daily routine. Cigarettes helped him relax. They helped him think. They made him more able to handle things. He drew deeply, heavily, and held it in. Nothing like a ciggy between classes.

The door burst open. It was Eliahu. Felix dropped the cigarette into the commode, flushed it quickly, and realized he had been caught red-handed. Wisps of smoke leaked from his nostrils. Then no longer able to hold his breath, he exploded in a smoky exhale. No sense denying anything at this moment.

Eliahu shooed away the smoke. "We were wondering who was stinking up the place. Rabbi Horowitz thought it was Gedolia. Here it is you."

"Well, sometimes a guy's gotta do what a guy's gotta do."

"You really should stop that bad habit."

"I wish I could," replied Felix. "I've tried several times."

"You should drink a glass of water whenever you want a cigarette. That way you won't want one."

"Why's that?" asked Felix.

"Because the cigarette is fire and your body wants that fire. So if you drink a glass of water, you put out the fire."

"Hmmm…"

"Now go get a drink of water and I won't tell Rabbi Horowitz on you."

"Thanks, man. You rock."

Runyon Canyon City Park, a web of steep hiking trails and dog paths on the steep slopes of the Hollywood Hills, was a soothing place for Beatrice. It helped her relax. Felix had first taken her up there, and after that she visited it daily. She liked the exotic dogs of the well-heeled who hiked there. She would occasionally stop and quiz the owner of a particularly fine breed, asking all the right questions that someone informed would ask.

She enjoyed eavesdropping on the chit-chat between the canines, the catty remarks the German shepherds made about the French poodles, the English bulldogs made about the Irish setters, the wolf whistles when an Afghan ambled by, the complaints of sore paws or dry mouths and the dog-tired. She would smile. She would get sore and tired, too. She understood them. She could communicate with them. As a child, she thought everyone could. But as she grew, others noticed her unique skill and she was sometimes called upon to translate Pekingese or Persian into the Queen's English.

She would park the Jag at the far end of the dusty lot off Mulholland Drive, a legendary road that rides the crest of the Hollywood Hills between the San Fernando Valley and the Los Angeles Basin. She would carefully adjust her straw hat and dark glasses and enter through the heavy black gates. "Beware of Rattlesnakes" signs reminded hikers to stay on the path, and Beatrice of the gentleman in her past.

On clear days, it was the best show in town. The tour buses and limousines would stop at the overlook on its northern border. People neck there. Marry there. Newscasters would do on-the-spot reports there. The panorama reaches from the Pacific Coast in the west to the Verdugos in the east, the Hollywood Bowl at its feet, the Griffith Observatory at its elbow. On some days, a brown fog would wrap around the city like a cat, adding an aura of mystery and anonymity and reducing the view to a few garish traffic lights along Hollywood Boulevard.

She would follow the wide trail to Cloud's Rest, where a tall park bench perches precariously atop a steep slope. Commissioned by the park system and christened Heaven's Bus Stop, it was tall enough for her to swing her legs like a child again. Here she seemed able to escape the inescapable. She could forget about the gentleman who had so dominated her life. Here she was in control again, holding dominion over a vast and powerful empire. Sometimes Felix would join her. She liked him. He made her laugh. He humored her. He was somewhat of a rube, though. He didn't know the starboard from the port, a port from a sherry, a Buick from a Bentley. When they sat together at Heaven's Gate, he would invariably point out the yeshiva. “See over there? That’s La Brea Avenue there. Just follow that all along to the tall clump of trees to the right. Yup, that’s where it is. That’s where I work. That’s Melrose right behind it.” Every time he would say it.

Heathcharlesharley couldn't believe it when Frankie told him. At first he thought it was just another one of those days. Frankie was always jazzing him about something. They had always been able to work out their differences before. Sometimes it was simple and easy. Frankie had purchased the refrigerator with his second paycheck from work and rented him the bottom shelf and half of the one right above it. The tape measure and a magic marker were used to insure accuracy and fairness. That was easy enough. Heathcharlesharley insisted that the air conditioner be set at a bone-chilling 50 degrees, but when the electric bill came in, the negotiations became more elaborate. Heathcharlesharley would pay the full electric bill in exchange for the use of Frankie's microwave oven two times a week, plus one small plate, one medium sized bowl, and one each of a knife, fork, and spoon. It really didn't occur to Heathcharlesharley that he never used those things, but it was all in the deal-making. After all, he was his father's son. Or his grandfather's son... or whatever he was.

Frankie didn't want to pay for all of those premium channels on the cable bill and since there was nothing much left to exchange, Heathcharlesharley made Frankie place his right hand on his Best Sunday Mass Bible and swear never to watch anything ever on that television, not even to glance at it when he walked past it, not even when Heathcharlesharley was gone, not even to touch it, not even the remote. Ever! “Say 'so help me god!'”

That were able to get past all of that. But this queer thing was different. There would be no negotiations around here about this. After all, he had asked up front on the telephone before he even moved out here, just to make sure that nothing like this would happen.

"Are you a queer?" he asked.

"No," said Frankie. And now it's happened.

"You can go to programs to reverse this," Heathcharlesharley had first offered.

"Why would I want to do that?"

"It's disgusting," Heathcharlesharley said, a snarl in his voice, his eyes two cold black marbles, his saber teeth unsheathed and razor sharp. "You know what the bible says about homosexuality? It's an abdominal pain of nature. That's what it says. You're gonna go to hell. I can't believe it. You better not touch me! I'll bust you in the face." He shivered to even think of it. "You're gonna pay for this. In the holy bible it sayeth my eye for your eye and my tooth for your tooth. Revengeth is mineth, sayeth the Lord."

He couldn't understand why Champ seemed so nonchalant about it. When Frankie had made the announcement last night that he had something to tell them both and then spit it out, all Champ did was pull the sliding glass door shut and light a Marlboro.

It was a different comedy club. A phone call here didn't work. Felix had to go down to Sunset on Monday morning and wait in line to see the guy with the clipboard, and answer some questions.

"Did you have an act?"

"Yes..."

"A blue act?"

"No." he said.

Not really. Maybe a little light blue here and there. But he didn't say that. No sense in pushing your luck. A blue act is all about bodily orifices and such, potty jokes. Dick jokes. They might be fine in some venues, but not this one. Clean folks come to this club, nice people with family values. Blue comics find themselves somewhat limited, with no chance of doing anything on a Disney channel, the Tonight Show, Letterman. No family shows, no resorts, no cruise ships. Save it for Vegas, Baby.

"Do you have ten friends to come, sign in at the door, pay the cover and buy the two-drink minimum?"

"Yes," he lied. He didn't have ten friends in LA. In fact, he would be hard pressed to come up with two. But this is common practice, not only in LA but everywhere else, too. Bring your entourage. Club owners trying to fill up the place. Pay a stiff price for a limp drink. Buy the appetizers. Musicians and singers wanting to play in coffee houses and bars have to face the same thing. At least it wasn't a pay-to-play club. Instead of the club manager paying you to play, you pay the club manager to play. For many, it was the only way to get stage time, to get noticed, to build a following, to have an LA showhouse to place on the old gig sheet. Fork over the money now and the paid gigs will come later. Maybe.

But he had to say yes if he wanted to be put on the list. He knew, too, that someone from the club would be asking ticket buyers if they had a friend appearing there that night and then place a little hash mark next to the performer's name. If there were problems later, well, he'd just deal with them then. Right now is the moment.

"Good evening, everyone," he began.

"Any smokers out there?"

"I hate to admit it, but yes, I'm a smoker. A closet smoker, mostly. It's tough because I'm a teacher. I have to sneak into the boy's room, stand in one of the stalls, flush the thing down the toilet when a kid walks in."

"Shoo away the smoke and blame it on the boy who just left." Felix held his nose in mock annoyance, fanning away the smoke in disgust.

"One time I found a joint on the hallway floor in front of some kid's locker. I took it into the teacher's lounge to show them, and by the time they were through with it, there wasn't enough left to show the police." Felix grinned innocently at the audience. Shrugged his shoulders.

"I remember when I was a teenager. Dad caught me smoking. He said, 'Son, I want you to take these three packs of cigarettes and sit in the closet and don't come out until you've smoked every one of them. That oughta stop that nasty habit."

"But Dad, you didn't make me sit in there with three cases of beer when you caught me drinking.

"You didn't make me sit in there with a bag of pot when you caught me with a joint! You didn't say, 'Son, don't you come out of that closet until you have smoked that entire bag!'"

"You didn't make me sit in there with a stack of Penthouse magazines when you caught me whacking off."

He lifted the palms of his hands up and shrugged his shoulders. "What's up with that?"

"You know that nicotine patch that gives you the benefit of smoking without smoking? "Well, I think someone should develop the pot patch. You know, just slap it on your arm right under the nicotine patch before you go to work. Then you slap on the Jack Daniel's patch. Now you're all set for that stressful day in the cockpit. Getcha through the day until you get home."

Heathcharlesharley first called his dad, who told him there wasn't really much he could do. "Make sure you sleep with one eye open all night just in case he gets some ideas about sneaking in and trying to get into your cookie jar."

Then he pounded on Felix's door, breathless, his face flushed with excitement and perspiration. "Frankie told me he came from a good Christian home. How can you be a homosexual and be from a good Christian home? The bible has rules against that stuff. You know, Slalom in Grenoble.

"Slolem in Grenoble?"

"Or whatever."

Felix wondered about people from good Christian homes. Anchors lead off the evening newscasts with tales of murderers or rapists or child molesters, and then add the surprise and disbelief when they announce that the criminal was from a good Christian home. He wondered if people would be less surprised if the murderer or the pervert came from a good Muslim home or a good Hindu one?

“What about that love thy neighbor thing?” asked Felix.

“A neighbor is someone you live next to. A homosexual is someone you DON'T live next to. Duh!!” He really got tired of explaining it to people.

Then Felix started mumbling about how an anvil just bounced off his head again, whatever that meant. Then he began to wonder if Felix was queer. But he knew one thing for sure. It was timeth for his revengeth.

Chapter 7

HAHAKAKAKROOM! HAHAKAKAROOM! HAHAKAKAROOM! ROOM! ROOM! HAHAKAKAROOM! HAHAKAKAROOM! ROOM! ROOOM! ROOM! AHEM AHEM!!" Beth Ann sat in her car in the handicapped parking space in the underground garage of the Villa Verdugo and waited. Surely someone would arrive shortly that could carry her heavy jugs of water and the jumbo-sized bag of kitty litter up to her apartment. People were in and out all day long. If need be, she could do it herself, but then she would be denying someone an opportunity to feel good about doing a good deed for someone. She decided it would be best to wait. She sat back and closed her eyes. Life had been such a challenge for her lately. It was a challenge for her to get that handicapped parking spot right next to the walkway. She thought, "Okay, problem solved."

But then came the pointed, no nonsense knock on her door, and there stood Tiffani, arms folded in front of her, flames shooting from her dark brown eyes. Well, almost immediately, the radar on Beth Ann's physiognometer blinked in urgent red, like a wind sheer warning on an airline control panel. "Danger Ahead! Beep! Beep! BEEP!" "I parked in that spot for six years now. It's MY spot!"

"That was because there had never been any handicapped people living here before, but now there is," Beth Ann tried to explain. “The numbness in my leg.”

“That numbness is not in your leg. It's in your head!”

Beth Ann had never seen anything like it. “HAHAKAKAROOM! HAHA KAKAROOM! ROOM! ROOM! ROOM! HAHAKAKAROOM! ROOM! ROOM! HAHAKAKAROOM ROOM! ROOM! AHEM AHEM!!!”

She felt badly for that poor apartment manager who had been caught between Americans with Disabilities and Americans with Distemper. But what could the manager do? She had that handicapped placard signed by the Bureau of Motor Vehicles and a doctor. It's the law.

Someone was coming. The gate was opening, at last. Beatrice’s black Jaguar sailed neatly into its space, Beatrice and Felix returning from Runyon Canyon. Some day she would like to join them. Felix had talked of the celebrities and their dogs, the view. Beth Ann had hinted a couple of times about being asked along, but Felix had to explain that there were no bathrooms and that pathway was steep and difficult even for a billy goat.

Beth Ann was interested in clutching Beatrice into her bosom of dear friends. There was a very favorable response in that good old subliminal sniffer of hers. She had been planning a trip to England to attend the wedding of a daughter of a dear friend and needed advice, especially in regards to her handicapped situation and all. HAHAKAKA ROOOM ROOM ROOM HAHAKAKA ROOM ROOM ROOM HAHAKAKA ROOM ROOM ROOOOOOOOOOOM! AHEM AHEM AHEM!!” But if the trails of Runyon Canyon were off-limits for her, her kitchen certainly wasn't. She would plan a lovely little dinner, after she got the carpets cleaned, after the holidays. In the meantime, Felix would bring the water and litter to her apartment and in the process bring peace and warmth to his heart.

It was early December and Hanukkah was nearing and with it came the annual Yeshiva fund-raiser. Negotiations for the use of the elegant Grand Ballroom of the Regency Wilshire had been completed and the room reserved and confirmed. The false idols Zeus and Hera and their consorts that encircled the ballroom had been tastefully converted to discrete ghosts in white sheets. The hotel kitchens had been closely inspected for adherence to kosher standards. The black suits and long dresses had been cleaned and carefully pressed at Saul's Dry-cleaners for the Stars. The thick program book, filled with ads and pictures of happy and healthy and smiling boys, was checked and double-checked for accuracy, the names of the most generous contributors embossed in gold ink.

Negotiations for Mendel "Squiggy" Weiss and the Squires and their Catskill Classics had been completed and the trio had been booked and confirmed. The most difficult decision had been debated and settled, undebated and unsettled, and re-debated and resettled. This year, the proclamation was proclaimed. The menu would be the same as it was last year. And the year before that. And all the years before that. A Crisp Tossed Salad to start off with, then The Boiled Chicken, The Boiled Potatoes, String Beans Almandine, Bread Rolls, all capped off with a nice dessert of Hot Coffee, Peach Sorbet, and Fancy Butter Cookies.

The tables had been arranged in precise patterns, with the womenfolk humbly taking their places with the other womenfolk at the rows of tables safely sequestered from the menfolk by a thick curtain. They could hear and see well enough, and they were alright with it. They were, after all, safe from the eavesdropping of unduly curious fathers and brothers and husbands and sons. They gossiped and checked and rechecked their wigs, careful to be in compliance with Talmudic law regarding the proper place and placement of women.

Orthodox Jewish people always have to have something covering the top of their head. The men wear the yarmulke, the little bowl shaped skull cap, some of them a plain and basic black, others richly embroidered in Hebrew lettering in a multitude of colors. They don't stay on the head very well by themselves, Felix noticed. He watched the boys always bending down to scoop up an errant cap when they hurried up a flight of stairs or over to the lunch room. It was a non-stop thing. Take three steps, bend and scoop. Take three steps, bend and scoop. Take three steps, bend and scoop.

The women keep their hair cut quite short, which they do with coarse and random scissoring. Felix had asked Rabbi Horowitz once about it, who explained in hushed and pedagogical terms that long, flowing hair excites prurient interest in the male so it is forbidden. And so since all women, young and old alike, are also required to cover their heads, they did so with wigs, all identical in modest length and styling.

Felix, doing as he was told, did not touch any of the women, offered no hand for handshakes, did not look them in the eye for too long, or stand closer than six feet. He wore his freshly laundered black suit and the requisite yarmulke, self-consciously checking every few minutes to see if it were still perched like a little tepee on the top of his head. The rabbis, in their long beards and long tails, finished their ablutions in the lavatory washing and muttering, then took their places at the table to sup while chatting in Yiddish.

Then after the tables were cleared, the lights slowly dimmed. There was an air of expectancy. There was no need for an introduction. The Rosh slowly and laboriously ascended to the stage, limping slowly and stiffly to the dais, and stood there. The spotlight roamed for several moments, then found its target. He waited. Soon the room would be his.

"Sssssshh…Sshhhhhhh...Sssshhh...the Rosh is up! The Rosh! Hush, hush, hush up now… HUSH!!… HUSH! THE ROSH!" Several banged their spoon against their water glass loudly and insistently until compliance.

The Rosh Yeshiva started slowly, pausing to gather his thoughts, looking for the link between the lesson he wanted to impart and the perfect words he needed to do that. Often times, those perfect words were only available in Yiddish or Hebrew, hammered home with karate chops of his right hand against the open palm of his left.

“In order to achieve the most spiritually satisfying **ףועה לשובמ**, we must first begin with the most essential ingredient, **תשש ףועה הזח םע רועה**..”

Karate chop. Chop. Chop. Chop..

“submersed totally in absorption of one's **ןיחתור**.”

Tilt. Chop. Rock.
“One must allow the opportunity to present itself to oneself in a complete state of compliance with its mandate, when the **רועה םצעה ןמ לפונ**.”

Whisper. Rock. Chop! Chopchopchop!!!

“Then we must comply with our mandate from the creator to add the **םיאושי, לצב, ירלס, יח רזג** and ultimately,”

Whisper.. shout... rock... chop chop chop!
“the pure and uncorrupted essence, the full measure of”
Pause... Survey the crowd...
The “**םוש**.
Yes, the **םוש**.”
Freeze. Glower.
Smile.
“םוש.”
“But the most important, most essential, most fundamental ingredient,”
Stomp. Shout. Chop. Rock Forward onto Tips of One's Toes.
“Without which nothing else works,”
Pause. Survey. Hold both hands high up. Look up.
“That final action that one must take to achieve perfection and to complete our universal fulfillment and bliss,”
Whisper. Wink. Chop. Rock Back onto Heels.
“That final step that leads to the true appreciation of one's

responsibility to maintain the long held mystery, the **המהות הטהורה של ההוויה שלנו**, if you will..."

Stomp. Circle the podium. Rock. Chop! Chop! Chop!
"That separates the good..."
Chop. Chop. Stomp. Lean. Tilt. Lean. Tilt. Rock! Rock! Shout! Tiptoe away from the Podium, Circle. Go Back Around the Other Way. Another Chop!!
"from the truly great,"
Chop. Stomp. Stomp again. Stomp one more time. Chop. Smile. Freeze. Feel the moment. Embrace the moment.
"is"
Chop. Chop. Lean. Tilt. Lean. Tilt. Rock. Shout. Tiptoe away from the podium. Circle. Chop.... circle.... chop...
"the..."
pause... survey... scan... hold the moment...
"הלב הלב הלב"
CHOP CHOP WEEP WEEP!
"Yes, the **"הלב הלב הלב!"**
CHOP. CHOP. CHOP. CHOP. CHOP. Whisper. Freeze. Stare Glower. Smile ....
"Yes,"
CHOP
SHOUT!!!!!
"הלב הלב הלב**!!!**
CHOP CHOP CHOP!
Lift. Lean. Rock. Stomp. Sob. Smile. Laugh. Rock Some More. Stomp. Tiptoe to the End of the Stage. Lift up onto the Balls of One's Feet. Chop. Chop. Smile. Survey. Spread the Hands out to the Flock. Sob Softly. Whisper Loudly.
"""הלב הלב הלב!!!!!!"
And the checks poured in.

Heathcharlesharley knew she was perfect when he first laid eyes on her, her long white fur, yellow eyes, her loving personality, one of those cats that likes to walk figure-eights around ankles, sits on people's laps or curls up with them in bed, purring madly and kneading, then wrapping herself around a warm leg or arm. With a little luck, she will insist that that lap or arm or leg be Frankie's. Frankie had lied to him, after all, in a big way, with that "not being a queer" thing.

He found her in a pet store. He whipped out the old man's credit card, stuffed her into a box, and drove her home. She wailed all the way back to Hesby Street in deep, sonorous tones, just what he had hoped for. What good would a cat be to him if it were quiet and aloof like some cats, sleeping under the bed all day long and refusing attention?

He decided that "Payback" was the perfect name, always reminding Frankie of his lie whenever he would call her name. "Payback! Payback, Here, Kitty-Kitty. Payback!" He introduced Payback to the place, concentrating much of his energy on the chair that Frankie sat in all the time, and on Frankie's bed and on all Frankie's clothes and towels scattered around the floor, like a hunter scenting his coon dog before the big hunt. He smiled broadly to himself. This was certainly one of his finest moments.

Tiffani woke early and angry. Her carriage had slipped down again. Sometimes it would ride down, sometimes ride up, sometimes veer to the left or to the right. She had acquired that condition from sleeping for eight years in those sagging army bunkbeds, and now the problem was becoming more of a problem as her carriage expanded, the curse of the middle-aged black woman everywhere, a hereditary thing, passed down to her from her mother, who inherited it from her mother who inherited it from hers and going all the way back to Eve. Nothing could be done about it.

Anyway, today things were riding down, way down and it was impossible to get comfortable. She would call Champ. He was always eager to come up and suck on her snake head. He would do it. She had taught him once and it became second nature to him. She would lay on her stomach and he knew just what to do. She had asked Felix couple of times when she first met him, but there was something she sensed, a hesitation like he didn't like touching her. She could feel his hands shake a little bit, seemed uncomfortable when she told him to put his hands right under her broad sagging buttocks and push everything up and back in place. "Okay, more to the center. Into the crack," she would have to remind him."Okay, now push up. OOOOOOO…Harder. Do it again. No, lower."

He'd never remember what he was supposed to do the next time it slipped so she eventually gave up on him. Champ would be off work in a few hours. They were birds of a feather. They would roll the dice and get high.

In the meantime, she would hobble down to her car at the far end of the garage, skirting the oil slicks and giving wide berth to the smelly dumpster and head for the 99-cent store just a few blocks down the street. Christmas was getting closer and closer, and she had only a few gifts so far. She would grab a cart and spend hours carefully looking at each prospect. She especially looked for games that had some instructional value, games that would teach young children and help them mold their creativity. She would opt for the paint-by-numbers, the sculpting clay, pre-school picture books of African animals, and things to put together. If she found something she particularly liked, she would buy ten of them. Sometimes she would find darling little tennis shoes or sandals, baby rattles and adorable little mobiles to hang above an infant's eyes. She didn't need to buy the gift-wrap or ribbons. Toys for Tots wouldn't accept them if they were wrapped. They wanted to make sure no one was passing on porn to little kids. There was always someone out there that thinks that would be a good idea.

Chapter 8

The sidewalks on the side streets and alleys of NoHo or Theater Row on the eastern reaches of Santa Monica Boulevard are filled on any given morning or evening with neophytes, rehearsing their lines for their scene studies, preparing for class. Some sit on the curbs and retaining walls of parking lots, with wrinkled scripts in sweaty hands, taking turns running lines with their scene partner. Some nervously pace, silently mouthing their lines, glimpsing at the script every thirty seconds, then swearing angrily at themselves. When the teacher finally arrives, they crowd in and take their place on the floor of the stage.

Most acting teachers are highly skilled and experienced actors themselves. Some are casting directors by day and acting teachers by night. Some work for Warner Brothers or Disney or Nickelodeon, coaching contract actors in preparing their daily sides. But other teachers are not so skilled. Some are failed actors who have had to resort to giving acting classes to support their rent habit, and they fail as teachers as well. Some are downright opportunistic frauds who accept anyone coming down the pike and then charge steep fees as they babble a bunch of nonsense about the methods of Meisner or Stanislavsky. Others are exploitive pseudo-psychologists who relish in delving into the extreme inner sanctum of their students to unlock the child within, to divulge their most intimate secrets, or to unleash unpleasant and forgotten memories in angry revivals, all ostensibly to create an emotional reservoir from which to draw on while creating a persona for the stage or set.

Frankie talked with his mother daily on the phone. Today he told her about the kitten, how he had come home from work and found her sleeping on his pillow. He told her he wished he had his sewing machine. When he was sixteen, his mom asked him what he wanted for his birthday and he said a sewing machine. A boy asking for something like that is a pretty rare occasion in the Midwest. She didn't think that a sewing machine was such a good idea so she bought him an electric piano keyboard instead. He was so disappointed and he insisted that she take it back and get the sewing machine, which she did with some trepidation. He liked to make hats and costumes, mostly. On Halloween, his nieces and nephews would sport his designs, and he made his little niece's first communion costume.

He was sure there would be some sort of opinion that Heathcharlesharley would have. But Frankie could handle it. He had been through that kind of stuff before. He took a sewing class when he was in high school and he was the only guy in the class. If any of the other guys made a big deal about it, he would stretch to his full six feet, eight inches, flex his canoe biceps discretely, and ask if they had any trouble with that. As it always turned out, they were cool with that. Mostly, though, he didn’t really much care what people said or thought, or he was completely oblivious about it. Perhaps a ramification of his dyslexia, his parents thought. They knew they had an odd little boy who was usually in a world of his own, concentrating on the color of a rose or a butterfly while others were playing ball. They probably should have put two and two together, but they didn't. The parents are always the last to figure such things out.

Frankie and Ricky talked daily, too, at exactly 1:00. Right on the dot, the phone would ring. Champ was usually at Epic Heroes and Ricky's roommate had his physics class so the two had their rooms to themselves. It was quality time for them both.

"Hey, what's up?

"I am."

"Mmm... me, too. How'd the test go?

"It's done with."

"Hard?"

" As a rock."

"No, I mean the test."

"Oh...it was okay."

"Whadda you think about coming out?"

"Not ready for that yet. Mom and Dad would shit a bri..."

"No, I meaning coming out to LA."

"Christmas break, I guess."

"When you getting off?

"In just a minute. I am so hot. Pant... ooohhh... ooohhh... close."

"No, I mean for Christmas break.?"

"Oh... December 15... oooooh.... ahhh.... ooohhh!

"I'm so pumped."

"Yeah, me too! Shiver. I don't know if I have the bucks."

"Shiver... awww....uhhhh.... ..ahhhh... uhhh..aaah. I can work some extra hours."

"Shiver... Yeah… oooooh... aaaaah...good..."

"Stay here for a couple of days , then maybe go back and meet the folks."

"Yeah.... Uhhh... Ahhh... Uuuhhh... Ahhh... Uhhh... Ahhh..."

"Okay…. I can't wait til you come. Pant. Pant."

"I am now. Oh... OOOHH! Yeah! YEAH!! YEAH!!! Phew! Boy! Wow! Man! Continental has cheap fares.

"Yeah…oh…jees…oh...jees...oh...jees. OH...JEES! OH!!! Phew... Okay. I'll look into it. Maybe a red eye."

"Wow, what a mess. I need to clean up."

"Yeah, me, too. I'll talk to you later. Love ya!"

"Love ya right back."

Barbara wasn't having a good day so Frankie and Heathcharlesharley weren't having a good day. She had been pretty patient about things up to this time, telling them softly and quietly when they did something wrong, trying to spell things out in simple terms for the both of them, but they didn't seem to get it, neither one of them. Frankie would reverse telephone numbers and call times and addresses when he answered the phone. Heathcharlesharley was always adjusting his tie in the mirror above the sofa, too busy to write down anything at all.

"Both of you! Don't answer the phone anymore. You hear me?!"

Frankie stamped the Mainstream return address on a full case of 500 manila envelopes, never noticing 500 times that he was doing them all upside down. Heathcharlesharley drove a child to an audition when the mother was unavailable. Not reading the map she provided for him, he drove around all afternoon. The kid got car-sick all over the front seat. Then a few days later he took an adult client to a commercial callback. She had to hang her head out the window with a handkerchief over her nose and mouth during the entire trip while trying to give him directions at the same time. She vomited too, not in the car, but in the holding room at Parkside Casting.

Barbara sat back in her chair. She had been working for months with Hayad, who would commute from Benedict Canyon to Sun Valley every afternoon to take his place at the glass-topped table next to her and the two would work long into the evening. It was a time-consuming project, but things had gone well and now Mainstream was ready for the pick and click thing, ready for the new world order. Most agencies were still in the process of making the change, seeing the writing on the wall and knowing that the alternative was failure. Then, of course, there were those who were reluctant to face the changing world, skeptical about the new system, or lacking the expertise and the resourcefulness to get the job done. They would be eaten by the hyenas.

Soon she could begin to recover her investments, saving on time and printer paper and envelopes and couriers and phone lines and fax machines and postage and such. The glass top table would become a dining table once again, the living room a living room again. There would be no need for interns or associates anymore, no need even for her clients to drop by with stacks of head shots or demo reels to fill in their files, no need to change out of her pajamas if she didn't feel like it. Everything would be done on line now. But for now, until the rest of Hollywood caught up with her, she would still need to have one foot in each world.

Every day in some far flung corner of LA, someone is doing a music video. Some are big productions involving a big name with a big label with big money to spend. They book through the regular channels of agents and casting directors and are shot in airport hangers in Santa Monica or in rented mansions in the Hollywood Hills, where limousines, rigging trucks, make-up trailers, diesel-pushing RV's, kitchens on wheels, and honey wagons park along the narrow, winding streets, where grips and gaffers and gophers snake long cables around swimming pools and through gardens and hoist sails of screens and reflectors over the ship of state.

Sometimes it is the effort of a regional band with some financial backing hoping to break out, to attract national attention, maybe sign with a label, maybe get played on television somewhere, maybe book a gig at the Standard or the Sky Bar on Sunset Boulevard. Maybe the Troubadour on Santa Monica. Sometimes it works. Sometimes they just remain a regional band.

And then there are the low budget music videos financed with a couple of hundred bucks borrowed from a buddy and shot in abandoned buildings downtown or in the working class neighborhoods of Sylmar or Compton. They are cast by word of mouth or fliers posted on telephone poles and pay nothing except for maybe a copy of the DVD and a line on a resume somewhere.

But there will be a story to tell.

They are all nonunion which mean there are no rules to follow. A featured role on a music video may pay $300 or $400, sometimes a bit more, but most of the time the work is background, atmosphere, extra for $60, before taxes and agent commissions. Struggling actors in a slump will subject themselves to the pain and degradation to stave off starvation. But only temporarily. Only until things get better.

Newly arrived actors from Wichita or Roanoke will book them and then report home to acclaim and success. But the blush soon leaves the bloom. For that $60, the extra will arrive several hours before any of the regular cast and crew arrive, lugging in his own wardrobe, often times four or five different changes of clothing to be examined by the wardrobe people, fill out the paperwork, then sit for sixteen hours on a folding chair somewhere out of sight, often times amid nonstop blabbers and pontificating show-biz know-it-alls, eating only after the cast and crew have had their fill, allowed to use only the less elaborate honey wagon when nature called.

The CIA recognizes that the quickest way to dislodge third-world dictators from their heavily fortified palaces is to assault their senses with the never-ending playback, the atonal, angry rap or the incomprehensible, discordant din of heavy metal, or the moronic, mind-numbing bubblegum played again and again and again for hours and hours and hours on end at ear splitting levels that brutalizes the very soul and sends even the hardiest tyrant to plead for mercy and the hungriest actor to realize that a slow starvation doesn't sound quite so bad after all.

"Father," Heathcharlesharley said,n"Barbara told me today that I had to take a class to be able to lose the drawl, she called it. That I needed to because it would limit my roles. That everyone on TV and in the movies has a Midwest accent and that I would have to learn it or else not get very many acting jobs." That cut was the cruelest of them all. A Midwest accent!? Talk like Frankie? After all, wasn't his tongue the tongue of Big

Daddy, Rhett Butler, Stanley Kowalski?

And then, as if that wasn't enough, just when he thought his day couldn't get any worse, Daddy Warbucks, who had never once mentioned a single thing about such things before, asked him how he had managed to spend $5000 in one month. He asked about the $400 for a cat. Couldn't he have found one for free somewhere? He asked about the bill for Sons and Lovers.

"What's that all about?"

"Sir! It's a literary club celebrating the works of a famous writer named D.H. Lawrence, Sir. One of my favorites, Sir."

He didn't think the old man paid much attention to those things. At least that's how it all went down in the past. Then his father said that maybe it was about time for him to start thinking about earning a living. Whatever it meant, it didn't sound good.

For that matter, nothing was going well for him. Frankie's reaction to Payback was not at all what he had hoped for. Not a word. Not one. At night, Frankie comes home and heads straight to his room. Not a word. Not one. Then Champ comes back late from Tiffani's, slips onto the balcony and slides the door shut. Not a word. Not a single one.

So he turned to his now best friend, Ima MacLaptop, who in turn introduced him to Sons and Lovers, which in turn introduced him to people who would appreciate his unique talents. Mature people, especially mature women. Older women were so much better than young ones. The young ones were so immature, only interested in themselves. What could he do to please them? With older women, it was just the opposite. What could they do to please him? And they were always so grateful to him, something he never got from anyone else ever, certainly never from Champ or Frankie or Barbara. He clicked on to his page.

No One Under 50
Older Okay
No Skinny-Minnies
No Long Term Relationships

He didn't include his picture, though. Someone might recognize him and alert the paparazzi. They would be all over him. His career ruined before it even got started. Best, too, not to tell Frankie or Champ. Some people just don't understand things like that. Trouble with everything nowadays is that people don't call a spade a spade anymore. They don't call a midget a midget. They call them a Little People. "Give me a break!" When he first saw Little People on a breakdown at Mainstream, he thought it meant kids. But no, Barbara said they were dwarfs. There's even a talent agency, she said, that only represents dwarfs or midgets or elves or runts or sawed-offs or little people or whatever people call them now.

He laughed out loud. This political correctness stuff is just going a little too far. Santa's little Little People. The Shriners in their Little People's cars. Dorothy off to see the spiritual consultant with a bunch of Little People. Snow White and her Seven Little People: Medical Practitioner, Jubilant, Special Needs, Somnolent, Irritable, Introverted, and Hyper-allergenic. Same thing with homosexuals. Now, it's called alternative lifestyle. Gays and lesbees. What was wrong with queers, fagots, fairies, twinkies, fudge-packers, switch-hitters, stump suckers, butt-buddies, hiney pokers, uphill gardeners, poodle jockeys, poo jabbers? Give me a break."

Beth Ann was beginning to think that she needed something more than the cane. It was somewhat of a problem to carry when she already had things in her hands. Sometimes, when she hadn't felt the numbness in her legs for a while, she would leave the cane hanging somewhere and then had to backtrack to get it. She had seen disabled people such as herself in those cute little motorized carts. They looked like they were having so much fun, whizzing in and out of here and there, gliding smoothly up those little ramps at intersections and whisking swiftly across parking lots and down sidewalks, zipping down the aisles in grocery stores, smiles on their faces, purchases safely stored in little luggage compartments under the seat. It reminded her of the dodge'm cars she enjoyed as a child at River Park. One of those just might fit the bill. She knew her health benefits would cover it. Her planned trip to England was coming up in February and she most certainly would be required to do a lot of walking and that could be a problem.

But one thing was clear and certain. She would NOT, under any circumstances share a room with anyone on this trip, or ever again, for that matter, especially NOT after what happened on that church cruise to the Bahamas. She had agreed to share the cost of a lovely berth with a dear friend from church. She didn't know her very well, but she registered very high on the physiogonometer. Well, within an hour that woman had petitioned the church cruise director for a change of roommates. It all happened right in front of her, that old woman begging, pleading, crying, demanding, threatening, talking about her like she had the plague or something. Boy, that was another day when her radarscope was on the blink. Then they brought in someone "with the heart and soul of an angel," then someone who was rather hard of hearing. In the long and short of it, she ended up having a room to herself when three ladies agreed to share a room for two. She sure did learn a lesson about sharing a room with the insensitive. It was all so traumatic. She needed to get a move-on. Time was a wasting. She had spent long hours last night on the computer looking at motorized chairs for the disabled and she knew exactly what she wanted.

Chapter 9

Eyes closed, and his arms comfortably at his sides, Felix lay flat on his back, the music of the ocean breathing softly in the back ground.

"Imagine," began the voice, hypnotizing, dreamy, "that it is early morning. The gulls call. The salty air is fresh and free. You are alone. Breathe. Lay back. Dig your heels into the soft, cool sand. Softly, now. Quietly now, relax. Breathe. Relax. Breathe. Be one with the beach."

There were so many to choose from. One right after another all along the LA coastline. Zuni, Malibu, Sunset, Will Rogers, Santa Monica, Venice, Hermosa and on and on, each one different, but Felix liked Manhattan Beach the best. So that's where he was for the moment, not in his acting class laying on a cold, hard floor on the stage in a darkened theater with nineteen others, but just a little south of the pier, where the surfers play, where the water is the cleanest, the beaches the sandiest, the sunbathers the nakiest.

"There is a long piece of string directly above your forehead. See it? It is slowly descending, slowly now... descending to your forehead. It lingers there, then softly sweeps back and forth, back and forth, back and forth. Sweep, sweep, sweep, sweeping away the tension. Feel the warm and comforting sand under your legs. The string gently sweeps down across your nose. Sweep. Sweep. Sweep. Slowly now. Hear the gentle waves. Breathe. Taste the salt. Around your left eye. Linger for a moment. Now, your right. Gently now… down across your left check…sweep…sweep…sweep over your nose to your right check. Peace. Shhh… All is quiet. The ocean is here. Its waves gentle, bathing away the aches. Calm…quiet…Let the string circle your mouth. Ahhhh…that's right. Now down to your chin. Shhhhhh, the sea birds call…to your neck…Let it sweep, sweep, sweep the back of the neck now. Sweep, sweep, sweep… The stiffness loosens…loosens… loosens…and now it is gone. It is all gone. No worry…no sorrow…no thoughts…All swept away. All is quiet. All is calm. Feel the warmth on your face. Your mind is free… Peace... Shhhhh... Breathe... shhhh.... You are free...free...free...free... free...free...free...free...free...free....sssshhh...

Tiffani sat sucking the snake head amid the towers of toys and games and dolls and tiny tee shirts and bonnets that lined the walls and hid the sofa and coffee table. There would be more yet. As usual, her pot donations picked up during the holiday seasons, what with friends laying in extra supplies and some even leaving thoughtful little tips like they do at the hairdresser. She made daily trips now to the 99 Cent Store and the bargain bins at Target.

Time was getting short. Soon she would need to load them all in the car and take them the few blocks south on Vineland Avenue to the fire station there. It would take most of the night. There were many, many full car loads to ferry over. She would wait until after midnight when people were at home in their beds. She didn't want any help. This was her gig. It made her happy to do this and she didn't want to share any of it. She would unload them at the back door of the fire house, out of sight. She didn't want anybody seeing her doing this. She just wanted to make sure there was plenty for the children. She knew how it felt to be short-changed. When she was a child, she heard the kids at school talk about all the gifts they got. She asked her mother why she only got one present. Had she been that bad? No, her mother would say. Their house was at the end of Santa's route and there just wasn't much left by the time he arrived. Every year she would beg her mother to move. She was just a kid then. Now, as an adult, she could do something. She would make sure that Santa could stop at the North Hollywood Fire Station and stock up when he started to run low. Plenty of room for sleigh parking there. Plenty of parking on her kitchen counter, as well, for an early Christmas Present to Tiffani, from Tiffani with Much Much Love, a Dark Chocolate Cake with Butter Cream Frosting Fresh from the Bakery of Albertson's Grocery, a sure-fired remedy for all the various and sundry ills that visit her daily.

The tens of thousands of homeless in Los Angeles County are predominately white, Christian, patriotic Americans with a strong and bewildering allegiance to a government and a religion that have basically forsaken them. They stand at the corner of Hollywood and Highland, holding a cardboard sign scrawled with biblical quotes and tributes to democracy in one hand and an empty Styrofoam cup in the other, which they shake in the faces of the drivers waiting for the light to change. No cardboard signs quote the Torah or Koran or ask for donations in the name of Allah or Mohammad or L. Ron Hubbard. No signs glorify the virtues of the Knesset or parliamentary monarchies. Just the lord and Lady Liberty. Often they suffer from drug addiction or mental illness, ranting and raving as they swipe through the air at imagined enemies. If their numbers swell to embarrassment in the streets of downtown, they are rounded up like a cowboy corrals stray dogeys and discretely relocated to the San Fernando Valley.

Many are military veterans, wearing the remnants of their fatigues and boonie hats, and never fully recovered from the trauma of war. They camp along the Los Angeles River in small communes or under the bushes in Panorama City or in the shadows of the Veterans Administration complex on Wilshire.

Some are actors and models and musicians who never found their spotlight. Too embarrassed or too busted to go home, they linger in the kindness of the southern California climate and dig coffee cups from trash barrels for 50-cent refills at the Java Joint and mix with those simply too drunk or stoned to think about any moment other than the one they are living in the instant.

Others are young teenagers, run-aways from unhappy homes in Chattanooga or Kalamazoo, who quickly and quietly stuffed their tee-shirts and jeans and teddy bear into a gym bag and scrounged up enough money for a one-way ticket on a Greyhound bus, taking up residence at the youth hostel near Hollywood and Highland when they first arrive, then relocating to the back alleys and abandoned buildings east of Cahuenga Boulevard, hanging with their kindred spirit for comfort and support, and working the late shift as prostitutes, the girls on the east end of Hollywood Boulevard, the boys a block or two south.

"I went to the dentist the other day. My teeth had been hurting," she told Felix. Beatrice knew she would be considered an anomaly in the United States. A Brit in a dentist's chair. Americans always seem to get such a laugh out of that. Her teeth were straight, white, and present, unlike a lot of Americans she saw. But Felix didn't make any comments. He was always on his best behavior.

"He told me I have six cracked teeth."

He stopped swinging his legs and looked at his reflection in her sunglasses. Then he turned to the sky and began counting the planes circling LAX, a cyclone of little glints in the far distance. If he were uncomfortable or mindless or anxious, he would count things. Silently. The number of steps in a stairway. The lockers in the hallway between classrooms. The ceiling tiles at the doctor's office. The number of people sitting in a theater with him.

"I never felt this way about anyone before. I've had my share of gentlemen, but there was never anything like this.

Where you hold your breath because you think it's too good to be true. So handsome, he was. Such a charmer. Walked on my right side. Held the door open for me. Loved to dance. Everything I ever wanted. I could scarcely believe that there was someone actually out there like that." She removed her owl glasses, blew a speck of dust from a lens, and slipped them back on.

Felix watched the jets and waited.

"So I decided to surprise him with a first-class cruise through the Caribbean. Every evening we wined and dined and danced and other passengers would notice and smile and wish it for themselves. Then we would return to our state room and make love all night long. One evening, he surprised me right back with a beautiful diamond ring, "a token of my love," he said. He purchased it at the ship's jewelry store while I was taking my afternoon nap and gave it to me over dinner. It was Valentine's Day. I was so happy."

She fell quiet as three hikers passed by. Unwilling to intrude on her thoughts, Felix looked down at his shoes and counted the eyelets in his left shoe, then the right. Then in reverse order. Then he counted every other one and multiplied by two and came up with the same number.

"A month later, I got my credit card statement and another surprise. He had charged the ring to my account. $25,000, plus another $10,000 in various other charges. Naturally I was shocked and I asked him about it. He said, 'Oh, yes…I had forgotten about it, darling. I'll take care of it.' But then not another word was said so I asked him again a few weeks later. He became a different man, turning on me and punching me twice in the mouth, a one-two kind of thing you would see in a boxing bout somewhere, knocking me out, even."

Felix glanced a grimace to her. She turned and stared into the distance toward the blue of the Pacific. She was so alone.

"I sued to recover my property so he hired some goons to break into my home and take my passport and immigration papers, refusing to return them unless I dropped the suit. But I wasn't about to buckle under such pressure. I hired my own attorney and placed my remaining assets under the protection of the bankruptcy courts, stashing some aside to hold me for a while until the whole bloody mess was over. But he wasn't the type who would give up without a fight either and that was when the serious threats began. The goons harassed me, trying to intimidate me to back off. And the bill collectors weren't far behind, calling in the middle of the night, banging on my door with violent and threatening language. Lawyers and bill collectors. In cahoots with each other, they are. The smell of money."

The wind picked up and she paused. Their legs dangled over the edge of the bench, like Edith Ann sitting in her oversized rocking chair in Rowan and Martin's Laugh-In.

"I didn't know what else to do, so I left in the middle of the night with nothing but a small suitcase. And that's when I became a girl on the run."

Felix bent back down and counted the eyelets in his shoe one more time. He had forgotten the earlier tally.

"The Brotherhood of Virginia Lawyers all know each other, buddies. They went through law school together, or sparred with each other in trials, or hung out in the same social circles. They share information, gossip, that I was a patsy, ripe for the plucking. Then I got a bill for $50,000 from my attorney, and nothing had really been resolved. No passport, no papers, no return of the money he owed me, the ring and the other jewelry he had taken. I asked for a breakdown of the bill, but was refused. So there is litigation about that, as well. An appeal to the Virginia Bar Regulatory Commission. It just keeps going on and on. I am dead weary from the fight, but I will not give up. Never!"

She took a deep breath, then smiled at Felix with an embarrassed grin.

"Sorry."

"See over there? he said. That's La Brea Avenue there. Just follow that along to the tall clump of trees..."

Yes, I know, Love. That's where it is. That's where you

work." She smiled and slipped off the bench.

"Will you be a love and shave for this evening?

"Okay."

"I want to get there at 6:00."

"Whatever you say, love," he said.

Frankie hadn't been real happy with the arrival of Payback, but he wasn't about to give Heathcharlesharley the satisfaction of victory. It would take much more than some cat from that cat. "Why the long face?" Beatrice had asked him in the garage so he told her about Payback and how he had disliked cats and how he could see the warm, friendly glow of successful retribution in the angelic face of Heathcharlesharley. When she asked him why he didn't like cats, he confessed to an abhorrence that stretched back to his early childhood. They are sneaky and aloof. They kill all the time, anything that flies, walks on two or four or six or a hundred legs or hops, crawls, slithers, or swims. Moths, butterflies, robins, rabbits, frogs, snakes, goldfish, anything that moves, including his pet toad. He couldn't believe it when he found Teddy. He would never forget that. Beatrice said that cats were a lot like people in that regard. Some people are sneaky and aloof. Some people kill anything that moves. Lots of cats don't kill. Lots of cats enjoy the company of people. Not all people are alike and not all cats are alike.

So Beatrice followed him down to their apartment, sitting on the very edge of the sofa, not quite willing to be embraced by any more of the sofa than was absolutely necessary. It was quite incredible, fascinating in an awful way, like the flats she would see in the tabloids back home of lonely old men who die in their beds and no one notices for weeks until the smell of death captures a neighbor's attention. The press would arrive then to take the photos of the piled debris, the bony cats, and the results of plumbing that hadn't functioned properly in decades. She would leave as soon as she solved this immediate problem.

She held the kitten in her lap and listened quietly, feeling her, nodding periodically. Then she turned to Frankie. Payback had several issues that needed to be resolved. She didn't care one bit for her name. Who would ever give someone a name like that? She said she preferred Lily. She had been called that by the nice lady at Pets for People. Her litter box hadn't been cleaned since she moved in. The food was okay, but could Heathcharlesharley flush the toilet every once in a while so she could have fresh water? She didn't like him. He was sneaky and aloof. She liked Frankie and felt like they were allies in a hostile world. Frankie softened. It seemed that they had common grounds. Perhaps this isn't the kind of barn cat he had experienced back home in Indiana, the one that ate Teddy's body, leaving only the gall bladder to dry out on the sidewalk in the hot August sun. He would try to be a little more positive about things. He would talk to Heathcharlesharley about the litter box. He would make sure there was fresh water for her. Beatrice handed Lily to Frankie, who held her in his arms softly. It was all so simple. She purred. Frankie purred. Beatrice purred.

Beth Ann pulled out of the handicapped parking space at Hurry-Up Health Supplies. It was a blessing, especially during this holiday season when parking spaces for healthy people were awfully hard to find. Her mission had been accomplished. The dear salesman and she had become such dear friends. He had helped her fill out the insurance forms necessary for reimbursement from her health provider. She had clutched him deep within her bosom and held him there. Then he loaded her brand new candy-apple red, motorized, human transport device into the trunk of her car, an early visit from Santa. She could hardly control her glee.

"HAHAKAKA ROOM! HAHAKAKA ROOM! HAHAKAKA ROOM! ROOOM! ROOM! AHEM AHEM HURRAY! HURRAH!!"

She pulled into the handicapped spot at the Villa Verdugo. Life was so much easier. She sat in her car, windows rolled down, enjoying the coolness and quiet of the garage, softly humming a Christmas hymn the choir sang in church the other day, waiting for someone who would be a dear. It wasn't much of a wait. The garage gate swung open. This time, though, Tiffani's old Taurus pulled in.

"Drat!" Beth Ann quickly slunk down in her seat, out of sight. She most certainly did not want to offer that grinch the opportunity to feel good about helping someone. She waited quietly, and slowly crouched deeper into her seat, scooting down until she was wedged under the steering wheel. Tiffani had to walk past her car. She could hear Tiffani's footsteps. They were coming closer and closer. Then they stopped. Beth Ann held her breath, drawing in even tighter, making herself as little as her imagination would allow, afraid to look. Tiffani peeked in at the expiration date on the handicapped placard hanging from the rear-view mirror. Then she spotted Beth Ann. Her eyes widened.

It seemed that the Christmas Express was running a little ahead of schedule for her, too, barreling down the tracks, its boiler coals stoked and glowing bright red, its big, bright eye scanning the track ahead of it.

"What are you doing down under there, honey? Looking for your keys or something?" the train whistle screamed, hissing white steam.

HAHAKAKA ROOM! HAHAKAKA ROOM! HAHAKAKA ROOM ROOM ROOM! AHEM AHEM!!!" Beth Ann offered.

The smoke stack blew black clouds, "HAHAKAKA ROOM! HAHAKAKA ROOM! HAHAKAKA ROOM ROOM ROOM! AHEM AHEM???" "HAHAKAKA ROOM! HAHAKAKA ROOM! HAHAKAKA ROOM! ROOM! ROOM! AHEM AHEM!!!" Beth Ann answered back.

The train chugged on down the line, its carriages swinging merrily this way and that, the caboose bringing up the rear, as it plowed through heavy snowbanks and skated across the frozen tundra to spread happiness and good cheer to good children far and near, leaving only a lump of coal in Beth Ann's stocking hung on her chimney with such great care.

Chapter 10

The Mayflower Club is a social club enjoyed by expatriated Brits. Beatrice had visited the one in Boston when she first arrived. She thought it was the only one over here. Boston, of course, but North Hollywood? There it was, right there on Victory Parkway. She stumbled upon it one afternoon during one of her drives. She had heard about the British Tea Room in Santa Monica, which she visited one afternoon, but it was filled with oglers hoping for a glimpse of someone famous. Keith Urban and Nicole Kidman were known to frequent the place. Russell Crowe when he was in town. If there were no stars to stare at, the quaint Brits drinking from cute little teacups and munching on little biscuits was a suitable substitute. She didn't feel too comfortable there. It was just a small square of the Old Sod. The Mayflower Club was the whole front yard.

So she signed up and diligently followed the social calendar. And now it was time for the annual holiday show, the Christmas pantomime, a tradition not only in the best theaters in London, but also in the village halls across all of Jolly Old England. Tonight's show was "Cinderella," one of her favorites.

"Cinderella, dressed in green,
Went downtown to buy a ring.
Made a mistake and bought a fake.

How many days before it breaks?
1-2-3-4-5-6-7-8," she would chant as a child jumping rope.

"Cinderella, dressed in yella
Went downstairs to kiss a fella.
Made a mistake and kissed a snake
How many stitches did it take?"

She could still sing songs about rings and fakes and stitches and snakes.

Felix had wondered why Beatrice had insisted in getting there so early, a full two hours before show time. There was no danger of getting lost or being late. It was just a mile or so up Vineland. But Beatrice persisted and Felix meekly submitted. When they arrived, the place was already full and noisy. They stood in small groups chatting up each other of the Queen and the Prime Minister and the Princes in familiar accents, queued up for shepherd's pie and bangers and plum pudding, washing everything down with long swigs of Boddington's beer. They were getting into character, after all, as they were expected to perform their role as well. It was one of those audience participation things and so tonight they would all be actors, and each of them were expected to be brilliant. But they all already knew their lines well, after decades of performing.

Felix watched as Beatrice rehearsed, belting down the ale and ordering the next before the one in hand was depleted. "You have to wet that whistle, get it well oiled because once the show begins, that's it," she told him. "And go to the loo, too, Love." There was no getting up and going across back and forth in front of people. That would be in bad taste and deserving of a public dressing down. Naughty behavior was reserved for the actors on stage, not those in the audience. She looked especially pretty tonight, Felix thought. She politely belched behind the long locks of her blonde wig. Several had complimented her on it and she let them run their fingers through it and smell it, as they told her how lovely it was and how lovely she was.

The lights dimmed and they took their seats, ever so politely saying "pardon me, love" as they passed across. The British were always on their best behavior. Nicely manner people, Felix thought. He liked how they called each other love. The place was full and extra folding chairs were being added at the last minute along the back wall. Near as he could tell, he was the only Yankee there. Then, slowly, the curtain opened. Beatrice was a Brit again, a child again. Everything else was left far behind.

Whenever each of the conniving, snitching and very ugly step sisters, played by fat and ugly men in outlandish costumes of floozy wigs and gingham dresses appeared on stage, they were roundly met by a chorus of boos and hisses from the audience. But when Cinderella arrived, a nice looking young fella in a dress of yella, she was wildly cheered and encouraged. "Watch out, Love, they're coming. Watch your back," Beatrice and the others shouted out in warning.

There were custard pies to be tossed and flying pots and pans targeted at each other by the villains as rightly well each deserved and plenty of falling over. As the ugly stepsisters dressed for the big ball, the ugliest and meanest of them all gazed into the mirror and boasted loudly, "I am the fairest of them all!"

"Oh, no, you're not!" the audience shouted on cue.

"Oh, yes, I am!" the man sister replied.

"OH, NO, YOU'RE NOT!"

"OH, YES, I AM!!!"

"OH, NO, YOU'RE NOT!"

"OH, YES, I AM!!"

Finally, a beautiful girl in princely garb arrived armed with the glass slipper. He first tried it on the feet of the fat old sisters, who struggled valiantly to slip their huge he foot into the tiny she shoe.

"No, no, Love, it is not she," Beatrice shouted out as each stepsister took his turn.

"Cut off your toes and your heel and maybe it would fit

then, Love!" someone behind them shouted.

And when the slippers slipped onto Cinderella's feet, the audience cheered wildly and the lovely she-prince kissed the handsome he-princess. The villains were defeated, the prince and the princess were led off the stage in each other's arms and the audience lives happily ever after. Beatrice and Felix lingered after the show, tossing Boddington's and darts until the lamps were lowered.

Champ sat between the purple walls, Ruby by his side, the snake head in his hand, thinking about home for the holidays. No money around for him and not much waiting around for him back home. Frankie's boyfriend was coming for a few days, then the two were going back home. Heathcharlesharley was leaving, too. He took a deep draw, producing a cloud of smoke, then erupted in spasms of coughing, choking, and gasping for air. Tiffani giggled. She liked to see people do that, get lungs full of that other sweet magic fixer-upper of all that is ugly and mean out there. Most of the time he would sit there with some kind of far away look, just glazed over. She would say something and he would say, "oh, uh huh." That was all. "oh, uh huh." She asks a question. "Oh, uh huh."

She clicked off the DVD. It was going to be a short evening anyway. She had a big job to do tonight. She had an hour or so before she had to start loading the car for her first trip. Dim-witted Harold would be coming home soon, too.

"Ruby have anything to say tonight?"

"Oh, uh huh."

"Ruby…She got a voice tonight or she just gonna sit there?"

"Oh, uh huh." He lifted Ruby up, caressed her neck, strummed her strings, tightened a screw, loosened another and centered her on his knee. He began softly, sweetly, his fingers expertly skating over frets and strings, listening to her voice and stretching his.

"Why did you go away? I'm lost today.
You know I couldn't say you'd have your way.
I didn't want to play your silly game to stay.
The price too steep. Too much to pay."

Champ was far away, alone and painful, soft and vulnerable, elsewhere. Tiffani hunched over her hookah and watched, a study in incongruities, like Marilyn Manson singing "Silent Night."

"Why did you go? Why did you go?
Why did you go? Why did you go away?"

With each question, he became sadder, full of mourning. Each word became a plea. Tiffani sat transfixed.

"Why did you go away? I'm lost today.
I lost my way. Another lonely day.
I cannot stand the pain. You've gone away.
I have to say I lost my way."

Champ played the melody softly. He was far, far away. Tiffani sat there warily, fearful almost.

"Why did you go? Why did you go?
Why did you go? Why did you go away?"

The strings were crying. The strums were stronger, the softness yielding to anger, a crescendo, a little bit at a time, but inexorably.

"Why did you go? I lost my way.
Another lonely day. Another endless day.
I wish you stayed, but you went away.
Another heart to break. Another game to play."

Tiffani sucked and stared. Ruby sang and screamed, the strums brutal now and pounding, Champ's voice raging in anger and anguish, in despair and abandonment, so total. So complete.

"Where did you go? Where did you go?
Where did you go? Where did you go away?"

The last lines were soft and quiet. The guitar became lovely again. The anger abated to sadness and loss.

"Why did you go? Why did you go?
Why did you go? Why did you go astray?"

Champ laid Ruby at his feet. "Yes, suh. Uh huh. She was one hot hooker."

Two floors down, Beatrice stood alone in the moonbeam on this soft winter night, among the sleeping birds of paradise and bougainvilleas, and softly sang, "Why did you go? Why did you go? Why did you go? Why did you go astray?"

Heathcharlesharley was beginning to get pretty busy, sometimes out several nights in a row as it got closer and closer to Christmas. Sex made him feel so much closer to the lord. He knew then that he was on a higher calling, that this was missionary work. He didn't recognize it at first, but the lord does work in mysterious ways. He took great comfort in it. He now knew how it felt to be Mother Teresa or Father Juniper Serra.

He would always ask the ladies if they were Christians, first, then double-checked their age and weight just to make sure before he left the Villa Verdugo. He knew from experience that they would usually tell a little fib. It was odd that they would make themselves younger or thinner when in fact he preferred the opposite. He just didn't want to go all that distance and waste all that time for some waif, some young, skinny thing. It's like having sex with a boy. No tits and a tight box.

The women would ask him about his shoe size and he in

turn would fudge a little. He knew that women knew that the size of a man's foot has a direct colonary to the length and the strength of his penis. So his nearly size eight foot was stretched nearly to size twelve, stretching his nearly four inches nearly to eight.

Often times he had trouble finding the place, leaving some desperate housewife in her teddy, peering out the drapes every few minutes at any approaching car until the wee hours of the morning. When he did find the place, the mood had already set below the horizon, the candles burnt to short stumps, the bottle of zinfandel nearly empty, Johnny Mathis still crooning softly through scratchy stereo speakers.

Sometimes she would want him to spend the night. There was no way he could do that. Half an hour was his limit. They would talk for the first twenty or twenty-five minutes, getting to know each other a little bit, loosening up little bit. Then they would spend a few minutes undressing each other. He liked that. He insisted on it. Both standing there, undressing the other. When she pulled down his underpants and he stood there with his glorious pecker pointing at Polaris, that was his favorite part. It got him really good and excited. Why, it would be just within a minute or two after they coupled up that he would explode in a heart-pounding orgasm. Then it would be time to leave. His father had once told him that when it came to women, the best advice he could give him was "leave them wanting more, my son." He was a regular chip off the old block. Yes, Sir!

There are few surprises for the yeshiva boys. They pretty much know what to expect day after day. The Talmud. The Hebrew. The Basketball. Their holy trinity. Each with the same intensity, day after day, except for Friday after sundown to Saturday after sundown for Sabbath.

During the morning break, they crowd around what is left of the sports section of the LA Times after the Rosh was done with the scissors, seeking out any news at all of their beloved Lakers, pouring over the photos of Shaq O'Neal or Kobe Bryant or Ron Artest in action, memorizing their moves, studying every word in the write-ups, and arguing among themselves about rankings and statistics and play-offs.

When the lunch or dinner bell announces their release from holy duties, they race from their classrooms to the asphalt, stopping quickly at the lunch room to grab a pizza bagel, a specialty that the cooks concocted for the boys to hold in their hands, a sliced bagel topped with pizza sauce and a slab of cheese, then toasted, which they can eat at court side while changing into their basketball shoes and choosing up sides.

There are three full courts carved from the back parking lot. Felix knew very well not to park on them or near them. They would be angry with him. And it was a true anger, something that didn't surface very often, unhappy about leaking truck juices onto the court, using up their valuable time by having to chase him down. They only have half an hour. The younger, newer students play horse on the least desirable court, the one with the drainage grate at mid court, and practice their dribbling and shooting skills under the guidance of the older boys who tutor in rotation. Every boy plays.

Prestige and honor are meted out for those truly gifted in courtmanship. On the best court, the best players race back and forth, executing sophisticated pick and rolls, give and go's, cutting and faking, testing, leaping, shooting, then deftly scooping up the errant yarmulkes and setting up defense on their return trip across the court. The only sounds are the bouncing ball, the shuffling feet, an occasional "yip!" the swish of the net, and the slap of high fives. There are no rabbis, no coaches, and no referees. The best player resolves questionable fouls without challenge, quickly and expeditiously. There is no time to waste arguing. They play in the dark in the short days of December, in the heavy rains of February, and in the triple digits of August.

Felix would stay after school to watch. He would never see any hotdogmanship, no fancy-schmancy showoffs, no one-man-shows, just a finely tuned and well-oiled machine like he'd see in a tournament game in the big arenas back home in Indiana, where the hoopla of high school basketball is king.

Woodrow couldn't believe it. He had been wary at first, thinking this was too good to be true. He rubbed his eye. But it was still there, parked right in the middle of the living room in front of the TV. He had watched Felix lug it into the apartment, pull it out of the box and unfold it. He grinned. His friends had warned him that sooner or later, he would be replaced by some sort of a robot. They were very concerned about losing their jobs, rendered useless, suffering the same fate as the slide rule and the typewriter, on the dust heap of the Industrial Revolution. "The Cane, a wooden stick once used as an assistant human leg." But Woodrow secretly prayed and prayed that they were right and that it would be sooner rather than later. He may have been the only one that felt that way, but there was no other way he could be extricated from this human bondage short of turning himself over to the toothpick factory. He wondered if those would ever be rendered obsolete. "The Toothpick, a sliver of wood once used to extract particles of food, such as spinach and popcorn, from between human teeth." You would see them only in museums next to the toupees. "The Toupee, once used as a device to protect one's hairless pate from bright suns and one's self-esteem from trite puns."

And now here it was, and it was just fine with him. He watched her sit in the driver's cage, making zoom-zoom-zoom noises through puckered lips, leaning left, then right as she raced around the oval and crossed the finish line at the Indy 500, barely edging out Mario Andretti in a photo finish. Sometimes, she was back in the saddle again, the reins in her fingers, whispering "giddy-up, little dogey," and snorting and whinnying, her eyes closed, her childhood on her face. Soon there would be no more trips or pokes or jabs or hooks or hoists. No more of that stale tale. There is a god and he does answer prayers. He would hang around home, just staying in the rack all day long. "Ahhh, Invention! Salvation is thy name."

Chapter 11

There were a lot of things Heathcharlesharley hadn't been able to understand lately, like what happened to Payback? She was always laying at Frankie's feet or on his lap. Frankie would coo softly and call her Lily. Didn't Frankie hate cats? It wasn't fair. He expected Payback to live up to her name. Another thing he didn't understand. Remembering his father's orders for financial responsibility, he returned to Pets For People, Payback in hand. The woman behind the counter refused a refund. "Too late," she said. Then she cuddled her in her arms, cooing and calling her Lily.

Payback always slept in Frankie's room, only coming into his when she had to pee or poo. He had to leave the door open so that Payback could get to the litter box. The other two had insisted that it be in his room. Frankie had even said it was supposed to be cleaned or changed or whatever. What does Frankie understand about cats?

When he first arrived in LA, he saw a girl walking her dog out front. Then the dog stopped, squatted down, got glassy-eyed for a few moments, then pooped in the grassy area between the sidewalk and the curb. "Then, right before my eyes, I watched the girl pull on a plastic bag over her hand, and bend over and pick up the poop! So help me god!!!" he swore again and again and again to his disbelieving father, who said that it was not a likely thing at all that he would be following his blue tick coon dogs around with a little plastic baggie when rabbit season opens.

Another thing he didn't understand was why Payback was peeing and pooing on his futon mattress. It was also most certainly not a likely thing at all that he was going to follow her around with a little plastic baggie either. Like father.. like....uh... whatever. He pulled the mattress into the closet and found it to be the perfect solution. Whenever he left, he would just slide the door closed. Amen. Payback could pretty much be free to do as she pleased. Then when he got home, he would head right for the closet, pull the mirrored sliding glass door closed behind him and spend quality time in peace and quiet, sprawled out on the mattress, watching television on the small screen set up on the other end of the long closet, humped over Miss Ima MacLaptop, isolated from the sounds going on in the other parts of the apartment.

Tonight, though, he had left the door open a crack. If he listened carefully, he could hear the debauchery of the sinful solemn knights or whatever you call them in the next room slapping each other, spanking each other probably, something that a mother should do to his son. Then he felt a curious warmth stirring in his pajama bottoms.

He hadn't been happy with the arrival of Ricky. No one bothered to tell him that an unfriendly, small, skinny, hairless girl-boy was coming. He looked like a little teacup in the china cabinet of his mother or grandmother or sister or whatever or whoever she is. Ricky didn't even spend the first night there, instead heading up to the couch in Felix's apartment. Then he showed up early the next morning carrying a fat roll of trash bags and bottles of disinfectants and bug killer, his face hidden behind a surgical mask, hands protected by long rubber gloves, like he was entering a leper colony or something. He made them stay out of his room, though. That night, Champ stayed out of his room, too, and slept on the sofa, like it was no big deal.

Ricky, for the first time, began to wonder about Frankie.

His dorm room back at college was usually disheveled, but harmless and quaint, like what someone would expect of a boy's room. After a little playful teasing, Ricky would spend a few minutes tidying it up for him and that was all that was necessary. But this was pathological, transcending any sensibilities at all. Frankie had never expressed any concern about it. It was clear, too, that Frankie had contributed his share. He asked Frankie how he could abide by this and Frankie said he hadn't really given it much thought. Champ just said, "oh, uh huh," slowly shook his head sadly, and went out to smoke, pulling the sliding glass door of the balcony behind him.

Ricky asked Heathcharlesharley about it. He said it was his art. Frankie had his art and he had his. That the heaps and piles were mountains and hills, his spacious skies oer amber waves of grain, his purple mountains majesty along his fruited plain. "If you look at it with an artist's eye, you could see it," he said, squinting his eyes and stretching his arm out in solemn presentation. Then he left for that important errand he almost forgot all about. Slowly, the purple mountains and fruited plains shifted to the dumpster, the carpet underneath the huddled masses of wretched refuse on the teeming floor napalmed, sending the ants and the roaches heading for cover in the trenches and foxholes while the bombs bursting in air gave proof to the sight that the Black Flag was still there.

Paramount, Universal, Warner Brothers, Dreamworks, Sony, MGM, Fox, and Disney, affectionately known as Mouschwitz by its employees, were swaddled in the warmth and hospitality of southern California. Everything is there. Whatever the script calls for, the location scouts will find the ideal place, wherever it is, the ocean, lakes, and rivers; the deserts, mountains, and forests; the downtown slums, ethnic neighborhoods, middle-class America, and the upper crust; the farms and small towns and the sleek, streamlined skyscrapers of a twenty-first century metropolis, all within a few miles and all with iron-clad promises of eight straight months of worry-free weather.

NBC, ABC, CBS, CNN, Nickelodeon, and other young upstarts moved in as youngsters. They all grew up next door to each other, intermarried, and became the aristocracy, the doyen of entertainment and news. They begot television shows and film and animation and on-air advertising and TV dinners. They enticed America into inviting them over for the evening, and they persuaded the cola companies and the telephone companies and car manufacturers and giant retailers from across the nation to come on out and pay for it all.

And the world came calling, knocking on the door, seeking the best and the brightest and their programming, their artists, their production professionals and their cutting edge technology, and learned from them, then returned to their shores and copied it, or used it just as they found it, and in the process, whetted the appetite of their own viewers for the smörgåsbord of American morality and culture.

The major studios themselves became fully contained, self-sufficient, fortified walled cities, not too unlike the walled cities of Medieval Europe. On the other side of those walls and spread out in full Panavision are the innards of the industry, complete with a Main Street, shops and restaurants, fully equipped police and fire departments, emergency care clinics, trash removal facilities, water towers, power plants big enough to heat or cool multiple large hanger-sized sound stages, warehouses, parking garages, lodging units, nurseries, sewing shops, carpenter shops and hardware stores, lumber yards, paint depots, office buildings, weather stations, travel offices, rows of big rigs for on-location shoots, car pools, museums, and amusement parks.

Thin, one-dimensional plywood facades mimic New York boroughs, brownstone neighborhoods on cobblestoned streets, courthouse squares, New England and Midwest villages and cowboy towns, two blocks long and two feet thick, their hidden ribs and spines stark skeletons of two-by-fours. It is there where lights and lenses make sunrise and sunset, where scrims and flats suggest sierras or prairies, where pipes and sprayers create London fogs and Kansas cloudbursts, where giant fans blow howling windstorms and blizzards of swirling snow, where a flooded parking lot becomes a sea for Moses to part.

"Okay, let's rise. Slowly now." Felix woke from his reverie, returning from the gently rolling dunes of Malibu to the hard cold floor of reality. He tried to visit a different beach every week. Maybe next week, it would be Zumi. Eventually he would have time to visit all the beaches. There were still eight more class sessions.

"Shake the sand from the bottoms of your feet. Vigorously now. Get all that sand off. Now your hands. Come on, give them a good shake. Now your legs. Shake! Shake! Now shake everything! Ahhhh, that's right. Good, good, good! Your back. Your front! Shake it! Shake it! Shake it! Good, good good. Now relax. Breathe deeply."

Felix filled his lungs. He wished that maybe they could go to the mountains some time. There were a lot of them around, too. He could develop his acting skills there, too, as well, he was sure. The San Gabriels. The Santa Susanas. The Santa Monicas. Lay around on a big flat rock with his eyes closed, smelling the forest and hearing the eagles call. "Shake those pine needles off your back now. Shake! Shake! Shake it!" she would have to say.

"Now stretch your arms to the sky. Nice and long, nice and long. Stretch for the sun. That's it. Stretch…Now relax. Okay, slowly, slowly bend over, from your waist down, bend slowly now, vertebra by vertebra, slowly now, until it loosens up, slowly, bend your knees ever so slightly if you have to. Reach for the floor. This shouldn't hurt. Drop, slowly, vertebra by vertebra. Slowly now. Bend those knees. Okay, hang there now. Say ahhhhhhh"

"AHHHHH," replied the class.

"Ahhhhhh..."

"AHHHHH"

"Ahhhhhh"

"AHHHHHH!"

While we're at it, the Mojave Desert would be cool, too, with its cacti and lizards and tumbleweeds. He could already feel the hot dry air warm his face and clean out his sinuses.

"Weave back and forth. Like a pendulum in a clock. Back and forth. Back and forth. Ahhh..."

"AHHHHHHH!"

"Hold it now. Ahhhh..."

"AHHHHHHH!"

"Now, slowly, vertebra by vertebra, lift back up. Slowly now. All the way up. Reach for the stars! Reach! Ahhhhhh...

"AHHHHH!"

"Okay, now you will drop into a heap between your legs, expelling your air as you drop. Then just hang there, just like you just did. Ready? "

"READY!"

"NOW COLLAPSE!"

"OOOOOOOOOOOOOOOOOOOOOOOOOOOOOOP PPPHHHH"

"Good. Now just hang there. Breathe. Breathe through your nose to warm up the air. Hang... Okay, now back up, slowly now, all the way up. Slowly now. Reach, reach for the sun. reach... NOW COLLAPSE!

"OOOOOOOOOOOOOOOOOOOOOOOOOMMMMPP PPHHHH!"

"Felix!"

So what about maybe going back to the old childhood crib? That would be interesting, too for a change. Imagining himself laying there in clean diapers, a rubber nipple cradled comfortably between his toothless gums, a little Donald Duck mobile hanging above his forehead, sweep sweep, sweeping away the pain and stress. Maybe he would ask her after class.

"Hang...swing...back and forth...breathe. Okay, now back up. Slowly now. Reach... COLLAPSE!"

"OOOOOOOOOOOOOOOOOOOOOOOOOOOOMM MPPPHHH!"

"Back up, slowly vertebra by vertebra, reach for the stars. "NOW DROP!

"OOOOPPPPHHHH!"

"Felix!!"

And for that matter, why not go all the way back to the womb, or with Eve under the apple tree in the Garden of Paradise, where everything is milk and honey and he could munch an apple and ...

"Felix!!!!!"

"OKAY!!!!!"

"Up...Up...Up...Up... DROP!"

"OOOOOOOOOOOOOOOOOOOOOOOOOOOOOO MMMPPPHHH!"

Christmas wasn't a real big deal at the yeshiva. There would be school as usual. But Felix has asked for Christmas Eve off and the Rosh agreed. Los Angeles loves all of her holidays dearly, but it is Christmas which she holds the nearest to her bosom. Felix smiled as he wandered through the Glendale Galleria and saw the cheerful menfolk in their Bermuda shorts and sandals sitting on the mall benches under the palm trees guarding the purchases with the other men while their wives shopped, then making multiple trips to the car with heavy bundles and bales of packages to stack carefully in the back seat of the convertible. Bing Crosby can dream of a white Christmas until the cows come home, but it ain't likely to happen. There won't be any dashing through the snow in a one horse open sleigh. Jack Frost won't be nipping at anyone's noses, not in the Southland. There will be the caress of the Pacific across her shores, the allure of the palms along her broad boulevards, the Beach Boys dreaming of Little Saint Nick, and children of all ages dashing through the dunes with a surfboard under tow.

Champ worked the lunch shift on Christmas Eve. It didn't really matter to him anyway. It was just another day. He arrived right at ten, just as Big Man was unlocking the thick plate glass door. Usually there would be no customers until around 11:00 or so, with the lunch rush not starting until a few minutes after noon, Pacific Standard Time. But this was Christmas Eve and things would be different. The place would be closing early. No one would opt for Epic Heroes on Christmas Eve, not when the tables back home were piled high with ruffles and truffles.

He did what he always did when he was doing lunch, ripping open the big ten pound bags of pre-prepared gray meat balls and pouring them into large vats of preprocessed tomato sauce. As they cooked, he pulled the ripcord on the thick plastic prewrapped ten pound blocks of processed American cheese, neatly presliced into small triangles for a perfect fit, and squeezed big bladders of processed ranch dressing into small squeeze bottles. He unloaded the frozen processed Italian bread dough from the big freezers in the back, lining twenty of them, two rows of ten, onto the large baking trays made perfectly to fit into the twenty slots in the backing oven, two rows wide and ten rows deep. While the bread baked, he poured the processed teriyaki sauce over the precooked, presliced chicken strips, put the wrinkles into the processed, precooked bacon, and sprinkled the dew onto the perfectly presliced green peppers and cucumbers and tomatoes.

Big Man came from the back room. He was leaving, had things to do. It was Christmas Eve and he had things to do. "I won't be back and oh yeah merrychristmasgottago. Ba sure ta douba check the back door."

"He probably didn't get anything yet for his wife," Champ thought. They weren't going to be busy today and the boss knew it. The office buildings and eye doctor offices lining Lankershim would shut down early. Most people wouldn't even go in, it being Christmas Eve and all. Those were the people who come in for lunch. They wouldn't come today. He stepped out front for a smoke.

Johnie was waiting around the corner where he usually stood, just out of sight of Big Man. Things hadn't gone well so he took up residence in the colony under the 170 Freeway North. "Under the overpass and over the underpass," he would say with a grin. “Lots of people living up there. Big enough to have its own zip code. But we don't need one. Mailman never stops up there. Nobody up there never getting mail from anybody anyhow. Lots of folks have something wrong with them, but the EMT never stops up there neither, 'less someone croaks.”

Champ met Johnie a few months ago on the sidewalk out front asking for change. One morning when not much was going down, Johnie told his story. Later, Champ walked down to the King's Pawn Shop and saw Johnie's guitar hanging in the window, swinging there with four or five other guitars, like the public gallows in a mid twentieth century village square on market day.

There was something about pawn shops and guitars, an attraction to each other, like boys and dinosaurs or girls and vampires. Johnie would stop by every night, late when no one was around much, and lean against the steel grid gate. “It is just a set back,” he would say. “Just a temporary thing.” Often he would fall asleep there, only to be booted away early the next morning by the pawnshop keeper. “You can't sleep here. One more time and I call the cops on ya.”

Champ would sneak him a sandwich when Big Man wasn't looking. He finished his smoke and went back in. What the hell. He pulled the bread from the oven and stirred the meatballs. He took the twenty bread rolls and laid them in two neat rows along the countertop, grabbed the long knife and neatly sliced the bread, like a surgeon, he thought, getting ready to yank someone's liver out. Then he ladled meatballs on ten, teriyaki chicken on the other ten, piling on the extras, then neatly wrapped each one in waxed paper. He loaded a big cardboard box with the heroes and headed for the door, then stopped. What the hell hell. He turned back around, fished around in back for another box and loaded it with bags of chips, oatmeal raisin cookies and liter bottles of water, sodas, and juices, then headed back to the door, then remembered the napkins and straws and a stack of plastic cups. He turned back to the door. Johnnie had to make two trips. Big Man wouldn't ever notice, and if he did, well, what the hell, hell, hell.

Back home, right about now, Paw would be gathering the younger ones and his handsaw, and they would walk out to the stand of pines in the back for the tree to decorate with garlands of popcorn and pecans and ornaments of handpainted crab shells. Later in the evening, there would be Midnight Mass and then the towering bonfires lining the levees along the Mississippi River would be set ablaze to light the night sky so that Papa Noel could find his way through the dark black bayous and backways with his heavy bags.

The Villa Verdugo slipped out of her cut-offs and flip-flops and into her best holiday threads of light, creating a warm halo of mirth and good cheer. Her halls and her gardens buzzed with the aroma of carols and cookies and calls for a merry Christmas, but on Christmas Eve, shortly after sundown, things become eerily quiet, vigilant, expectant, hopeful. Everything on tiptoes. The music would cease. Windows, sliding doors, front doors gaping widely, phones on vibrate, televisions mute. Bottles of Christmas spirits opened, poured, and waiting, marijuana smoke wafting heavily through the bougainvillea and the birds of paradise, all of the cars parked on the street moved into driveways or yards or to Ralph's down the street. All is bright, all is calm, but above all, all is quiet.

Then it happens.

"IT'S COMING!" someone in the front apartments shouts first.

"IT"S COMING! IT'S COMING! IT'S COMING!!

Instantly the halls would fill.

"Do you hear it?"

"Yes, I think I do. Shh."

Then the faint sounds in the far distant.

"Listen. YES! IT'S COMING!"

Everyone can hear it now. It can be heard for miles. Hesby Street and Otsego Street and Morrison Street and Houston Street fill. All the streets of Toluca Lake and the south end of North Hollywood fill, lines of Angelenos, many clutching glasses of wine, and others with a beer in the hand and two in the bushes out front.

"It's coming," everyone shouts.

"Soon, now. Soon!"

"Maybe twenty minutes or so! But it's coming! "

Adults become children again. And children become younger again. Babies become cuter. Spirits run freely. The sidewalks continue to fill. It is near, near, nearer. Now, the next street over. Now, the hush. It's all been said. It's coming.

The advance crew in orange vests arrives first, on foot, checking the flight path, the runway, mumbling into walkie-talkies, gently reminding the crowds to remain on the sidewalk, eyeballing, measuring particularly narrow streets or steep turns, and if necessary, muscling an uninformed automobile up, lifting it up over the curb and onto a yard and out of the way. The way clear, the signal is given to more orange vests, more walkie-talkies. This is serious business, no room for error here. It is Christmas Eve in Los Angeles.

Then, the mammoth cab emerges, its windshield trimmed with twinkling lights, its fenders and hood bedecked with wreaths and buntings of pine and holly, booming loudspeakers and bright floodlights mounted on its top, and slowly it creeps forward from around the corner, in inches, the seasoned teamster behind the reins directed by more walkie-talkies and swinging orange-tipped flashlights with the precision of the ground crew directing a jumbo jet into its gate on a foggy midnight at LAX. On the flatbed trailer as big as the deck of an aircraft carrier perches an Alpine Village, its chimneys smoking, the windows and doors of the colorful little chalets and storefronts lined with revelers in Santa hats singing and waving and wishing greetings, the bubble machines bubbling, twirlers twirling batons, and dancing Santa elves, and pretty young girls in red vests and white leotards passing out candy canes.

Tears of comfort and joy would flow down cheeks, unabashedly, and scores follow the spectacle, unwilling to let go just yet, and grateful that it came once again., This year, it was the Magic Kingdom once again. Then the village would move on, disappearing like a mirage into the evening mist and the streets would empty as quickly as they filled, and the Halls of the Villa Verdugo, decked with Boughs of Holly, would once again be alive with the Sounds of Music. Fa la la la la, la la la la...

Beep. "Hi, there! Did you know..." Zip. Zap.

Beep. "This message is for Felix. This is Ashley Brooks Saint Tropez calling from Osceola..." Zip. Zap.

Beep. "Tired of high medical bills? Then..." Zip. Zap.

Beep "Hi, Remember me! I met yo..." Zip. Zap.

Beep. "Hi, there! Did..." Zip Zap.

Beep. "Hi, there..." Zip Zap.

Beep. "Hello, Felix. This is your mother. Hope you're okay, honey. I think of you all the time. Well!. So...! It's hard to believe another Christmas is on the way, huh? I put the tree up this evening. The ornament you made in fourth grade. It is so pretty. It's hanging where I can see it whenever I walk by. So... Well... Hmmm... I miss you, Felix. I thought maybe you'd call on my birthday like you used to so I stayed around the house all day. Afraid I'd miss you. Maybe you can call on Christmas Eve or Christmas morning or something. Your dad and I'll be here all day. He said to say hi. I think he feels bad. You know, he really didn't expect you to do what he told you to go do. You know how he is. I miss you, Felix, and I love you very much. Goodbye, honey."

Click.

Barbara had shuttered Mainstream for ten days or so. Most of her clients had booked out to return home for the holidays and there would be few audition calls coming in. She could relax. Hayad had left for London so the final touches on the point and click technology would wait until after the holidays. She pushed back from her computer screen.

She liked being by herself, especially during the holidays.

The sun had set behind the neat cottages on Cohasset Street. The evening was crisp and clean and every home in the neighborhood was brightly lighted. Each had a nativity scene. Soon a posada would arrive at her door. During each night of the Twelve Days of Christmas, a different family in the neighborhood was assigned to reenact the Holy Family's search for lodgings, going from house to house and turned away at each. Barbara would open the door, then sadly shake her head no and say there was no room in her inn for them, and the family would leave for the next house. Then later in the evening, she would hear the children whack at papier mache piñatas filled with peanuts in the shell, oranges, tangerines and small hard candies while the parents sipped on ponche con piquete. Gifts wouldn't be opened for a few more weeks, not until January 6, the Day of the Kings.

Her archways and door frames were lined with colorful Christmas cards, some handmade, some store bought. Others sent her gift certificates for Trader Joe's or the Aroma Cafe. Heathcharlesharley brought over a case of wine, unaware that she was a teetotaler. She opened the case and sent out bottles with the courier to deliver to her favorite casting directors. Frankie painted her a little picture of a farmhouse on a snow covered hill. Poinsettias and boxes of cookies and fudge and date nut bread covered the glass-topped table and lined the path from the front door to the kitchen. She leaned back in her rocker in the darkened room, and smiled. Maybe she should consider putting a stable in the back yard next Christmas.

In the heart of WeHo is the Cock-A-Doodle-Doo, a buffet-type restaurant noted for its healthy chicken and candied yams, feel good gumbo and string beans, French style. It is the place to be on Friday nights. It is then and there that the rich old queens of the village showboat their young thoroughbreds, the elegant and well-kept stallions in their stable. Their French pastries. Their French horns. Cock-a-doodle doo. But not any cockle do, though. These cockles are breathtakingly handsome, sophisticated and meticulously groomed. Most are imported, but sometimes there is a stallion from Iowa or Oregon. They drive handsome and sophisticated imported Porsches or Mercedes coupes. They wear handsome and sophisticated diamonds on their ears and wrists and fingers and toes and neck, and handsome and sophisticated Italian and French dressing. French silks. French cuffs. French scents.

"Eau de Toilet."

"Water of the Toilet?

"Oui! Oui!"

"Wee wee? A la Pepe Le Pew? Oooo! Adieu!"

"Non, Monsieur."

"Man's sewer! Poo poo?"

"Parfum

Wilted gay octogenarians, their jism yellowing in antique testicles, attempt to outdo their competition with the most bountiful beau, often times wooed away from rivals with handsome and sophisticated bonuses and extravagant vacations to the south of France, pockets lined with plenty of French bread, showing both their rivals and possible prospects that their wealth has no limits.

The young concubines are evaluated, sized-up, and scrutinized for fashion triumphs and boners, ogled, and groped as they line at the counter, two trays in hand, one for Daddy back at the table and one for themselves, posing as they picked from the pans of steaming potpies, then pirouetting back to their masters with the practiced grace and poise of a Miss America finalist.

Chapter 12

The Glendale Galleria was the perfect place to test drive the sporty new wheelchair, a sprawling mall in complete compliance with the Americans with Disabilities Act. There would be ramps and wide aisles. Felix and Beatrice had been such dears and loaded it into the bed of Felix's truck. But things didn't go quite as well as she had hoped. It was different from the dodge'm cars back in her Akron youth. In those, if you ran into something, the car would just automatically bounce back and move ahead in a different route. No harm done. And those little cars didn't go quite as fast when you put the pedal to the metal.

Both Beatrice and Felix shrieked with laughter every time she collided with a pole or knocked over a display rack or sent manikins toppling or caught some shopper unaware with a butt to the rear, or rolled over someone's toes. Then she got the tuckle in her throat. HAHAKAKA ROOM HAHAKAKA ROOM HAHAKAKA ROOM ROOM ROOM! AHEM AHEM!"

A couple of people started to videotape her. Others tried to catch the action on their cellphones. Then someone started the rumor that they were shooting a movie. Soon there were hundreds of people following her and watching, screaming with delight and jollity, forgetting about their shopping woes for the moment and joining in the merriment, as she bowled her way down the wide aisles out of control, zigzagging and swerving, racing full speed backwards, sideswiping trash receptacles, spinning around in circles. One time she even flipped over, which really sent everyone caterwauling. Then she got caught sideways in the handicap stall in the bathroom and had to send someone out to get Beatrice. HAHAKAKA ROOM HAHAKAKA ROOM HAHAKAKA ROOM ROOM ROOM! AHEM AHEM!!!"

Later, when she told Beatrice about her plans to use it in England in her upcoming trip there to attend her dear friend's dear friend's long lost daughter's marriage, Beatrice warned her that it was a horrible idea. Americans are much more sensitive to the disabled than the Brits are. There is no Brits with Disabilities Act. And the Brits have zero tolerance for them, angrily telling wheelchair-bound people to move out of their way. If they didn't, the Brits would grab the push handles on the wheelchair and shove them out of the way, often times with enough force to send them careening fifty feet down the walkway, well out of everyone's way, excuse me.

"When Brits see people in wheelchairs in the streets," said Beatrice, "why, they jeer at them, telling them bluntly to get up off their fat arses and walk, that it would do them some good. Besides that, how are you going to navigate that wheelchair across those cobblestone roads? Why, you'd never make it. You'd be a nuisance to everyone."

Beth Ann had to admit that she hadn't thought about any of that. Perhaps it should be back to the cane. Lately, the numbness had been coming and going with more frequency, but she never knew when to expect its arrival or departure.

The New Year arrived and brought with it Heathcharlesharley a few days ahead of schedule. He headed straight for the closet, rejuvenated and ready to resume his missionary work. There hadn't been many souls to save in Louisiana as everyone there was already out doing missionary work all the time and all, but there was certainly a lot of catching up to do here in California. He was eager to get started.

It wasn't easy. He never knew what to expect. It was those mysterious ways of the lord thing again. Sometimes that poor soul needing rescuing was an ignored wife, a widow, a divorced lady, a spinster, or someone "deeply disappointed in my husband." Sometimes it was something easy and simple, like a desire to be released from the bondage of boredom. Sometimes it was more complex, a soul that needed a special and intimate connection to a loved one from her past, like a teacher and her student, a doctor and her patient, a gentle minister and one of his conjugants.

Sometimes in the heat of passion, she would order, "Beam me up, Scotty," or repeatedly call him Father Flannigan or Sergeant Preston. Sometimes he was called on to say things, like, "Frankly, my dear, I don't give a damn!" or "Bond... James Bond." There were a couple of occasions with diapers and talcum powder, and he was okay with that. Some had favorite little gadgets they kept hidden in a little space behind the bed stand. One soul had a special mist that made everything feel all warm and wet and tingly and she sprayed him while he was standing there. Well, Katie bar the door. Wham bam, thank you ma'am. That's all it took. His four banger began firing up. Bang bang ban...g ba b b bb...pfft.... It was great. He just pulled his pants right back up and was out of there in the matter of just a minute or two. So now, he was very ready to make up for lost time. He clicked on. There was so much work to do. He sighed heavily.

Trader Joe's is the place where yuppies, flower children, artists and musicians and actors, the literati and glitterati, the doting daddios and smothering motherlings carefully read labels before tossing the salt-free, fat-free, cholesterol-free, sugar-free, MSG-free, hormone-free cookies and crackers and sodas into their carts, alongside the color-coordinated clumps of blooming buttercups and lilies and the homegrown pumpkins, the vegan dog food and black olive pizzas, organic eggs and butter and Chinese greens, and Two-Buck Chuck, a sobriquet for their

$2.00 bottles of Charles Shaw wine.

Beatrice would begin every day there for chat with the amiable clerks as she breakfasted her way through several sample-sized cups of Bolivian coffee and sliced Caribbean papaya. Later in the day she would visit the free sample tables at Sam's Club for more chat and noshing, puffing up the clerks who would serve her bigger portions of free pasta and mini-tacos and petite sausage sandwiches, then polish it all off free-sampling her way down the counter of any good ice cream parlor, conversing with the counterperson about the distinctive peaches and their Georgian or Michiganian nuances vis a vis the subtleties of Tennessee mint in a deep Peruvian chocolate.

Then it would be back to Trader Joe's on Saturday afternoon for their weekly free wine-tasting lessons, presided over by a friendly and officious oenophile who appreciated someone with Beatrice's particularly discerning palette and would answer her intricate questions about the origin and unique qualities of that particular wine as she wooed her way through the wine wagon, instructing Felix as they lingered long and sampled deeply from each of the ten or fifteen bottles and munched heavily from the sophisticated cheese and crackers arranged neatly on trays among the bottles, and then fully satisfied and very well schooled, would weave and wobble their way back down the winding sidewalk to the Villa Verdugo.

Beth Ann caught her boss rolling her eyeballs and sighing heavily when she left for her doctor's appointment. Then she caught Felix rolling his eyeballs and sighing heavily when she asked him to be a dear. Then she caught the refund guy at Hurry-up Health rolling his eyeballs and sighing heavily. Then she caught the doctor rolling his eyeballs and sighing heavily when she asked for the handicapped placard. Then she rolled her eyeballs and sighed heavily when he said "Acid Reflux. Acid Reflux. Awk... Awk." Then she rolled her eyeballs and sighed heavily when she saw Tiffani's Taurus back in the handicapped spot.

Lily was delighted to see Frankie walk in the door. Sure, Champ fed her, occasionally wiping his hand over her head in a timid pat, and saying “Nice Kitty,” but that was about it. Mostly, he just sat on the balcony with the door shut. So it was just the two of them. She and Ruby. They had nothing in common, except they lived together. But the ice melted when everyone was gone. Lily would toss and turn and cry in her sleep so Ruby would sing softly to her and she would become peaceful. Then on lazy afternoons, Lily would sit on Rocky Top and listen to Ruby making funny comments about Heathcharlesharley and the two of them would just roll on the rocks and howl like banshees.

And now Frankie was back. She watched him put the heavy Singer sewing machine down on the kitchen table with a thud and unpack his bag. Then he presented her with two gift-wrapped packages. She couldn't believe it. Nobody had ever given her a present before and here there were two. She unwrapped the first one and found a really fine ball that tinkled when it rolled. The other present looked like that kind of stuff Champ rolls into little cigarettes. She just took one whiff and was immediately hooked, utterly simply delirious. For the next ten minutes there was nothing else on the face of the earth. Then she fell into an intoxicated slumber.

Later when she woke up, Ruby told her it was cat weed. Humans call it catnip. “Lily have a lil catnip, Lily have a lil catnap,” Ruby teased.

“Now ya'all really a Kool Kalifornia Kat. Maybe ya'all could just step out onto the balcony with Monsieur Beauchamp and the two of ya'all get high together.” Then they both squealed and gave high-fives. Ruby was so witty. Lily felt a little bad that Frankie didn't think to bring anything for Ruby so Lily said she could have the ball since they both had such lovely voices inside of them. Ruby thanked her and told her she could play with it whenever she wanted. Lily sighed. “Friends is great, ain't they?”

After the holidays, everything slowly returned to normal.

Felix began the year by making a long, detailed list of New Year resolutions, and then checking it off the list of things he had to do. Tiffani continued her cruise, examining every inch of the ship as she sailed to her doom, closely checking the positions of the life boats, the knots in the ropes, the music sheets and instruments as the band played on. Her red Taurus was back home where she belonged. Beatrice took long afternoon drives along Pacific Coast Highway, checking the rearview mirror habitually, watching her back. Beth Ann began to weary of her long drives back and forth to work everyday and wondered why Archie and Veronica had started to pee on the carpet. She resolved to finish writing the documentary about those fabulous pyramids and the probability that they were giant refueling stations for extra-terrestrial travelers. Woodrow was unceremoniously yanked from the rack and redeployed back to the war front and not one iota happy about it. "No 'scuse me's, no how do you do's. Such bad manners. So much for early retirement." Heathcharlesharley was deep into his missionary work and starting to gain a reputation while Champ slowly rocked back and forth on the five gallon bucket, deep in thought.

And Frankie signed up for an improvisation class. In fact, Frankie lived it and breathed it. In college he knew all the other improv actors. They all competed with and against each other. They all lived it and breathed it. They would work out while they walked to class in the morning, and in the hallways between classes, and in their dorm rooms every evening. They knew each other's strength and weaknesses, and how to fill in the gaps when someone was off their game. It had a lot to do with mental wave lengths and intuition and trust and not so much about thinking.

One of the things that Frankie wondered about was why improv had rules. Why would you have rules for something that was different every time you did it? But they were there and you had to follow them, like Felix and his lists. The Golden Rules of Improvisation. Do Not Deny. Do Not Argue. Do Not Question. And his favorite rule of them all: Do Not Plan Ahead. You were limited only by your own limitations and the rules allowed you to be free from limitations. You would never have any idea where something was going. Whatever was offered was required. Maybe it was something like "this is the day Virginia decides to leave her husband." It was a spontaneous creativity. You have to run with it. You couldn't deny it, argue it, question it, or plan it. You had to be quick to set up the who, the what, and the where, establishing the things the audience needed to know up front, the characters, the environment, painting the picture in the mind of the viewers, pantomiming the actions, all in an instant. It was like a big rubber ball rolling down a hill, bouncing this way and that, finding meaning when it rolled and closure when it stopped.

Chapter 13

Felix continued his learning ways, headshot in hand. He didn't have to consult his map much anymore. He had been in just about all of the casting studios several times now. He knew how long it would take to get there, how many miles he would need to record in his log, where to park to avoid the meter. He knew nearly all the casting directors, those who ran a tight ship and those who didn't, those who were the heavy hitters and those who weren't. And they knew him, too.

He learned that for being such a big business, the entertainment industry is actually quite small, like an Cecil B. DeMille epic in a can. Most everybody in the business who matters knows everybody else in the business who matters. So one has to be careful about what one says. Someone always knows someone who is willing to pass the word along. Legend has it among the troopers in the field that some casting directors have hidden mikes and cameras in the holding areas to weed out the careless tongues, the complainers, gossips. Other accounts have commercial casting directors sitting in an unseen office somewhere in the wings with several monitors in front of them, watching casting sessions being conducted simultaneously in their various suites by their casting associates and videographers, checking to see how well actors treat their staff, which ones ask a lot of stupid little questions, which ones can follow directions, jotting down casting notes for callbacks at the same time.

He learned that show biz people spend most of their lives looking for work. After someone is wrapped, the gig is done. Time to start looking for another job. Network. Make some calls. Ask around. Check the wires. Anyone looking for a PA, gaffer, grip, gopher, grubber? Usually something comes along, sometimes right away if the economy is good and your connections and credentials are solid. Sometimes it's a long wait so you take anything else that comes along. But only for a little while. Only until something bigger and better comes along. The bills still need to be paid.

In the Hollywood royal family of entertainment, pornography is a popular prince with hosts of loyal subjects, adding tens of billions of dollars annually to the economy of Los Angeles County. Prostitution may be illegal across most of America, but pornography is not. Production companies in North Hollywood and Chatsworth engage in the mating ritual, discreetly luring the porno industry into their beds, to keep their sound stages busy, the income coming in, the overhead paid. Freelancers regularly keep their ear to the ground to do the hair or make-up, do some gripping, gaffing, or grunting. But only until something else comes along.

Major reputable hotel chains add extra tens of millions of dollars annually to their bottom lines by offering porn in their rooms where the traveling sales rep will pay handsomely to tune it in, putting it on the company's tab, watch it for an average of sixteen minutes, and then turn to a Disney movie. Small towns across America have movie rental shops with a lucrative little back room featuring art films for adults only. Legitimate international Dow Jones-listed television cable companies delight their directors with handsome bonuses earned by their adult-only channels. Hugh Hefner is a venerable Hollywood prince and an invitation to one of his rollicking parties at the Playboy Mansion is one of the biggest prizes in town. Larry Flint sits in a penthouse suite in a gorgeous and prominent skyrise he owns on some of the most valuable real estate in Beverly Hills, ruling over his vast fortune and hustling his eclectic menu of the popular porn de jour.

Pornographers who are budget conscious learn that it doesn't cost much to produce and it makes a lot of money. There is not much overhead, no union dues to pay, no expensive writers, no wardrobe people, no complicated set. A backyard or a swimming pool, a quiet cornfield somewhere will do. A simple hand-held camcorder gets the picture. You get it on tape. Someone out there will buy it. Whatever it is.

Then there are those who have some bucks to spend, who hope to be a contender for the Grabby or the AVN Award amid much hoopla and red carpets in Las Vegas. They have full scripts and often shoot in large mansions of people who need a little help with their large mortgages. "Yeah, sure. Come on over." So how do the neighbors feel about something like that going on next door? Do they get a little weirded out? If they do, someone will toss them a bone and the weirded outness goes away as fast as they can pocket the unexpected windfall. Sometimes they even ask a few discrete questions about hosting the next big affair or hint around about possibly performing in one. Big budgets will buy what is needed, a lighting guy good enough to shed light into deep, dark crevices, a soundman good enough to capture all the slurping and slipping and sliding and sighing, post-production people good enough to get the best possible edit of all the best angles.

Then there is the talent, the god-given talent, the kind of talent that can't be developed in an acting class somewhere. There are auditions to find just that. Show up at 2:00 for show-and-tell time. Certain things are important. Size, for one thing. The poorly hung need not apply. Little hard-boiled egg knockers? "Sorry. Not what we're looking for. Next!"

Agility is important, the ability to maintain dizzying acrobatics and contortionisms for several minutes at a time. Staying power is important, too. There are down periods between shots, during camera resets, lighting changes, lunch.

The talent has to be able to stay up. He stands at the craft service chatting with the prop mistress, munching carrots and celery with the left hand, stroking with the right, maintaining that boner at all costs. Once it's gone, it's hard to get it back. There is Viagra, but it was a heart pill before its rebirth as an aphrodisiac and so caution must be exercised. Pacing is important. Problems with premature ejaculation? Try something else. The soaps, probably.

It is hard work. Sore muscles. Blisters. Exhaustion. Then you clock out. Go home. Shower. Make supper. Watch Wheel of Fortune. Call Mom. Pay the bills.

Frankie stood there, waiting to go. Tonight, though, it wasn't the day that Virginia leaves. It is the day that Mama takes Junior shopping. "DO NOT PLAN AHEAD," Frankie thought loudly in his head as he began to set up the scene. He began dusting and sorting and straightening the store racks. His team members pick up his direction and assume the characters. Mama walks in resolutely, with Junior in tow.

"Yes, may I help you?"

"Uh, yes, my son here needs a little support for gym class."

"A little support?" Oh, the boy needs a jock strap. OOOOO!" Frankie squeals with delight. "Well, let's see. What size does he need? Shall we measure it or weigh it?" OOOOOOOO!! HA, Ha, Ha!!!"

He eyes Junior's crotch. Then Mama eyes it, both thinking, measuring, weighing it in their minds and scratching their chins. "Hmmm," said Mama. "Could you stand up a little straighter for me?"

"Awww...Mama…"

"Could you arch your back ?"

"Awww..."

"Hmmm, " she wondered. Then turning to the clerk, "What sizes do they come in?"

"OOOOOOO…what sizes do they come in? OOOOO…Well, they come in all sizes. Colors, too. Step right over here." He leads them to the imaginary long display table. He sweeps his arm to indicate that the row goes on and on.

"We have the largest selection in town. Beginning here with extra-extra extra super-duper extra small. We call this one," and he holds one up with two dainty little fingers, squinting with one eye to see it, the "Mister Muscle Beach."

"Why the Mister Muscle Beach?" asks Mama.

"Well, you know what steroids can do to a man's unit. OOOOOOOOO!!! Hahahah! Wheeee! He holds up an equally small camouflaged one with his two pinkies. "The Governator." Snicker. Snort. "Same reason." Snort.

"Well, I think…or at least I hope that we can go a little bigger than that, unless you're just like your father," said Mama, again eying his crotch. Junior stares at the floor, ruing the day he was born.

"Okay…well then," Frankie counting them off on his fingers, "for those who want the perfect fit, we have the short short, the medium short and the long short. The short tall, the medium tall, the tall tall. The skinny skinny, the medium skinny, the fat skinny. The garden snake, the garden hose, the fire hose, the anaconda. And the general sizes over here. The large small, the extra-large small, the super-sized small, the small medium, the medium medium, the medium medium medium, the large medium, the extra-large medium, the super-large medium, the grande, extra-small large, the small large, the medium large, the large-large, the large large large, the super large-large, the venti frappachino..."

"Why so many sizes?" asks Mama.

"Well, you know, honey, not all men are created equal, in spite of what they say. HA HA! Wheeeee! Same thing as with a woman's boobies. As if I would know. HA HA HA!!"

"Uh, what is that tiger-striped one called," asked Mama.

"Oh, that's the Lounge Lizard. Doubles as a G-string. HEE HEE HEE HEE. Wheeeeee!!" He held it up to his waist. "GRRRRR…," he snarls.

"Oh," said Mama. And that pink one"?

"That's the ever popular The Boys Night Out. We sell a ton of these in our store in WeHo. "WHEEEEEEEEEEHOOOOOOOOOOOOOOOOOOOOOOOO!!!"

And over here," Frankie continued, "is our Big and Tall." This is our largest, the super-dooper no-larger-than-this-extra-extra-super-extra large extra very large large extra heavy duty large circus maximus." He picks one up heavily with both hands, pants audibly, sighs wistfully, and begins fanning himself.

He eyes Junior's crotch again. "No, not right now, Honey. Maybe in a couple of years, if you get some good luck, a lot of good luck, a whole lot of really, really good luck! Or you run for congress. HA HA! If that happens, honey, you come see me. Right now, you'll be tripping over it all the way down the basketball court. HA HA HA!!!"

"And what's it called?" asked Mama.

"This one's the Peter the Great, but we also have the Grand Ballroom."

"Oh, I see. Hmmm," she said, then stooping down within six inches or so to eye Junior's package more closely.

"Let's try a small small medium short tall, long short," ventured Frankie. After all, he is only thirteen. Those boys are still dropping. So now…. will there be anything else? Maybe a cute little cup? They start with the Peter Pan over here and go …"

"No, I think that will be all." She pulls out her imaginary credit card. Frankie swipes it, bags the jock, and hands it to her.

"Come on, Junior, let's go home. I want to see if it fits you properly."

Panic visits Junior as the ball stops rolling.

Beth Ann was deep in thought as she wound up the narrow and treacherous Laurel Canyon Boulevard. The days were shorter now and evening was descending over the Hollywood Hills when she left work. A light rain was falling. She was a little depressed. She had to cancel her doctor's appointment. It was an important appointment, a new doctor. But her boss said she couldn't spare her today. There was much to be done. It was the first of the year filled with new agendas, revised business models, and long term objectives to be planned out.

Two years ago, when her boss Harriet left her old job at Cinematix in Toluca Lake and moved to Vidematics in Century City, Beth Ann cheerfully went with her. She was still a valued employee then, quite a skillful writer and composer, undaunted by any of the new and sophisticated computer software. And she was a maestro, a veritable Arturo Rubinstein with the keyboard, far eclipsing her nearest rival. She had gotten a nice raise, a stellar evaluation, but in the process traded a five-minute commute for an hour long one.

Things were just getting worse and worse. She began to detest the long drive back and forth to work. Traffic was always bad through the narrow pass with its winding curves and steep hills. She couldn't do this too much longer, but she couldn't quit either. She needed the salary and couldn't live without the health plan. Surely there was a way out of this jam and the traffic jam at the same time.

She crested at Mulholland Drive and headed north down the hill, toward Studio City. The road was wider here, the curves a little straighter, the pavement smoother, no more heavy cement walls or thick oaks lining the street, just pleasant, pretty homes with friendly landscaping. "The road always seems a little slicker here when it rains. Good thing there's a fire station with its emergency crews just a short half mile or so down the hill," thought Beth Ann. She tucked her seatbelt in a little tighter, and placed both hands on the steering wheel.

Gasp! Gasp, Choke!! Choke!!! HAHAKAKA ROOM HAHAKAKA ROOM HAHAKAKA ROOM ROOM ROOOOM!!! AHEM AHEM! Gasp…Choke…Strangle… Gasp…Gasp…Strangle…Choke! Gasp! Ahem…hem… Gasp! STRANGLE… GASP… CHOKE! CHOKE!! CHOKE!!! CHOKE!!!!!!!

"Quiet, everyone! QUIET!"

"Scene seven, Take two!" called the script supervisor.

"Scene seven, Take two!" repeated the assistant director.

Rolling!"

"Rolling!" echoed the assistant director.

Sound?"

"Sound!" answered the soundman.

"Speed?"

"Speed!" answered the speedman.

"ACTION!"

Felix sat on his stool inside the manager's cage at the seedy down-on-its-luck San Moritz Hotel, deeply involved with his magazine of big boobed babes spread on the counter in front of him. The front door is open and late-night bowery smells and sounds fill the air. Sirens wail in the distance. A screeching bus pulls to the curb, its door hisses open. Two down-on-their-luck residents sprawl on a wretched sofa facing a television in what functions as the hotel lobby.

Jimmy enters and limps rapidly to the cage. He was excited.

"I need a cigarette."

Without looking up, Felix said, "twenty-five cents."

Jimmy flips him the coin over the partition. Felix picks a cigarette out of a package and slides it through the slot. Jimmy lights up, enjoying the moment. "Eddie's comin' in tonight. Ten long years and now he's a free man." Felix says nothing and turns to the next page.

"He's coming in. Stayin' with me."

He takes a puff from his cigarette.

Felix grunts, looks up at the man. "You know it costs extra to have a guest here. Five dollars."

"Eddie'll pay when he comes." He disappears up the stairs.

Felix bends back over the boobs.

"CUT!"

Nice…good…check the gate."

"Gate's good."

"Okay, Put it in the can. Let's move on."

It was a night shoot in downtown LA, starring an aging actor whose sun had long since set into the black ether. Opposite him was an American darling of 1980's television, but her bad choice of men mixed with her bad choice of drugs rendered her well-suited and affordable enough to typecast as a drug-wasted prostitute plying her trade at the San Moritz.

Johnie had come from Iowa, America's heartland, with a heart full of hope and a future full of promise. His friends had encouraged him. "Go to LA, man. Someone with your talent needs to get out there. Be seen. Nothing for you here in Oskaloosa." The local newspaper ran an article announcing Johnie's going away party at the Cabin, a popular bar and restaurant on Main Street where Johnie got his start, playing on Friday nights after the dinner crowd had finished their spaghetti dinner special or rib-eye steak and sauntered home, toothpick wedged between relaxed lips. After the famous salad bar had been dismantled for the evening, safely packed into large plastic tubs for Saturday night's dinner crowd, after the tables had all been wiped down, the younger crowd would arrive; young, well-scrubbed farm boys in freshly laundered jeans and closely cropped crew-cuts and smelling of Right Guard, finally free from a full day of tilling fields and flush with Friday's paycheck, standing along the bar and swigging from long-neck bottles of beer; giggly, jiggly young ladies in red lipstick and summer blouses arriving in small groups a little later and sit at the tables, resting tired feet from a long day of cutting hair, slowly sipping strawberry margaritas and tapping their toes to the beat of Johnie's guitar while they wait for the boys to loosen up.

They all came that night for Johnie. Most had known him all his life. The dinner crowd lingered longer than usual, wanting to shake his hand and sign their name on the card, get their picture taken with him. His old teachers were there, neighbors, people he hadn't seen for a while, cousins and nieces, the bar regulars. They were all there. Nobody from Oskaloosa had ever done this before, heading out to Los Angeles, California, U.S.A. to make it big. Someone strung up a banner along the back wall and taped red, white, and blue balloons to the large mirror above the bar. They all said he was a natural with his nice looks, his nice voice, his nice guitar. He would go now and come back later in a frenzy of success, put Oskaloosa on the map. There would be a parade, a sense of local pride.

Welcome to Oskaloosa
Childhood Home of Johnie Sorenson
Ya'll Drive Carefully Now

He left very early the next morning, handing the large, black family suitcase to the driver for storage down below, and carefully laid his guitar case on the rack above his head and sat in the front seat. Through dirty bus windows, he watched the cornfield become prairie, the prairie become mountain, the mountain become desert, and the desert become North Hollywood.

Felix marveled at the depth and perception that his students had acquired in their use and understanding of language. But then again, he knew that his students were appointed by their parents at a very early age to become the family rabbi so it became incumbent upon them to master the holy scriptures, starting as soon as they were able to read. Rabbis would pore over the books with their young charges, using only the Hebrew text to ensure an uncorrupted originality of intent, asking probing questions, leading them through the words of Moses and David with the wisdom of Solomon and the patience of Job. They would become adept interpreters of the law of god and in the process, the law of man. They became excellent and accomplished teachers and authors and attorneys and negotiators as well as rabbis in the process.

They learn of literal meanings and the figurative ones buried in subtlety and nuance and double entendre and intuition. They examine each word for color and texture, swish it around, sniff the bouquet, take a sip, roll it around on their palate, then swallow carefully and solemnly, thinking, judging, then reaching for the next vessel.

But they also learn that that which was not said was often more powerful than that which was said, that worthy silence helps to protect against the profane. The yada yada yada effect and all of its variations. Not quite saying the whole yada yada yada, but enough to yada yada yada. Lord becomes l-rd, god becomes g-d. L-rd g-d, what do we have here? A sacred quintagrammaton in its own right. But with their study comes the residue of their human frailties, a humility or an understanding that all was in the person of g-d.

"How are you?" Felix would ask.

Always the answer was "Baruch Hashem!"

"Pretty day, isn't it?

"Baruch Hashem!"

"Nasty day, isn't it?"

"Baruch Hashem!"

"How's the Boiled Chicken?"

"Baruch Hashem!"

He heard it dozens of times each day. He lived with it as long as he could and then he asked Rabbi Horowitz.

"It means thank g-d."

"Oh."

"Baruch Hashem!"

And they respected the dead enough not to refer to them as being dead. They were not pushing up daisies. They did not leave the planet. They had not transitioned. They were OBM. Of Blessed Memory.

"My grandfather Ezra Of Blessed Memory."

"My Persian cat Esther Of Blessed Memory."

"My mother-in-law Naomi Of Blessed Memory. Baruch Hashem."

Chapter 14

Beth Ann's Grand Am came to rest between two crouching tigers in a particularly nice front lawn. She slunk down in her seat. Cars were stopping, their drivers reaching for cell phones, hopping out to see if she were okay.

"PANT!!! GASP!!! CHOKE... GURGLE... HAHAKAKA ROOM HAHAKAKA ROOM HAHAKAKA ROOM ROOM ROOOM AHEM AHEM!!!!"

"Must be a heart attack!"

Within a few short minutes, the ambulance had arrived. Three very strong EMT's lifted her from the seat, and dropped her heavily onto the gurney.

"PANT! GASP! CHOKE! GURGLE! HAHAKAKA ROOM HAHAKAKA ROOM HAHAKAKA ROOM ROOOM ROOOM!!!! AHEM AHEM!"

"Get the oxygen mask on her. Take the readings. Get out the defibrillator. Check the pulse."

"Color looks good. Heart rate steady. Normal."

"Check for ID!"

"Insurance card!"

" Let's roll!"

The ambulance wound through the snarl of stopped cars on down the hill toward St. Joseph's Medical Center in Toluca Lake, its siren screaming and lights flashing and blinking and strobing red and blue and yellow and white flashes echoing off the shiny pavement and into the evening air. Beth Ann could hear the radio operator calling in the call. “Possible asthmatic attack or seizure. No symptoms of cardiac problems. All systems reading normal at this time.”

“HAHAKAKA ROOM HAHAKAKA ROOM HAHAKAKA ROOM ROOOM ROOOM! AHEM AHEM!”

She watched through the little window as cars scrambled out of the way, marveled at running the red lights and driving on the wrong side of the streets, and arriving at St. Joseph’s, where the gurney was quickly pulled out, the wheels dropped, the emergency room personnel waiting, everyone on duty for her arrival. She was wheeled with rapid response into the rapid response room for the rapid response tests.

She waited, figuring that it was going to be a while. She would be spending the night at least, and perhaps days as the physicians consulted with each other, ran additional tests, sent inquiries to all the experts in the field to determine the causes of these puzzling anomalies on her test results. Her thoughts were interrupted when a harried practitioner hurried into her room, quickly scanned a clipboard she was holding, double-checked the green armband on Beth Ann's wrist, asked her to recite her social security number, double checked one more time.

“Everything looks clean here. Probably just a reaction to some of your medication. After you get dressed, stop at the desk and sign some paperwork for us. You can pick up your purse and your cane there, too.”

“Is this all there is?”

“One more thing. There's a police officer in the hallway. Wants to ask you some questions. Be sure you see him before you leave. After that, you're free to leave. Need me to call a cab?”

“Your car's in Van Nuys, Ma'am.” said the cop. “Here's a card with the contact information. Your medical reports says that you stated you blacked out. Is that correct, Ma'am?”

“Yes, sir, officer.”

“You will have to surrender your driver's license until

your doctor can determine what caused the blackout and provide us with a clean bill of health. It's the law. If you have a medical condition that makes you an unsafe driver, we don't want you on the road, Ma'am."

The nice police officer looked so nice in his crisp blue uniform. She buried him into the deepest reaches of her bosom as she murmured about her generous donations to the Police Activities Program, and he smiled and turned on the blue and red flashers for her on the short trip back to the Villa Verdugo and she was pleased that her troubles had so brightened the evening of another.

"Maybe Santa Monica," Felix had suggested to Champ. Champ had asked him what he thought. Nothing out there seemed quite right for him. It was always one thing or another, no money to buy stage time, no room on the long list for a open mike somewhere, no friends to bring with him to pay the cover, no experience in playing with others, no one much interested in his kind of music, no one much interested in him.

"You're not what we're looking for."

"No, that's not what people want to hear. Next!"

"Quit wasting my time."

He had heard it all. And now Felix's telling him to try Saturday evening in Santa Monica. The Third Street Promenade. A street performer. What the hell.

Santa Monica prides itself on being the most liberal city in the nation, besides being one of the richest. The homeless and nearly homeless are welcome to hang out there, unmolested by the authorities who manage the peace, and no effort is made to remove them from the well-kept parks and palisades overlooking the Pacific. Dozens of hapless men and women lay sprawled out on the grass, dozing in the shade of the magnificent royal palms on Ocean Avenue, surrounded by everything they own stashed in black plastic bags, or the bedrolls and backpacks of the more well-heeled homeless. They are allowed some access to the storefronts along Fourth or Fifth or Sixth or Seventh Streets, but the Third Street Promenade is strictly off limits to them.

A few blocks west is the famed Santa Monica Pier, the official end of Route 66, the Mother Road of the nation. Heeding Horace Greeley's advice to go west, they came, the Forty-niners prospecting for gold in the streams of Sutter's Mill, the Okies and the Arkies seeking work in the fields of the San Joaquin Valley, the star-struck panning for gold in the Hills of Hollywood.

The Third Street Promenade extends for several blocks, crossing and connecting Colorado, Broadway, Santa Monica, Arizona, and Wilshire Boulevards with a tree-lined, brick and concrete public walkway, lined with trendy retailers, art and music and book shops; kiosks and booths featuring handmade jewelry, scented candles, new age art and music; movie theaters, bistros, cafes, and creperies; a MacDonald's safely hidden in an obscure nook for the finicky palate of Midwest tourists.

But it is also a stage, open to the public for those who have the proper street performer's permit, available from City Hall down the street. The permits are limited and the acts scrutinized. They don't want too many acts, or too many of any one type of act, and certainly nothing that would unsettle the sensibilities of the rich liberals living in the high-rises surrounding the Promenade. There are the regulars who renew their permits with no questions asked, the dude who covers his entire body, skin, clothing, props and all, with silver paint and stands motionless on a small pedestal and becomes a statue. Then when a tourist moves in for a closer look, he startles him or her by engaging in a quick robotic jerk, changing his position, then freezing again in total stillness, leaving the tourists interested enough to linger long enough to see it again, or to verify that they had seen it the first time, then discovering that it happens only when someone tosses a donation into the bucket in front of him.

Circles of people gather around young jive dancing teams who spin and gyrate on their heads and shoulders on the concrete and red brick walkways, or an organ grinder with a monkey that scurries around taking coins from the outstretched hands of tourists, and shaking hands with those who give him the kind of money that folds. Acrobats spin plates on sticks, and singers sing Sinatra and Dylan and solo pianists and cellists and violinists play concertos and rags. Occasionally, a noisy parade passes by, small groups of a dozen or so banging on drums, chanting and carrying placards and banners protesting the unethical treatment of animals or the Dalai Lama or women in Yemen.

Champ applied for his performer's permit, but was denied. This was something a little bit too unsettling about the sensibilities, not quite in synchronicity with the level of liberalism of Santa Monica. All of those piercings and tattoos, and the chimney-sweeper's goatee? "Hmmm... Uh... No, thank you. Not today. Next!"

"Your voice is an instrument that needs to be stretched and exercised as well," she said. "It should receive just as much attention as your body and your mind. After all, if your audience cannot understand you, then you have failed as an actor. And it doesn't matter what language you are speaking, what dialect, what accent. Diction is important."

Felix hiked up his baggy jeans. Maybe it was time for a belt. Working as an actor in Hollywood was a good way to lose a few pounds, but he wasn't sure what was so useful about a lot of this stuff; laying on the floor pretending to be on the beach, reaching for the stars, then collapsing in a heap; running through the jungle with a man-eating lion hot on his tail; the psychological autopsies. All that kind of stuff. Every time he took an acting class, it was the same, whether it was back home or out here. He thought it all a little artsy fartsy.

Okay, now," she said, "let's stretch that voice. Repeat after me."

"The teeth, the lips, the tip of the tongue."

"THE TEETH, THE LIPS, THE TIP OF THE TONGUE."

“The flea infested feline.”

“THE FLEA INFESTED FELINE”

“The flesh of freshly fried flying fish.”

“THE FLESH OF FRESHLY FRIED FLYING FISH.”

To his recollection he never summoned up these spirits when he was in a scene study. He just sensed things out.

“Felix!!“

On the other hand, all of the roles he ever had were just quick walk-on things anyway. He hadn't been called upon to be a John Barrymore.

“Felix!!“

He had never been expected to carry an entire epic film. Maybe things were different at that level. He wondered deeply whether that was...

“Felix!!!“

“OKAY!!!!!!!”

“The big blue bug bit the big black bear and the big black bear bled blue blood.”

“THE BIG BLUE BUG BIT THE BIG BLACK BEAR AND THE BIG BLACK BEAR BLED BLUE BLOOD.”

“You love New York. You need New York. You know you love unique New York.”

“YOU LOVE NEW YORK. YOU NEED NEW YORK. YOU KNOW YOU LOVE UNIQUE NEW YORK.”

She offered her honor, he honored her offer, and all the night long he was on her and off her.”

“SHE OFFERED HER HONOR HE HONORED HER OFFER AND ALL THE NIGHT LONG HE WAS ON HER AND OFF HER”

Sheofferedherhonorhehonoredherofferandallthenightlong hewasonherandoffher.”

“SHEOFFEREDHERHONORHEHONOREDHERO FFERANDALLTHENIGHTLONGHEWASONHERANDOF FHER.

Through the haze of her hookah, Tiffani squinted at

Champ. He was drunk again. Every time he came up, he was drunk. Melancholy. On the oil rigs, he couldn't have alcohol or drugs so he was forced into periods of sobriety and a clear head induced from the two week tour of duty forty miles out to sea. Here there was no one in charge, no restraints, no two week break to clean up a little.

He called women hookers. She figured he referred to her as the hooker up there in 213. He called guys pussies. He called himself a coonass. She had never heard the word. Of course, she heard the word "coon," more than just a couple of times back in southern Illinois. She knew what an ass was. She had known a lot of them, too.

"What's this coonass you keep talking about?" she asked. "I never heard that before. It sounds like something racist, like you're referring to yourself as the rear end of an African-American. It isn't, is it?"

"Nah, it ain't nothin' like that. My whole family's coonass. It's south Louisiana Creole. Some of the white folk down there call us French niggers, Cajun injuns."

He told Tiffani of a childhood where they went to bed when the sun went down and went to work before it came back up. On Sundays after church, the family would gather for a pitch-in dinner at his gramma's house. They were poor, but there was always plenty to eat. Smoked ham. Barbecued shrimp. The children would climb trees in the backyard, and the grownups would sit on the back porch and chat among themselves in a blend of Indian, French and African.

Most of them farmed small plots or fished or trawled for shrimp and they lived in the bayous and wetlands. They were a quiet people who kept to themselves. If they found themselves thrust into the business of city folks, they would avoid eye contact with them and talk among themselves in a simple secret language that those outsiders couldn't understand. He taught Frankie that language so that the two of them could discuss stuff without Heathcharlesharley butting in all the time. Heathcharlesharley thought they were just toying with his head.

“Well, what is it?”

“It ain't no big deal. You just spell everything out, putting an “ong” on the end of the letter, except for the vowels, which you just say.

“Huh?”

“Tiffani would be tong i fong fong a nong i. When you say it real fast, it's Tong-i-fongfong-a-nong-i. Mine's Chonghong-a-mongpong. After a while, you get real fast at it.”

He told of how some of his kin were forced by economics to leave the wetlands, expatriated to the kitchens in the French Quarter or the laundry rooms in the hotels on Canal Street. Others left because they wanted more, like himself. He left for the bigger paychecks on the oil rigs. He was only eighteen then, raw and unschooled, impressionable, eager to learn of the life that resided outside of the bayous. And it was on those derricks and in the whorehouses and barracks that lined the gulf shore docks where Champ learned that other way of life, where he first heard the flatlander's language of hookers and pussies, where he learned how to escape the misery of his existence with their rum and their whiskey and their opiates, where he acquired his piercings, his tattoos, his goatee, where he first tasted of a woman, where he took his first steps in leaving his past behind. Now there was very little of him left.

Mann's Chinese Theater holds court in the heart of bustling downtown Hollywood. There, Judy Garland, Marilyn Monroe, and Charlie Chaplin pose for pictures for a dollar or two a pop. Sometimes Oprah or Cher pop up. Crowds gather there for flashy star-studded movie premieres, craning their necks to get a glimpse of an A-lister and then cheering wildly when they see one. The sparkling Kodak Theater for the Academy Awards is nearby and the stately Hotel Roosevelt where it all started, Disney's El Capitan Theater, where the Jimmy Kimmel Show is taped. Frederick's of Hollywood is there, too, offering a full menu of edible flavored G-strings and crotchless underpanties in strawberry or chocolate or banana. Souvenir shops peddle head shots of the stars and maps to their homes, and tee-shirts and fake little Academy Awards for “Best Boss” or “Best Brother.”

And, of course, there is the Walk of Fame where pilgrims speak in hushed voices in front of the Chinese Temple, and place their feet in the footprints of the pantheon of idols immortalized there, then pay solemn homage as they slowly walk, heads deeply bowed, reading the fame names that stretch for blocks and blocks along both sides of the Boulevard. Most names have been forgotten, anonymous again. But a few live on. Donald Duck. Mickey Mouse. A few others. Superman. Spiderman. Ageless. Telegenic. Perfect for their roles. Forever.

It is all not too unlike the cemetery on Santa Monica Boulevard behind Paramount Studios where Cecil B. DeMille and Douglas Fairbanks and Rudolph Valentino sleep, or the one down a side alley in Westwood where Marilyn Monroe remains, or the granddaddy of them all, Forest Lawn, cut into the Hollywood Hills above Toluca Lake where countless others hide in unmarked graves. Felix had visited those cemeteries, the Walk of Fame, the Chinese Theater, Madame Tussaud's Wax Museum countless times, when company from the Midwest arrived. “I want to see a star,” they would say. So he would take them there.

“I want to see a real one now, a live one,” they would say later, like they thought they all gathered at a local Starbucks every afternoon at 4:00 for easy viewing for folks to gawk at them and snap their photo and get an autograph and have a story to tell the folks back home. Some of the rich and famous actually do put themselves on display. They drop anonymous tips to the paparazzi of their whereabouts or they hire publicists to do it for them. They hang out at the latest rage on the Sunset Strip. They cultivate an image with shiny cars and showy mansions, gussy up before venturing out, telling themselves that they were actually only investing in their future, making themselves a hotter commodity to market at hotter prices. But in spite of their best efforts, fame is a fleeting thing, fickle and fast on her feet. Hollywood has a short memory and she could care less.

Chapter 15

For the fiftieth time, Barbara carefully removed the invitation from its large envelope, unwrapped the silk paper and undid the white satin ribbon. Inside was a laced invitation, its words in India ink calligraphy, and one lovely rose, a single spectacular handpainted red rose. She felt it, weighed it in her hands, moved her fingers along the lines of words, scrutinizing it. It helped her to focus, to picture the environment and the role she would be playing in it.

Elie and Matma Singh
Request Your Presence
To Celebrate the Rose

Barbara listened to Hayad, as they worked side by side at the glass covered table fine-tuning the point and click system, happily talk about the family gatherings, the children, the music and the laughter when his parents were in town. He told her of his mother's love for roses and her beautiful gardens in London and LA and how she loved to cook. They would always host a grand party when they were in town at the home in Benedict Canyon. His mother would prepare all the food herself, with the help of the two houseboys who would do the chopping and dicing under her watchful eye.

Hollywood loves a good party and any reason is a good

reason. Armani's new fall collection is considered a good reason, or a birthday party for a five-year-old in Bel Air with a special appearance by Dorothy from a fly-over state, or Goldilocks or Cinderella, but no wolves to blow down the thick brick walls of Mommy's and Daddy's house or eat little girls wearing little red hoodies. And there are theme parties. The Singh party is to be a celebration of the rose and the guests are expected to fully comply with the wishes of the hostess. A simple rose pinned to a lapel would not be considered enough effort. She carefully slipped the invitation back into its envelope, then leaned back in her chair, deep in thought.

It hadn't taken Champ long to figure out that it wasn't going to be as easy as he had been led to believe. He began to think he had come to the wrong place at the wrong time. LA had a music scene, but it was just a scene in a music video somewhere. LA is a place for actors and writers and television and movies. LA is Hollywood, not Nashville. Now most of the music was being birthed and burped somewhere else, New England, the South, the Northwest. The music makers would still come to town occasionally to meet with the big shots at the Warner Group, do their music videos or post production work behind high windowless, whitewashed walls in quiet, air-conditioned studios along Magnolia or Burbank Boulevard in the Valley, and then head back out of town when everything is wrapped.

While an occasional music act does still rise out of the hot concrete of Sunset Boulevard, most of the current music scene revolves around preprocessed pop, overly-produced to camouflage weak voices, or taped techno-music spun by celebrity DJ's and strobe lights and smoke and mirrors in Off-Hollywood or Off-Off Hollywood venues. Crowds pack karaoke bars, like Dimples in Toluca Lake, to watch television celebrities play singer-wannabes. But nothing is at all like the heydays of the 60's, 70's, and the 80's when the music scene in Los Angeles rocked and rolled, filled with raw, original, and live acts performing in front of standing room only crowds along Sunset and Santa Monica and down the side streets and alleys in between. The legendary Whisky a Go Go became a household name when it introduced the go-go boot and the go-go dance to America, its stage promoting the futures of the Byrds, Alice Cooper, Buffalo Springfield, The Doors, the Turtles, The Monkeys, the Kinks, Nirvana, Cream, Led Zepplin, Guns and Roses, Metallica, and Motley Crue. Then there was the Rainbow Bar and Grill with Grace Slick and Janis Joplin. The stage at the Troubadour helped launch the careers of Elton John, Linda Ronstadt, The Eagles, Joni Mitchell, Bette Midler, Bruce Springsteen, Arlo Guthrie. James Taylor and Carole King performed together there. The Viper Room featured the likes of Oasis, Pearl Jam, Iggy Pop, Tom Petty and the Heartbreakers. You didn't need to ask where it was happening. It was happening everywhere. But now you have to look around, ask questions that didn't need to be asked a generation ago. So, the problem right now, thought Champ, is not only when does it happen, but where does it happen.

Heathcharlesharley sat in his closet, the door shut tightly. No one loved him. No one understood him. No one listened to him. Payback had been driving him nuts, rolling that idiotic ball through the broad canyons and rocky arroyas in the living room. Back and forth. Forth and back. Jingle. Jangle. Jangle. Jingle. Day and night. Night and day. It was such a bore that he finally took it away and Frankie and Champ ganged up on him and made him give it back to her. Payback was his cat, after all. Did they care anything about that little fact? Then there was that stupid sewing machine taking up all the space on their only table. He couldn’t believe that a guy would actually use a sewing machine. Whenever he said anything about these things, Frankie and Champ would start talking that king kong ping pong hong kong stuff, then laugh loudly like they understood each other and had a private joke going on or something. He could hear the two snickering in their room late at night. He was sure they were thinking up ways to make his life a living hell and they were getting pretty good at it.

Then Daddy Warbucks called with the devil in his voice. "How in the hell did you spend $450 in parking at LAX?" Give me a break, he thought. How was I to know what they considered short term parking? Long term parking is for long terms, like your sophomore year. Two weeks is not a long term. Duh! But, boy was he hot. Then he asked about the $600 case of wine. Since when did he start drinking wine? And what about that $1200 for new head shots "Didn't you just have new head shots made a few months ago?" Well, yeah, but didn't he think that people look different as they get older? Am I the only one in this world who ever thinks things out? You can get them done a lot cheaper, but then that is what you have. Cheap head shots He was going to mention that, but then decided to let it drop. That Sons and Lovers thing came up again, too. Didn't he already explain that? But he didn't say that because his father was an angry father. All he could say was "Sir! Yes, Sir! Sir! Yes, Sir! Sir! Sir! Sir!"

And then the ax fell. That was it. "It's time you learned a little about the value of money," said Daddy NoMore Warbucks. His father told him that from now on, he was on a budget. He had heard of the word, but had to go ask Felix, who told him it was where you only have a certain amount of money to spend every month and when it was gone, you couldn't buy anything else. So he had to be careful to make sure it lasted until he got more. Heathcharlesharley was doubtful about Felix's explanation, as he had never heard of such foolishment.

The drug business is the dirty little whore who resides on the mean streets and back alleys of show business. She is not fickle. She seduces the young and the old alike, wrapping her lips around the weak and the strong, the tough and the vulnerable, those who have too much, those who have too little, the unknown and the known, whoever they were. But there were those who underestimated her lure, those like John Belushi, Judy

Garland, Marilyn Monroe, River Phoenix, Heath Ledger, Janis Joplin, Jimi Hendrix, Jim Morrison, Michael Jackson.

In her Hollywood heydays, she visited the studios, tidied up in her designer labels and ushered in the front door, summoned by an adjunct of the commissary or an ambitious assistant director. There was always someone pimping her. Then she fell out of favor, her spotlight dimmed. But she is still around, slipping unseen in the back door, doing the trick and slinking out. Sometimes she dresses in a lab coat and has a stethoscope hanging from her neck and an office in Beverly Hills.

Felix occasionally smelled marijuana on the set, and saw the huddles, but it was always after the martini shot, after the work had been wrapped for the day. They were on their own time then. But he knew that he didn't see it all. He didn't see the American Darling of 1980's television alone in her trailer on her first night on the "San Moritz" set. It was late and she was lonely and the whore dropped by. She opened the door and submitted to the power, losing her own in the deal. In the morning, there was another huddle, this time, it was the producers, the director and another ax fell and Miss American Darling limped home to bed and pulled the covers over her head. The rags reported it and the spin doctors did what they could. It was just another night in Hollywood and two days later, nobody really remembered anymore.

Beth Ann did what she could to overcome the trauma of her accident. She knew the therapeutic value of talking about it. It would help her. There were a lot of people who needed to be notified. It would help them too, making them feel good about feeling bad for her and that would make her feel good about feeling bad. They would be worried and she would need to calm them. She would relate in vivid detail the second-by-second series of events that landed her in the emergency room of the hospital.

HAHAKKAKA ROOM HAHAKAKA ROOM

HAHAKAKA ROOM ROOOM ROOOM! AHEM AHEM! She would tell of the blackout, the extraction from the car, the harrowing rush to the hospital, the cadre of doctors and nurses who waited for her arrival. She would exclaim in solemn tones that her car had been completely totaled, then pausing to look sadly into the distance, letting the implications solidify in their minds of a mass of mangle-tangled steel and sharp shards of broken glass and the trauma she had experienced. She didn't reveal the boring details, except to Felix when he had driven her to the car to retrieve the bags of cat litter and the jugs of bottled water from the trunk, that the old car was barely damaged, but totaled anyway because the transmission had been nudged out of place when it bumped over the curb. The numbness was beginning to return to her legs and her walk was becoming wobbly and Archie and Veronica were still peeing on the carpet.

Beatrice was coming down for dinner, a girls only night. She would ask about the cats and tell her about her near brush with death. HAHAKAKA ROOM HAHA KAKA ROOM HAHAKAKA ROOM ROOM ROOM! AHEM! AHEM!

It would be the first time she cooked for her. She would serve her legendary spinach soufflé. All who sampled her cuisine considered an invitation for supper a real treat. She carefully laid the delicate filo leaves in neat layers over equally neat layers of spinach leaves. Wait until Beatrice gets a load of her double chocolate walnut supreme fudge brownie delights. It was the chili powder that gave the recipe its triumph. They were in the oven now. She always made a double batch. She was exquisite with her timing, pulling something from the oven or the refrigerator at precisely the right moment, like a conductor directing a symphony. Her recipe for the iced tea was borrowed from a Venice Beach café she had visited years ago. No one could touch it. Beth Ann slid the soufflé into the oven. She peed, swished the toilet, then sprayed Fabreeze one more time on the dampnesses in the carpet.

Chapter 16

There were certain things that just weren't ever funny. Johnny Carson always said that about the assassination of Abraham Lincoln. No material there. Once, Felix decided to do a routine about adolescence. He thought the whole experience was funny, but all of his friends with twelve and thirteen-year-olds in the house said there was nothing funny about it, not a single thing. But he persisted, incubated that baby for months and got four full minutes out of it. Then he delivered it for the first time in a Cleveland bowling alley lounge. It was the longest four minutes in his life, the biggest egg he ever laid. Beads of sweat formed on his forehead. All the moms and pops just stared at him, reminded of what was waiting for them at home after their evening out. "Please hurry through this," he read in their faces. "Get it over with." He ended up throwing it all away, keeping nothing from it and wasting all that time in the process. That was one of the challenges of writing comedy. It was just tough to know whether what he thought was funny would be what an audience thought was funny. The only way to know for sure was to throw it out there. If an audience laughed, you kept it. If they didn't laugh you tried it again with another audience, and it still just laid there, you would bury it somewhere, dead on arrival.

Then only certain people could tell certain jokes. If you are a fat person, you can tell fat jokes. If you are Jewish, you can tell Jewish jokes. A self deprecating kind of thing. If you aren't, then don't go there.

Anyone from Indiana out there?" Felix asked. When you're from Indiana, you can do Indiana jokes. There usually was. Even if no one responded, he would pretend that someone in the back had raised a hand. Tonight, though, someone got him off the hook, responding by clapping and who-whoing.

"Boy, I miss that place. There, things were safe. Out here, I have to lock the car door all the time, even if I leave it for just a few seconds. In Indiana, the only time I ever have to lock my car door is in August."

The audience sat there with a "wonder why" look on its face.

"Make sure none of my friends or neighbors sneak over at night and leave a sack of zucchini in the front seat."

Everyone laughed. This was a Midwest crowd. Lots of Indiana types. You have to be from the Midwest to understand the zucchini problem. The Midwest folks wouldn't understand his joke about Forest Lawn, but they would about zucchini. The bowling league crowd always loved it.

"I tell you, people who grow zucchini should have something that eats zucchini. There should be a warning label on the little packet of seeds. Caution, this packet of seeds will produce 5.4 metric tons of zucchini." Everyone nodded in agreement, smiling, happy to be watching a comedian who understood their everyday problems.

"You can feed all the starving children in India with just a couple of packets of seeds."

Laughter.

"Let them eat zucchini bread!"

Not so much there. Same thing as usual. Not really funny enough for the effort of laugh. He knew it wouldn't get much, but he did it for himself. Just enjoyed it. Didn't care if it wasn't a real knee-slapper.

"Martha Stewart said one of the nice things about zucchini is that it has so many uses. I'll say. Zucchini muffins, fried zucchini, pickled zucchini, stuffed zucchini, breaded zucchini sticks, zucchini soufflés, zucchini salads, zucchini barbecue, zucchini pizza, zucchini on the half shell, zucchini cream pie, zucchini gumballs, zucchini wine, double chocolate walnut supreme fudge zucchini brownie delights. Anything to use up that zucchini." The audience laughed. He was sure they would have their own to offer.

"But she didn't say anything about zucchini doorstops." Laughter.

"She didn't say anything about their use as ballast for ocean vessels, or loading the rear end of your pick-em-up truck with zucchini for better traction on those winter roads. Or paving the driveway with them." Joy was running rampart. They knew how important it was to have good traction on those southern Indiana Januaries.

"She didn't say anything about zucchini skeet shooting." Felix holds an imaginary shotgun, follows an imaginary clay pigeon, squints through an imaginary sight, and pulls the trigger.

"Wham." Every guy and most of the gals in the audience had their own shotguns at home. Laughter, excitement. Here was one of their own. Here in Hollywood. But enough already about zucchini. A comic has to know when something has been tapped out.

"You know, everything nowadays needs to be politically correct." The audience all nods in sympathy.

"Indiana has probably the biggest problem. Do you see, we don't call Indians Indians anymore. We call them Native Americans." The audience waits expectantly, nodding and knowing that Felix was right.

"We need to change the name of that state of Indiana. It has to be called Nativeamericana." Groans and laughs.

"Home of the Nativeamericanapolis 500." More laughs.

"Have to change all those lyrics in their songs." The audience waits.

"Back home again, in Nativeamericana…" Laughs.

"If god didn't make little green apples, then it don't rain

in Nativeamericanapolis in the summer time..."

The table had been cleared and Archie and Veronica had finished with the dishes.

"They get them so clean that all I have to do is stack them," she said..

"Ha Ha...HAHAKAKA ROOM HAHAKAKA ROOM HAHAKAKA ROOM ROOOM ROOOM!! AHEM AHEM!" Beth Ann stuck her index finger into her mouth and deftly cleaned her gums on the left, then used her other big finger to clean the right, dislodging a couple of errant walnuts and chunks of brownie. Beatrice believed that it lived up to its name, every bit as good as promised. Properly primed, she would now be expected to live up to her end of the deal.

Beth Ann began with the cats. Both Archie and Veronica had been peeing on the carpet. Beatrice held Archie on her lap and listened calmly, softly stroking him, massaging his neck, nodding.

"I see, Love. I understand. Oh, that must be dreadful."

Then she picked up Veronica for more of the same. "You poor dear. Yes, I'll tell her." She turned to Beth Ann. "You had the carpet cleaned recently."

"Yes."

"It seems they both have the same complaint. The carpet cleaner used some sort of cheap chemical cleaner and it's stinky and always giving them both headaches. They pee on the rug to make it smell better."

"Remember," Beatrice reminded her, "the cats live down there. You can't smell it, but they can. You need to bring someone else in to reclean the rug, and tell them to rinse it real well."

That was easy. That will take care of that problem. Then Archie and Veronica complained bitterly about the hahakaka-roomhahakakaroomhahakakaroomroomroomaheamahemming "Couldn't there please be something to be done about that. PLEASE!"

"Yes, my dears. It's giving all of us a headache, too."

She knew how to handle that problem, too. She wasn't a life coach by choice. It was a natural talent. When she was a child, she thought everyone else had these abilities. But as an adult, she found she was a rara avis. She had had a rough time as a school girl, always in trouble and taken to the headmaster's office for a dressing down. Some of the teachers thought she was a loonie and they were afraid of her. She always saw things, like easy solutions and teachers didn't like it. Things had to be the teacher's way, and there was no other way but the teacher's way.

"I'm finished," she would tell them when they scolded her for sitting there idly. You were suppose to sweat through things just like everyone else. You were always supposed to do things in the correct order. Her father was called down for a conference.

"She's always taking shortcuts," one teacher told him

"She doesn't follow my directions," said another.

"Everyone else in class is working on a problem and she is just sitting there, twiddling her thumbs," said her math teacher.

"It sets a bad example for the other children in the class," said the headmaster.

Her father understood her. They were birds of a feather. Problem solvers. He had suffered the same affliction when he was a child. He pulled her out of that school and hired a private tutor. The problem was solved in just five minutes.

Her talent was quite useful when she started her own business, but she did have to admit it wasn't much help when it came to her relationship with men. Men feel threatened sometimes by a woman such as she. And this mess she was in right now is a matter of the heart. There are never any quick and easy solutions for that, no short cuts, no set of directions to follow or not to follow. Too bad, she thought. She could make billions if she could.

But right now there was a challenge sitting in front of her on the red sofa. HAHA KAKAROOM HAHAKAKA ROOM HAHAKAKA ROOM ROOM ROOM! AHEM AHEM! This won't be real hard. She'd seen stuff like this before. It was a simple thing to just redirect the route.

"Whenever you feel that you're going to cough, just put your hand up like this, " Beatrice explained, making a fist, "and tap on your chest right over your heart and count one, then tap and so on up to five. Like this, love."

"One." Tap

"Two." Tap

"Three." Tap

"Four." Tap

"Five." Tap

And although Beatrice had told her she did not need to count out loud, Beth Ann thought it better that she should. It helped her keep track of things. The pesky little ahems were still around, though, but since they were so less invasive, less intrusive, Beatrice allowed that vestige to remain. It kept things interesting. Ahem. It was like amen to the problem. Ahem. Amen.

"One," thump.

"Two," thump.

"Three," thump.

"Four," thump.

"Five," thump, "AHEM AHEM," she coughed,

Chapter 17

as Barbara worked on the breakdowns. It was a tricky thing and it was difficult to do them quickly. Even with the new system all in place, there were things that she would still have to watch carefully, the human element, for one.

There were conflicts to avoid. They were clearly listed on the breakdown and the talent agent was expected to avoid sending someone over who had one. If one of her clients did a Coca Cola commercial, then he or she may not do a Pepsi commercial or even audition for one. That actor would even be asked to sign a document saying that there were no conflicts. If an actor did a Chevy spot and then a Ford spot and nobody said anything, then there would be hell to pay. Some actors don't reveal a conflict because a national commercial is too lucrative to be too honest about things, and they figured no one would ever notice anyway. But someone always would. Ultimately, it was left up to the agent to keep tabs on things and report them if necessary.

Some of the commercial breakdowns were confidential and the shoots done in closed sets. Maybe a pharmaceutical company didn't want its competition to know of a new marketing blitz, or maybe a restaurant chain had invested a lot of time and money to develop a new angle and didn't want it compromised. Same with actors who had to sign confidentiality agreements not to release any details about an upcoming episodic.

And there were other things that she had to look for as well. Most of the time when production companies were looking for actors to play drug pushers or pimps or whores, they would always request black actors. Most of her black clients pretty much refuse now to accept those auditions, and she knew enough not to submit them. Same with Jihad, her Lebanese client, who was always being called in to audition for the role of a terrorist. She had actors who weren't quite ready to be submitted for an above-the-line role, too green yet. Others refused to work for anything less than $300 a day.

Some breakdowns stated that simulated sex scenes were required of the actor. There was really very little of the simulated sex scenes that was actually simulated. It was complete with the nudity and the moaning and the rubbing and stroking and the humping and panting and the sweating and the screaming. The only thing simulated about it was maybe an actual penetration or orgasm. Clients of hers who may not have fully understand the requirements when they accepted that kind of role would usually take a pass on an opportunity to do another one.

Some of her clients had principles. During political campaigns, Democratic clients would not do commercials for the Republicans, nor the Republicans for the Democratic causes. Conservative clients would not take a role in a movie or television show in which the discussion of an abortion was part of the script. Sometimes, though, if a client were in danger of having the car repossessed, or being evicted from the apartment, that maybe it would be okay just this one time. But it's just a one-time thing, something to hold them over for a while until things got a little better.

Lily sat on her haunches in the middle of the room, watching Heathcharlesharley adjust his necktie in the reflection of the sliding glass door to the balcony, then stepping into his hat, making the careful adjustments to ensure the proper angle, the brim tilted slightly to the right, just so. "Always make that good first impression," he told the others, winking.

Ruby leaned against the wall, her arms akimbo, a smirk on her face. "Why is that child winking at me?"

Frankie sat on the sofa, sewing a button onto one of Felix's shirts. "Where do you go all the time?" he asked.

"On missions," Heathcharlesharley replied.

"Missions?

"Missionary work. That's what missionaries do. They go on missions. Duh! Am I the only one around here that knows anything at all?"

Champ snuffed out his cigarette and walked into the living room. "Tonghong-e pong-u-songsongyong i-song a hong-o-o-kong-e-rong," he said.

Heathcharlesharley poked around for his briefcase, then slid the closet door closed with a bang. He was getting awfully tired of being treated like a fool by two morons.

Lily ran to Ruby. "What did he say?"

"Monsieur Beauchamp said that Heathcharlesharley is a kitty who goes out at night."

"Heathcharlesharley is a kitty?" she asked, her eyes two big milk saucers. "Where are his whiskers, his fur and his purr?" She paused and thought for a second. "Excuse me for a second," she said, then slipped quickly into her bedroom to make sure her catnip was still safely hidden in the corner under Frankie's bunk, then returned to the living room in time to see the briefcase disappear behind the front door and to hear its resounding slam.

"It's a different kind of kitty," Ruby said with a benign smile. "Don't worry about anything, honey."

Champ pulled the sliding door shut, lit a cig, and leaned back on the bucket. Frankie made a neat, quick snip with the scissors and held the shirt up for inspection. Lily crawled into a ball at Frankie's feet to wonder for the rest of the evening about what other kinds of kitties there were out there.

It was the last of the late night shooting schedule. The streets were creepier then, when the rats chewed on the squalor of the back alleys and human shapes lurked in the shadows. The rotten stench of humanity permeated their very essence, affecting them, repulsing them, and they worked faster so they could go home and stand in the shower for a long time and then go to bed to dream of it. Felix squeezed in among the others hunched around the playback monitor, set up on the sidewalk under the darkness of the San Moritz. Everyone gathers to double-check, scrutinize for boom shadows, uninvited sounds, loose threads, uncurled curls, flaws in focus or framing, dropped lines. The script supervisor checks her notes and her Polaroids for the correct amount of water in the glass, the location of the fork, doors open to the same width, the correct time on a clock. There was always someone who would notice if something weren't right. If they all gave the nod, it was in the can. If not, then a reshoot. This one looked good and there were high fives. Time to move on to the martini shot.

Suddenly, a spray.
A splat from over their heads.
An open window,
An anonymous toss.
Unknowing. Unmindful. Routine.

Confusion. Puzzlement. Realization.
No one escaped.
A direct hit.
The bedpan was full.
A shit and piss cocktail.
Cheers.

Some laughed. Some screamed. Some stood motionless, incredulous, looking at each other, then looking up, searching for the window. Then slowly and silently they moved into the light and began using their fingers to rake the clumps of pinkish fecal matter from their long golden locks, or pulling the long sleeves of their shirts across their brow from left to right, leaving an orange trail of urine on their cuffs. Some sobbed, not knowing what else to do. Felix pulled a large soggy spitwad of toilet paper from his left arm. There was something on the back of his neck. His pants were wet. There was something in his left shoe. He felt sick. Then he vomited on the sidewalk.

The LAPD Hazardous Material team arrived in their masks and sterile suits and their Hazmat vans and whisked them all away for showers and shots, and the rats abandoned the dumpsters in the back alleys for the greener pastures on the darkened sidewalk in the shadows of the San Moritz.

A small stage leans against a brick wall at the alley's end, removed from the bustling boulevard in the same way that most of the musicians who hung out there were removed from reality. Apart from it, but a part of it. It is the hang-out place. There is an open mike and a beer stand and if you buy a beer, you can sit on one of the benches under an awning in front of the stage.

In the afternoon, Lookie-Lews lookie in and walkie on, tourists stop to rest their feet before continuing their journey, and others with not much else going on sit on the curbside in the sun and drink colas and watch pretty country girls sing country fried music, and new agers and Christian rockers and Yoko Onos. Whatever it is that someone brings with them. But it becomes a different place when the sun drops and the afternoon acts head for the subways to the suburbs and supper and tourists flee to the shelter of their hotel rooms. The night shift arrives. Loose, stoned bagmen jam, unrehearsed, screaming heavy metal, train wreck music, pulsating, panting, getting-things-off-your-chest music. They play for a little while and then yield to the next act sitting on the dark curbside waiting and watching through pale night faces.

Near the entrance to the alley is a large bulletin board crowded with tattered notes and scribbles. Bands looking for gigs. Vocalists looking for back up bands. Back-up bands looking for a front man, amps for sale, open jam sessions, club playbills, free concerts. Others looking for buddies who disappeared. “Where are you, Bro?” Lines of poetry. Notes left to those passing through. “Left for Detroit 01/09/08.” Life lyrics. An adventure novel. An autobiography. A history book. A road map. Hieroglyphs on a stone wall. Timeless. Universal. Lives through millennia. Five thousand years ago and today. Living the life. All kinds of things. People at Work. People at Play. Discovering. Inventing. Courting. Singing. Whatever it is. A life story. Sometimes the road is smooth and fast and easy. No sweat. Life is great. Sometimes there are potholes or steep hills. The going is slow. A struggle. Setbacks. False starts. Champ played, but no one heard.

But you're supposed to keep swinging. “Brush yourself off and get back up onto that horse!” “Pull yourself up by the bootstraps!” Everyone says that, Champ thought. Felix always telling him that if you throw enough mud against the wall, some of it will stick. It has to, he says. The law of probability promises it. Just wait. Just keep throwing it. It'll come. Frankie assumed it with no effort of thought. Heathcharlesharley believed it with no effort of question. It was the one single thing they all had in common with each other. It's coming. It's coming. It's coming. Just hang in there. It's coming. It might not be tomorrow, but it's on its way. On rare occasions, it comes right away. A one in a million shot, but it happens. The other 999,999 have to bide their time, but in time it comes. “You're supposed to pay your dues. You'll appreciate it more if you come up the long and hard way.” That's what everybody says. Everybody knows the story that Jim Carrey carried around a check in his wallet for a million dollars made out to his father for ten full years before enough mud stuck to be able to present the check to his father. But it arrived and it was spectacular.

So you have to believe. “If you don't believe it, it won't happen.” That's what everyone says. “If you can dream it, you can live it.” The message is everywhere. The Field of Dreams of Kevin Costner. The Sweet Dreams of Patsy Cline. Dorothy’s dreams really do come true. Maria Von Trapp climbs any mountain, crosses any sea, follows any rainbow, til she finds her dream. And she finds it in the end. She waited long enough, worked hard enough, and got the full Count.

Champ thought about all of this and he thought and he thought, but where were the answers? Where is that mountain he's supposed to climb? That sea to cross? That rainbow? And just how exactly long is that wait?

Besides, isn't a dream something you have when you're asleep, when you've escaped from consciousness? What the hell. So you can have a dream, if you like. Dream as much as you want. Then wake up and smell the coffee. And if he is wrong and dreams really are real, then what do you do if the dream really does come true? Was it worth the price? Okay. You're there. So now what? Ho hum. All that for that?

And Johnie didn't have any of the answers even. But for Johnie it was not that complicated. It was something else. something real simple. A single moment of weakness, a moment of whimsy, seemingly small and unimportant, can send you careening over the guardrail. You take your eyes off the road for just a second. You say yes when you should have said no, or no when the right answer is yes. Just one wrong word. But no one has a crystal ball. You do what you do and it's done. The nice looking young man with the nice voice and the nice guitar said yes one late night to the dirty little whore who sat in the darker blackness behind the small stage. Just one time was all it took. Yes. It was as simple as all that. Just one time. Goodbye, Sweet Dreams. Hello, Bitter Nightmare.

Felix did not teach on Fridays. He wouldn't have much time with his students before the sun would begin its quick descent over the Pacific Ocean and the Sabbath would begin. Everyone hurries home at the time ordained by the special daily calendar that tells them precisely what minute the sun will complete its run for the day. All work ceases. The family gathers around the light of candelabra in the darkened dining room. It is a sacred time with an elaborate meal prepared beforehand and traditional rituals to follow, hands to wash, songs to sing, and prayers to chant.

They may use no electricity or push on buttons. No ovens, toasters, microwaves, coffee pots, air conditioners, lights, television, radio. On some Saturday afternoons when the Southland sun burns hot over the Jewish community, it may be acceptable in some circles for someone to fan oneself and mention to a goyem about how hot it is, hoping the hint would be picked up to push the button on the air conditioner. They may not open an umbrella, but if it is raining as they walk to the temple on Saturday morning, it is generally considered permissible to walk under one if one is offered. Elevator cars in apartment buildings where many Jewish people reside are automatically programmed to stop at every floor from sundown on Friday evening until sundown on Saturday evening. It takes a while getting to the penthouse on the thirtieth floor, but it sure beats taking the stairs. Appliance manufacturers market the Sabbath Oven which can be programmed beforehand to turn on and off so that no pushing of buttons would be required. There is no travel permitted, no planes, trains, or automobiles. Walking is okay and the tieing of shoes is pretty much okay, as well.

They cannot touch money or credit cards. One of Felix's students discovered a $20 bill lying in the grass near an ATM machine one Saturday morning. He knew he couldn't touch it and he knew he would like to have it, so he deftly used his shoe to kick up enough loose grass and dirt to completely cover it, being careful not to let his shoe make any contact with it at all, then returned to it on Sunday morning to find it safe and secure.

Heathcharlesharley had made it to his first audition okay, mainly because it was just a mile down the street. Then the callback came in and the long wait began. Heathcharlesharley spent the time in deep, fervent prayer, promising that if he got the booking, he would be able to fulfill a secret lifelong dream, establishing the first of several We-Will-Give-You-Something-To-Eat-**AND**-A-Place-To-Sleep-**IF**-You-Accept-Jesus-Christ-As-Your-Lord-and-Savior Orphanages for all the starving children in India. It seems the lord was listening. You just have to know what rings his bell. Well, now he can ring his own bell for a happy day.

Felix helped him work the twenty lines or so, then dug out the surgical mask and rubber gloves to help him kick through the Great Smokey Mountains for the clothing the wardrobe department required. He showed Heathcharlesharley what a washer and dryer looked like and offered him fledgling instruction in ironing. But Heathcharlesharley knew it as the slippery slope of distaff. One thing always leads to another and before you know it, he would be flirting with Frankie and wanting to borrow his sewing machine. Rather than to risk that possibility, he gathered up everything and went to Kay's Korner Kwicky Kleeners down the street. Felix drove him to the shoot to make sure he would be at the right place at the right time.

"Molotov Cocktail" was about a Midwest kid building a soap-box derby car to enter into the race in Akron. Heathcharlesharley had to ride a bicycle alongside the Molotov Cocktail during a test run and engage in a dialogue with the driver. "Duh," he replied when the director asked him if he could ride a bike. Well, it turned out that Heathcharlesharley could ride a bike, but he could not ride a bike and deliver a line simultaneously. As soon as the director said, "action!" all of those words right between his ears disappeared right before his eyes. After a morning of take after take after take, the producers and director huddled and decided on Plan B. Heathcharlesharley would abandon the bike and trot alongside the soapbox car.

Well, it turned out that Heathcharlesharley could not trot and deliver lines at the same time, either. So Plan C was sent in. Heathcharlesharley would do a slow walk. Another huddle and the coach sent in Plan D. Heathcharlesharley would stand in place next to the Molotov Cocktail and deliver the lines. Plan E. Plan F. Plan G. Plan H. card. Plan I. "Read the card, idiot! Scene Eight-A, Take 183."

Beth Ann liked her Chevrolet Malibu. The insurance company didn't give her much, but a church friend arranged a good deal for her and she was happy that she was made happy. "It was nice to have a car named for a place she knew, and such a nice place, too," she thought. Chevy Malibu. "See the USA in your Chevrolet." It sure was better than her Trans Am. Why in heaven's name did someone think that was a good name for a Pontiac? Pontiac was a Native American chief, after all. Didn't anyone think about the Pontiac Tomahawk, the Pontiac Calumet, the Pontiac Papoose? No, but they did think of the Pontiac Trans Am? "No wonder that company folded."

And speaking of companies, Beth Ann was starting to feel betrayed by Harriet, who seemed ungrateful for all of her sacrifices, becoming increasingly insensitive about her delicate health issues. Today, Harriet said some things about coming in late and leaving early all the time and all the days she was taking off and that it wasn't fair to the rest of the people on the floor. Apparently someone on her floor was even passing around a petition about the tuckle in her throat. She couldn't figure out what the big deal was all about. She always got all her work done and even had time to sneak in a few hours a day building her fabulous pyramids, quickly changing screens anytime anyone came close enough to see what she was doing, just so that no one would pass around a petition about that, too.

In fact, that whole job thing was becoming an annoyance. Maybe it was time to nip this whole thing in the bud. She was not a well woman and she was working for an insensitive boss who didn't understand these situations. She was pretty sure that she would no longer be able to make that long drive over the hill. The possibility of having another bad accident on Laurel Canyon on a wet, winter evening was too great to risk.

"One," thump

"Two," thump

"Three," thump

"Four," thump

"Five," thump, "Ahem Ahem."

But the day wasn't a total wash. She was driving her Malibu. That nice policeman who had brought her home from the hospital was such a dear, arranging for her to get her license back. She was so grateful that she obliged his suggestion that she set up an automatic monthly payment to support his PAP. He told her to be sure to call him if she ever needed anything. Then that nice-looking young doctor in Sherman Oaks, just fresh out of medical school, obliged her request for the handicap placard she needed. She felt like driving up to Ojai and treating herself to an aural massage there. She pulled into the garage and took her rightful spot. She was sure that Apartment 213 would have something to say about the whole situation, but it was Apartment 103 that had the paperwork.

"Try the Venice Beach Boardwalk, Felix suggested. "Sunday afternoons. Maybe that's more for you." So Champ once again gathered up Ruby and his five gallon bucket seat. It's crazy, Champ thought, that Felix had all this advice. What does Felix know? Santa Monica was a wash. Is this the blind leading the blinder? Then again, you never know. It's always the big quantity out there, the unknown. So what the hell. What did he have to lose? The unexpected comes from unexpected places.

Don't worry. Here there are no sensibilities in Venice Beach to be sensitive about. Don't worry. No one will come around and ask you for your permit. It is an ocean of movement and colors and sounds and smells. It is a place of the Other World, the jagged edge, the unafraid, the uninhibited, the raw; truthful, but creepy and overwhelming to the timid and the untested, the Disneyland tourist, the Hollywood starbird.

"Ladies and Gentlemen! You asked for it and now you got it! Right here on this boardwalk! The t-shirt shop that has what you have been looking for! ANYTHING you want airbrushed directly onto any size tee shirt, as long as it's large, in any color you want, as long as it is white! Ha Ha! Now don't be bashful. We've done it all. Yes, sir! Nothing shocks us. Looking for that special something to take back to that special friend back home? We gotcha covered. Or uncovered if you like. Ha! Ha! Just say the word. Your wish is my command!"

You can take your place along the concrete boardwalk, wherever you can find a space. Right across from the pizza-by-the-slice place or under the high-flying dragon kites snapping and flapping in the strong Santa Ana's, perhaps right there next to that famous Muscle Beach workout place where freakish body builders in baggy Speedo's measure their bulging biceps, or over there where the fortune-tellers are.

"My crystal ball will look into your future."

"I will read the tarot and uncover the mysteries of your life."

"I will see your destiny in the palm of your hand."

"I will feel the bumps on the top of your head. They will tell you what you want to know."

"Ladies and Gentlemen! Take a lookie-lookie here! Yup, this gentleman and his lovely wife. Both eighty-five, they are. Absolutely! I tell you the truth. Check their ID if you like. Both of them. The lovely wife there. Those tiny pasties barely cover her nipples. Her tiny little g-string struggling against all odds. Her handsome husband there in his itsy-bitsy teenie-weenie yellow polka-dotted thong. Stand back just in case it gives! You don't see anything like this very often, folks, so look all you want for free! Wanna take a picture for the folks back home? Just toss five bucks into the bucket there and you'll have THEE photo to show the boys back at the shop. Tell'em you been to Californy, by god! Hurry, folks, before they pass on!"

Uncle Sam in hotpants and roller blades zig-zags through the crowded boardwalk playing the national anthem on his battery-powered Stratocaster. Stilts walk and pogo sticks hop and squads of roller skates line-dance in perfect precision to hip hop. Chalk artists chalk sidewalks and sand artists sculpt recumbent nudes. Tinsmiths snip cola cans into Cessna's and ships, and henna tattoo artists paint poseys and pot leaves. Ultra-environmentalists and vegans and pagans and wiccans and PETAns and Buddhists and Hare Krishna vend their scriptures and scents among the hemp dealers and horoscopologists and the Ouijas, the iconoclasts and poets and sitarists and satirists and political and religious zealots and atheists and prophets of doom and New World Orderites loudly broadcast though portable bullhorns amid troops of placards standing at attention in the sand amid the perfumes of marijuana and tobacco and beer and ocean air and bananas and coconut and incense and the sweat of humanity.

And out on the sand, amid the dunes on the shore, the throbbing of drum circles, the dancers and dreadlocks, the influence of the West Indies and Africa and Polynesia and Native America, communicating across language barriers in brotherhood and sisterhood by rhythm and cadence, and drowning out the voices of Champ and Ruby. They both knew that this wasn't the where either, but lingered late anyway in the kindred phantasmagoria that is Venice Beach on a typical sunny summer Sunday afternoon.

Felix and Tiffani would watch American Idol together, but then he started to make excuses, saying he had to memorize lines or that he was expecting an important phone call or that he wasn't feeling very well. She knew he was still watching it because she stood at his door checking and sure enough, he had it on. But he couldn't tell her.

"There! Look! See right there?!" she would say.

"What?"

"It's touched up!"

"What is?"

"Her mascara! See it?" Zip. Rewind. "See! Now look! See! Look. The little place here! See!"

"Oh...yeah. Uh huh."

Then thirty seconds later. "Look at the Coke glass there. This one. See how full it is?" Rewind. Zip. Zip. Slower. Slow. Slow. Slow. Stop. Advance Slowly. Frame by frame. Slow now. Slow. Slow. Now freeze. "See where it is here? Not the same. They edited this part. See!!? The assholes. This isn't live! How can they say this show is live when it's not live?"

"Oh... Yeah. Yeah. I see it. The idiots." But he wanted to

scream, “So fucking what!? Who gives a rat's ass? Let's watch the goddammed show!!”

But no. He just said he wasn't feeling well so could he go? Felix figured that sometimes, it was just easier to lie. He didn't want to hurt her feelings. And he didn't want to spend four hours watching the show.

But he had to admit that she had a good eye for the details, that she didn't miss much. She certainly did notice the car parked in her space. She noticed it was white and it was a Malibu. She noticed the handicap placard hanging from the rearview mirror and she noticed the thirty day expiration date on it, and she knew that it was time for Round Two of the Villa Verdugo Battle Royale.

Chapter 18

During the daylight in downtown Los Angeles, the sidewalks are filled with immigrants, many dressed in the colorful garb of their nationality. At Metro bus-stops, long lines lean in the shade against tall buildings, bags gathered around their feet, occasionally a jug or two of milk perched precariously on a head. They sit on street benches in the sun and lunch on gyros and tacos or hotdogs from the food vendors lining the grand avenues. Talking rapidly in foreign tongue, they dicker prices at the mercados for fish and cheese and cilantro and they weigh tomatoes in worn, tired hands. They shop in the clothing stalls on Main Street and Sixth Street and Broadway and peer through the windows of jewelry shops that line the Diamond District.

The nighttime streets are surrendered to the nighttime people, who glean the streets for spillage and leave their mark and their art on the heavy metal doors pulled down tightly over the store fronts and padlocked, separating the worlds of day and night. With the first light, they withdraw from the broad avenues and boulevards and return to the sanctuary surrounding the San Moritz, like Dracula returning to the safety of his casket.

The Garment District is downtown, too, where mostly Central and South American immigrants work at sewing machines in the sweat shops or as clerks in the outlet shops run by Jewish and other Mideastern immigrants. It is a massive district where gigantic bolts of fabrics and stuffing and padding and bindings of every composition, texture, weave, size, color, and pattern are stacked to the rafters between narrow aisles and rest against outside walls in side alleys. Display cases are filled with buttons, snaps, clasps, hooks, zippers and sewing tools. Racks bend under the burden of rolls of trim and lace and other frilly stuff. Frankie found what he needed, the green shirts and pants and matching green ties, gloves, belts, and socks. He felt the felt and found it fine, the corduroy, the pipe cleaners, the little doll-eye buttons and thread and yarn, the sizing and the stuffing. Then he hurried back to North Hollywood.

Tiffani wasn't some schmo, but a force to be reckoned with, especially today. She was in a foul mood. Her carriage had continued to drop and it would be several hours before Champ would be back to offer his strong hands. But she could handle this problem. She had a long history of handling problems, letting people know how it felt to be treated poorly, giving them a taste of their own medicine. She knew how to play the game and cover her tracks. That English woman on the second floor that Felix said made $500 an hour in Virginia finding easy solutions didn't have anything on her. She gave easy solutions to people all evening for their problems for free. Just a simple donation was all that was needed.

Losing is for chumps. Thumper can crawl into her cave and lick her wounds. You don't tug on a lion's tail and you don't mess around with Tiffani. She would begin with the zucchini. One good thing about zucchini is that they come in so many sizes. No matter what you needed one for, you could usually find one that would be a perfect fit. Just the right size slipped into the exhaust pipe and pushed up far enough as to be out of sight would be a good first step. The car would refuse to run properly, and mechanics would need to be called, and several noses under the hood ahemming and ahawing about what the trouble is. A zucchini up its butt hole, a simple case of constipation, having gas and unable to fart.

When Felix went to pick up Heathcharlesharley, he expected to find Heathcharlesharley wrapped and happy. But what he found was unwrappiness and unhappiness. They had lost the light, which was already well behind the tree line in the west. Heathcharlesharley was not happy. The cast and crew were not happy. Many of them were sitting on the curb, some laying on their backs in the grass along the sidewalks waiting it out, others on their cellphones canceling or delaying evening appointments.

"It's my attention-defecate disorder," he admitted, in the ride back home. Felix thought that it was quite a bit more than just a disorder, more like an apocalyptic, cataclysmic catastrophe. On the stage, Heathcharlesharley could get by with it. It wasn't that big of a deal. He could just jabber away with anything that came into his mind because no one would stop the show and say, "Cut! Back to One!" Most of the time, the people in the audience didn't catch on anyway. It was better to say something than to just stand there ahemming and ahawing. If some in the audience did catch on, they would always find his version much better anyway. Eventually someone would always jump in and get him back on track.

Everyone back in college still talked about the time he played Marc Antony in Shakespeare's "Julius Caesar." Even though everyone had heard the story a million times, they would still burst out laughing and slapping their knees as if it were the first time they heard it. He had spent hours learning the lines as he lay on the futon mattress in his dorm room, night after night after night. He had it all down real well and there were no problems in rehearsal. On opening night, though, he got a little distracted by the audience. He did alright with his one line in Act One, but then he got to that long "Friends, Romans, Countrymen" monologue.

"Friends, Romans, Countrymen," he began.

"Lend me your ears. I came to …uh…conquer Caesar

As he had tried to conquer me. Ummm…
Now I know that some of you are thirsty for blood, but you will have to
Wait until lunch. Because right now all we have are the evil bones that are left
Over after we have chewed the fat. It is good that the bones
Are then buried in the evil backyards of Rome.
And we have to find those who did this more than brutal act.
It was the brutal butcher Brutus, the bread baker Bocephus
The clever, conniving candlestick maker Cassius Chaos
Along with the lying witch in her ugly wardrobe.
We do not want to wrong these honorable men who did this terrible deed.
And we do not want to dig up the bones under the elms.
We do not have to call for Stella or strangers.
We do not have to go gentle into that good night.
We do not need the iceman to cometh. There is not a dagger that is leading
Me the wayeth I was goingeth. Caesar dearly loved Brutus and that is why
Brutus killed him. That was the kindest cut of them all.
He was not light in the sandals. He did not want to cometh.
He wished not for the Roman hands and Russian fingers
To go wandering under his toga on the banks of the Tiger.
He was not Greek so he would not lend him his rear.
And that is why Marcus Brutus was an honorable man.

And that is why he killed him."

That was the best he could muster up under the circumstances. The audience all knew this famous monologue, having read and reread it multiple times under the tutelage of teachers in their sophomore year of high school and they knew that wasn't how it all went down. The audience sat there, dumbfounded, staring at Heathcharlesharley standing there on his bare, skinny legs in his toga and his awesome overbite. Heathcharlesharley returned the stare, sheepishly. Dead silence. Then a little tee-hee, and another and soon the entire audience was rolling in the aisle. The friends, Romans and countrymen on stage in their togas joined in, slapping the sides of the plywood Roman Forum, and dabbing away tears with edges of their togas. Then one of the Romans finally reached the presence of mind to shout "Mutiny!" and the play continued. Everyone enjoyed the moment. No harm done. They even cheered him at the curtain call. Then the next night the audience was overflowing. They wanted to see what else he had up his toga.

They were not nearly as touchy as these people. There were no bravos when he finished. He had not been treated honorably. Someone called him a moron. Another rolled the eyeballs. It hadn't been pleasant. If they had let him do it his own way, they would have had everything they needed.

How and why, when his lineage was so sophisticated, his workmanship so exquisite, did he get reduced to this? Of all his contemporaries who were on display that day, why was it he, Lord Woodrow, who was pulled out of the line-up, like a good fellow pulled out of a line-up of shady characters and falsely ID'd? He was not your typical, ordinary garden variety leg. He was top shelf, bred to be a gentleman's gentleman. Instead he was bread for a woman starving for attention. Had he done something to upset his creator?

He hadn't been polished since he first joined her. He

smelled of cat pee. His neck was sticky with something brown and chunky. His foot was shod in a wad of Wrigley's Doublemint gum. "It just doesn't get any worse than this," he sighed.

He watched Beatrice focusing on the wobbles. That was where he would fit in, or, if he had any luck at all, where he wouldn't fit in. He hoped that Beth Ann could just count and thump on something when she got the wobbles.

"Okay, dear," Beatrice told Beth Ann. "When you feel that you are wobbling, keep walking, put one foot in front of the other like you are a tightrope walker. Hold your cane straight out in front of you with both hands, like a balancing bar, parallel to the ground." And Beatrice demonstrated. Beth Ann was soon taking a few steps, wobbling, then extending him far out in front of her, holding him tightly, choking him like an acrophobe would choke the guardrail on the observation deck of the Empire State Building, and not looking down, place one foot in front of the other and hurry quickly, as though she was racing to the safety of the tightrope platform high above the circus tent.

"Rats!" cursed Woodrow. "Foiled again! It does get worse than this! It's a veritable Greek tragedy! Aeschylus, move over."

The producer called Barbara the next day to file a report about Heathcharlesharley's shortcomings, his inability to deliver a line and the hundreds of retakes they had to do at a dollar for each foot of film, the overtime paid to the cast and crew, and the penalties for the missed deadlines on their shooting permits. He would pay his basic rate, but would not fork over any more money for his overtime, and furthermore, he would never consider renting another donkey from her stable.

Barbara was a reasonable and shrewd businesswoman and she knew right away she was the underdog in this discussion. She apologized for the situation, explained that he was one of her new actors and this was his first booking. She waived Heathcharlesharley's fee, apologized, and the producer softened. They ended on an upbeat note, and she knew she had dodged a bullet and she knew it was time to cut the cord.

"Boys," she told them, "Your internships are over at the end of the day. Thank you for all of your hard work." Then she turned to Heathcharlesharley, "Take your headshots with you when you leave. Sorry things didn't work out for you, Heathcharlesharley."

After he had time to sort things out, he felt shortchanged. He hadn't expected Barbara to cut him like a hot tomato, just like that, with no warning, not after all he had done, all of the sacrifices he had made, moving all the way out here from Louisiana, having to live with a homo, having to listen to the jing jong coming from Frankie and Champ all night long. Payback going over to the dark side.

The internship was over, but he was certain that he would be kept on as an associate, like Felix, sitting there in the fatbird seat. Powerful. Needful. But if nothing else, she would continue to send out his new headshots. But no. All of that was over. All gone now. All of his chickens in one swell poop.

When he called his father to tell him, all he had to say was, " Sorry things didn't work out for you, son."

"Go figure that one out, Jesus. And, oh yes! While we're at it, what happened to you in the deal? Let's put the blame where it belongs. So, it's hasta la pasta, baby, to the whole WWGYSTEAAPTSIYAJCAYLAS Orphanage. Sorry things didn't work out for you, JC. Now you know how shortchangeation feels."

Tiffani had legions of friends from all walks of life. There was a minister, a teacher, a bus driver, a masseuse, show biz people. And there was a doctor and this was his night for a visit. Every Friday, just like clockwork, he would drop by after he left his Toluca Lake office to lay in his weekly supply, leaving the usual donation and his usual tip on her kitchen counter top. Theirs was a quick and easy friendship. They enjoyed each other's jokes as she carefully held her finger scales up to the light to measure out his week's worth. If he were watching her closely enough to see, she would throw in a little extra.

"Absolutely," the good doctor readily agreed. "Drop by the office any time Monday." And she did that. There was no waiting three months for an appointment, no sitting in the waiting room for hours flipping through last year's Today's Health magazines. "Absolutely," he agreed. Tiffani returned to the Villa Verdugo, and neatly pulled the old Taurus into the garage. Plan B implemented.

Heathcharlesharley was not the only one who had a visit from Ma and Pa Misery. They were out making the rounds that day, all dressed up in their Sunday best, paying visits to people they hadn't seen in a while. They stopped by to say hello to Beth Ann and ended up staying for most of the day. First, she had only gone a couple of miles or so on her way to work when the Chevrolet Malibu sputtered and died, right at rush hour at the busiest intersection in the universe, Laurel Canyon and Ventura Boulevards, leaving her at the mercy of others. Then all these damned fools behind her honking angrily and flipping her off when they finally got around her. That was not the way to make people feel good about feeling bad.

But in spite of it all, she tried to do what was right. She called Harriet to tell her that she would be unable to get to work today because of car trouble. No mercy there, either. Harriet arranged for someone to shoot over the hill and pick her up and deliver her to her desk. The path to perdition is paved with politics, potholes, and full time positions. Then she called AAA and a tow truck was summoned and her car was lifted up and carried away to the garage and she was lifted up and carried away to the job. Then she had to arrange for a ride after work back to the garage to pick up the car where the mechanic showed her the zucchini and explained where he had found it. Then he gave her the bill. So long to any goodness floating around in the air on this day. Thank the ethereal impulses this day is finally drawing to a close, she thought, as she headed home.

Tiffani's carriage had slipped to its lowest level in record, like the barometer at Galveston Bay in 1900. But this was worth the sacrifice. No slipped carriage would cloud up and rain on this parade. She hid behind the concrete pillar and waited until the big black gate finally opened and the white car descended into the darkened garage. She watched as it cruised in, pulled up, then stopped with a quick jerk. Then, a few moments later, she stepped out.

"One," thump.

"Two," thump.

"Three," thump

"Four," thump

"Five," thump. Ahem. Ahem."

Tiffani stood grinning to herself. She had turned the handicap placard for optimum view when she hung it on her rearview mirror. She watched Beth Ann reach back in for the cane, and then begin the tightrope walk to peer at the blue placard.

"Be patient, now," Tiffani told herself. "Let her see it. Let her digest it. Hold it... Hold it... hold it... Wait for the right moment... NOW!" She jumped out from behind the pillar and grinned broadly, like the Cheshire cat, her beautiful white rows of teeth gleaming in the soft darkness.

Oh…dear me," trumpeted Tiffani.

"One," thump

"Two," thump.

"Three," thump.

"Four," thump.

"Five," thump. "Ahem, Ahem. Some dear is parked in my parking place. Whatever should I do? Dear me!"

Tiffani began the high wire walk, her arms stretched out. She wobbled and tiptoed then careened into the support column in the middle of the garage and clutched it, panting heavily and thumping her chest.

"One," thump.

“Two,” thump.

“Three,” thump.

“Four,” thump.

“Five,” thump. Ahem. AHEM… Oh my goodness! Someone else has a disability now.”

By now there wasn't very much charity and kindness left in Beth Ann's tormented soul, not this day. It was time to fight fire with fire. Sometimes you have to do bad to feel good. There aren't very many secrets in the Villa Verdugo. Everyone generally knew about the living conditions in the boys' apartment. Everyone knew that the guy in 209 had filed a lawsuit against the Villa Verdugo for the backaches he suffered from having to walk up and down those flights of stairs all the time. Everyone knew that the two old women who shared Apartment 111 had not spoken to each other in twelve years. And everyone knew what was going on in Apartment 213. When they sat in the pool or the hot tub beneath her balcony, they could hear the conversations and smell the earthy cloud emanating through that open bathroom window or a sliding glass door left ajar behind the Venetian blind on balmy spring evenings.

Beth Ann stepped forward, then leaned back, holding an imaginary snakehead up to her lips. She started sucking, huge and exaggerated sucking, tapping the same huge reservoir from whence came the powerful and hefty harrooming and ahemming, sucking in her cheeks until her eyes nearly popped out of their sockets, then erupted into an imaginary dialogue amid apoplectic fits of coughing.

“SUUUUUUUUUCCCCCCCCCCKKKKKKKK…

Cough…hack….hack…hack…hack…cough!…Cough… COUGH!

Giggle…Giggle.

SUUUUUUCCCCCCCCKKKKKKK…

Hack… Hack… Man, this is good shit, man. Hack! Hack… Cough… COUGH!!

Giggle… Giggle! Hand me that snakehead, would ya?!

SUUUUUUUUUUUUUUUUUCCCCCCCCKKKKKK

KKK…!

Don't forget to make your donation, please.

SUUUUUUCCCCCCCCKKKKKKK… Cough… Cough… Hack… Hack…

Giggle… That way, if the POLICE come, I can tell them I am not SELLING it.

Giggle…Giggle…!

HAAAAAAAAAAAAAAAAAAAAAAAAAAACCCCC CCCCCKKKKKKK!!!"

A Venetian blind closed over those two rows of white and a carriage dropped further down into uncharted territory. Mr. and Mrs. Misery continued to rule the day.

Chapter 19

Los Angeles hosts great hotels, the Beverly Wilshire of "Pretty Woman" fame in the Rodeo Drive District, the eponymous pink Beverly Hills Hotel on Sunset Boulevard, the Mondrian, the Hotel Bel Aire, the Sofitel on Beverly, Shutters on the Beach in Santa Monica, the Four Seasons in Beverly Hills, the Renaissance Center in Hollywood and they all have separate kosher kitchens, well staffed and stocked for any needs of the second largest concentration of Jews in the United States. They are inspected regularly by Jewish kosher authorities to insure that the Laws of Leviticus are followed, the special tools and separate kitchen are used, the procedures in place to insure that the meat is not mixed with the dairy. Orthodox Jews shop the kosher delis, grocery stores, and bakeries in the Fairfax District. Beverly Boulevard and Third Street are dotted with kosher Chinese and Mexican restaurants, intimate cozy kosher Italian cafes, pizza shops and burger joints that deliver.

On the first Thursday of the month, the yeshiva boys think about it from the moment they arise in early morning, while they pray their morning prayers, while they sit in their Hebrew and Talmud classes. All day long, they confer with each other, diagram things out, measuring, deciding, voting, then revoting. There are plenty of decisions to make. Should the cheese be real and the meat be fake, or should the cheese be fake and the meat be real? Should it be sliced into wedges or cut into squares? How much for each slice? How much for each wedge? Onions on two slices, olives on three, green peppers on one slice, double extra extra garlic on the whole enchilada. Finally, when all the details had been ironed out and the money collected, the boys gather around the pay phone in the front hallway to place the order. Kovi, their best negotiator, would be sent to the sidewalk out front to wait for the delivery guy and when it arrived, he would inspect the pizza, count the pepperoni slices, the olives, examine the thickness, weigh its heft, measure its circumference and then hammer out the deal. The others wait quietly behind the gate, eager to hear of the deal as they are to eat of the meal.

"How much," they would pepper him when he reappeared with the greasy, white box. "How much, how much, how much?!" Kovi would raise his hand to quiet the multitudes, take the dramatic pause, lean forward on the tips of his toes, rock back and forth, then proclaim to all that the $20 pizza was purchased for $17.50 to a hail of "baruch hashems" and "matzel tovs." The refunds were carefully calculated, counted out, and pocketed. It was a routine thing, the same every month, a battle of the wits and strong wills between the Jewish owner of the kosher pizza shop and the boys of the yeshiva in training to become owners.

There were other strong wills struggling with each other. Harriet spent a lot of time thinking about what course of action to take. When she brought Beth Ann over with her from Cinematix, everything was fine. Beth Ann was the best assistant she ever had, computer savvy, an excellent writer and composer, good on the phone with the network executives in New York, top-drawer memory, very attentive to the fine print, able to grasp even the most complicated legal language in the most complicated legal documents. Harriet had given her rave reviews, and plenty of praises and raises.

Harriet wanted to give Beth Ann the benefit of the doubt.

There were times in the past when Beth Ann stayed in the office until late in the evening when Harriet was in a pinch with some complicated, urgent last-minute snafu. At one time, they had even been good friends, with Beth Ann going to Harriet's home for Fourth of July barbecues, and Beth Ann bringing in double batches of double chocolate walnut supreme fudge brownie delights. Boy, were those good. She shook her head sadly. It's funny how sad things can get. That was a huge loss.

But it appeared that now she was becoming a liability, wanting to do a full time job part time, with full time salary and benefits. She always got her work done, so what can you say? If that was all there was, it would be one thing, but there was much more. Increasing demands about needing a desk closer to the bathroom and lunch room, the elevator, the water cooler, claiming that it was becoming increasingly more difficult for her to get around, that she needed extra time for this and that, a better parking place, leaving early or coming in late. And now the other employees were beginning to get ugly about things, suggesting that perhaps Beth Ann was getting preferential treatment. Many of her employees had been broken down by the hahakakaroomroomroomahemahemming, which disappeared mysteriously overnight, to be replaced by the incessant onethumptwothumpthreethumpfourthumpfivethumpahemahems, which were driving the rest of them to the brink of insanity, much worse than the typical squeaky wheel on a chair or the chronic sniffing and heavy breathing from the person in the next cubicle. There was none of this nonsense when they worked together in Cinematix. If there were, she would have never invited her along to Vidematics.

Harriet knew she should start building a case, keeping a file, jotting things down, verifying things, just in case things got ugly. This was going to take some pretty fancy footwork. There was always the due process that had to be followed. This wasn't anything about incompetence. She was certainly able and capable, and she did her job. How do you make a court case with that? Beth Ann could sue for wrongful termination, drop a tear or two, and juries would side against Vidematics, believing them to be an unsympathetic and ungrateful corporation who wants to get rid of someone who is handicapped because it's such a bother to them, then hand her an expensive settlement package costing Vidematics millions.

Harriet decided she would discretely ask for affidavits from her other handicapped employees, none of whom ever had any complaints about mistreatment at Vidematics. She would confer with human resources about offering her counseling to determine if the problem could be fixed before more drastic action was taken, just in case there was some hot potato rolling around out there. They would do whatever they could to show that they were a compassionate company, trying everything to accommodate the special needs of every one of their employees. They would pass everything through legal to make sure that everything and anything would hold up in a court of law and a jury of her peers.

Tiffani wasn't in the best of moods when Champ came up. He was sweating heavily and she complained that he smelled, telling him he needed to shower more often. He straddled Tiffani, who sprawled face down on the floor, holding her pillow to her face to stifle her screams. He began by kneading her buttocks to loosen them, then girding himself for attack, braced his legs against the side of the sofa, then pushed with Herculean strength, shoving the carriage back into the garage. “Auuuuggggghhhh!” Then she fired up the hookah. Her mood hadn't improved. She complained that it was tough for her to have a sensible conversation with him, that he seemed to be in a different world somewhere.

She was right about that detail. What the hell. Tonight he was packed and ready for another journey. He never knew where he was going. Sometimes it was just resting on a quiet, peaceful cloud in Nirvana with Kurt. Sometimes he went on a Magical Mystery Tour with John to the Strawberry Fields to lay there and eat of the fruit. Sometimes he boarded the zeppelin to the heavens to soar through the ether with Lucy in the sky with diamonds, or knocked on the doors of Jim and his LA woman to break on through to the other side. Maybe he would step through the looking glass to ask Alice for a little time in wonderland. There was always a stopping off place. If Tiffani wanted to have a sensible conversation with him, then she needed to buy a ticket and hop onto the tour bus with him.

The picture of America presented by American media to the world outside of its borders is that of a peace-loving, violent nation. The gentle American father who knows best has an insatiable appetite for glorious wars and guns. The vicissitudes of family ties are laced together in inane situations in idle comedies. Peaceful and quiet night times, after the kids are tucked safely in bed and kissed goodnight, feature violent and noisy dramas portraying a nation rift with lurid sexual exploitation, drug abuse, domestic violence, and monstrous crime. Reality shows give the illusion of a rich and spoiled American youth as easily corruptible, conniving and greedy, with the justification that "I am not here to make friends; I am here to win a million dollars or marry the prettiest girl or the most handsome boy, at any cost." And the world loves it and wishes to emulate what they see. The Italians shoot spaghetti westerns in the big cowboy boot that is their nation. Daytime dramas shot in Mexico mimic the yearnings of the American young and the restless and all their children. Often time, in an effort for authenticity and needing American actors and local color, film crews from around the world travel to Los Angeles to shoot footage to be consumed by their own domestic markets.

Felix had booked an episode for a Japanese drama, playing a young and married J. Edgar Hoover living in Washington. There were no mike booms or lines to memorize. It didn't matter. Japanese voice-over artists would dub in all that later. It didn't matter that Hoover never had a wife, either. An unmarried Hoover did not fit into their story line. The director approached them and bowed respectfully. "Okay, you two," he said in his best English to Felix and the actress playing his wife. "I wan you un you to do typical Amelican spousal abuse. Okay? Any questions?"

"No…"

Turning to Felix, he said, "I wan you to smoke cigalette. Smoke! Smoke! Smoke! All time." Then turning to the actress. "I wan you to dlink maltini. Sip. Sip. Sip. All time. Dlink... Dlink...Dlink. Smoke...Smoke...Smoke. Okay?"

"Okay."

"Okay! Camela Lolling!"

Felix and the actress weren't exactly sure what typical American spousal abuse entailed, so they faked it, chasing each other around the set, periodically pausing to puff on the cigarette or take a hit from the martini, then resume taking hits from the other, pummeling each other with pillows and threatening shouts, jabbing fake punches, taking stage slaps and prat falls, tossing each other onto the sofa, throwing whatever was available in each other's direction, exhausting every possibility, desperately waiting for the director to call "cut!" Finally, after an interminable half hour amid the clamor of the entire Japanese crew who had gathered ringside to offer their cheers and whoops of encouragement and excitement and make bets on the side, the joyous director had given his obliging and reluctant "Cut!"

J. Edgar and his wife collapsed heavily into a heap of exhaustion and perspiration onto the sofa in the heavily trashed living room of their Washington D.C. apartment, under the shadows of the capitol building framed in the window above the sofa in the back lot of Universal City in Los Angeles for the fine folks of Tokyo, Japan, who will cherish a firsthand glimpse of a typical, happily married American couple at home.

Champ remembered the first time he had smoked Tiffani's California weed. There was nothing like this floating around in the oil rigger's barracks along the gulf-front. It was far different from the dulling numbness of the cocaine he snorted in the dingy motel rooms there. In fact, he had never been so high in his life. He lay spread eagle on the apartment floor that night, his heart racing and pounding, then moved to a cold shower trying to come down. He had gradually become accustomed to the pot and didn't get quite so wasted. But Uncle Jack helped him along. Good old Uncle Jack, the answer man.

After he parked her carriage and sucked on her hose, Tiffani sent him away. All he caught was a buzz and a bad mood. He rocked on the bucket and waited, his bags packed. He wondered where he would land tonight and he sucked on Uncle Jack for that answer. He wondered what the hell he was doing in Los Angeles. Ask the answer man. There was no answer. He wondered again when Engine Engine Number Nine would come barreling down the railroad line and he sucked on Uncle Jack for the answer.

"Soon, my boy, soon," answered Uncle Jack.

He looked between the smudges on the sliding door. Ruby dozed quietly in the corner. Frankie snipped at the table. Lily lay under the table, quietly toying with the scraps of yellow and red felt. Champ wondered what it was all for and turned to Uncle Jack. Jack didn't know jack about it either. Heathcharlesharley surfaced, hat in hand. Champ looked at the pussy and hated him. Then he hated himself for falling for it all. "Snip, snip snip," snipped the scissors. "Tick, tick, tick," ticked the clock.

"Where is the spaceship, Mister Sir Uncle Jack Daniels, your Holy Highliness?" he demanded.

"All Aboard!" roared Uncle Jack.

Champ wasn't present when Ma and Pa Misery dropped in there for a quick visit, too, while making their rounds. He wasn't there when Heathcharlesharley suffered a broken arm. He couldn't tell you what happened to Ruby. He was out of town, visiting Dante in the Inferno. What the hell.

Tiffani noticed a small drop of something that looked like it might have leaked from the pipe directly over her car. It looked corrosive. Maybe it was something from a sewage line.

Whatever it was, it didn't deserve to be dripping onto her car. She definitely would not park in that spot ever again. If Thumper wants to park there so badly, she's welcome to it. Let her be the patsy here.

Chapter 20

It was time for the World Talent Championship. Felix would judge the various acts on Friday for the Saturday night showcase and conduct the one-on-one interviews on Sunday. This one was a little different from the typical showcases he had worked. This was an international affair for those fortunate enough to live in a country that had strong enough diplomatic ties with the U.S., nations that could issue artistic visas and have American authorities honor them. Normally athletic visas were issued and recognized handily from countries virtually worldwide with few questions asked, but things would get a little sticky over artistic visas.

They had traveled from the eastern European block, Russia and Poland and the Ukraine, primarily, to showcase their talent in Hollywood. Most did not speak English, or spoke it poorly. It was unlikely he would find someone here for Barbara. In the early days of Hollywood, it didn't matter. Many actors with thick accents were able to work in the silent films, but when the talkies arrived, they often found themselves out of work.

But on the other hand, many foreigners arrived in Hollywood and the mud they slung against the wall stuck. Arnold Schwarzenegger, the body builder from Austria. The Gabor sisters, Eva, Magda, and Zsa Zsa with their thick Hungarian accents. Many others like the modern day Charlize

Theron, who moved to the United States by herself as an eighteen-year-old from South Africa, learned English by watching The Love Boat on television. So he could not rule out any possibility. What is there to judge anyway in an ocean of unpredictable waves that take a certain surfer? What is the perfect wave and what surfer does it choose?

Felix knew he would have to sit through the interminable preliminaries of every act imaginable, the jugglers, hula-hoopers, ethnic dancers, ballroom dancers by the scores, actors, singers, comics, clowns, models, musicians, magicians, mimes. Many were young children accompanied by mothers and aunts and older sisters. Felix would sit at the table with the other judges, gradually whittling them down to those who would be spotlighted on the Saturday evening showcase. Anyone who could pony up the money qualified. But it would be their only shot at it. There were no more resources left, after selling the silver candlestick holder, the golden wedding ring, Papa's glass eye. They didn't put all their eggs in one basket because they only had one egg and they didn't have a basket to put it in. That egg was carefully wrapped and carried to America where the streets are paved with gold. It would be accompanied by the brood of hens in babushkas, all there to keep the egg warm, to see that it hatches into a goose that would lay a whole big basket full of golden eggs.

The big competition would be performed on the main stage in front of an audience of hundreds, mostly the families of the participants. Everyone would be awarded something, big certificates for all the first place winners in each category and little certificates for everyone else. It was something to take back with them. Felix saw the same judges from before. They were all there and many more beyond that. Here he was, Mr. Felix NotYetMadeIt, sitting with the rest of the best of the NotYetMadeIts. They would mingle in the green room before the show, wolfing down the crackers and punch, exchanging fancy business cards, bringing each other up to speed with the latest news of their latest venture. Everyone was right on the edge of victory.

"This is the big one, Baby!"

"Cha Cha La Bore's people have been snooping around."

"Steven Shpellbound wants first look!"

"Da fodder of Quatro Tarantula, da guy who did 'Dime Store Novel.' He's in!"

Then they would solemnly take their seats at the judges' table, and when introduced would stand, do a full turn to face the audience, wave, bow, and flash their dazzliest smile. Everyone would cheer loudly after each introduction, lending for a short while a gravitas and validity to the dignity and value of the assemblage of judges, and thinking perhaps that the louder they cheered, the more likely the egg would hatch. The emcee was some ancient game show host from Chatsworth, and yes, of course he was available and, yes, he would condescend to the honorarium offered him if a car could be sent for him and he would have his own dressing room.

Everyone, the big and the little certificate holders, would be invited to the follow-up one-on-ones on Sunday. Circles of padded chairs were arranged around tables in the main banquet room where an agent or manager of sorts sat, a sign posted at each. "Models." "Actors." "Dancers." "Fire Eaters." "Bear Baiters." When the doors were finally unlocked at noon, the alpha hen of each brood would creep in like a lioness to the kill, alert and circling each agent, smelling the air, pawing the ground, testing the herd, seeking the weak, the meek, stalking until the advantage was theirs, then pounce with fury and determination, dividing and conquering, bombarding their prey into submission with whatever it took. Pleas of mercy, begging, weeping, bribery, flattery, cooing, cajoling, coaxing, threats and shouts and screams.

"Whatever it takes, whatever you want, whatever you got, just name your price." "What will it take? The casting couch? You want it? You got it."

"No English? No problem. We learn it."

"No work visa? No problem. We get one."

At the end of the day, Felix left, wishing sincerely for some peace and quiet and a cigarette. He found the peace. He found the quiet. He found the cigarette and he blamed it on J. Edgar. He found no talent to take back to Mainstream. The Slavs and the Serbs, the Poles and the Russians returned to their villages to check every five minutes to make sure the only phone in town was in good working condition, then in a few days interrogate the local postal official about lost mail, then after a week begin their daily litany of prayers to Saint Sophia, and then after a month, start the long and tedious process of finding a lonely American to marry.

It is the best kept secret that everyone in Hollywood knows about. The Casting Couch. Hollywood officially denies it, saying that the modern corporate Hollywood no longer needs to rely on the bottom feeding tactic of trading sex for success, dismissing the practice as an old wives' tale or acknowledging it as a relic of the days gone by, when there were whispers about Charlie Chaplin, Alfred Hitchcock, John Wayne, and Clark Gable.

But it is not in today's business model. Hollywood is too professional, too transparent, they will tell you. The companies are run today by committees and boards of directors and MBA's from the nation's finest business schools who haven't the power to unilaterally cast a lead role in a $200,000,000 blockbuster in exchange for a quick hummer. Likewise, the actors are MFA's from top university fine arts programs and are hired for the strength of their talent and not the length of their unit. The old school is passé, they tell their shareholders, who insist on maintaining a squeaky clean corporate image because it's good for the bottom line. Anything else wouldn't be prudent. Not at this juncture.

Times and pedigrees change, but sex is still sex. When someone new enjoys a meteoric rise with little or no experience or talent, the whispers surface. When a director or producer is seen in seemingly unseemly company of the hot, new commodity, there are still whispers, just like in the good old days when men were manly and girls were girly. Only the names change. Arnold Schwarzenegger, Don Johnson, Steven Seagal. All ardently denied. But most suspect that there is not a day that goes by somewhere in Hollywood, whether it is in a big corporate corner office suite of a major studio or in the dingy back broom closet in some small production company on some small side street in Hollywood when the scene is played out.

"You can do it the easy way or you can do it the hard way. 'Sup to you.'"

"It's how show biz operates, my boy. Wake up and smell the roses."

"You produce. I produce."

"I make your dreams come true. You make my dreams come true."

"It looks just like a strawberry ice cream cone. It tastes just like a strawberry ice cream cone. You like ice cream, don't you, Kiddo?"

Johnie lay awake, listening to the night noises, the snores and snorts of the sleeping, the moans of the ill, the jerks of apnea, the sobs of dreams in tatters and rags, the howls of sirens in the distance, the tires of the semis beating overhead on the I-170. In a few hours the scream of the low flying jets would resume, heading for the Bob Hope Airport a few miles east, and leaving behind the smell of fuel in its wake. Then he would pull on his boots and head down the slope to Magnolia Boulevard and follow it to its intersection with Lankersham, to catch the early morning crowd in line for coffee at the Starbucks there. "Brother, can you spare a dime?"

He stayed to himself, avoiding the idle conversation and the huddles around small, smoky campfires during the cold, wet mornings of January. The others would leave him alone. They understood and shared the same fate. Failure is a deeply personal thing. You just don't go there. You don't ask questions. You know the story anyway, the unmindful, uncaring poker dealer who deals you a dead hand, designing your destiny with a shuffle of the cards. You already anteed up. You either fold or you play, but either way, you lose. Nobody cares whether it's fair or not. It's just a game anyway.

But they still dare to dream. Their current condition is only a temporary thing. “I'll be back on my feet real soon now.”

“Soon as I get to feeling a little better.”

“Soon as my brother sends for me.”

“It's just a little while longer,” they tell each other and themselves and they believe it. They have no other choice. And they come and they go. Maybe because their brother did send for them. Maybe because they did start to feel better. But probably neither. Mostly they just go wait somewhere else for a little while. Maybe because they got tired of those around them and decided to move to the next neighborhood and a different underpass to look at. Others would arrive to take their place with another shuffle of the cards and another hand to play. Johnie dug for the cigarette, lit it, took a couple of hits, then snuffed it to save the rest for morning. It was very dark, but in a few more hours the sun would come up over the Verdugos and the colony would slowly waken to another day of waiting.

Frankie sat quietly at the table, cutting pieces of red felt and yellow felt into small flower petals. He had been working on it well into the evening and now it was late night. He would stay up as late as he needed to finish the petals. He had plenty of time to wonder about things. He wondered about Heathcharlesharley, who hadn't said a single thing to him about being cut from Mainstream Talent. He wondered about Heathcharlesharley's new budget. He had overheard the conversation he had with his father and wondered if Heathcharlesharley would think to pay his half of the rent.

He wondered about a couple of nights ago when Heathcharlesharley had asked Champ how things were going at Epic Zeroes, then laughed like it was a funniest thing he ever said, then making that little gesture that he always makes when he thinks he is being entertaining, pointing with his two index fingers in a row, one in front of the other like he saw a stand-up comic doing one time on a stage somewhere. He remembered how Champ rose and grabbed Heathcharlesharley by the arm and in one brutal twist, snapped it in two places, then went for his neck to snap that as well, like he was intent on doing some serious harm.

Frankie had risen from the sewing machine and tackled Champ, who fell back into Ruby, breaking her body like it were an eggshell, like a Humpty-Dumpty. He thought about how he drove the sobbing Heathcharlesharley at three in the morning to St. Joseph's to have the arm set and put into a cast, how he had picked up the broken Ruby and labored, like all the king's horses and all the king's men, painstakingly putting all the pieces back together again, then carefully matching the pigment from his paint box to help hide the cracks in her shell. Still, she would be disfigured, scarred for life.

Champ hadn't known what he had done until the next morning when he found his baby. Then this squat brute of a man, with his piercings punctuating his bald fat head and face, this scary tattooed man with his stiff black whiskbroom of a goatee, this big hardened ox of a man from the poorest part of Creole country, this self-proclaimed Coonass from the school of hard knocks, who had seen it all, who had done it all, who had taken a bullet to the thigh without flinching one late night at a convenience store; this traumatized man who had responded to a taunt with such brutal force, sat in the middle of the floor bobbing back and forth like a baby on his blankie, cradling his beautiful little girl in his fat, stubby paws against his stocky body, cooing and crying and apologizing, kissing her wounds like a mother kisses the boo boo's on her child's knee, explaining over and over again that everything was just a terrible mistake, just one big, terrible, awful mistake.

Beatrice knew how strong the human mind was, and how to unlock many of the mysteries within it, but this was one of the biggest mysteries, rivaling something shown on Masterpiece Theater. In a way it was fascinating, like a case study for some psychologist to write a book about, something that some Hollywood producer would look for. No matter how she long she thought about it or how much she worked it, there just didn't seem to be a sensible explanation.

Out in public, Beth Ann was still quite a spectacle, but she was much more user-friendly and interesting. Little children would watch her and then do the walk themselves along imaginary tightropes, their arms extended out, chanting "wouldyoubeadears" and cutting into lines and found it far more fun than the old hopscotch game they were used to playing. The hahakakaroomroomroomahemahems had moved over to make room for the onethumptwothumpthreethumpfourthumpfive-thumpahemahems, and diners would watch their watches, trying to predict how often the contractions would occur and when the next one would be expected and placing little side bets.

But Beatrice was unsure about some of the other mysteries, like the willingness and wherewithal to cut into lines, to sit in her car and wait for some dear to come along to carry the bags of cat litter and the jugs of water up to her apartment when she was perfectly capable of doing it herself, to shop around until she could find a doctor who would sign off on her disability. Beatrice knew she did not understand all of the travesties of the human heart. This may even be something entirely outside of the appliances of her art.

There were all sorts of mysterious human behaviors out there. Beatrice wasn't sure why wonderful and lovely people who seemed normal in all ways had a penchant for hunting and killing endangered wild animals, or stalking children on line, or trading blowjobs in public bathrooms, or why billionaires underpay their staff, or the saintliest of nuns hurls stones and shouts "Jesus Killer! Jesus Killer!" at young Jewish children walking to school in the morning. Maybe it was the tragic flaw, the harmartia, inherent in the human condition, that everyone has to have something wrong somewhere, that no one is without some kind of original sin. Maybe people don't feel complete unless they are incomplete or flawed somehow. Maybe it's the Primitive Thinker who has trouble determining what is fair and what is not fair. Or maybe it's just not that complicated. Maybe it's just boredom, something to get the old heart stimulated, raise a sweat, throw the spice of variety into an otherwise uninteresting life.

But probably it is a matter of the heart and not the head. Emotional abnormality has to be repaired before behavioral normalcy can set in. Beth Ann had tearfully divulged to her one afternoon over a nearly empty bottle of Two Buck Chuck merlot that she had never been kissed on the lips. No man had ever put the move on her. She had never seen a real live man naked, unless she wanted to count the time she saw her father when she went into his bedroom without knocking. She tried so not to stare, but it was just too fascinating not to get an eyeful. She did see other men naked, but they weren't real men, just men on websites she visited late at night occasionally when she was bored and needed stimulation. She would wear her lacy panties and new bra and when she saw someone she liked, she would close her eyes and pretend she was Scarlett O'Hara in the arms of Rhett Butler.

"What kind of man are you looking for?" Beatrice probed.

"A southern gentleman, maybe. A nice looking slender young man with strong convictions and a belief in a higher authority," she replied. Someone intelligent with a nice sense of humor."

"One," thump.

"Two," thump. "

Three," thump.

"Four," thump.

"Five," thump. "Ahem, Ahem."

"Well, where have you looked?" asked Beatrice.

She told how she had searched at church and their social clubs there. There were clubs for the congregational gays and lesbians, but she wouldn't find what she was looking for there.

There were clubs for the drug and alcohol dependent congregants, but that wasn't for her either. She tried the CWWWD, The Club for the Widows and Widowers of Our War Dead, but they were too red, white, and blue. The Coupon Clippers Club didn't work. They really were there to clip and trade coupons and nothing else. She attended a couple of dances of the Lonely Hearts Club. It was wonderful to be there. It was certainly a thrill, but she found no one who liked to take her home, no one who'd love to take her home. Except the older, overweight, and desperately lonely bulls, and she would thump and count and sadly shake her head and point to her cane and they would saunter off to greener pastures.

"Well, why don't you look on line for love, Love?" There were lots of dating services where every flavor was the flavor of the day everyday. Whatever she wanted, it was there on her fingertips. Beth Ann decided that as usual, Beatrice was right, but she would wait until she returned from the wedding in England. No sense starting something that would end up coitus interruptus.

Beep. "Hi, there! Did you kn..." Zip. Zap.

Beep. "Hi, there! Di..." Zip. Zap.

Beep. The message is for Felix. This is Charlie Wilson. Sir! What is it about you that makes you not want to return my phone calls? Are you stupid or some..." Zip. Zap.

Beep. "Hello, Felix. This is your mother calling. I hope you had a nice Christmas. Ours was okay. Didn't go anywhere. Just stayed home. Well. It's all over now for another year." Pause. "Uh, Felix, honey, I just wanted to call you to tell you that your father isn't doing too well." Longer pause. "The doctor said there wasn't too much more he can do." Pause. "I think you should call your father. Talk to him for a little while. It might make him feel a little better." Pause. "It'd make me feel better too, honey. Please, honey. Call him. I miss you and I love you very much. Goodbye, Sweetie."

Beep. "Hi, there." Zip. Zap.

Beep. “I am so excited. Thank you so much for saying you'd help me. This is Trudy Karazuski and I am ready to leave South Bend just as soon as you can call me ba...” Zip. Zap.

Beep. “Hi, th...” Zip. Zap.

Lily stayed by her side, wrapping around her to keep her warm, and softly crying, hiding her sniffles in her paws, not wishing to disturb Ruby who lay under Frankie's bottom bunk in the warmth of the darkness there safely hidden from curious, her neck in a brace, the gaping wound in her side sutured and bandaged, her vocal chords in a box next to her.

Champ would look in on her hourly, laying on his belly and stroking her head, and apologizing again and again and again and saying that everything, everything had been one big, huge, colossal mistake. Champ was broken, broken like Ruby, more broken than Heathcharlesharley's arm. He stayed by himself, accepting no visit from Jack or X or the Snake. Radio Head was off. He took no trips by train, steamship, rocket, or dirigible. He sat on the bucket, rocking back and forth, thinking, rocking and thinking. Lily would go to him and caress his feet with kisses. “You can't keep a good girl down. This is just a temporary thing.” she would whisper to him. “Everything will be alright. Just wait a little while and everything will be okay.”

Chapter 21

But no one stroked Heathcharlesharley's head or cuddled him or rocked him back and forth, or apologized. No one kissed his feet or whispered in his ear. No one listened to his side of the story. Plus that budget thing was odorous. He had tried to explain to his father that living in LA was not like living back home.

"Father!" he pleaded. But his father, a Creon of a man who preferred the role of steadfast oak to the flexible willow, had laid down his law.

"Sir! Yes, Sir!" So he sat down and did his figuring. His father said he had to prioritize so he figured in the important figures first, the high speed wireless Internet connection, the Sons and Lovers worksite, the cellphone, the cable bill, the air conditioner bill, the thrice weekly gas fill-ups, the delivery boy's twice daily visit, the movie tickets, the pocket money. Then Frankie asked him for the rent, which he had completely forgotten to figure in so there wasn't anything left. But he was good at figuring out solutions and this one was right in front of him. He knew that when he was scheduling his nightly missionary trips, women would invariably ask him what his fee was. He would shake his head in amazement that somebody would think such a thing. A Christian going around doing the lord's job for a fee? Give me a break!

There certainly were a lot of odd ideas floating around

out here. The other day he saw some old goof balls in North Hollywood picking up trash at the park and he shook his head again. That's what the Mexicans are for. Then there were those people who pay good money for plastic bottles of just plain old water at the supermarket and carry them with them everywhere they go, taking swigs every fifth or sixth step. He would call his father whenever he saw anything goofy like this and the two would just sit and tsk tsk tsk together.

Champ told him once how he got his pot from Tiffani for free. All he had to do was just leave a donation on the counter. Felix told him once that he got something called an honorarium instead of a fee for judging talent. He remembered, too, going to the annual free church breakfast where all he had to do was throw a free will offering into a basket on the way through the line.

He knew that when he was doing the lord's work, he couldn't pass around the collection plate like they did at Saint Theresa's whenever the church needed a new roof or furnace or something. He couldn't take a big shiny plate in with him and hand it to just that one person. That would seem goofy unless he considered getting a bigger conjugation.

Plenty of possibilities out there, and since it just simply wasn't the right thing to do to ask for a fee, the idea about a donation or an honorarium or a free will offering might be the perfect solution. He would be able to continue to be fruitful and copulate. The word honorarium sounded right. It has that word honor right inside of it. It couldn't be any clearer or cleaner than that, an honorable man doing an honorable deed for an honorarium.

He had long thought about becoming a man of the cloth. On Career Day in grade school, he wrapped himself in his father's big, long white terrycloth bathrobe, tied his cowboy lasso around his waist, then walked around with his hands clasped tightly behind his back, his head bowed in deep theological contemplation. He often dreamed of hearing people's confessions on Saturday night, listening to all their sins about impure thoughts and actions and learning a bunch of new stuff, maybe even writing a book about it all, then telling all the penitrants to say three hail marys and three our fathers. One time he even went trick or treating dressed as a Franciscan friar. When someone answered the door, he would cast a blessing and chant BOX OF NABISCOS AHHHHHMEN!

Perhaps he had missed his calling. Maybe he will rethink things if this Hollywood thing doesn't pan out, maybe become a missionary in Russia even, where all the women have real curves. But then again in the pictures he had seen in National Geographic, a lot of the women looked a lot like a lot of the men and he didn't want to risk making the bad mistake of discovering too late that the woman he thought he was with was a lot more like a man than he had bargained for. One time he saw a photo of Nikita Khrushchev and his wife or her husband or whatever, bundled up against the frozen Russian hohum and he had sat there for hours trying to decide which one was Nikita and which one was his wife or her husband, or whatever.

But back to the roof over his head. He clicked onto his Sons and Lovers home page and bowed his head over the screen. It was time to set the plan into action, time to shake things up a little bit, take charge of his life, refine some things. He typed in his secret password, BFF4JMJ and hit the edit key.

No Fee Required.
Donations Only.
Honorariums Accepted.
Free Will Offerings Appreciated
Services 24/6
No Services on the Lord's Day

He wasn’t sure how much of a donation, honorarium, or free will offering to require. He did the figuring, but had too many unanswered questions. This wasn’t the same kind of thing that Tiffani did. It wasn't the same kind of thing Felix did. It was different from the church breakfast. He was on his own with this.

Felix had told him one time about the young men and women who worked the sidewalks at night along the east Hollywood, Santa Monica and Sunset Boulevards doing the lord's work, only he didn't refer to it as the lord's work, but rather something very unchristian-like. It might do Felix some good to get out there and do a little prostituselytizing himself for the lord.

As a child Heathcharlesharley listened to his father talk shop at the supper table about price quotes and mark-ups and mark-downs, and profit margarines. He figured he would need to do the same thing. Get the goods, his father would say. He would travel over to the east side on Saturday night and ask some questions about their donation policies. He was quite a chip off the old block. "Sir! Yes, Sir!"

Beth Ann was beginning to believe that there was no hope left. When she informed Harriet that she was being summoned to England to administer the inspirational benediction to a loving couple on their day of betrothal, well, frankly, Harriet was not at all sympathetic to her or to the occasion. She just flat out said NO, in capital letters, then sent her down to Human Resources, where someone in a quiet room started asking her questions about her younger life, her disappointments and failures, what made her tick and the like. She, Beth Ann, had been specially trained in those matters as a metaphysical counselor, so she knew a rat when she smelled one.

But then she found her salvation at church. There he was, sitting right next to her in the pew and she marveled at the rapture of his attention to Brother Joseph. He was truly connected. Her physiognometer was flashing spinach soufflé green up and down the radar screen. After the service, he offered his arm and assisted her to the parking lot. He was a doctor, he told her. And indeed he was, a Dear Dear Doctor. When she tearfully told him her tale, he sternly advised her to come over to his office first thing on Monday morning for a look-see. It sounded a lot to him like there was some hazard in the workplace that was precipitating these conditions. It is not too unusual for chemical solutions, dyes, plastics, lack of sufficient fresh air, the dizzying effects of working high in the sky, and many other factors that affect the health of the employees who are forced to work in little cubicles in those new modern high rise towers. “Often times,” he told her, “these allergies and reactions only affect certain employees and often times even with different manifestations of the same symptoms, which then become difficult and confusing to identify and diagnose. That could be why no doctor has been able to find anything out of the ordinary. Sometimes they even seem almost silly to the uninformed or the insensitive. Furthermore,” he added, “medical experts are uncovering more and more hazards of the modern day work environment, but concerted efforts by manufacturers, engineers, and construction companies manage to squelch any attention from the media.”

Later, in his office, he conducted his tests, his bushy black eyebrows furrowed in concentration and concern as he reviewed his findings. “Hmmm... my, my. What have we here,” he murmured softly, then clutched her deeply into his broad bosom, holding her there as he murmured quietly into her ear his apologies for the unforgivable treatment she had received from a medical system that was becoming increasingly more and more devoid of sympathy and understanding of the emotional and spiritual needs of the patient, of a medical system that is unconnected and unconcerned about the complexities of the modern work environment, about a medical system that has become a medical industry more concerned about protecting the bottom line of their stockholders than the better health of employees across the country.

She knew immediately that the good doctor was right as rain. She hadn't thought about the possibility of such things. Now things were becoming clear. After all, these symptoms really didn't arise until after she moved with Harriet over to one of those cubicles in one of those new modern high rises in Century City.

“Another thing,” he added, handing her a business card.

"You will need to retain this attorney. He has experience in this kind of problem. He can help you."

In return, Beth Ann clutched him deeply within her bosom, lingering there for several moments, wishing indeed that he were a younger, slimmer man, maybe one with a distinctive accent. But that would be entirely too much to ask for. But she was grateful for what befell her there.

She slowly left his office, thumping and tightroping to the elevator down, at long last at peace with her convictions. Sometimes help doesn't come until the darkest hour. To think that she would actually find her salvation right there in church, sitting in the pew right next to her and not standing in the front next to the organ. That dear, dear doctor. He had been sent to her by the Divine Intervener, she was sure. No more "OH MY GAWD" 360's. No more "WHATS!?" No more "NOT AGAINS?!?! Now it was YES YES YES to Jolly Old England. Sometimes life is good.

Felix arrived at the yeshiva to find dirty wretched chickens stuffed into dirty, stinking cages stacked five high in the courtyard, and he knew that his students would not be in his classroom on this day. Instead they will be receiving instruction on how to hold a chicken by its head and swing it around over their heads in ritualistic death. Felix walked up to his classroom, preferring not to be a witness. Later the boys would enjoy the chickens prepared under the strict supervision of the rabbi in charge. Felix would skip that as well.

It seemed there was a ritual for everything, with each rabbi claiming his own specialty, that rabbi down there in the courtyard sharing his chicken swinging expertise. A fat rabbi on the second floor specialized in kitchen kosherness. A wispy, elderly rabbi, Rabbi ZZ Top, came equipped with a super-long, razor-sharp, notched thumbnail to perform circumcisions. Zip, Zip, Zip. Just like that. He had done it a thousand times as a young rabbi in Russia. He could do it in his sleep. Although more modern techniques and equipment are now used, he kept his tool in tip-top shape, should there ever be a request for the more traditional approach. There were rabbis who supervised the bar mitzvahs for the boys and bat mitzvahs for the girls, celebrating their coming of age and their responsibility to adhere to Jewish law on their own rather than under their parent's supervision, and they would often rival a wedding celebration in extravagance. There were administrative rabbis and rabbis who were strictly teaching rabbis, and others who spent all of the time in deep meditation and prayer, surfacing only when an expert opinion on intricate doctrine needed rendering.

But they all performed something simply called a mitzvah, an act of charity and kindness performed anonymously. One time, someone changed a flat tire on Felix's truck when it was parked at the yeshiva and it was done in the rain and dark and he never learned who had done it, even though he had asked some discrete questions on who and how. Sometimes bagels or cookies were left for him on his desk or on his truck seat, or a pay raise that nobody fessed up to. So Felix was kind to all of them, just to make sure he had all the bases covered.

Felix spent a lot of his down time up on his balcony, enjoying his fix of the poseys that were always in bloom under his feet. From there, he had a bird's eye view of the courtyard and the walkways on the two floors. It was like watching the nightly news, coming on every night, right at 6:00, everything predictable one day after another, just like clockwork, people leaving for work every morning at precisely the same time, then returning in the early evening precisely at the same time, their routines so finely perfected that they know within a minute or so how long they need to get to work, and deviating only on Fridays when the commute required an extra seven and a half minutes.

Sometimes it was like comedy on demand, starring Beth Ann tight-roping down to the garage for her doctor's appointment; or Heathcharlesharley following his overbite across the second floor walkway, leaving on his nightly pilgrimage, his black fedora on his head, his briefcase swinging at his side; or

Tiffani's clients moving quickly, stealthily up the back stairs, then retracing their steps ten minutes later, not so quickly and quietly, but more happily.

Tiffani would enjoy the shows that aired under her balcony, as well. A little porno here and there, a little Candid Camera, spying on those who did fun little things in the pool or the hot tub beneath her when they didn't think anyone could hear them or see them. She would quietly slip onto the balcony, camouflaged by the dark, whenever she heard someone switch on the whirlpool motor in the late evening when it was safely dark. Then she would wait for the action. One evening, she watched Felix spanking the monkey and she succumbed to the temptation. Taking careful aim, finely tuned from all the precision egg tossing at the Otsego Arms directly behind the Villa Verdugo, she lobbed her big, black rubber dildo into the boiling, churning water. He hadn't noticed until it bobbed up to the surface. He picked it up to see what it was, dropped it quickly, glanced up at her darkened balcony, grabbed his towel and hurried off. She hid behind the Venetian blinds, struggling to stifle her irrepressible laughter at such a show, then when the coast was clear, went down to reclaim her property. Sometimes life is good.

Beatrice watched a different channel from her balcony late every morning after she returned from Runyon Canyon. She would brew tea and sit in the shade of the towering jacaranda that hovered over her head and watch the drama on Hesby Street unfold in front of her. It was a little bit Leave it to Beaver, a little bit Joe Friday. The Villa Verdugo was surrounded by quiet bungalows where men mow their lawns and spray water on their roses. She would watch short, thick legs carry Champ down to the lunch shift at Epic Heroes. On trash day, she would watch the homeless or the underpaid pushing overloaded supermarket shopping carts down the middle of the street, stopping at every trash container to scavenge for recyclables, sorting them into huge billowing white bags attached to the cart, then redeeming it all for cash at Ralph's around the corner at Vineland and

Magnolia. She would watch Tony, the guy who lived in Apartment 106, fix cars at curbside, hunched under the open bonnet, a flashlight in one hand, a screwdriver in the other. She knew the cars of the neighbors, the cars of their friends and relatives who visited on regular schedules. She knew when someone got a new car. She knew that people parked their cars in the same space in the evenings. She knew what time they came and went. She knew when she saw a car that didn't belong.

It all served in helping to keep the home front safe, watching for things out of the ordinary, or for intruders who knew how to slip in when the automatic gate was opened in the garage by someone coming or going, or who would walk in behind someone who was buzzed in at the front door. If someone did breach the perimeter, the alarm was immediately sounded, everyone on full alert, a weapon of sorts in one hand, a cellphone in the other. A high wire fence wrapped around the property, and there were highly visible security cameras at all of the gates and entrances, but there wasn't anybody sitting at a gray steel desk somewhere watching a monitor. The cameras weren't really hooked up to anything. There was no filming going on, but they did have a blinking, glowing red light on them. “Uh oh, security cameras. Let's go somewhere else.”

Frankie had finished with the red scraps and the yellow scraps. They were all sewn together and laying in two gigantic heaps in the middle of the table. Lily had admired them and obeyed Frankie’s orders not to play with them, not to knock them off the table and not to sleep on them. The green pants and green shirts hung on big wooden hangers from the overhead ceiling fan. Frankie sat there with a needle and thread and the scissors, clipping and sewing little snips of black and green and brown and orange, sculpting bodies, stitching wings, attaching thorax, creating, ripping out, recreating. Felix told him he was like Epimetheus hunched over his work table creating the lower animals with all the really good parts and leaving nothing real cool for his twin Prometheus to create man.

He worked long into the evening every evening. Time was running short, and he had to make everything twice, once for himself and once for Ricky. Barbara had cleared the way, receiving permission to bring a couple of additional guests along with her to the affair, so Frankie and Ricky had been added to the guest list. Ricky would fly out for the long Valentine's Day weekend. They could hardly wait. It was the social affair of the season and they were invited guests and everything needed to be just perfect. Frankie called Ricky and insisted that he get undressed and measure everything, then Frankie jotted down the numbers on his note pad.

"Inseam. Check."

"Waist. Check."

"Chest. Check."

"Shoe. Check."

"Hand. Check."

"Sleeve. Check."

"Neck. Check."

"Hat. Check."

Then one thing led to another and other measurements were made on both ends of the line and they were the same measurements as before, but it's a man thing, always double checking to see if age or the pull of gravity was having any beneficial influence at all. They giggled as they played. Such was a long distance relationship. Then he called his mom to tell her all about it, the party, that is, and she asked him to get George Hamilton's autograph while he was there.

Barbara found her dress in a vintage clothing shop on Melrose. Felix had been with her and they went on a Saturday afternoon when Mainstream was closed and all the shops along Melrose were open. Felix knew all the shops. He worked in the neighborhood and after school would stroll the avenue, stopping for a Cuban steak sandwich at an Argentine restaurant there, or visiting the Groundlings Theater for an improvisational show, then stopping for an apple turnover and coffee at the bakery across the street afterwards. He told Barbara about Sosi's little shop, So N' So's. It was there that they found the dress, which had been born in the Roaring Twenties and nodded an acknowledgment to the elegant influence of a Louis Comfort Tiffany vase. She had had her season in the sun, and then retired quietly from public life, hanging out in a cavernous closet of a Norma Desmond on Sunset Boulevard until finally released by estate executors and consigned for sale. Barbara was not a broad broad so Sosi at So N' So's sewed and sewed so that the red red rose rose readily, rosily from the stem at the hem to the bud at the bust.

Chapter 22

Beth Ann was fully packed a week before her plane left LAX for the long non-stop flight to Heathrow. She checked her passport and the amount of unused credit still available on her charge card. She had selected the necessary herbs and aloes that she couldn't live without from the long row of bottles on her counter. She never did travel very well so she checked and double checked to make sure she would have what she needed to make the journey a little more comfortable. She knew she would become crabby so she packed her anticrabby supplements and her pillow, and the two Gideon bibles she always traveled with. She had her cane for comfort, conversation, balance, and long airport lines. She packed her new bra and her lacy undies just in case lightning should strike. Be prepared, like a good girl scout, and leave nothing to chance. She smiled at the prospect of serendipity, stumbling into a young, nice-looking, slender Brit with a charming accent, someone with a belief in a higher authority and she didn't mean that old queen sitting on a throne.

She had informed the airline when she bought her ticket that she was a handicapped person and inquired if they would be a dear and have a wheelchair waiting for her at curbside. "Please make sure it is not one of those damn motorized things," she warned them. "I know what those are all about, thank you very much," she told them with a chill and a shiver.

“One.” Thump.
“Two.” Thump.
“Three.” Thump.
“Four.” Thump.
“Five.” Thump.
“Ahem. Ahem.”

Beatrice had promised to drive her to the airport and Felix reluctantly agreed to shout “Mama's Home! Mama's Home!” twice a day when he went in to feed Archie and Veronica. Then she moved on to what would be expected of her once she arrived at the wedding, an event that must be celebrated with special ceremony. She knew she would be expected to evoke the grace and beneficence of the spirits that minister to such matters upon the gathering assemblage. She would make the sacrifice of the time and the money and the ordeal of an arduous voyage nearly halfway around the world to insure the marital bliss of the betrothed. But that is the price to pay when one has a special calling. After all, she had received exhaustive instruction on that duty as a student practitioner of her church in Santa Monica. She would dig deeply into her repository of skills and do everything necessary to ensure the perfect peace and prosperity of the pair and all who gathered for them.

Felix would not be going to the big, big bash in Benedict Canyon. Instead, he was opening act at a club on Sunset, Saturday night, Valentine's Day, to boot. The place would be packed. Already, a full week before the show, he was sweating about it, thinking about it long into the night as he lay there waiting to fall asleep, thinking of every possible worst case scenario. He always did that. He asked himself why he put himself through this ordeal if it frightened him so much, costing him hours of sleep as he tossed and turned, unable to eat or drink anything, unable to hold the mike, always eying that big black door with the green exit sign above it, always running his routine through his head again and again and again, waking up in the middle of the night with the routine running through his head. It exhausted him.

It was the same battle every time he booked a commercial or a role in a movie or a TV show, running the lines through his head all night long, even when it was only three or four words, like thinking of all the ways that the words “just right for the handyman” could be delivered, again and again and again.

But it was on a comedy stage where he fought the hardest. He was always afraid that he wouldn't measure up to someone's expectations. It was residue from the past, but this is now. So why can't he grow up and grow out of it? On the other hand, maybe it is because people will listen to him now, if he has something funny to say. People like him when he makes them laugh. They find him attractive, sexy. Who doesn't like to feel that way? Maybe everyone is a stand-up comic at heart. They remember their favorite jokes to tell at parties. They feel great when they get a good ad lib off. “I want to make you laugh. I like you to like me.”

Thoreau was right, that all men do live a life of quiet desperation. Desperate to make others laugh. A desperation to please others in order to please themselves. Perhaps a desperation to laugh at themselves. John Donne meditates that “No man is an island, entire of itself,” and therein lies the problem. We are not finally free from desperation and need until the eclipse of final consciousness. So which is which and what is what? Maybe it's just better to leave things like that for other minds. One can get lost in the labyrinth if one goes too deeply into it, and there is a minotaur lurking in here somewhere, as well.

He thought of the time he told Beatrice about his trouble with stage fright, hoping that the answer girl had a trick up her sleeve. She said it was simple. “Just put it out there for the audience to see. Use it as part of your act,” she advised.

“What do you mean,” he asked.

“Make it your own.” Just go out there and tell them that you are nervous up there and the only way you can combat that is by imagining that they are all naked down there. Then just eyeball the room for a little while from left to right. Ogle. Stare. Smile. Frown. Shake your head. Let everybody get a good laugh out of it."

He thought it sounded like a good idea, so he tried it out on a Friday night show in a club on Melrose. He took the stage, looked around at the audience for a few moments, then, in his nervousness, told the audience, "Okay, you are all nervous down there and the only way I can combat that is by being all naked up here."

So there he was, trapped, going right from the fry pan and into the fire and he was stuck there. So he ended up having to do his entire act with his hands in front of his crotch, hiding his privates from prying eyes. But the audience thought it was hilarious. Someone in the crowd shouted out at him to join a gym and everyone goes ha ha ha. Then a cute babe approached the stage and handed him an unfolded bar napkin to hold in front of him and asked if he would be a dear and everyone thought that was a hoot, to boot. Ha ha ha. Everyone's a riot. It seemed like it took forever to get through his routine and when he was done, he had to exit the stage, sidling sideways like a horseshoe crab, and they all thought that was funny, too. Beatrice said there was no hope for him. That it is what it is and will always be. "We don't live in a perfect world," she told him.

Tiffani sucked on her hookah, pushed the pause button, and sat deep in thought, taking a break from the Gigantica Titantica Atlantica Disastica. The monitor stared motionless in the darkness, frozen in place like a great silent, unblinking eye of an Edgar Allen Poe character, waiting. She was finding it a little difficult to concentrate. This new development was weighing heavily on her, a lot like the old times back in East Saint Louis. She didn't want to return there.

Things weren't easy back then. But she was just a little girl taking things in stride. You just rolled along. Nobody really had much. Everyone else she knew was in the same boat, the kids at school and the others out in the streets, just rolling along, pretty much powerless to do anything about it anyway. You have a different eye for things when you're a kid. Things happen that you don't understand until later, when you're all grown up and look at things with a grown-up's eye.

Her mother lived with a dead end man in a dump of a place on a dead end street, one that even Santa dreaded, saving it for last and then hurrying through with what little bit he had left in his bag, basically, the little kernels left over at the bottom of the popcorn bag, before heading back north, glad to be all done with that section of town for the year.

Back then, about a week or so into each month, there would be a banging on their door and Mama would open the curtain a crack to see who it was, then quickly turn off the TV and hide behind the sofa until the pounding stopped. It was the landlord coming around for the rent. She grew weary of that so she and her boyfriend did decide to move. Tiffani was excited. Christmas would be far better now. But when her mama moved, she didn't take her little girl with her, instead telling her that she would be back to get her just as soon as she could. So she stayed put, living with her uncle. She waited and waited, daily looking up and down the street, hoping that each time a car approached, it was her mother. Whenever the phone rang, she was sure it was her mama and she would race to pick up the receiver. But she never called.

Then one afternoon her uncle told her he thought he knew where her mother was. She begged him to take her there. He didn't want to at first, saying he didn't have the gas money, but she didn't let up until he finally agreed. At first they didn't know if they were at the right place, but then she saw her mother's car. She was so excited and happy. It had been a year since she had seen her. She ran to the door and knocked. Then she saw a curtain move, and heard the TV go off. She knocked again, louder, but there was no answer. She kept knocking and knocking, and shouting, “Mama, Mama! It's me! Tiffani!” Then she went around to the side of the house and climbed up the electric meter to knock on the window. There she saw her mother hiding from her behind the sofa like she did whenever the landlord came by for the rent.

She was only thirteen, but she became an adult that day. She cut the ties. She didn't talk to people much after that, and when she did, she didn't trust anything she heard. She didn't believe a thing. As soon as she could, she was out of there. It was the U.S. Army the first day after she was done with high school. Then LA. Now, whenever someone would ask her about her family, she would just tell them that all of her people were gone. They were all dead, that she was the only one she had left. If they pressed for the details, she would make up stories all the time that seemed to satisfy their curiosity. She was so convincing that she would often bring herself to tears, stepping out of the reality of things, telling how she wished it had been as though that was the way it had been. There was comfort there. The truth just wasn't anybody's business. She knew now what the truth was. She's all grown up now and has the adult eye thing going on. Sometimes mothers aren't meant to be mothers. They don't know how to be mothers. They didn't learn from their own mothers, or they learned the wrong way about things. But all that was in the past, and there was no sense going back. She didn't just have to roll along taking things as they happened. She controlled the roll of the dice now. Someone push her? She push back double time. Simple as that.

Right now she just needed a little time to gather her thoughts about the matter. She was careful at first, making sure the blinds were closed, the scented candles lit, the windows shut, the door locked. They would huddle in the bedroom behind closed doors in fellowship. But after so many years of safe sailing, she relaxed a little bit. This was LA and people are more tolerant. But not everyone was. So she would need to tighten things back up. The last thing in the world she wanted was a visit from the POLICE!

Beatrice was beginning to feel uneasy. She wasn't sure why. There wasn't anything to support the uneasiness. It was just that kind of feeling you sometimes get when things are going too well. Who and what do you trust? Maybe it was her inner voice. Maybe it was just the smog in the air. But there was no need to panic just yet, not until there was something more tangible. She left Richmond in the middle of the night. Then she left Miami in the middle of the night. Then it was off to Phoenix. She grew more careful, but she ended up growing a tail there. She had underestimated him. She didn't think he would want to spend so much time and energy finding her, that he would move on to another target. She left in the middle of the night again and headed to Las Vegas. She wasn't there for very long until his goons showed up. She thought she would be safe there. People go there to hide, but some creep found her anyway. The place was creepy with creeps. She had been tripped up by her cellphone. They send out a traceable signal when someone is talking on one. Police use it to locate people all the time. A lawyer knows lots of police types. All he would have to do is call in a marker, or bribe or blackmail someone. She left in the height of the Friday evening rush hour to make it tougher to be tailed, and before she left, she mailed her cellphone to her old pal Peaches in Atlanta and asked him to use it for a while. Let the creeps waste a lot of time looking for her there. It's a big town and it would take them a while to realize that she wasn't there.

Then it was four hours down the road to Los Angeles and the Villa Verdugo, where things had been safe and quiet. LA is huge. If someone were looking or listening for her, she would be hard to find here. Eight months now, her longest stay yet. She was beginning to think that maybe the gentleman had thrown in the towel, given up, moved on to someone else for his amusement.

Then yesterday her phone rang. She had an unlisted number and caller ID, but the incoming number had been blocked. “Restricted,” it read. When it rang again later, she just picked it up and listened. There was a hesitation on the other end and then the hang-up. It could just be a coincidence. Maybe it was just bad phone manners. Lots of Yankees are guilty of that.

If they dial a wrong number, they don't apologize. They don't say, "Sorry, love." They just hang up without a word if they don't recognize the voice.

It had all made her uncomfortable. She had learned as a young girl to put total trust in her intuitions. She knew the brain could pick up subliminal messages, things that didn't surface right away, but were rolling around in the subconscious. Something had tripped a neuron, perhaps. On the other hand, perhaps it was just that time of the year, the February blahs. Maybe it's a biorhythm kind of thing. Was she becoming paranoid, suspicious? Maybe it was nothing at all. But she couldn't be sure about that and she did trust her basic instinct.

She would be even more careful now. It might be a good idea to take different routes in her routine. She would always be ready to go, not doing anything that would restrict an abrupt departure. She would buy only what she needed for a day or two. She would make sure the Jaguar always had a full tank of petrol, ensure that her new derringer was well oiled and loaded. She wouldn't let her guard down, though, until she knew for sure. She would be a little more careful about hiding behind loose disguises. Her owlish sunglasses, the long blonde wig that made her look so fetching, her floppy straw bonnet that signaled who she was and that she wore to Runyon Canyon and Trader Joe's, would all need to be changed.

Change is always good, she always told herself, in the best of times and in the worst of times. She tried to see this predicament as a game. It helped her deal with things, added a certain funness to it, pretending sometimes to be a movie actress taking on different roles, different guises, becoming someone else.

True actors hide from who they are, externally as well as internally. They are all impersonators. Liars, pretenders, hypocrites, charlatans, quacks, fakes, forgers, ringers. All actors. She can do that. Live a life as a liar in a town full of liars. Maybe that's why the gentleman hadn't come calling. He couldn't find out the truth about anything here. "Beware, all ye seekers of truth." On the other hand, a good liar can spot another good liar. Maybe it's just a matter of time. He is spot on in his game and so is she, a battle between the liars and so far she is the better liar of the two.

Like the other times, when the time comes, she would leave in the middle of the night. She doesn't need any sloppy goodbyes. It's all just a part of the illusion. She would be gone. She wouldn't be missed for a few days. Then it would dawn on someone. Where'd that girl go? That girl in the long blonde wig and the sunglasses. Someone would look through a gap in the Venetian blinds and see nothing but a cheap plastic Adirondack chair. Someone would show up later asking about her whereabouts and no one would know. Her role in that movie would be over. The list of credits would roll off the screen and the script would gradually fade from her memory. The slate would be clean. She would step into a new role in some new picture show set somewhere unknown out there where she would learn the new lines, play the new play, lay the new life.

The Mayflower Club was having their Valentine's Day Dance tomorrow evening. She would be British again. Be Beatrice again. She hummed as she dusted and polished the cobwebs from the corners of her carefully guarded core.

Felix saw the young boy swinging a bottle of vodka back and forth as he strode down the hall. In any other school across the country, the parents would be summoned immediately to pick up their child at the local police precinct. But at the yeshiva, it was nothing unusual, just another ritual. It just simply meant that a farbrangen was in the offing, a religious ritual meant to lead the young acolytes into an inebriated state so that the walls of inhibition would come tumbling down like the Walls of Jericho, allowing them the freedom to release their carefully concealed doubts about some doctrine, to express their pent up frustrations about their roommate or the bad breath of a rabbi, to give voice to family secrets, to reveal who had hidden the bicycle in the bushes for an after-hours excursion off campus.

The typical farbrangen would begin in the late afternoon. Sometimes it was planned and sometimes it was spontaneous. But it always meant that once again Felix would have his classroom to himself, and that tomorrow and perhaps even the day after that, they would lay in bed still under the influence of its theology. The boys sit around the Rosh Yeshiva in the third floor shul in solemn silence. In front of them stand liters of vodka, like soldiers in the Salvation Army, and stacks of small paper cups, the size used by In-N-Out Burgers for single servings of ketchup. Each student pours his prescribed dose and then waits respectfully for the leadership and the requisite prayer. Then with a nod from the Rosh, a slow sip is sucked between testing lips, followed by grimaces and gasps as the vodka keeps its 100-proof promise.

It starts slowly. The boys sing softly. In unison.

"Hava nagila, hava nagila."

Between sips. They pray. They sway. Back and forth. Gently. Like a raft in the lake. They sing.

"Louder, boys!"

"HAVA NAGILA! HAVA NAGILA!"

They pray.

"Louder!"

HAVA NAGILA ! HAVA NAGALI! VI NIS' MECHA!"

They warm. They drink. They dance arm in arm around the table, lustily. They stomp. They pray.

"Drink up, boys!"

Shots are tossed. Like learned sailors.

"Play, boys!"

The dancing. Oh, the dancing!

"On the tabletops, boys! Sing, boys!"

Shake! Rattle! Roll! Crescendo! Dionysus!"

Phew! Time to rest.

"Quiet, boys!"

The purpose met, the boys are free. The walls have fallen. The lips are loose. The confessions begin.

"You tell me a secret. I tell you a secret."

The Rosh, who had Cyclopean walls to breach, who bore the heaviest weight, who held the strongest inhibitions, who harbored the greatest doubts, who had the most to release, leads the charge, bursting forth with long and plaintive wails that resonate far beyond the ivied walls confining the boys to the campus, walls that no cases of vodka, no fanfare of trumpets would ever bring tumbling down. The vigorous investigations and inquisitions stretch late into the night and into the early sunrise of the next morning. Then the youngsters, their mind free from the guilt of unkempt secrets, their conscience rid of unkept promises, their soul purged of the stain of doubt, their stomachs tossing their salads and pizzas and breadsticks and vodka along the way, follow the walls down three flights of stairs and across the back parking lot to dormitory rooms to fall into neat beds and messy slumber.

Chapter 23

Lily adored Frankie. Frankie left the toilet seat up so that she always had a fresh supply of water. That certainly wouldn't have been an option in Heathcharlesharley's bathroom, where the toilet seat was always up as well, but there was no fresh water there to enjoy. Heathcharlesharley said it was an ongoing study called Moonstones in the Sea of Tranquility. Frankie had discovered her tickle spot and nightly before bed, he would oblige her and she would lay at the foot of his bed and giggle away. He was still staying up late at night. The snipping continued, but Singer was silent now. Lily had to admit that she missed Singer's singing. Funny that he would be called a singer when he was actually more of a hummer, knowing only one note and all. Ruby was the singer. She and Champ. Maybe when Ruby was back on her feet, the four of them could get together for a jam session. She, Lily, would bring the jam. It would be a Strawberry Jam Session.

One of her friends back at the adoption agency once told her of another member of the human orchestra, if you wanted to call it that. It wasn't a humming or a singing. It was a horrifying HAROOOOOOOOOMMMMMing. Then her friend lowered her voice and whispered so that no one else would hear it, like when humans lower their voice when they say the word cancer.

"He's called Hoover." But the others heard and trembled.

One screamed. Someone else fainted. Another ran into the arms of his brother. No worse or more frightening sound anywhere on the world. As soon as Lily heard about it, of course, she wanted to hear what one sounded like. She was curious about things like that. In fact, she was curious about just about everything. But she would never know, though, for as long as she would live in Apartment 107, the voice of Hoover.

Lily watched Frankie stand in front of the full-length mirrors for the entire evening adjusting things, intent on his work, oblivious to anything else, fixing, snipping, stitching until everything was perfect. He would have to do it again when Ricky arrived. Now the finished project was hanging carefully on the backs of two chairs, two enormous, magnificent hats of roses in full bloom, one red one and one yellow one. And resting softly on the petals were monarch butterflies and beetles and smiling ladybugs, cut carefully from the red and brown and black velvet and whiskers and feelers of black pipe cleaners, and button eyes and bushy eyebrows and curly eyelashes, caterpillars that accordioned in and out, fireflies with aluminum fire. Attached to the green gloves were hummingbirds that fluttered when the hand moved. Pale green Luna moths hung delicately from the neckties; the pants and shirt studded with thorns fashioned from brown felt, and trains of black ants lined all the way up the pant legs in single file and up the green shirts and along the sleeves and up to the rose heads. Lily had to hand it to him. They were spectacular. They looked like they should march in the Rose Bowl Parade down the middle of Colorado Boulevard in Pasadena.

Heathcharlesharley made comments, of course, like "Some flowers never lose their flagrance." He couldn't believe it. It was another thing to call his father about. "Sir, you wouldn't believe it." No man in his right mind would ever dare wear anything like that back in Louisiana. They would be hanged, lynched from the big American elm tree on the lawn next to the courthouse. The whole town would attend. Someone would even set up a few rows of folding chairs for the old folks. People down there think about the needs of others.

Valentine's Day was looming large over the Southland. All stops would be pulled. The restaurants and nightclubs would be full. Tiffani had quite a day. The phone began ringing exactly at 3:00, nonstop. People get horny when they smoke pot. It all adds up to a pretty decent roll in the hay on the most romantic night of the year. She was worn out. This evening she asked her friends, one at a time, to be less visible. She locked the door, checked the balcony door and windows, and talked in a low voice.

Champ had talked to Frankie, who had used some of the left over costume material to dress the hookah up to resemble a fat Buddhist deity holding a fistful of serpents. One would have to look quite carefully to determine that it indeed was a hookah.

But for now, things were quiet. Business was closed for the rest of the evening. Dim-witted Harold was out guarding a mall loading dock somewhere, making sure no one would rifle through the dumpsters in the back area looking for stuff they could use or sell or eat. She returned to the computer screen. It was a big job, but someone, somewhere out there had to hold these people accountable. No one else seemed so inclined or thought it was so important. But that was what separated the sheep from the shepherd.

It hadn't been easy for Frankie to get the night off, the busiest night of the year for The Coral Reef, and the entire cast and crew were expected to be on duty.

"I won't ever ask again," he promised his boss. "Just this one night."

He was willing to quit if he had to, but he didn't tell the boss that. It would sound like a threat and he was a man of action and not threats. He could find another job if he had to. But the boss caved and so he didn't have to follow that route.

Ricky arrived for the weekend so Lily did not occupy her

usual position at the foot of Frankie's bed. She understood. She would be in the way. She knew that the heart wasn't the only thing that grew stronger in absence, and that they would be working well into the late night slaking their appetite for each other, that the heat would be intense, that the pistons would be pounding. They had a lot of catching up to do and not much time in which to do it. It was an interesting and amusing thing to watch. She had to admit that she was baffled during Christmas when she first viewed the human mating ritual, and she watched unabashedly from the front row seat until she received a wild heavy blow to the side of her face from an errant foot. Her curiosity satisfied, she slept with Champ on the sofa.

Heathcharlesharley had rolled open the closet door a foot or so so that he could hear the loud, sharp slaps against bare backsides, followed with the yips and the yelps. He would shake his head with disgust. It sounded like a couple of dogs in heat under his bedroom window on a hot, muggy spring evening in south Louisiana. He would certainly never feel closer to the lord doing that sort of thing. He wasn't HEATHENcharlesharley, after all. He called his father in the morning with a full report while Lily watched the two slip into the roses and listened as Frankie gave fledgling instruction to Ricky in butterfly fluttering, petal rustling, moth motion, lady bug bustling, and worm inching. Lily, unable to resist the temptation, leapt at the prey and Frankie had to chide her.

But this morning, things were not quite right. Frankie was nervous, tense, not himself. Lily had heard Ricky talking in a loud voice from behind the closed door and she didn't hear Frankie say anything. And when Frankie made the adjustments on Ricky's costume, Ricky didn't say a single word the entire time. Ricky just stood there continually pulling his shirt up over his nose and Frankie just knelt there, continually pulling it back down. Lily thought about getting the Dodge out of hell.

It was a big crowd, just as he had expected. Servers carried precarious trays of umbrella drinks and light lagers through narrow footpaths. Eight tiny cocktail chairs were wedged tightly around each tiny cocktail table. Pack 'em in. Make hay while the sun shines. The house lights were still on. People were still being seated. Once the lights went off, though, it was nearly impossible to navigate the route to the bathroom, having to excuse yourself all the way through the maze to the back of the venue and risking the public embarrassment of a trip, or raising the wrath of the comic in the process.

His hands were shaking. He wished they wouldn't. Just one time, he wished they wouldn't. After all these years, they still tremble. When will it ever be done with? Let no one see. “Remember to keep your hands in your pocket the whole time, except for the clapper part.” He wanted a cigarette, but there is no smoking in there, no more smoking in bars and night clubs anymore. Get used to it. All he had to do was twenty minutes. And then it would be all over, except for the next time, and the time after that, forever and ever after that.

Felix eyed the green exit sign above the big black back door. “You can leave now, if you like. Just walk right back there, push open the door, walk out into the back alley and be all done with it. Just disappear into the night. No one would come looking for you. No one would call the next day to ask where you went. People would already know.”

“He went out the back door,” they would say. He knew if he did that, that he wouldn't leave them hanging. Some fledgling comic could drop everything and be there in five minutes. No worry about that in Hollywood. Someone was always out there, on a list somewhere just in case. Ready at the drop of a hat, eager to take your place. “Sure, yeah, I'll be right there.”

Kappy Kipper was the headliner. The Kapper had put in his time. Some mud stuck, a sitcom being developed by Warthog Sisters. “You can do that, too, if you just stay. Get used to that, too.” It just wasn't fair, doing stand-up comedy. Whoever thought that was a good idea. It was especially so when you were having a bad night. There was no one to share it with, no one to blame it on. If you were on stage in a play that didn't go well, you could blame it on the director, or a ham actor that was particularly porky that night. If you were a singer and the crowd wasn't connected, you could blame it on the song or the arrangement or the conductor. There was always someone else involved so it didn't all fall in your lap. Like gang warfare. Share the blame, spread it around. But on a comedy stage, it was just you, by yourself, naked, alone, the spotlight on you, you, you, no one else. Nothing else is visible. When it went wrong? Guess what? It's You. You. You. Everything is your fault. You planned the menu. You set the table. You boiled the chicken. It was you who wrote the script, arranged the jokes, directed the action, performed the show, pulled the trigger. No one else. No one to share the blame with."

The people out there crammed around those tiny tables paid $40 to park, $40 admission. Then there is always a tip to lay on someone. If you're going to pay a lot of money for a ticket, you might as well go the rest of the way to insure a good seat, especially if you want to impress your date for the evening, especially on Valentine's Day. Shrewd insiders know how the system works. You carry two five dollar bills, one in each hand. You give the first five dollar bill to the usher and say, "What can you do for this?" He leads you to a seat close to the stage, but off to the side. Then you offer the second five dollars. "Okay, now how about this one?" and suddenly he spots a table in the front middle. Then there is that pesky two drink minimum, each person, appetizers, the twenty percent tip to the server, eight percent tax. At the end of the night, another five dollar bill helps the parking valet find your car much faster.

So the comic better be funny, better be worth it. Felix had heard other comics tell about being hit with flying shot glasses from disappointed audience members who thought they were being ripped off, or someone who thought he could add his own punch line, or they would find fault with something in the routine. Some of his comic buddies had performed on stages where chicken fencing protected the performer from the audience. He thought that only happened with bands playing in red-neck joints, but it doesn't. Anyone on a stage anywhere is fair game, actors, singers, dancers, piano players, bear baiters.

One night Felix worked with a comic who was getting heckled. The comic made the mistake. "If you're gonna be a heckler, you might as well be a good heckler," the comic said. Felix knew right away he had left himself open to the heckler. "If you're gonna be a comic, you might as well be a good comic," replied the heckler. That pretty much destroyed the rest of the comic's routine. That was the wrong way to shut down a heckler. Felix felt bad for the comic. "Awww... too bad. Sorry about that, Bro." It doesn't help much though. It's a personal, internal thing that a few nice words can't fix.

He had seen good comics deal with hecklers. They were cruel and ruthless right up front. Sometimes they stopped their show right in the middle of a joke and asked the bouncer to remove the offender. "Don't try to banter with them because they often can out-banter you," his friends told him when he was just starting out. Say something mean, like "Why don't you put a condom on your head. If you're gonna act like a dick, you might as well dress like one."

He needed a heckler like a moose needed a hat rack. So far, he had been lucky. There had been no moose around, but he knew that somewhere, at some time one would saunter into the picture. It was that old law of averages. Sooner or later, it was going to happen. One time, though, he did have to ask a table if they had learned how to whisper in a sawmill. Fortunately the table was good-natured about it and got the idea. But there was a first time for everything.

When he first got the idea that he would do stand-up comedy, he would memorize the jokes from Jay Leno's monologue from the night before and then deliver them to himself standing in front of his bathroom mirror. He didn't get nervous. There was no worry about hecklers. But he learned a lot from other comics when he moved from the bathroom to the clubroom. For a while he went on the road, crisscrossing the Midwest with Four Bucks Four Bucks, a group of four guys who would each do about twenty minutes in some roadside tavern or bowling alley for the four-dollar admission, split the money four ways, then drive to the next town and do the same thing all over again. It was a tough way to make a buck buck buck buck and the group disbanded when the wives of the two married guys in the troupe didn't think they were all that funny. And Two Bucks Two Bucks didn't work, no buck buck for the surviving buck buck. But the whole experience was good on-the-job-training, an opportunity to hone the craft, to learn how to deal with the vicissitudes of the biz, to learn how to handle the club managers who short-changed them, who slipped out the back door themselves when it was time to fork over the dough. He learned how to sleep in a Volkswagen Beetle, iron a shirt on the back seat, manage with bad sound systems and poor lighting, the drunks, the talkers, the juke boxes. It never did help with the nerves, though. No iron could press out that wrinkle, it seems.

Harriet sat at her desk at Vidematics, drumming her long fingernails against the glass top of her desk, the letter from Beth Ann's lawyer laying in front of her. She hadn't expected things to go this far. It all seemed rather sudden in some ways, but on the other hand, she should have seen this coming. With Beth Ann taking the first legal step, they would no longer have to be so discrete. It will bring things out in the open. Beth Ann had tipped her hand. Vidematics now had a clear path. They had been down this path before and knew the territory. The legal department would take one step at a time, first sending out an official letter to Beth Ann's lawyer, advising them that the notification of the pending lawsuit had been received and that they begin their investigation of the case. There would be nothing particularly nasty at this time. They would save that for later in case they need it.

This was simply a formality, the usual path taken when similar such situations arrived in their office. In the meantime, she would be approve Beth Ann's request for a leave of absence immediately until the situation could be appraised, in effect, removing her from the chessboard. It would give the petitioner time to rethink things. Sometimes people try to do something a little funny, thinking it's just a walk in the park, something they could get away with. She had seen it before. Someone files a suit, gets a doctor somewhere to sign off on it, maybe fib a little bit about chemicals in the carpeting causing chronic headaches and such things, thinking that the employer will accept some sort of settlement to avoid a costly legal battle, then kick off their work boots and slip on their loafers for the rest of their life. But when no settlement is offered and the principals are faced with the probability of an exhaustive investigation, their documents scrutinized, their doctors questioned, their friends and neighbors interviewed, and it looks like things are not going well, they start to get cold feet and back down, and the problem goes away.

In the meantime, the legal department would start to produce a defense. Security would put a little tail on her, follow her around for a little while, see what she's doing, check her computer to see if that turns up anything. It was a shame that it had come down to this. She sighed heavily, stared out the window momentarily at the Pacific Ocean visible from her twenty-fifth story corner office, and opened a valentine.

Heathcharlesharley thought that Valentine's Day was the perfect time for all the necessary footwork to determine how much of a donation to demand in his business of doing the lord's work. He knew that they would all be out in multitudes, searching the sidewalks and street corners and back alleys in the eastern reaches of Sunset and Hollywood Boulevards, looking for lonely souls to rescue, giving them a one-night valentine. He would ask the necessary questions. He had it all written down on paper and attached to his clipboard. He wistfully wished he had thought to bring along his priestly garbs from back home, the outfit he wore at Saint Theresa's High School production of “The Bells of Saint Mary's.” He thought he should keep it in case he actually did decide to become Father Superior Saint Thomas Aquinas, JMJ. Tonight he would wear his business suit. His name for tonight, the Right Honorable Superior Mr. Heathcharlesharley, LL Bean.

"What is the typical honorarium? Did they give money-back guarantees? Did they give little cards to be punched for each visit and then award freebies for the tenth time?" They did that where he got his haircut. One time, Beatrice told him they do that at the carwash down the street. Even though he never took advantage of it, he thought it was a good idea, good business practice. He was becoming more and more like his father, who built up a successful auto-parts store in Louisiana with "several locations conveniently located nearby for your convenience" by starting small and asking the necessary questions. He, too, would start small, ask the questions, get the roof built overhead, and pull away from his father's nipple at the same time.

Chapter 24

The three of them arrived together, arm in arm, a bouquet of red and yellow roses. A white-gloved footman opened the door for them, and then reading from the embossed card, announced their arrival. "Miz Barbara McGill, escorted by the Misters Frankie Anderson and Ricky Johnson."

Elie ran up to them, her hands over her mouth, speechless with excitement and pleasure. The orchestra softened, then stopped.

"Good evening," said Frankie.

Elie squealed, "Matma! Matma! Come see the talking roses!"

The orchestra broke into "Everything's Coming Up Roses." Aunts and uncles and exotic nieces circled the three, snapping photographs and posing with the three, talking excitedly in their native tongue while fingering the luxury of the lime green silk of her dress, gaping and gasping as a caterpillar inched, a butterfly fluttered, a ladybug danced, and ants flickered feelers. Everyone circled around them. And that is what Barbara wanted. After all, show biz is all about appearances. Making entrances.

Felix fingered the little index card in his pocket. It held tonight's line-up, his routine, the intro he had to make for Kapper

Kipper, all printed in his neat hand, meticulous. It was damp and limp now, but it was there. He would use the clapper routine, then his dog story. He knew them by heart, every little nuance, every little gesture, and every little look. He had to be careful though, not to be too practiced, act like it just popped into his head, like it was all just natural to him, like he was just one of those spontaneous guys who could just make it up as he goes along. He knew those who could and he was envious of them. It took him so long to develop a routine that worked. He could save so much time and maybe even his hands wouldn't shake. The folks back home loved the clapper thing. It always worked, like the zucchini thing. It seemed like an easy crowd tonight. He said hello and teased the audience for a little bit. They were cheerful. You never can tell. Friday night audiences were always the best. But this was Saturday night when anything can happen. He could do a show on a Friday night at a club and absolutely slay them. Then he could do the same show at the same club the next night and absolutely bomb. There was no figuring such things out. It was just the way things are.

"Lots of you wearing roses tonight."

Everyone looks around. Smiles and warmth.

"Every girl loves a rose. My mama always wears a rose. Every day. Back when she was eighteen, she had a red rose tattooed on her right breast. Of course, now it's a long stemmed red rose." Groans and chuckles. Good natured, it's fun. It's kind of worn, but no one takes any offense.

"My momma says I don't work hard enough. She says, "Son, I was in labor with you for twenty-four hours on the day you were born, and I haven't gotten twenty-four hours of labor from you since the day you were born."" He did it in his momma's voice and then kept the stern face, the poise for a long count. His face was good for this kind of stuff. The crowd connected. It was gonna be okay tonight. He relaxed a little.

"I told her I wasn't born on Labor Day. It's all her fault. She's not perfect. My mama's not perfect. She thinks she is," he says with a sneer. Folks think it's funny when he picks on his mama with a spoiled little brat persona. It's crazy how comedy works. Everybody thinks his own mama is perfect and everyone knows she isn't.

"You know what she always gives me for Christmas? What she always gives me for my birthday? What she always puts in my Easter basket? "You know the clapper? Yeah, the clapper. It's always the clapper. She gives it to me all wrapped up and says "Guess what?" Felix repeats it for emphasis in his mama's voice, "Guess what?"

"Oh, I don't know. I give up."

"Open it, honey!"

"I keep telling her. 'Mama, I already got fifty of those things.' She never remembers."

I have those things spread out all over the house."

"You remember the commercial on TV?

Felix sings. He takes his hands out of his pockets, needs to for this gag. "Clap on..." He clap-claps. "Clap off..." Clap-clap. "Clap on, clap off... the clapper." Clap-clap. The audience knows that ad. Someone usually sings along. It's on a million times a day on all the channels during the Christmas shopping season, along with the cha-cha-cha chia pet.

"The TV ad shows a little old lady lying in bed. She claps her hands and her TV goes off, the lights go off and she pulls the covers over her head and goes to sleep."

Felix eyes the audience, then solicits their sympathy. "Well, that's a problem for me. Every time I'm watching TV and that commercial comes on and she claps her hands, it turns off my lights and my TV."

It's cute. The mood is mellow. The house is humming. They sympathize with him.

"But that's not the worst of it. Whenever there's an good old fashioned gully-washer of a thunderstorm banging and clapping overhead, well, then I really have problems." Felix pauses. The audience imagines. Felix looks up at the sky warily, with fear and trepidation, ducks imagined lightning bolts, spooks at imaginary thunderclaps.

"Turns on the stereo, defrosts the refrigerator, warms up the soup, sets the alarm clock, the vacuum sweeps, the garage door goes up and down, the phone dials my girlfriend, the computer checks my email, the coffeepot brews coffee, the toaster makes toast, the bathtub fills up, the drapes open and close, the shower goes on, the lights go on and off, the toilet flushes."

This always works. It's not total knee-slapping material, but everyone always appreciates it. They can picture it. It's basically a no-brainer.

"I have to go around and clap everything back off. Takes an hour and a half." Felix starts walking around the stage, clapping here and there and everywhere, high and low, hither and yon, with great concentration, sincere and honest and busy.

"By the time I've finished, the dog is dancing in the middle of the living room. A long-stemmed red rose between her teeth. Ole!" Here he does a flamenco dance, making a complete turn while stomping his feet and clapping his hands above his head. "Ole!" The audience loves it, and applauds.

"I'm gonna put one of those clappers on my mama." He clap-claps.

Felix moves to the dog. He knows he has to move on. Keep things fresh. Keep the pacing. The light from the timer in the back of the room is still green.

"Yes, I have a dog. A golden retriever. I got her when she was still a baby."

A few people clap-clap. They have goldens, too.

"I thought I would earn some extra bucks. Breed her." He smiles benignly.

"Well, soon the time was right and she was ready and all the sixteen-year-old pimply-faced coon dogs from around the county were ready, lined up all the way down the driveway, halfway around the block, carrying little six backs of Busch Lite under their arms, cigarettes dangling from their lips, t-shirt sleeves rolled up, reeking with whatever they roll in that makes them smell so good."

Felix continues the persecuted persona, feel-sorry-for-me-attitude, the nothing-goes-right-for-this-poor-tortured-victim. The audience loves it. They laugh at the image and Felix's face. The yellow light in the back of the club switches on, time to wrap it up.

"She goes out for an hour or so and then comes back in."

Pause. Set it up.

"Her back dripping with saliva."

The folks groan and moan and laugh. They know what he means. They get the picture. Time now to wind things up.

"About eight weeks later she had thirty-two puppies. All with buck teeth. Big ears." Groans and laughs.

" Be careful tonight, ladies." Good exit.

The red light just in time.

"Okay, folks, speaking of buck teeth and big ears, time to introduce this next guy."

Felix finished up and took a seat to the side. It was okay. For a Saturday night, it was good. He didn't take any big risks tonight, didn't try to introduce any new material, no sense in tempting fate, no harm done. He was done. There was nothing to be ashamed of. He would hang around and close the show, reminding the folks to tip their server, then head home.

Champ was working the supper shift at Epic Heroes. Most of the staff had begged off. The place wouldn't be busy. No pussy in his right mind would take his hooker to Epic Heroes for Valentine's Day, not even the cheapskates, not unless he wanted to cut himself out of any fringe benefits that would come later on for good behavior. What the hell. He didn't have anything else to do. Nobody would be around at the Villa Verdugo, except for the hooker upstairs. But she was always busy watching some movie over and over and over again, eyes glued to the screen, stopping, rewinding, and watching again. He knew others who did that, watching the same movie until they knew all the words in it. Then they drive others to distraction, making them sit and listen to them recite it all.

It wasn't for him. He never went to movies. Movies were for pussies and hookers. That's all that people did around here. Movies. He'd rather be hanging out somewhere, with Ruby, or shooting pool, riding his motorcycle. He made a foot long Southwestern meatball hero and took it out the back door, propping the door open with a corner of the foot mat just enough to hear the ding-a-ling of the front door. That's what everyone along the boulevard did after the supper rush was over. Jimmy from Dairy Doodle. Barista Bob from the coffee shop. Eddie, the pie guy from Pizza Pizzazz. Teddy from Spaghetty-Freddi's. Lennie from Lankershim Tobacco, Liquor, and Lotto. They would all gather in the darkened alley behind the row of shops and lean against the wall or sit in the shelter of the delivery doors, keeping an ear posted, all the doors along the back propped open just enough. There would be no supper rush this evening so everyone would be out there early. They would trade. A deluxe epic hero for a loaded pizza or a venti mocha frappacino for a super-sized banana split. A pack of menthols for a pasta marinara. Someone would always have a doobie. They couldn't do that during the daytime though, when Big Man was on duty, and with the delivery trucks coming and going.

What the hell. Big Man didn't see everything. He didn't work nights. When he left, then you had your freedoms. Nobody was watching you. The night belonged to them, the night crew. There were no airs, nobody pretending to be someone else, nobody really giving a shit about stupid stuff. Sure, they had to play by the rules of Big Man, for a while anyway. They had no choice, except go back to Wheeling or Whiting. But Big Man rules there, too.

Parking is always a messy thing in LA, but particularly messy in the side streets of East Hollywood. Everything on those side streets there is messy, the debris of the sex trade; the sidewalks messy with expired hypodermics and yellowish Trojans, the butts of cigarettes, the empty pint bottles of Jack Daniel's and crumpled cans of diet Coke; the curbs messy with black Buicks and BMW's bucking and rocking, their windows steamy from the pantings of the pantless; the bushes and back alleys of seedy stucco bungalows messy with newspaper kneepads from anonymous blow jobs, the occasional pair of panties and mateless black socks.

Heathcharlesharley drove those messy side streets, cruising. He needed to park. He needed to go to The Boulevard where the souls were seeking salvation, to stand on the corner under the street lamp, to ask the questions, to conduct his research. He wondered if it were always like this, traffic stacked up on the boulevard, parking nonexistent, the sidewalks a temple with lonely Christians negotiating the lord's business. He felt alive, purposeful. He prayed for a spot as he circled. The lord heard him. "Thank you, Jesus," he ejaculated.

Woody was exhausted from the trip to England. He had received quite a workout, on duty full time at the two of the world's busiest airports. He had a backache from the heavy load he supported and blisters on his foot from jabbing Japanese travelers in front of her at the counter who were always asking far too many questions and those "annoying zigzagging lallygagging scalawags" who were always wandering around in her way, looking at television monitors and not watching where they were going, not caring that she was trying to get around them. And the embarrassment, oh the embarrassment! People would look at him as an accomplice, with a sneer, like he was a willing partner in all of this. He would shrug his shoulder and give a sheepish "don't blame me" grin and try to make the best of it.

Then at the Wakefield Arms, the check-in clerk, peering up over his reading glasses from under the darkish shade of his desk light, stared at this curiosity and wrinkled with incredulity as she thumped and counted. He shook his head and mumbled something inaudible which sounded a little like wanky fanny or Yankee fanny or something like that. Woody hung on the edge of the counter wishing he were firewood somewhere. Then up in the room, he sprained his leg when she used him to jack up the bed to slide a Gideon bible under each of the two legs of the headboard for the proper slant required for a good, healthy night's sleep.

But that was only the beginning. What happened at the wedding was something he would recount to his friends for decades, and they would shake their head in wonderment and disbelief. A day that would live on in infamy, a day that he thought he was actually, positively, absolutely, indubitably, unequivocally, inexorably, totally going to crack. He really should write a book about it all. It would be a venerable war story, but one with no medal for meritorious service. Maybe call it Citizen Cane. But that title was already taken. The Cane Mutiny. In his dreams... Already taken anyway. Cane and Abel. Cane and Unable? Raising Cane. Hmmm...

Frankie stood alone in the cool evening by the pool, its smooth surface dotted with red rose petals. Wafts of "The Days of Wine and Roses" emanated from the ballroom. The coolness of the evening was welcome. The air was clean and scented from the pines beyond the gardens. He felt free. It was a curious, strange feeling, a different kind of freedom even more than the one he felt on National Coming Out Day. Maybe it was the wine. He had never had wine before. People back home didn't drink wine. If they could see him now, they would talk about it. Frankie goes to California. First he becomes gay and now he drinks wine. Will wonders never cease. Then again, maybe it was the rose. Maybe he became someone else when he donned it, like Cinderella in the glass slipper. Maybe because Ricky, who was there, wasn't there. He moved quietly through the grass. In the evening shadows of the gazebo, the roses rested peacefully. He stepped gently into the garden and paused. He stooped, then knelt, feeling the greenness of the leaves, the power of its spikes, the sculpture of its spine. In the earthly aroma of its bed, a moth fluttered.

She saw him when he slipped out the back door. While

he lingered at the pool, finishing the last of his wine. Elie's talking rose. She watched with ancient brown eyes as he stepped into the yard and followed him as he found the circle of gardens. The creases in her face deepened when he bent over. She gathered her gown around her. Her daughter would remain in the big house, to play the hostess, to enjoy her friends, those with the painted roses on their toes and fingernails, those with the henna rose tattoos on their cheeks and on the backs of their hands, the nosegays on the wrists and ankles and rose leis draped around necks and wrapped around waists, the exotic roses in Valentino lapels and hand-painted rose ties and rosy gowns of raw silk.

In the gazebo, she sat, calm, serene. And she watched him, natural, young, pure, belonging in the garden among the others. And then he saw her. A worm inched. A ladybug lifted. An ant winked. Her dark eyes, young and fun again, beckoned him. “May I?” With a soft bow, he handed her the hat. For the moment in the rocky canyon of this America was she no longer the royal princess, the sister of a king, but a lullaby of pleasures, of her past and her presence, of her childhood and her children, of his magic and her majesty. She smiled, returned the hat, then turned her gaze back to the high ridges and dark pines in the sweet black air.

Beatrice pulled the shiny black Jaguar into the parking lot. It was already quite full. If she had waited any longer, she would have had to park a few blocks down Victory Parkway. She knew it would be. Brits always arrive early at the Mayflower, eager to reclaim their authority of being English. They would spend the time double-checking to ensure that all the conditions were right, doing little practice steps on the dance floor to see that it had been properly waxed and sanded, that the orchestra would pass muster, that the cooks in the kitchen were Brits and not Yanks, to check the bar.

“Make sure you have plenty of brown ales from New Castle and Marston's Pedigree. Boddington's. None of that damn Yankee beer, Love.”

Young children in English schools learn how to dance at a very early grade. Same time they learn the A, B, C's and the 1, 2, 3's. Her father filled in the gaps, showing her the fancier moves during the blistering, blustery cold winters on the Island of Jersey. The two would roll up the rug, move the table to the side, slip on their shoes, then swing to the tunes of Tommy Dorsey and Glenn Miller on the old Victrola. When it was all over, they would fall together into a heap in the middle of the living room in sweaty warmth and merriment.

Like the Jaguar, her high heeled black dancing shoes were freshly waxed and polished. She donned her long blonde wig one last time, and the black pullover turtleneck sweater that made her boobies boobier. She would move easily on the floor and off the floor. There were no strangers there that night. They had known each other for centuries. The Lord. Lady. Chambermaid. Barrister. Butcher. Courtier. Pipe-Fitter. Tory. Baker. Episcopalian. Candlestick Maker. From Londonderry or Swansea or Kingston Upon Hull, Birmingham and Manchester, worked in the East End or the West Side or Underground. But in America, they were all of one. They were all peers. They were all Brits.

The Charleston. She accepted the hand of a dapper man, quite like that man that had so dramatically changed her life. But this chap was a Brit and wouldn't be at all like that well-dressed Virginian gentleman with impeccable manners who could order properly from a wine list.

Where was her trusty old reliable radar during all of that? The answer was simple. “Really quite simple, Sherlock,” she told herself. “Cupid’s Arrow.” Perfect Aim, Right Smack in the Heart, Deep, Dead Center, Head Over Heels. What could she do? She did not choose to fall in love. No one ever chooses to do that. No one wakes in the morning and says, “Well, I guess I’ll go out today and fall in love somewhere.” Or, “I guess I'll fall out of love this morning. Shop around and see who else I can find to fall in love with. Then stop somewhere for lunch.” She did a nifty traveling kick. And there are no ground rules.

Anyone and everyone is fair game, the possibilities unlimited when Cupid's arrows go aflying every which way. The woman falls for the man. The man falls for the woman. The young fall for the old. The man for the man, the woman for the woman. The thin for the fat. The tall for the short. The young and the skinny for the old and the fat. The man and the family dog. We are Brits, after all. She giggled, then bowed to her gentleman and returned to her seat. She loved her wig, but it sure was hot. She lifted the edge of it a little bit and mopped up.

Oh, the Lindy. "Yes, Love. I would love to dance. Thank you, Love."

Heathcharlesharley leaned against the street lamp on the corner, huddled with the others like the hungry throngs that had gathered long ago for the loaves of bread and the few fishes. There were others in suits and ties besides him. He was glad there was still some decorum left in the world, something hard to come by in Los Angeles. "Dress for Success," his daddy always told him." The left sleeve hung empty, his clipboard cradled on the sling. He really hadn't needed the sling for quite a while, but he found it really quite useful. "It was cute," someone said. People were more tolerant and understanding about things if he had a sling on his arm. They wanted to stop and talk to him about it. They wanted to give him a hand. So with his pencil cradled in his right arm, he asked the questions, listened, and scrawled. Someone in a cowboy hat and boots walking by, stopped, looked at him curiously, looked at the sling on his arm. "I bet that was a nasty crack," he quipped lasciviously, smacking his lips into the evening air, his laughter melting into the din of the darkness.

The negotiations were fervent, devout. Donations, he was able to figure, depended on the nature of the services rendered and by the amount of time required. Nobody made money back guarantees, or accepted coupons or frequent flier miles. It was cash only. "Most importantly, get that money up front!" every single person told him. "In the hand, down and dirty. Lock it up. Put it away. Hide it somewhere. Make no exceptions, take no

IOU's, no checks, no credit. It was business before pleasure, just like his father always said.

Most told him they advertised in one way or another, on web pages, fliers, bus stop benches, the few public phone booths left on the planet, bathroom walls in bars, word of mouth. They knew their demographics. Some had agents and managers. Some were freelancers. Some were family businesses. Some had regular routes. Some had specialties and special equipment and commanded a higher donation. He took careful notes. He didn't realize there was so much involved, things he hadn't thought of, like business expenses, advertising, public relations, branding. There would be paperwork and slogans to figure out. A few had mentioned overhead. He already figured that out, the roof overhead. But the equipment? He didn't understand that. He'd have to figure that out. And specialization? Missionary work was special. He figured that was what that meant. He had asked several if they felt closer to the lord when they worked and they all fervently agreed. He knew he was on the right path.

He had the satisfaction, too, of knowing that he was participating in the salvation of the souls of others. The destiny of his own soul had already been settled long ago. He already had a buy into heaven. The nuns of St. Theresa's had told him that if he went to church the first Friday of every month for nine months, that he would die with a priest at his side to perform extreme unction, the ticket to heaven. So he did that, although he didn't like thinking about dying. They told him that if he went to church the first Saturday of every month for seven months, he didn't even need the priest. He had a first class express ticket with no layovers in Purgatory, no stops in Limbo, a gold pass to go to the front of the line, like they do for VIP's at Disneyland. So he did that, too, just in case the paperwork for the nine first Fridays got lost somewhere. Wishing not to leave any stone unchurned, he made a handsome weekly contribution to the Ransom Pagan Babies Fund at school. His dad had always told him to cover all the angles and he listened to the old man.

"Sir! Yes, Sir!"

So now he could spend his time concentrating on his missionary position and he felt particularly good about that. He could do it on a much wider scale, world wide, even. Staff Sergeant Sister Saint George Michael told his fourth grade class that if every Catholic in the world said a "Hail Mary" at the same time, all the Jews in Israel would be converted, rescuing the Holy Land from the Infidels. It had worked before, when Russia was converted. If he could make a lot of money, he could make that happen, run ads or something announcing a set time.

Sister SSSSGM didn't say a thing about all the Jews in Los Angeles, though. A major little slip-up there. Duhh!! He had asked Felix one time about how he felt about teaching Jews. Didn't he feel a little guilty? Did he forget what the Jews did to Jesus, hanging him on a cross between two crooks right before the weekend and then poking him in the side with a sharp sword for good measure? Felix just muttered something about how he wished someone would come and poke a sharp sword into his side for good measure.

He knew there would be no first class ticket to heaven for Felix. He wouldn't be going north, but south where the temperature was a lot warmer. A place that rhymes with jail, and it begins with an H, just in case there was any doubt about things. That was the price he would have to pay. Amen.

Chapter 25

Gabby was the cabbie; flabby, shabby, crabby. He eyed the exotic costumes warily. He had seen it all before. In Los Angeles, you see it all. Just when you think you have seen everything, something else pops up. Hard telling what this one was about, two kids dressed like big flowers. He kept one eye on the road and one eye on the rearview mirror. It was late, very late, and they were young and drunk. The little, skinny one was rolling down the window, probably getting ready to upchuck his cookies. Gabby had expected trouble and he got it, but not the kind he had expected, though. This was different. It never happened before. Always a first for everything. Just five minutes into the ride, before he could do or say anything, the little one jumped from the cab. In less than five seconds, rolled down that window and slipped right out. Just slipped out the window and into the darkness.

"Just like dat!" he told Louie and Dewey back at the garage. "Poof! Here now, gone now. Boom-boom-boom…just like dat. Right out da winda. Dint open da door or nuttin." He slammed on his brakes. The other rose rose up in his seat, looked back, jumped out, raced to him, the petals and leaves and thorns and ants and butterflies and ladybugs all atwitter, aflutter, aflitter, afluster, aglitter, aglow. Gabby, the blabby, flabby, shabby, scabby, grabby, crabby cabbie was no dum-dum-dum. Boom-

boom-boom, he took a Louie, made a U-ey. "Jus like dat. Here now…gone now. Jus like dat. I dint need dat kinda trouble," he told Louie and Dewey. "Hooey Phooey!"

It was a lovely wedding, a dignified one in the lovely English tradition in a lovely little cottage. The wind was brisk. The sun shone that day for the first time since October, she had been told. Good auspices. She felt responsible for it, a metaphysical thing, bringing the warmth of sunny southern California with her in her handbag. Open it up and share the wealth of warmth with the world. Wherever she went, she brought happiness and goodness. And she intended on sharing it with all that were attendant here at this sacred gathering to place these two in wedlock.

A dear in a trimmed and proper European suit opened the front door for her and she entered a lovely parlor. A young girl with daisies in her hair handed her a darling program of hearts and cupids. She saw no familiar faces, but she had expected that. She had never met any of the gathered personally, but she knew them all. They were all a piece of the universe, involved not within themselves, but in mankind. The preacher and the congregation as one, the husband and wife as one, the gathered and she as one.

"One." Thump.

"Two." Thump.

"Three." Thump.

"Four." Thump.

"Five." Thump.

"Ahem. Ahem."

She took the seat in the front, the big comfortable one that had been reserved for her. She heard the murmur as she sat. She had expected that the gathered guests would notice her arrival, that they were holding their programs up to their faces to whisper to each other that the celebrated guest from Los Angeles, California, the United States of America, who had journeyed long to attend the blessed event, had arrived and that now the ceremony could officially begin.

She had prepared her words carefully. It was a meditation built around her strongest metaphysical belief that we are never alone, that we share our past, our present, and our future with every other soul in the universe, on this planet and when we leave this planet. Furthermore we all, each and everyone of us, have the responsibility of sharing not only in the pleasures of the universe, but in the responsibilities of this universe, as well. And that it is incumbent on each and every one of us to present others with the opportunity to help one another, including within this holy union being witnessed here this afternoon. By allowing others to help us in times of need, we are allowing them the opportunity to participate in the greatest experience of human life and loving that is possible.

She knew from experience the pleasures she received when she allowed others to help her achieve happiness and humanness, making sacrifices such as waiting in her car endlessly on hot summer afternoons or hobbling way up to the front of long lines at movie theaters, all done to help others achieve the happiness in knowing they were providing happiness and humanness in reciprocity. It was vital that others follow in her footpaths, the same footpaths expounded by those who came before her, the Great Prophet Moses, the Great Prophet Jesus, the Great Prophet Mohammad, the Great Prophet Zarquon. It was these precepts that allow her to serve as a paradigm for others, that allows others the opportunity to help, even when it's a great inconvenience, whether it is monumental or mundane, leading a revolution against a dictator or carrying a bag of litter or a jug of water for the handicapped.

She had everything carefully committed to memory, ready to test the limits of her years of training as a metaphysical practitioner. Now all that was left was the opportunity to give her thanks for giving her the help in giving. She had attended enough funerals and weddings to know that there was always a moment of awkwardness, when someone was at a loss for words, when someone forgot what he or she was going to say, a gap in the ceremony when nothing was happening. She had stepped in often, like Super Woman, to rescue a floundering service. It was always so appreciated by those gathered. "The angel with the tact, the saving grace." Others would nod. She would abide by things as they were until it was her time. There was always a time when it was her time. And she was always ready.

"One." Thump.
"Two." Thump.
"Three." Thump.
"Four." Thump.
"Five." Thump.
"Ahem. Ahem."

Ricky landed in a heap in the middle of Coldwater Canyon Boulevard, under the greenish light of the streetlamp. It wasn't the way this fairy tale was supposed to end. There was nothing Frankie could do. Help was behind high impregnable walls.

The white-gloved Peace officers
Arrived.
Circled.
Spotlights.
Panic!
Flee in Flight.
Into the Black Nightness.
Chase.
Catch.
Cuffs.
Back Seat.
Drunk
Disorderly.
Underage.
A boy.
Resisting arrest.
They charge.

“I come along?”
“Against the law.”
“Call me a cab?”
“ Pay phone.
At the park
Down the street”
My kingdom for a quarter.
Walk.
A flutter.
Far.
A flitter.
Think.
A glitter.
Long.
Fairy tale
Over.
Home.
Dawn.

Lily lay at his tired feet as he cried. So she cried, to, for Frankie, for Ricky, for Ruby, for Champ, for Heathchar...naw..., for herself. When Frankie awoke, he silently packed Ricky's suitcase, then drove to Benedict Canyon in the sunny afternoon to deliver his red, red rose to the front gate for the Princess in the Gazebo, then slowly through the early evening traffic to the Beverly Hills Police Station, picked up a Mister Ricky Johnson to deliver, in silence, the yellow, yellow rose to the gate at LAX. That chapter closes and another one begins.

Chapter 26

Beep. “Hi, t...” Zip. Zap

Beep. “Hi, Felix, this is Trudy calling again. I am thinking you lost my telephone num...” Zip. Zap.

Beep. “Hi...” Zip. Zap.

Beep. “Felix. Your father died tonight. He said to tell you he was sorry. You can come home now, if you want. The funeral's Saturday. I'll make your bed up for you. Bye, honey.”

Beep. “Hi, there. Did you know the warranty on your car is about to expire? Don't be left with expensive car repairs. Act now before it's too late! Call 1-800-C-A-R-S-A-F-E. Yes, that's 1-800-CARSAFE. Yes that's 1-800-227-7233. Our operators are on the line, ready to help you RIGHT NOW! Don't delay. Call NOW and save THOUSANDS. Call today. Again that's 1-800-CARSAFE. 1-800-CARSAFE. Don't be sorry later. ACT NOW! Call 1-800-C-A-R-S-A-F-E RIGHT NOW!

Beep. “Hello, Mr. Felix. Could you give me your address so that I can send you my new headsho...” Zip Zap.

Beep. “Hi, there...” Zip. Zap.

“Hi...” Zip Zap.

Woodrow had never seen anything like it in all. He thought he had seen everything. Even in his wildest imagination, he never would have been able to come up with this.

"Something like this just couldn't be made up," he told his friends later. He knew there was a place in the Land of Canaan for him, a special spot right between the Canes of Charlie Chaplin and Franklin Delano Roosevelt. After serving Beth Ann for the past year, he was especially sure of it. And now this was the climax. None of his friends would ever be able to top this, and they all had stories of their own.

The lovely ceremony was reaching its climax in that ivy-covered quaint cottage. The Vicar of Wakefield had paused in his duties to gaze fondly at his favorite niece and her betrothed. This was the moment for the formal pronouncement that would forever link the two as husband and wife. He paused to reflect for the moment, to remember when he was fresh out of the seminary, when she had asked him to perform the service at her marriage. She was only seven then. Now here she is, all grown up and he was fulfilling the solemn promise he had made to her, uniting her in wedlock to the man of her dreams. He dabbed his eyes with his embroidered handkerchief. All eyes gathered were centered on that moment. All was quiet and lovely and soft …and still.

It was her time, the moment, the inevitable, awkward break when one has dropped his words. Beth Ann rose solemnly from her seat of honor, beatific, angelic, purposeful. She etched the pain and sacrifice of the long and arduous journey deeply into her face. She grimaced her wisdom as she tight-roped up to the landing platform, her cane carefully horizontal to the floor, then turned to face the celebrants and congregants, leaning heavily on Woody. The prophets of love and harmony dwelt there within her. Another moment of giving. It had been difficult, but it was her duty. She solemnly cleared her voice. The elegy was ready. Take your time, take it all in, take the moment. Carpe Diem.

"One." Thump.
"Two." Thump.
"Three." Thump.
"Four." Thump.

"Five." Thump.

"Ahem. Ahem."

All eyes were fixed on her. Outside the sky suddenly darkened, transforming the sunlit parlor to a cloudy pallor. Something was stuck. Perhaps it was the dampness, the sudden chill in the air, the stress of her travel, the momentous occasion.

"One." Thump.

"Two." Thump.

"Three." Thump.

"Four." Thump.

"Five." Thump

"AHEM!! AHEM!!"

"Get out of there, you silly wanker," a three-piece tweed hollered.

"Yeah, and stay out of that chair, too," threatened a Windsor knot.

"Watcha doing up there? Get that big fat arse of yours outa there!" shouted a big hat.

And then the dam broke. The storehouse, the reservoir, the oceans of backlogs, in all of its power and force that had piled up like steam in a factory boiler about to blow, erupted in volcanic fury, exploding like the Grand Finale of the Fourth of July Fireworks over the Brooklyn Bridge during the Bicentennial Celebration.

"AHEM…AHEMMM!!! AHEM HAHAHEM AHEM! AHA! AHA HAHEM! HAHAHAAHAHAHAHAHAHAHA-HAHAHAAKAKAKAKAKA! HAHAHAHAHA KAKAKA-ROOOOOOOOOOOOOOOOOOOOOMMMMMMMMMMMM! ROOOM!! ROOOOOM!! ROOM!! AHEM!!! AHEM!!!HAHAHAROOOOOOOOOM! ROOOOOOOOOOOOMMMMMMMMMMMMM. Gurgle, Gurgle, gasp, gasp, hack, HACK, HACK! HACK HAHHAAHAHAHAHA HAH HAH AHAHAHAHAHAHAHA HAROOOOOOOOOOOOOOOOOOOMM! ROOOOOOOM!!! Ahem… Gargle, gurgle, gasp, hack…Hack…

HACK!!! Ahem...!

Woody sensed that there was stormy weather ahead inside as well. This was not going to end well. He braced himself.

"What in Bloody Bethlehem is that?" shouted a woman wearing a lily.

"Get that crip out of there."

"Who does she think she is?"

"Piss off!" yelled an elderly lady. "Go!"

"I am not a well woman! Can't you see?" replied Beth Ann. "AHEM!!!

Oh, yes, you are," shouted someone else.

"OH, NO, I'M NOT," Beth Ann shouted back.

"**OH, YES, YOU ARE**" shouted the audience in unison..

OH, NO, I'M NOT!!" shouted Beth Ann back.

"**OH YES, YOU ARE**!"

"**OH, NO, I'M NOT! Gurgle... HACK... GASP... SOB**!"

Poor, Poor, Poor Woodrow. It all happened so quickly. Before he could even react, someone snatched him right out of Beth Ann's hand, grabbing him by his foot and bouncing him off her head with a swift and resounding thonk. She stood there, dazed, startled, unsure exactly where that all fit into the universe of things. Then the crook in his neck crooked around the crook in her neck to pull her gurgling and gasping out into the coldness of the cloudy, windy, wintry air outside. He had never felt so humiliated, so abused, so indignant as he lay there among the dead leaves, the dormant roses, and the discombobulated Beth Ann in the Garden of Wakefield Cottage.

Motes of dust floated in the peaceful sunbeam. Lily lay at the foot of Ruby. All was quiet. The place was theirs, alone at last.

"Thank you, honey," hummed Ruby.

Lily purred softly. She knew.

"We both orphans, Child. Abandoned, then sold like

street children in Rio," reminded Ruby. We in this alone together, you and me, sisters forever. "

Lily didn't have much of a recollection of life before Ruby. She had no memories of her mother and father. She did remember the nice lady who called her Lily. She remembered the words of advice about Hoover. She remembered when the beaver boy came in, and that was about all.

Well, frankly, Ruby had seen her share of things. Became quite worldly. "Been around the block a couple of times, me and Monsieur Beauchamp," she said quite proudly.

"Oh, tell me," cried Lily. "Are there really flutter-bys?"

"Butterflies, my dear."

"Are their aunts with six legs?"

"Ants, my dear."

"Are there bugs with red polka dots and moths made of lace?"

"Uh huh."

"Do night bugs carry lanterns that flicker in flight?"

"Fireflies."

"Are there worms in wool coats with whiskers of wire?"

"Ya betcha booties, caterpillars."

"Are there roses with thorns and leaves like green fire?"

"Yes, and much more!" rang Ruby.

"Oh, please tell me!"

"Evening skies studded with juju-bees and jelly beans."

"Oooo, lala!"

"Summers and back porches for mint juleps, and pots of tulips.

Pumpkins and watermelons sprawling wet in the dewsy."

"Oh, that's so silly! Are there lilies?" purred Lily. Naturally curious she was of everything newsy.

"Easter lilies and day lilies and tiger lilies and lilies of the valleys. Cat tails and pussy toes and pussy willows and Spanish moss for a pillow, too, my dear.

"And?"

Japanese lanterns ands silver coins hanging from money

plants.

"And?"

"And lilacs, blue violets, baby's breath, and snotwort."

"Oooooh!"

"Sweet Williams and Johnny-jump-ups and Johnny-come-latelys and black-eyed Susans and Queen Anne's lace. Forget-me-nots to help us rememberin', and morning glories and go-to-bed-at-noons, and four o'clocks to help us keep time in. Columbine covers Corinthian columns. Phlox and foxgloves and coxcomb and ox-lips and ox-eyes cover the cow pasture. Sprigs of butter-and-eggs and sweet catnip and clover cover green meadows.

"Mmmmmm…catnip. I love it. Frankie says it grows near the barn of his. Hmmmmm… I wonder… I reckon I don't know really whatever a barn is…"

"A barn is a place where the owl asks whoo, whoo, whoo's robbing the cornfield.

"Not I," chuckles the raccoon, her fingers a busy a shucking.

"Not I," clucks the duck with her six baby ducklings.

"Not I," caws the black crow, her beak a busy a plucking.

"Not I," sighs Lily, her eyes all a slitter.

"A blue moon, a white moon in sliver or platter. Children and puppies a pitter and patter. Chickens and roosters a clatter and chatter."

"Oh…" cries Lily. "Oh…oh…oh…oh…oooh…oooooo! I just knew it would be that way."

She purred in full power, yawned as big as a sunflower, licked a tickle on her tummy, then lay in the sunbeam to think of farms and barns and to dream of cat matters.

Chapter 27

"Please talk with your grandfathers and grandmothers," Felix had ordered. The boys would return to their families in Miami and Brooklyn and Chicago and Houston for Passover, Pesach. At home they gather from far away places for this holiest of Holy Days, nieces and nephews and aunts and uncles and fathers and mothers and sisters and brothers from across the nation, grandmothers and grandfathers from Haifa, Kiev, Johannesburg, Paris. Their kitchens and cars would be purged of yeasty foodstuff and alcoholic beverages, then double-checked in dark night by candlelight, feather and wooden spoon, the candle for lighting corners without casting shadows, the feather for dusting the tiniest crumbs from hiding places in the cracks of kitchen counters and corners of cupboards, the wooden spoon for collecting the crumbs to be burned the next day. The Seder meal is planned and the first born son will begin his long fast, unless he was delivered by a C-section.

Felix always had a sense of family and ancestry. He didn't know exactly why because he was raised mostly to fend for himself and there wasn't much he knew of his ancestry and heritage. Maybe that's why. He didn't want his students to suffer the same fate, even if that meant requiring his students to sit down and interview their grandparents during the Holiest of Holies, when all would be gathered. "Ask your grandparents about their grandparents." "Both sides of the family now. Call them and tell them to have their scrapbooks, their bibles, and their family histories ready." He wanted his students to see their grandparents as mothers and fathers and sons and daughters and brothers and sisters, instead of patriarchs and matriarchs and rulers of tribes and judges and arbitrators of family matters, to learn of their lives back when they weren't old wheezing geezers who smell of Fix-o-dent and Ben-Gay.

The boys in class eyed each other nervously, each waiting for the other to handle this hot latke. Felix had seemed so eager to announce the assignment, so expectant of celebratory kudos, so convinced of its virtue. They turned first and looked at Kovi. He was the class negotiator and a class leader, but his frankness could be brutal. This would call for a softer touch, a social sensitivity. Tzi excelled on the basketball court, but his deftness and agility there did not translate into the world of words outside of the white lines. Yossi, by nature, always avoided anything confrontational. Yitzi always wrapped everything in dizzying metaphor. There was no virtue there. Everyone else was just there. So the burden fell on Lazer. He had nothing to lose. He was leaving the yeshiva, not returning after Passover, instead heading for Tel Aviv, taking with him any of the collateral damage that may arise from hurt or embarrassment. After all, Felix was goyem and didn't know of such things.

Felix stood there puzzled. The boys enjoyed writing, enjoyed telling Felix long sagas of their family gatherings. They loved long litanies, relished in relating the long list of famous, and the infamous, Jews throughout the ages. Jews like Cheese and Crackers, they said. Christopher Columbus and Leonardo Da Vinci, and Leonardo D' Caprio, they would claim. The Warner Brothers and Fox. "And don't forget Albert Einstein and Emma Lazarus and Franz Kafka and Carl Sagan and Karl Marx and the Marx Brothers and J. D. Salinger, and Marc Chagall, while you're at it," they would say. And then there are Dear Abby and Dear Ann and Sigmund Freud and Stan Lee and Jerry Springer and Jerry Seinfeld and Mike Wallace and Joan Rivers and Howard Stern and Paula Abdul and Ayn Rand. Bob Dylan and Simon and Garfunkel and Arlo Guthrie and Elvis Presley and Barry Manilow and Al Jolson and the Beastie Boys and Phish and K.D. Lang and Beverly Sills. Leon Trotsky and Allan Ginsberg and Slash and Itzhak Perlman and Isaac Stern and Paul Shafer and The Frogs and Barbara Walters and Katherine Graham and Alan Dershowitz and David Berkowitz and Bugsy

Seigel. Harry Houdini and Nostradamus and Albert Sabin and Jonas Salk and Hyman Rickover and Alan Greenspan. And too many more to remember them all. So what was the big deal?

"Uh…Sir," opened Lazer.

"Yes, Lazer?"

"Uh…Sir, Uh… We have no grandparents. Most of us, that is."

"What do you mean, you have no grandparents?"

"Uh…Sir...Uh...Auschwitz One and Auschwitz Two and Auschwitz Three and Birkenau and Treblinka and Buchenwald and Dachau and Theresienstadt and Bergen-Belsen and Sachsenhause."

"Oh… Well, then… uh… Hmmm…Never mind… Forget it…. Forgive me…"

They could forgive him. But they would never forget it. They would never forgive it. The stories are Revered. Recited. Repeated. Recorded. Whispered. Shouted. Wept. Written. Etched. Inscribed. Tattooed.

Felix asked Rabbi Horowitz about it one time. If the Jews are g-d's chosen people, then why did g-d allow this horrible thing to happen to them?

"Oh," he said. "We are asked that all the time."

"Ooops…" apologized Felix.

"He didn't allow it," the rabbi responded. "He had merely nodded off for the moment."

Memorized, Memorialized, Condemned. Avenged. Never. Ever. Again. Forever never forgive. Forever never forget.

Tiffani pushed back away from the screen. Her eyes hurt. She was nearing completion. The Villa Verdugo was still in her pajamas. Soon the place would stir and she would head for bed. She always marveled at how fast time passed when she was absorbed in a project. Hours would fly by in mere minutes. It had been an especially fruitful night, smudges on camera lenses, mispronounced words, doors opened at different widths. But tonight she found a goldmine, the reflection of a production assistant in the glass of a framed picture on a desk. Of all the stupid, asinine, pointless, no-one-watching-the-road pieces of trash, this one takes the cake.

She sat on the edge of her bed and lit the quickie pipe. The day hadn't started out so well, though. After her visit to the 99 Cent store, she drove down Cajuenga Boulevard through Toluca Lake and got behind some honky driving too slow in the fast lane. Today just wasn't the day to get in her way. There was another honky to her right driving too slowly. No way around. Then they got to Warner Brothers Studios. So here they were, driving even slower now, rolling down the window and gawking. She knew they would gawk and stare, then head over to Buena Vista Avenue to do the same thing at Disney. All there was to see were just tall walls and guarded gates. Then there were three cars. She had places to go. Things to do. Her car was loaded with gifts to carry up three flights of stairs. She honkied at the honkies, then politely gave them the hurry-along gesture. They didn’t get it. Then she gave them the get-out-of-the-way gesture. They didn't get that either. Out the window with the politeness. She honked again, this time, a mean I-mean-it-and-I-mean-it-now honky honk. It didn't help.

She knew there was a left turn lane coming up that fed into a Warner parking garage. She used that lane to swoop around, but she ran out of lane and bounced off the curb in the median, smashing the geraniums planted there. She got in front of those slowpokes and that was all that mattered. Then she slammed down hard on her brakes. The out-of-towner behind slammed down hard on his brakes. Then the driver behind that driver, then the one behind that. Screech! Screech! Screech! She jumped out of her car, stomped to the back of her car, stood there with her hands on her hips and stared at them, icily through their dirty rented windshield. The three cars quickly rolled back, the windows quickly rolled up, and they quickly rolled away. The gawkers didn’t wanted trouble, not with her. And they would have a story to tell once they got back to Ypsilanti. Then when she rolled away, the front left wheel of the Taurus began to wobble.

And that wasn't the worst of it. Her friend who donated the pot to her so that she could donate it to her friends was arrested and sitting in a downtown jail cell for trafficking in illegal drugs. What happened to his so-called donation defense? The only time she didn't verify something and now she has time to regret it. Somewhere out there was an answer to her problem. She could live without the parking space. She could find a way to fix the wheel. But she couldn't live without the pot, and she couldn't live without the donations. She would find a way to have her pot and smoke it, too. She exhaled deeply, laid back and waited for Mister Sandman to take care of the rest of the day.

Beth Ann had arrived home the worse for wear and tear. The large lump on the top of her head had gradually disappeared, but now the tuckle was becoming a struckle. The whole thing was entirely unfortunate, but it was behind her. She would spend her time now with Those Fabulous Pyramids and forget what happened in England. All that time and money and effort was wasted. What a disappointment. She didn't get to utter even a single word of her homily there. No one there was much interested in her giving them the opportunity to help her help them help her help them. "So help me god," she sighed. She had limped back through the sleet and the numbing wind to the Wakefield Arms to learn that she had attended the wrong wedding. The Wakefield Cottage was not the Wakefield Manor. They were two different places. The stuffy hotel clerk sent her to the wrong place. When she told him about it, he shrugged his shoulders, turned around and walked away. "Jolly Olde England. Ha!"

When she returned to the Villa Verdugo, she found her mailbox chocked full of the usual ads and circulars, mountains of them, which people are forced to look at one by one, lest they accidentally toss the gas bill or the tax refund. Beth Ann stood there in the foyer, thumbing through, dropping the circulars into the recycle basket there. It was the typical beautiful, sunny day in the San Fernando Valley, but bad weather was once again gathering in the darkening skies off the coast of Santa Monica, heading inland and gaining strength like a North Carolina hurricane.

Heathcharlesharley finally had all the pieces figured out. He had expanded and enhanced his ad, revising the full page in living color to attract the eye. He had briefly considered asking Frankie for advice, but then realized that he would need to share some of the glory of its success. He had carefully lined up his digital camera to get just the right photos, setting up the automatic timer, trying to leave just enough for the imagination. He had to take several shots before he got things just right. A photo of his nice smooth, slim, naked chest from his neck to his navel. He had to stop and do a couple of quick sit-ups first to dress up the package. But the other photo was the bread and butter shot, as Barbara would say when she saw a particularly good headshot. It was a shot of himself lying shirtless on his belly on his futon mattress, his head under the pillow, his pants pulled down just far enough to reveal his youthful buttocks jutting up, tantalizing, tempting, inspired by the painting he had seen Frankie make for Ricky. A crescent moon. Then he wrote the ad:

A Spoonful of Sugar

No Fee!

Donations and Free Will Offerings Required

Cash only.

No Credit Cards. No Debit Cards. No Checks. No IOU's. No Food Stamps.

Open 24 Hours a Day. Seven Days a Week. 365 Days a Year

Big Feet!

No one under 50. No Exceptions.

No Skinnies. No Chest Hair. No Drugs.

Spanking Ok.

Christians Only (Duh!)

He had to add that no chest hair thing. It never crossed his mind that he would encounter something like that, but he did. There she was laying naked, hair growing in a circle around each nipple, another circle around her belly button, looking like a big bagel with chocolate sprinkles on it. It was shocking, disgusting, and worse than anything else, deflating. He didn't want anything to do with some hairy football linebacker of a woman.

He sat back and looked at the final product, eyeballing his ad from the left eye, then the right, with the light on and the light off. He stared at it, squinting, looking at it upside down, crossing his eyes, looking at it cockeyed, trying his best to see it through the eyes of a woman. It was a little hard for him, being that he was not a woman, and once again he thought of asking Frankie to look at it. Then he changed his mind about that, as well. Frankie would just start asking questions about what that had to do with missionary work, then talk Hong Kong to Champ and they would both wiggle and giggle. They didn't understand anything. It was too complicated for them to understand. Same thing with Mumble and Grumbles upstairs. It was just one of those things only he could appreciate. He liked what he saw anyway. He had to admit that he even got a little rise out of it himself. If he weren't a he but a she, she would sure, he was sure, head for him for her bed. Or head for her for his bed. Or head for his bed for some head, or however that goes.

Next, he would call on Ima MacLaptop to make him some colorful, attractive business cards to place in neat little stacks next to the mints in teashops or at hair salons, pastry shops, ice cream parlors, See's chocolate counters, and other places full-figured mature Christian ladies visit regularly. He would design attractive, tasteful little fliers to leave under the windshield wipers of Crown Victrolas and Cadillac De Villas in Macy's parking lot. Daddy Warbucks would call it smart coupleage. He would plant his seeds everywhere, then sit back and wait for the crop to grow, for the harvest to ripen. His father would be proud of him, his first efforts to make something of himself, to put a roof over his own head for a change instead of relying on the kindness of strangers, like Blanche De Bois had to do, a woman who certainly drove a Caddie.

It wasn't hard to miss. The official looking envelope with the red, white, and blue rainbow logo. The return address embossed in gold lettering:

Vidematics Communications
2000 Avenue of the Stars
Twenty-fifth Floor
Century City, CA 90067

Her attorney had advised her that Vidematics may be eager to make their little problem go away. Make an attempt to resolve the conflict. The progression of the condition from a tuckle to a struckle was pretty serious business and needed to be attended to. Vidematics would just admit defeat and comply with the mandate and move on, eager to close the book on the entire affair, before others caught wind of potential little problems. Beth Ann ripped it open and stood there in the soothing warmth of a particularly benevolent Toluca Lake sunbeam. "It was great to be back home," she mused as she filled her lungs with southern California sunshine.

"One," Thump.

"Two." Thump.

"Three." Thump.

"Four." Thump.

"Five." Thump.

Ahem. Ahem.

She unfolded the paper, and leaned against the tiled wall.

To: Beth Ann Mueller:

Vidematics has long maintained a healthy and whichfore yada... yada... yada… slip... skip… zip… its employees enjoy the hereon yada… yada… yada… zip… skip... every effort is yada… eventhough whatsoever whatever... yada… yada… zip… skip ship… holds the position that its employees are an asset… evennonethelessmoreover throughout in conjunction to the yada

yada yada benefit of responsibility...

However, concern afore hereafter yada... yada... yada... skip shift...safe and healthy work environment yada yada yada. Furthermore… the ability of petitioner to endure the hardships... international travels…midnight dreary...to wit thusyet... inability to maintain... responsibility to Vidematics… Party A...immediately upon hereafter thereafter. Personal business.... Party A … proprietary … nevercandomore, those fabulous pyramids prohibited.... in violation... subsequent retaliatory... compensation of that which is yada yada yada...

Further actions forthcoming hereto forthwith as yet to date...for claims of … medical conditions...hereto forthwith the chamber door sofar uponwith in accordance to withwhich for which the afore mentioned below in Addendum 132-76.1, Paragraph H1E company policy… forevermore, Lenore... yet evermore, yet nevermore... warrants further investigation… decision pondered weak and weary. Questions concerning… medical reports... Vidematics policy. Party B... Henceforever supply us with uponwhich erstwhile test results…our medical experts compliance… human resources furthermore wherevermore... Be advised... possibility... probability... sue your pants off... liability… legal neverfore... forenevermore... neverfore... forevermore... moreforever... nevermore... no more.

Sincer... yada yada yada.

"Mama's home!!! Mama's Home!!!" She hurried to her balcony, yanked open the balcony door and scanned left, then right, looked with the left eye, then the right, up and down Hesby Street. The sky had darkened, one of those sudden and unexpected storms moving in from the Pacific. Was someone watching her every move? Was someone out there with a lens or a listening device? She knew about those listening devices. They could just aim a big round horn, something like what the old deaf people used to use long ago to hear things. They could pick up anything even from a mile or two away. All you had to do was just point it in the direction. She had seen them used on CSI.

Did someone follow her to LAX? Check to see what

plane she was getting on? They must have seen her with the cane. They couldn't miss it. They had to know that she was not a well woman. "Further investigation," the letter said again when she read the letter again. A door of opportunity, perhaps. They must not feel like they had an open and shut case if they think they need to do further investigation forevermore. Well, she would meet them head on. She would gird herself for battle. She loved a good battle and this one would be the biggest of her life. She opened the sliding door to its widest width. It would be a good opportunity to let them hear and see all the heartaches and trials and tribulations of an American with Disabilities. She could give them plenty. The smell of lightning filled the heavy afternoon air and thunder rumbled to a noisy crescendo. **HA HA HA HA HA HA HA KAKAKA KAKAKA ROOM ROOOOM ROOM ROOMROOMROOMROOOOOM!! ROOOOOM!!! ROOOOOOOOM!!! AHEM!! AHEM!! Gurgle** and **Gaggle!! KAAAABOOOOOOOOOOM!!!!!**

"Yes, Sir. Mama's home! Mama's Home!"

Buddha shifted his arms, adjusted his robe, and gathered his snakes around him. Finally, for the first time in what seemed like centuries, he had the time to kick back and clear his head a little bit, enjoy the world around him, no more friends sucking on him. Tiffani would visit his temple once in the morning, once in the afternoon, and then late in the evening to worship, and he had to admit that he admired the depth and sincerity of her devotion. His snake heads were gradually healing, no longer red and blistered like the nipples of a mother with three-month-old quintuplets.

"No, not anymore," she would say to the person on the other end of the line when the phone rang. "No, I don't know anyone else." "No, I never sold it. Who told you I did!?" It was well into the second week before the long parade up to Apartment 213 dwindled, then disappeared, and, at long last, she no longer had legions of friends.

Buddha sat quietly in the corner and listened as she talked

with the doctor, who had hurried over from his Toluca Lake office for this emergency. As a rule, he never made house calls, but there is a first for everything. Then he arrived right exactly on the dot of the appointed time, another first in a career spanning decades.

California had passed that medical marijuana proposition and so it was all legal, she told him, ironclad, unlike that donation thing that didn't hold up in court. Doctors didn't even need a reason. All they had to do was sign off on the form. A bad hair day was good enough. Aching feet from tight fitting shoes was enough. She had double and triple checked it and found it to be the case.

Now, all she had to do was head down to that special drugstore on Sunset and place that prescription form right there on the counter top, right in front of everyone. No need to lock the door behind her or to talk in hushed tones, no longer have to fear the POLICE! Just sit there on the vinyl chair by the counter while a pharmacist in a white lab coat fills the prescription, then calls out your name.

"Then we divvy it," she told the doctor. "Cheap, good, and legal," she said. They would both win. It was a this for a that thing between friends. Buddha liked the peace and harmony of the moment, the quintessence of his existence, offered a snake and the pact was sealed with a toot and a snort.

Frankie wondered why he was asking Felix about such things. Felix was a loner who was never seen in the presence of a love interest. There was never any shy little boy talk from him about a fling or an old flame. But he did read a lot and that's probably where he got all of his information about such things. He would quote straight from the lips of the immortal lovers, Romeo and Juliet, Elizabeth Barrett and Robert Browning, Eros and Psyche, Achilles and Patroclus, whoever they all were. Sometimes Professor Felix didn't know when he was in a classroom and when he wasn't. Too bad he just couldn't take a rest from it sometimes.

Frankie had gotten his first knowledge about love and sex not from reading any books, but as a fifth grader riding the school bus every day. So he wondered ever since about some of the unanswered questions he had, some of those things that the seventh graders sitting in the back of the bus talked about, but had no answers for, like what happens when a man doesn't release his seed in decades, like the pope or something. Does his scrotum hang low and heavy and full, like the udder of a fat Wisconsin cow that hasn't been milked in a month? He decided one time to see for himself, but he could never go any longer than four hours to find out for sure. But he wasn't going to ask Felix for the answers to those questions. He would just grumble and mumble something about asking somebody to come and shove him off a cliff somewhere. He was there because he wanted to talk about Ricky. And himself.

Frankie told Felix that Ricky said that Frankie wasn't Frankie anymore and it made Frankie, well... cranky... frankly. Frankie told Felix that Ricky said Frankie insisted on being the husband, leaving Ricky barefoot and pregnant, pans in one hand, glans in the other. Then Frankie said a little too quickly that Ricky was... uh... picky... persnickety. Thought too much about things that didn't matter. And that was why that chapter ended.

Chapter 28

"But I want to be the same Frankie I was back home. I don't want to change."

"Circumstances change, but people stay the same all their life. The way they're born. Everything is already there, but it just grows bigger as the person grows bigger.

"What do you mean?" asked Frankie.

"A person is born gay, just as a ricky is born a ricky. An artist is born an artist just as a frankie is born a frankie. An idiot is born an idiot just as a heathcharlesharley is born... uh, never mind."

"What do you mean?"

"Well, it's like this. People have things inside of them that they don't know they have, but they were always there from the beginning. They just didn't find it for a while. Sometimes they never find things there."

"Why?"

"Too deeply wrapped in freezer paper, or they hang around uninspiring people for too long."

"Oh."

"Then there are things that people have inside of them that they know about, but they don't like to talk about."

"Why?"

"Too painful, maybe. Frightened. They don't want to get

hurt. Or they are confused about how they feel and they don't want to look stupid.

"Like in high school," Frankie thought.

"A lot of people let things dribble out a drop at a time. Drip. Drip. Drip. In little puddles. Sometimes it becomes a cesspool, sometimes a calm little pond. Sometimes a great big ocean with breakers and tides and you find yourself needing a bigger boat and a wider berth so you cast off the mooring lines and sail away. Anchors aweigh!"

Frankie wondered if this meant he had to go out and get boots or a boat somewhere now. Then he wondered when Felix would begin dripping, and what his puddle would become.

"So that's the way it is. Wondering about things that you said or did is just a big waste of time. You can't unring a bell."

Champ had to go home, back to the Louisiana mud. He carried it in his pocket, scrawled in pencil in his mother's hand, "Paw needs you come home." But it was more than just a short note on tablet paper. It was a summons, condemning him to continue his father's sentence in that prison. He would go. He told Big Man at Epic Heroes he needed his pay. Now, that this was it. Big Man paid him, then told him that someone had gone up and down the boulevard the other day and taken every tip jar from every counter along the way. "Take care of yourself," Big Man said, handing him his check, "and take a hero with you."

And he walked. It was easier to think when he walked and he had a lot to think about. The marine layer hung late and heavy and gray. He passed the shops, past the gyro place where the surly shop owner would never give back the correct change, then act like he didn't speak a word of English when challenged, past the Academy of Television Arts and Sciences with its big open concourse paying homage in bronze statues to the likes of the late greats, Jack Benny, Bob Hope, Milton Berle, others forgotten by now. Someone was always putting up a statue of someone. He passed the new Metro station and the glitzy new faux lofts surrounding it, Sunshine Ford, empty lots, walking, thinking, then over to Tujunga Avenue, past the Amelia Earhart Library. Someone was always naming something after someone. He crossed Magnolia to North Hollywood Park and its 78 trees planted for each of the California victims of the World Trade Center attack. Why don't they plant a tree every time anyone dies? Why does it just have to be just certain people? Certain occasions? "Who decides those things?" he thought. Probably no bronze statue of him standing in the middle of a fountain somewhere, no library named after him, no tree planted.

He passed under the overpass over to the underpass.

"Johnie?"

"The guy with the meth marks on his face."

"Lots of people with meth marks. They come and go. In and out."

The one who brought the heroes on Christmas. The kid from Iowa."

"Oh... Corncob."

No one knew his real name. Corncob from Iowa.

"He kept by hisself all the time. Didn't say much. He ain't here. He left. Carryin' his bundle. They come and go. Got a smoke?"

Champ passed back over and under to the pawnshop on Tujunga. Johnny's guitar was gone, no longer hanging there. He went in. The guy with meth marks on his face came and got it, spilled a large plastic jar of pennies and dimes and crumpled one dollar bills on the counter, slung the guitar on his back, then walked out the door, heading toward the highway. Gone, disappeared. No one noticed. No one is watching. Come to LA. Be left alone. Be anonymous. Enjoy the loneliness. Revel in the salty ocean of emptiness.

Champ thought about the hard work his father did all his life. He had thought that his father and his grandfather and all of the others before him had wasted away their lives trawling for shrimp in the increasingly stingy waters around Saint Charles, repairing worn nets in the early morning dawn before setting out, then returning too often with barely enough catch to buy fuel for the next day, or often idled by threatening weather, oil spills, or worn out parts in the old diesel engine. There was always something to work against. Always some obstacle in the way.

But his father, like his father before him, accepted it and embraced it. His father would return home in the evening, laughing loudly as he roughhoused with his children, ate heartily, and slept lustily. He remembered his father's deep, resonating voice filling the church on Sunday services, his heartfelt prayers of thanks to god for his goodness and gifts. It was all pure and simple and true.

Champ never experienced those pleasures when he returned from the oil rigs, instead turning to the whorehouses and the bars for his comfort, a short, artificial escape from the loneliness and isolation that were his constant companions, then ending up here in the ultimate House of Smoke and Mirrors, Tinseltown. The home of epic heroes. There wasn't anything here, or anywhere else he had been, to fall down on his knees and thank god for. There was no reward, no fulfillment. Perhaps the old man knew the truth all along, and that it was he, Ronnie, who was the prisoner. He had grown up free and became a prisoner of his own devices.

His father was fifty-five now and the hard work had eaten away his strength. He was tired now and needed the help of his first born. So the prodigal son would return to the life of his father and his people, repentant, and free at last to experience truth and triumph. Champ headed back one last time, east on Magnolia, past Ralph's, past Sorrento's Bar, past the pensioner apartments, a right turn at Friendly's, three blocks down, right on Hesby. There she stood, the Villa Verdugo, proper-like. Blessed is the fruit of thy womb. What the hell.

And down off Hollywood Boulevard, down where the alley cats gather nightly in their own quest for the truth, a note flutters in the afternoon breeze, "Johnies gone home, love and peace."

"Are you anybody?" people would ask him. "Beg

pardon," Felix replied when he first heard the question.

"Are you somebody?"

"Am I somebody?"

"Yeah, you know... somebody?"

"I think I'm somebody. Are you somebody?"

"Naw... We's just here from Kentucky. We thought maybe you was somebody. Ya look kinda familiar."

They meant SOMEBODY. Somebody rich or famous. Somebody they should get an autograph from. Even those out here struggling to get in would ask him, "are you somebody," meaning, of course, is there something you can do for me? Somebody who could propel them into stardom. They would be on their best behavior at first, just in case, searching his face for familiarity, hopeful, unsure. When they found out he wasn't somebody, then they let their guard down, didn't care anymore about hanging around, left, looking for somebody. "Are you anybody?" "Are you somebody?"

"And who are you?" asked Felix, pinching his nose and mimicking a tired, nasal-voiced receptionist.

Who am I?" asked Felix's voice.

"Yes, sir," answered the voice on the other end of the line.

"Joe Schmo," replied Felix.

"And Mr. Schmo, what company are you with?"

"Well," replied Joe Schmo. "I'm not with any company right now.

Felix knew his comic pauses. Set it up. Pause.

"I had some company earlier today, but they left. I'm expecting more company tonight. I can call you back then and tell you who I'm with, if you like."

"Thanks, everyone. You've been great. Drive carefully, y'all. And don't forget about your server."

Heathcharlesharley had remembered to remind god in his prayers about the sins of Felix. Heathcharlesharley prayed frequently. It was a thing expected of all good Catholic boys at Saint Theresa's. They had plenty to chose from, long prayers, medium prayers. Short ones, called ejaculations, were his favorites. You just spit them out, like "Lord Help Me!" or "Thank You, Jesus!" They were fast and easy. He began and ended each day with an ejaculation. He began and ended each meal with a medium prayer. He prayed all period long in each of his classes, deep in contemplation. He had special prayers he prayed before and after each test, before and after each basketball shot during recess, whether it went through the hoop or not, which it almost never did, when he needed to find a parking space. In fact, Heathcharlesharley began and ended each prayer with a prayer.

He wrote a little "JMJ" on the top of all of his papers. Jesus. Mary. Joseph, with a little cross above it. Sister Attila The Nun wouldn't accept the paper if any of that were missing. It was worth five points when he did put it up there. He wondered why paper companies didn't sell whole reams of it with that detail already taken care of, like how they drill the holes in the paper or put in the little pink margin line. They could just as easily stamp JMJ and a little cross right on top in the center, maybe even in purple ink. It would save everybody a lot of trouble.

He wore sacred little medals and scapulary around his neck and used little holy cards with pictures of saints on them for bookmarks and carried more in his wallet next to his lunch money to protect it from loss. He blessed himself with holy water when he entered and left the small school chapel, making sure to dip the tips of each finger well into the sacred water to amply anoint himself. He genuflected generously whenever he passed each station of the cross in the sanctuary. He religiously blessed others when they sneezed. He was a regular little pattern for others to follow in the proper preparation and practice for priesthoodiness.

Maxine peered through her reading glasses at the computer screen. She had worked hard on her way up the administrative ladder to the position of chief decision maker at the VA Center. She was a person of color so she secretly believed she had to work just a little bit harder to get there. But she did and she felt particularly blessed by the lord. Now she had the power to give a yes or a no. She was the go-to person, the final say-so person. She wasn't an easy touch and she weighed every decision before making her final decision. She took seriously her responsibility to balance the concerns of the taxpayer on one hand and the needs of the military veteran on the other. But once she clicked her mouse, the case was considered closed. The situation was resolved.

She felt particularly sad for the Army veteran sitting across the desk from her. Like her, the African-American woman shared the curse of the expanded carriage and she empathized. She knew and well understood the trials and tribulations of trying to get comfortable in those tiny chairs in restaurants or airplanes. She understood the problems of finding good fitting clothes from the long racks at Marshall's or Dress For Less. She understood the stress on the knees and the ankles, the swollen feet, the depression one feels while gazing into the mirror, the sadness caused by the insensitivities and unkind remarks of others. White women had their problems, too, of course. Some had the expanded carriage as well, but most had trouble with their hair. Black people's hair just turns white when they age, but white women's hair just turns loose. “Ha Ha Ha,” she smiled as she typed. She usually tried to find things to smile about. She had to, since hearing daily of the multiple woes of the military veteran can be extremely trying most of the time. Catch a smile when you can.

To hear the sad tale of an expanded carriage was sad enough, but to hear of a sagging expanded carriage was enough to break one's heart and certainly not a laughing matter. She listened as Tiffani tearfully told of her chronic pain, made worse by walking on hard surfaces like sidewalks and parking lots, the spasms of pain from walking up stairs or getting in and out of her automobile. She listened as Tiffani told of laying long uncomfortable nights in the sagging bunk beds in Fort Gordon, Georgia; Fort Leonard Wood, Missouri; Fort Knox, Kentucky. There was no escaping them. When she expressed concern to her commanding officers, they treated her, well, like, she was just some homesick crybaby. So the problem just kept getting worse until her carriage no longer had any recollection of where it was parked anymore, slipping this way and that, riding this way and that, swinging this way and that. Maxine didn't need to hear another word and with a swift, easy click on the mouse, checked "Approved." And Sergeant Tiffani Rae Wright, 318-79-9032, had solved the other problem. Just like that.

Beatrice pulled in her perimeter as much as she felt was necessary. But there was one part of her routine that Beatrice refused to change, the daily experience of Runyon Canyon. The old regulars hiking there wondered where the blonde in the floppy straw hat had gone, then wondered who the new gangly brunette was, her pageboy topped with a Dodger's baseball cap and steamy, black-rimmed glasses perched on her nose. But people come and go around these parts and the blonde was soon forgotten.

It was a panacea for all her troubles. The fresh air cleansed her mind and she saw things more clearly. The view offered from Heaven's Bus Stop presented a city of birth and rebirth, of reach and retreat, marking the progression of time across the face of the Southland, of superstructures of buildings rising from the floor of Los Angeles, others meeting their demise with the wrecking ball, their importance no longer important, their usefulness no longer useful. The ever present circle of jetcraft hovering over LAX in the far distance bringing and taking with routine nonchalance and anonymity, those who need to come and those who need to go. Move in. Live. Learn. Move on.

She continued to eavesdrop on the chatter between the canines leading humans up and down the gently winding slopes. Spring time had arrived and so the collies, poodles, German shepherds and others still fortunate enough to have the capacity for such matters were on the lookout for a hot bitch or a well hung stud. Bassets and others built low to the ground like sleek Lamborghinis would pass on warnings as they passed on the path. "Hey, Bro. Watch out! On the right. A cactus! Poke another hole in your fanny," or "Careful! Rocky road ahead. Knock those boys around like the balls on a billiard table."

On most afternoons, she still motored her Jaguar through the streets, and as always, keeping one eye on the rearview mirror, taking circuitous routes, memorizing license plate numbers of cars that looked too familiar. She was unfearful that her own car would betray her. Most people would notice a Jag on the street in any other part of the nation, notice it and stop and look at it. But not in Los Angeles, where practically everyone has a black Jag, common as rusty Ford pick-em-ups in Indiana.

Heathcharlesharley at first thought that he indeed had the Midas touch, that he was a chip off the old block, like grandfather-father, like son. In the first few weeks of his new business model, he received hundreds of hits from lonely, full-figured, mature Christian ladies. He trekked to and fro and hither and yon happily those first few weeks, morning, afternoon, evening, late night, learning to get around Los Angeles County, Orange County, Ventura County, San Bernardino County, returning home with his cash drawer filled with the largess of generosity. It became increasingly difficult for him to rescue every soul. His skanktity had its limits. He took a pass on those who would require too much time. The invitation for weekends together, like trips up the coast or excursions to Disneyland. Sometimes there were invitations for long leisurely evenings together featuring double batches of double chocolate walnut supreme fudge brownie delights. He didn't eat those kinds of things. So he would take a polite pass.

For a while, he considered selling franchises, like what his father did with his auto parts empire, like hire extra help, and maybe even go national. But then things went into the sewer and pretty quickly at that. There was the downside that he never anticipated. He didn't understand it at first. When he was donating his services back before he became the businessman, it wasn't too much of a problem. Now, when he showed up in his business suit, his briefcase with a good solid lock on it, his arm slung in the sling, well, frankly, at first, the ladies thought it was a gas, a new gimmick they had never heard of. It was cute and different. They would giggle when he asked up front for the donation envelope, when he punched in the numbers on his calculator, and when he locked everything up with a crisp snap of the clasp, real business-like. But now, well, things were different. People just seemed to expect more. It was that customer satisfaction problem. Nowadays people just seem to expect a whole lot more than they used to.

"Is that all you got, honey?"

"Is it in yet?"

"Big feet, my foot!"

Then there were the days when he had multiple missions, and he found it hard to rise to the occasion. Some demanded their money back, but it was too late. He had already locked it up in the briefcase. Besides that, he would tell them, donations and free will contributions were not refundable, only fees were, and that made some of them get cross with him.

"Take that sling off your broke arm and put it on your broke dick."

"You go over to the pharmacy, young man, and get you some of that coxaphalen."

It wasn't long before the world got wise to the ways of Heathcharlesharley and his little bit of sugar. The advisories were out, like weather bulletins before a South Dakota blizzard. "Beware of the businessman with his briefcase and broken arm." It was saturation coverage all over again, but not the kind that was good for business. On the Sons and Lovers Rating's Page, he got zero stars out of a possible five. There were strong gale warnings about him in every chatroom and lonely hearts club across five counties. The Better Business Bureau was notified, the Chamber of Commerce. Complaints were filed by the League of Women Voters, the Louisa Chitwood Literary Guild, the Daughters of the American Revolution. The hits went from a torrent to a trickle to a drip. Things would be whole lot easier for him if he were one of those hermaphrodikes or whatever you call those people with both sex organs. Then he could just stay home at night with himself, put a little Johnny Mathis on the CD player, and do all his missionary work right here on the comfort of his own futon. No more of all that driving around anymore. No more having to listen to all that complaining going on all the time. And speaking of complaints about things, he had his share of issues to share, particularly like his deals about the conversion of Israel. Payback seemed to be pretty much nonexistent out here any more, from cats to gods and all points in between.

Chapter 29

The students at the yeshiva always wear their prayer shirts everywhere, on the basketball court, in the classroom, in bed, taking them off only when they bathed. They were thick vests, called tzitzit, from which suspend a series of long strings punctuated with knots. The boys would finger the commas and semicolons throughout the day, like one would finger the beads of a rosary or Hindu mala or Muslim misbaha, reminding them of their sacred covenant with a higher authority. At sun-up the boys would rise up, pull on their black trousers, button their white shirts up over their tzitzits, and head for the shul, the cavern-like tabernacle in the yeshiva to chant their morning prayers before the ark. They would wrap themselves in prayer shawls and don their tefellin, phylacteries comprised of little wooden boxes containing biblical verses. They would solemnly unwind the long cords which held them securely in place in the center of their forehead and the arm opposite their heart, and then entwine the leftover straps seven times in and out of the fingers on their left hand. Felix thought they looked a lot like the old AC adapters with the box and the long cord you plugged into the wall to recharge your cell phone. They probably were a lot like that, but recharging their souls instead.

He would watch them on occasion as they did their daily ablutions, using little cups to pour spring water over each hand three times and mumbling certain prayers before they ate bread. Occasionally, at some predetermined moment, the students would all rise in unison, turn to the east and daven, bobbing up and down from waist to pate, palms joined, eyes closed. The students would rotate the charge of leading the chant and the other boys would echo in chorus. Felix would stand discretely and respectfully in the rear corner of his classroom until the ritual was completed, then continue on with his lesson as if nothing out of the ordinary had occurred. To them, nothing unusual had happened.

"Blessed are You, G-d Almighty, the King of the World, that You haven't made me a Woman." When Felix first heard his students fervently praying that prayer, he had to admit that he was a little disappointed. In Judaism, were women second-class citizens? He could live with the womenfolk sitting apart at the temple or the fund-raiser at the Wilshire Regency. He knew the women preferred to hang with the other women; the men, the men. Since ancient times, in medieval times, modern times. Sisters with their sisters. Brothers with their brothers. Together. Apart. Gynaeseums and Andraeseums. Gynarchies and Andrarchies. Convents and Rectories. It was true in all religions, all societies. But how could they teach their young men to begin each day with such a prayer?

"Thank G-d I'm Not a Woman!" sounded to him a lot like the gynophobic rantings and ravings of a rollicking, frolicking, whooping and hollering misogynist cut off by a female driver on busy traffic day on the 405 or some sourpuss passed over for a promotion by a woman. It might even be the way that some menfolk feel deep down somewhere under wraps, but they sure wouldn't utter it out loud as part of a fervent prayer of thanks to their creator. Finally, he cornered Rabbi Horowitz.

"Isn't it sexist?" Felix had asked. "How do the women feel about that sort of prayer?"

"The women?" He brushed the words out of the air with a wave of his hand. "They're grateful. They don't want to be a man anymore than a man wants to be a woman." They begin their morning with "Blessed are You, G-d Almighty, the King of the World, that You haven't made me a Man." He smiled. "You see," he said, his didactic finger pointing to each word as it wafted in the air between the two. "G-d wants a man to do what only a man can do and he wants a woman to do what only a woman can do. G-d made man and woman for two very separate reasons. And that we are thankful to be able to do what he wants us to do as a man or as a woman."

The marine layer had burned off and soft sunbeams filtered through the leaves above the balcony. Champ sat for the last time on the bucket in the corner, like a boxer in the ring who had gone twelve rounds, leaning against the ropes, too spent to paw or jab any longer. The fight was over. The decision announced.

Ruby told Lily for the millionth time about the catnip in the meadows and the owls in the barn, the thosers and thatters and pitters and patters and chitters and chatters and platter and clatters and other catter matters. Then they cried for themselves and they cried for the other and Lily begged to go, but it couldn't be so. And so it was said, "I love you. Fair-thee-well, my friend. Ta ta. Adios. Adieu."

Beatrice awoke on May 1 on a day when her mood was sunnyside up. It was her birthday and she would spend the day in celebration. She knew that Denny's would have a nice free breakfast of eggs and pancakes and that the Carwash of the Stars down the street on Magnolia street offers a free birthday carwash. But this May 1 was not going to unfold in the way that she had expected. This May 1, her first birthday in the City of Angels, was the same day that the millions of immigrants and their supporters stayed home from work in protest, or were downtown for the big Mayday demonstrations against pending unfavorable immigration legislation in Washington. So not much was open. Denny's was closed, no one to cook the food or wash the dishes. The carwash was closed, no one to vacuum out the cars and wipe them dry after they emerged from the tunnel of water. Every place else in town was closed as well, the freeways deserted. No one to drive the busses. The cabs. The delivery trucks. Places of businesses all closed. No clerks. No cooks. No where to go. No way to get there. Los Angeles stopped dead in her tracks.

Undaunted and determined, Beatrice arose early the next day to claim what she could not on the day before. Denny's coughed up the plate of eggs and pancakes and she headed next for her free wash. A tired, aging Asian sat leaning from her stool onto the counter.

"Good Day. I am here to claim my free car wash," said Beatrice cheerfully.

"Free car wash! What for?"

"My birthday. It's my birthday! I read where it says you give a free carwash if it's your birthday. See, it says right here." Beatrice stood there with confidence and pride, beaming widely and pointed to the ad. "Well, it's my birthday."

"Lemme see."

I have it right here. See!" Beatrice held the open paper to the woman. The old woman muted the television on the ledge above her head, snatched the flyer, pulled down the glasses roosting atop her hair and leaning into the light of the window, examined the advertisement closely, and then grunted.

"Okay, lemme see ID."

Beatrice held out her driver's license.

Snapping it from Beatrice's hand, she mumbled "Where? Here…?"

"Yes, it's right there. You can't miss it. See it?"

The old woman leaned back in her light and examined it closely, reading every word and number on it, then in a burst of triumph of catching a cheat, "Hah! It say May one! This is May two. Your birthday was yesterday, May ONE! See, it say right here, MAY ONE! Today MAY TWO. You no get free carwash. It too late."

"Well, I came yesterday and this place was closed. So I

came today. You were closed yesterday. The immigrants didn't work. Remember? You were closed yesterday. I couldn't get my free car wash on my birthday."

"Your birthday was yesterday. No free car wash. It say free carwash on your birthday. Your birthday no today."

"But you were closed yesterday!"

"That no my fault! I no go on strike yesterday. I no march in no parade. I no open. Too bad it your birthday. We no open, you no get free carwash. So you lose."

"Why, I believe you have just lost a customer! So you lose!"

"Big Deal! Look out there." Rattling back the blinds, she pointed to the parking lot and sweeping her hand over the vista, "Big Deal! Look out there! See all those cars lined up? We have plenty customer, too many customer. Big Deal. I no care. "

"I will never come back and I will tell all my friends about this place, and you!"

"You no come back? Your friend no come back? No big deal. Just look out that window. See all those people. I no care. Big Deal! Look! Look at all the people! We have plenty of customer, too many customer. You no come back? No big deal. We still be in business."

Looking the old woman squarely in the eye, Beatrice shouted, "you are a wanker, you are," turned curtly, and took long angry strides to the door.

Smiling, she switched the sound back on the television set, leaned back in her stool. "You no cheat me! Ha!"

Chapter 30

The heat of July baked the San Fernando Valley, sending temperatures thirty degrees higher than the coastal cities. Felix would fight through the heavy tourist traffic to Manhattan Beach, seeking a place in the sun amid the packed beach. The yeshiva was closed for the summer so there were no students to teach. Most of Hollywood was shut down for the summer and the folks back in the nation's midriff were fed a daily diet of reruns. There were few auditions, but the showcases continued and Barbara continued sending him to look for someone. "I need the boy next door," she would tell him, or "See if you can't find an edgy Latina in her twenties."

And he would go and he would still tell them, "Run as fast as you can. Go home!" But they wouldn't listen to him. They would go ask someone else until they got the answer they wanted, like a young child who asks his mother who says no so he asks his father. They won't take no for an answer because they think they are entitled to it. They think they are the exception to the rule. There's a fairy godmother somewhere out there with a magic wand to grant their every wish. Or Hollywood will discover them sitting on a stool at the soda fountain in the drugstore on the corner of Hollywood and Vine. Or they have the "It" factor, "Just get me out there," they say to Barbara. "Everything else will fall right into place. I'll be off and running within the month."

So it was all pointless, like trying to keep a moth from flying into the campfire. It was too big for Felix, his small voice drowned out by the moneychangers in the temple. There was nothing he could do. They would have to learn it themselves the hard way. And if they're lucky and they are able to get back home, they arrive damaged, but alive, broken like the promises that had carried them there. And they would warn the others, "Don't Go! Don't Go!" Like Daedalus calling to Icarus, "Come back! Come Back," to ears that won't listen and eyes that won't see.

Beep. "Hi, there..." Zip. Zap.

Beep. "Hi, Felix. This is your mom. Just wanted to call you to tell you I sold the house. It was so dark and empty living in that big old house all by myself. I'm okay now. Things were hard for a while. But I'm all right now. So guess what, honey? Good news. I bought a small place in a retirement community in Tampa. Thought I would give you my new phone number so that if anything comes up, you could call me. I have it written down here somewhere. Oh, yes, here it is. It's... Oops. Can't read it. Let me get my glasses. Ok. Silly me! Ha ha. Here they are, right on the top of my head. Okay, Got a pencil or something to write with? Okay, here it is. 1-813-790-6379. I miss you very much, Felix. I love you. Maybe some day you can call me. Bye, honey. I love you."

Baruch Heshem! Baruch Heshem! Baruch Heshem!

Beep. "Hi, there..." Zip. Zap.

It was early in the evening. The black sedan, its windows tinted into anonymity, rolled slowly down Hesby Street, then pulled to the curb a few houses down and lingered, returned the next morning and lingered again. It was reported that cameras poked through open windows. Beth Ann limped up and down the sidewalk, her cane horizontal, keeping her balance. Pausing every few feet, ahemming and harooming, thumping and counting. But then she fell from the tightrope. No safety net below. The blue and white and yellow and red lights wailed and blinked. One last smile. One last ahem. Then all was quiet. The lights were stilled. The siren silenced. Reunification with the universe. Mama's home. Mama's home.

No
Sad
Tata's.
Jaguar
Taillights
Disappearing
Into the darkness.

And the location scouts in the black sedan moved on as well, their mission complete. They will report back to the producers at Warthog Sisters. Sure, the Villa Verdugo, with its typical Los Angeles look in the daylight and nightlight, in its neighborhood of green squares and quaint cottages drawn behind white picket fences, its easy presence in the foothills of the Verdugo Mountains, its lanky palms, the bougainvillea and the birds of paradise abloom in the courtyard, the overpasses and the underbellies in the hip NoHo just down the street, all fit in the script, and will certainly suffice as the perfect place to shoot "That Damned Human Race."

In the Community for the Warmth, Harmony and Longevity of the Golden Agers, Woodrow dozed on the lap of the gentleman during long lazy afternoons in the sun room and spent evenings at the fireside bent over bridge and backgammon. "Yes, Virginia, there is a Santa Claus." And Heathcharlesharley was discovered, with no name change necessary, in the halls of the Villa Verdugo by the producers and offered his place, his skills of ad libbing, his way with words, his gentile Mississippi drawl, his overbite just exactly what was needed, the roof over head becoming larger and larger as his star rose higher and higher over Hollywoodland and Barbara sat quietly on a hard folding chair looking for the next Heathcharlesharley on a makeshift stage somewhere, and Tiffani, her Disabled American Veteran license plate and disability check secured for the rest of her life, sucked medication from the snake head during long easy evenings, surrounded with picture books and jigsaws and the cutest little dolls lining the walls and stacked to the ceiling and pulled her chair closer and leaned over "Gone with the Wind," dim-witted Harold snoring noisily in the background. And one late Friday evening on the twenty-fifth floor offices of Vidematics in Century City, Harriet sat at her desk and felt a tingle in her throat that became a tangle that became a tungle that became a cha cha cha choo, cha cha cha choo, cha cha cha choo, choo, choo. Aachoo. Aachoo, then noticed a peculiar numbness in her right arm.

"Hello, who is this?"

"This is Annie. Who is this?"

"Felix."

"Felix!! Oh! Felix! Oh! Oh! Oh! Felix! Oh! Thank god!"

"I'm so so sorry to tell you this. You have the wrong person. It is my name, but I am not your son. I am so sorry. I wanted so much to call you, but I had no phone number. I am so sorry."

"Oh." A long pause. "Oh..." A heavy sigh.

"I am so so sorry," whispered Felix.

The investigators arrived one morning at the Royale Grace, armed with their official credentials, warrants, and photographs. "Have you seen this woman pictured here?" they asked. A lovely lady in a long fetching blonde wig, owlish sunglasses and floppy straw hat. "Or here?" A priggy and pert brunette in a pageboy cut, thick, heavy spectacles hanging from her nose, an LA Dodgers baseball cap topping it all off. "Or this?" a closely cropped curly red headed lass in a blue-striped hospital gown. "Considered armed and dangerous."

"On the run," they claimed. "A tall, slender thirty-four-year-old female with an English accent. Killed a prominent attorney in Richmond, shooting him dead with her derringer as he slept. Captured, interrogated, tried and found to be broken. Sent to the Virginia State Institution for Those Who Have Been Terminally Destroyed by Love, but checked out during movie time one Saturday evening when no one was watching the door. Fled in the director's black Jaguar. "Pictured here," they offered. "Believed to be residing at this address. Nothing there but a white plastic Adirondack chair."

"You know, I noticed that the ladies out here in LA like to wear tight jeans. I like ladies in tight jeans. You know the reason they buy them that way is because they think they're gonna lose those five extra pounds."

"But ladies, think about us guys. We see you looking good in those tight jeans, we buy you those expensive margaritas, we take you home, blow in your ear, get you all hot and bothered, then reach down there and loosen that top button, and POOF! Like a car airbag inflating."

"Have you ever noticed that some TV commercials are geared for men and others for women. For example, commercials for diarrhea always seem to be addressing the men. Probably because they drink so much. Right guys?"

"Women, on the other hand, are always the constipated ones. There is a reason. Women are three times more likely to be constipated then men are. It's all those iron tablets they take. So I tell you what guys, between the PMS, the menstrual cycle, their headaches and their constipation, there are only about three days of the month that you can approach them."

"And those are the days they get pregnant."

"I tell you, the world is changing so quickly. Nowadays, when you get mad at your lady, you can't scream and yell anymore. That's abuse. You have to be more subtle. You gotta do things like go to the bathroom and take her toothbrush, swish it around in the toilet and then put it back in the holder. Then when she goes up to brush her teeth before bed, you just stand in the doorway and smile sweetly. But you don’t kiss her for a while. At least not until the blue is gone from her lips.”

“What's the matter, Mac. You don't like girls?”

“Boo,” said several others.

“Go home,” shouted someone in the blackness in the back of the room.

Felix walked out the big, black back door and into the vacant alley, a lone light bulb above the door casting a dim spotlight over his head and sending long shadows across the littered pavement. It was all over. He was free at last. “Go home,” he said. “Tell yourself that it's the journey itself and not the goal that offers the greatest rewards.” So he went home to the warmth of his farmhouse in the valley's end of the gently rolling hills of Blue Creek, to run with Maggie, to count sunflowers, and to have long chats with Annie in Tampa. Frankie, too, too tall for Hollywood, to paint Hoosier autumns and sunsets to sell in olde shoppes, and Archie and Veronica came along. And Lily, to lay under evening skies studded with juju-bees and jelly beans, to drink milk on the back porch, to hear at long last the voice of Hoover, which lived up to its reputation truly, and to chatter about matters with the owl in the barn, to catnap in the catnip and dream about Ruby.

The End

Mark McLane spends most of his time in a classroom somewhere, either standing behind a desk or sitting in front of one, and like most English teachers, dreams of someday having the time and energy to put into practice what he teaches to others. And so that time came, culminating in *The Impersonators*, based on his experiences as a struggling actor and stand-up comedian who paid the bills by teaching orthodox Jewish young men at a yeshiva in the Fairfax District of Los Angeles and working as an associate for a Hollywood talent manager. Mr. McLane lives in Brookville, a small village in rural southern Indiana, where he teaches composition at a local community college and when he has the time and energy, continues to write.

You can email the author at Mark@MarkMcLane.com
Follow him on FB: www.facebook.com/writerMarkMclane